Now I'm Found

Theresa Hupp

Copyright

Dedication

This book is dedicated to my husband, who once said my writing was a "nice, inexpensive hobby." I dispute this description and love him anyway.

GOLD MINING IN CALIFORNIA, CURRIER & IVES, C. 1871

Chapter 1:   An Oregon Cabin

What have I done? What have I done?

The words reverberated in Mac's head to the beat of Valiente's hooves as he rode away from the cabin. It was barely light on Friday morning, March 3, 1848. A low Oregon fog sifted between tall evergreens bordering the wagon path ahead.

Mac had been awake twenty-four hours. At dawn on Thursday, he'd ridden to Samuel Abercrombie's claim to help with the barn raising. All day he lifted lumber and pounded nails, until his back was stiff and his palms blistered.

When the barn walls and rafters were in place, the men ate their fill of Abercrombie's food and drank enough whiskey to soothe their aching muscles. Then Mac headed home, accompanied by his friend Zeke Pershing. They arrived at Mac's cabin, where a light burned in the window.

"You're a lucky man, Caleb McDougall," Zeke said to Mac. "Your wife and son are waiting for you."

Mac almost blurted out the truth. That Jenny wasn't his wife. That William wasn't his son, though the baby bore his name. But he caught himself, realizing alcohol dulled his brain, and merely grunted.

"See you next time," Zeke said, then rode off with a quick wave.

Alone and inebriated, Mac stared at the cabin window, watching the lamplight inside flicker. The past year had not gone as expected. He'd left Boston in early 1847, bound for Oregon. He traveled to escape his parents and seek adventure in the West. He needed a wife to join a wagon train with an experienced captain. So he asked Jenny, who'd been alone in the

5

world and pregnant, to pretend to be his wife.

They'd made a good team on the six-month journey, he thought, smiling. Jenny did her part and then some, handling the wagon after Mac took over as company captain. Zeke Pershing and others helped, but Jenny managed well on her own.

Mac staggered when he dismounted outside the barn, then he lit a lantern and stabled his stallion Valiente in the stall next to Jenny's mare. The mare was pregnant with what he suspected was Valiente's foal.

As Mac removed the saddle and bridle from the horse and wiped him down, he murmured, "Shall we head back East, boy? Spring is almost here. Can't stay much longer."

No, he couldn't stay. Not alone in the cabin with Jenny—their only chaperon a five-month-old baby.

He'd built the cabin for Jenny last autumn after they'd arrived in Oregon City in mid-October. Jenny deserved a home after toiling on the wagon train. Mac always planned to return to Boston in the spring. He would have to face his parents sometime.

Dousing the light to return to the cabin, Mac noticed a gray knit bootie on the barn floor. He picked it up and stuffed it in his pocket. "Jenny will wonder where this has been," he told the horses.

He paused in the barn doorway before heading to the cabin. To Jenny.

It had been hard to live with her all winter. She wasn't his wife or lover, but sometimes he dreamed he was as lucky as Zeke and the rest of the world thought he was. Sometimes he dreamed of Jenny's blue eyes, the golden glints in her brown hair, and her gentle hands when she'd bathed his fevered brow.

She'd been an obligation when he first met her, maybe an atonement for his sins in Boston. But after living with her daily and watching her croon to William as she rocked and nursed the baby, all he could think about were the soft curves of her mouth, her breasts, her hips.

Mac spent as much time as possible away from the cabin through the winter. When word of the Indian massacre at the Whitman Mission reached Oregon City in December, he joined the militia formed to seek revenge. He'd been gone until late January, when a larger force went after the Cayuse.

In a few more weeks the mountain snows would clear enough for travel, Mac thought, shaking his befuddled head. He could last that long. He shut the barn door and crossed the clearing.

He pushed the cabin door open. Jenny stood across the room with William held to her shoulder, her hair glowing in the firelight. "Shhh," she whispered, a finger to her lips. "He's asleep." As she lowered the baby into the cradle Mac had made, her round buttocks under her skirt curved toward him. Then she turned to Mac and smiled, her shawl falling off one shoulder.

In two strides Mac reached her, pushed her against the wall, and kissed her as he'd thought of doing so often. One hand pulled Jenny's hips to his, the other molded a breast. A fine breast, the first time he'd touched it, and it was as desirable as he'd dreamed.

Jenny gasped into his mouth, softened against him, and her hands clutched his waist. Then she went rigid in his arms.

Mac pulled back to look at her. A tear rolled down her cheek.

The lust cleared from his head at the sight of that tear, and he pulled in a shuddering breath. "Sorry," he said. "I'm sorry." He willed himself to let Jenny go, rushed out of the cabin, and returned to the barn.

He had to leave. Now. He couldn't stay or his hands would be on her again. It didn't matter how much Mac wanted her, she didn't want him—she'd said as much when he'd asked her to marry him shortly after William's birth. He'd wanted a real marriage, not a ruse. She'd said she didn't want marriage to any man, not after being raped before Mac met her.

Back in the barn Mac lit a lantern, found his saddlebags, and packed what he could. He took a scrap of paper and a pencil and wrote:

> *Jenny,*
>
> *I'm leaving for Boston. The gold coins under the loft floor near my cot should keep you and William until the crops come in.*
>
> *I'm sorry.*
>
> *Caleb McDougall*

Mac found hammer and nail and pounded the note to the barn wall.

He needed to return to the cabin to gather clothes and money for the journey. He delayed until his fingers were numb and he shivered in his coat, hoping Jenny would be asleep when he went inside.

When he couldn't bear the cold any longer, Mac saddled Valiente and left the horse hitched to the barnyard rail. He stole into the cabin with an empty saddlebag. Jenny lay in bed, covered by a quilt.

Mac quietly climbed the ladder to the loft and packed clothes and his bedroll. He pried up the floorboard, opened the bag of gold coins he'd brought from Boston, and shook half of them into a sock, which he packed. The rest of the coins he returned to their hiding place.

Then he crept back downstairs, out the door, and mounted Valiente.

"Mac," he heard Jenny cry behind him, as he kicked the horse into a canter.

What have I done? What have I done? The question echoed in his head to the beat of Valiente's hooves.

Chapter 2:   Abandoned

When Mac lurched out of the cabin after kissing her, Jenny sank into the rocking chair beside her bed, gripping its arms. William slept in his cradle nearby. Jenny's world had turned over, and the baby hadn't even stirred.

Mac had scared her. He hadn't meant to, she knew, but he had nonetheless. His arms around her had felt splendid at first, warm and comforting on this early March night. Then he pushed her against the wall. Mac never treated her roughly, and she was confused. His eyes had been glazed with drink, his breath smelled of whiskey.

She touched her mouth, feeling again Mac's lips descending to hers, his tongue thrusting inside her mouth. He'd never kissed her before. It wasn't a gentle kiss, but demanding. His hands roved over her body, rising up her sides and forward to cup her breast. A thrill went through her. Mac was her protector, her friend. She trusted him more than anyone in the world.

But his hands tonight were no different than those of the men who had raped her. The memory pushed its way forward.

She couldn't deny Mac anything, not even her body, if that's what he wanted. But she couldn't give in either. Not ever again. Her eyes welled as she froze in his arms, while his mouth and hands claimed her.

Then he'd stopped. Unlike the men in Missouri, Mac stopped. He drew a deep breath, shuddered, and said, "I'm sorry."

He left, and she felt a pang of regret. Regret turned to worry. He must have gone to the barn, but he would return. What would happen then?

Jenny sat in the rocking chair waiting. When the fire dwindled and the cabin grew cold, she went to bed. But she couldn't sleep.

Hours later Mac crept into the cabin and climbed the ladder to the loft. She longed for him to talk to her, but prayed he would wait until morning.

She was still confused, her body tense and achy.

Mac rustled around in the loft awhile, then left the cabin again.

Jenny slid out of bed, slipped a shawl around her shoulders, and ran to the doorway. When she threw open the door, she saw Mac riding away on Valiente, barely visible in the early fog.

"Mac," she cried. "Mac!"

He didn't look back. She didn't know if he even heard her.

It was close enough to dawn that she dressed and climbed to the loft to see if she could determine where he'd gone. His bedroll was missing, as were many of his clothes.

Frantic, Jenny ran to the barn. No sign of Mac or Valiente, though her mare Poulette pawed restlessly in her stall. A piece of paper hung on a nail on the wall. A letter.

Jenny read it and swallowed a sob. They'd talked of Mac leaving in the spring. But she wasn't ready for him to go.

Mac hadn't stayed with her much this last winter. In fact, it seemed he'd taken every opportunity to leave William and her. He joined the Oregon volunteer militia and made frequent trips to Fort Vancouver. He spent time working on other men's claims—like the Abercrombie barn raising the day before.

Jenny thought Mac had been trying to get her used to living alone with William. She hadn't realized he might have wanted to avoid her for other reasons. She wondered what would have happened if he'd stayed in the cabin last night. Would he have kissed her again? More?

If he had fondled her again, what would she have done?

Jenny wept as she let Poulette out to graze in the small paddock beside the barn. When she returned to the cabin, she clambered up to the loft again and found the coins mentioned in Mac's note. She left them under the floorboard. She wouldn't use them, not yet.

She took Mac's pillow off the cot and breathed in his scent. Then she carried the pillow down the ladder to the room below and pulled out her journal, a small bound book Mac had given her when they left Missouri. She wrote:

Friday, March 3rd—Mac left for Boston.
William and I are alone. What will I do now?

Chapter 3:   To Portland and Beyond

As Mac rode away from the cabin, he put his last minutes with Jenny aside and tried to think, though his head still throbbed with the aftereffects of drinking. He had to decide what to do, without any time to plan.

If he returned to Boston, his father would pressure him to join his brother's legal practice. Mac had a law degree from Harvard, but office work didn't interest him. He chafed at doing his father's bidding after living independently for the last year. But without his own income, Mac would be beholden to his father and to the trust fund his father controlled.

In his addled state, he couldn't think of any alternative to returning to Boston. He slowed Valiente to a walk and tried to consider the supplies he would need for a long journey east.

The early fog had lifted by the time Mac reached Oregon City, an easy hour's ride from the cabin. He skirted the swamp south of town to ride north along the muddy main street. Stores were just opening. At Abernethy's store, a two-story brick mercantile building, Mac hitched Valiente to a railing and went inside.

"Need food and ammunition for a trip to the States," Mac said to the clerk behind the counter. He'd met the man—Mr. Hamilton—several times through the winter.

"Returning to Boston?" Hamilton asked, seeming ready to chat. "You'd said you was, but I thought maybe the mild winter here would convince you to stay."

Mac shook his head.

"What about your wife?"

"She's staying."

"You'll be back next year, then?"

Mac ignored the question, not wanting to explain himself to the clerk. "Not much selection on your shelves," he said.

"Sold almost everything through the winter. Heard tell yesterday the first ship of the season just berthed at Portland. Don't know yet what Abernethy will buy from its cargo."

"There's a ship in Portland?" That was news worth chatting about. "Where's it headed?"

"Come from the Sandwich Islands. Bound for California next. Then around South America and back to the East Coast. That's what I heard."

Mac decided on the spur of the moment. "Never mind the supplies. I'll ride to Portland. See how long it takes to travel to Boston by ship." He'd left money with Jenny, but he wanted her to start fresh without him. He handed two gold coins to the clerk. "Let's settle my account," he said and watched while the man made a notation in the store's ledger.

Mac remounted Valiente and rode to Portland, covering the fifteen miles to the outpost at the mouth of the Willamette River by noon. Portland was smaller than Oregon City, little more than a wharf with a log warehouse and small wooden houses nearby. The wharf teemed with activity. Men unloaded cargo down gangplanks from a small barque.

"Who's in charge?" Mac asked a dockhand.

"Pettygrove," the laborer replied, waving at a well-dressed whiskered man in a topcoat.

"Caleb McDougall," Mac said, extending a hand to Pettygrove. "From Oregon City. I emigrated last year, but I'm heading back to Boston. Is your ship bound for the East Coast?"

"First to California, then around the Horn. As soon as we unload here and get the pilot on board, she's heading to San Francisco," Pettygrove said. "Tomorrow morning, I hope."

"How long will it take?"

"Three weeks to San Francisco, maybe less, maybe more. Depends on the wind. Don't know what goods she'll take on there, so can't say when she'll head south to Panama and beyond."

"Do you have room for a paying passenger and horse as far as San Francisco?" Mac could think about his future as well on an ocean voyage as while traveling overland. And he'd never been to California. He'd decide in San Francisco whether to head east by land or continue on the ship. Whether to go to Boston at all.

Pettygrove eyed Valiente. "Long voyage for a stallion like that one."

"He's been on steamships on the Ohio and Missouri. He'll do fine."

"Ocean's rougher than a river." But Pettygrove gave him a price. "You can board now. Captain plans to leave on the first tide after the pilot's here."

After Mac settled into his tiny cabin on board, he took out his journal:

March 3, 1848. It seems I have embarked on another adventure. I have left Jenny and William on the claim with the Tanners. I now sail south to California, en route to Boston, unless another destination reveals itself.

The ship's progress down the Pacific coast was rough—early spring seas tossed the boat like a bobbing cork. The captain sailed far from shore to avoid the rocks near land.

"Need at least seventy fathoms to travel along the coast," he told Mac. "Rocks ain't been charted in these parts yet. And there ain't no lighthouses like in the East."

Mac was a good sailor, but gripped lines and railings to move about as waves washed over the deck.

"You done much sailing?" the captain asked when Mac climbed to the deck one morning, staggering from side to side on the steep ladder.

"Mostly small yawls and ketches near Boston," Mac said. "And one voyage to Europe. I always enjoyed the ocean."

Mac went down to the hold every morning and afternoon. Andalusians were calm by nature, but Valiente grew agitated at confinement below deck, particularly in rough seas.

As he curried the stallion's coat one morning, Mac wondered how he would fit back into Boston life after fleeing his family the year before.

"It wasn't right, you know," Mac told his horse, reflecting on his mother's treatment of Bridget, a maid in his parents' home discharged when she became pregnant. "Mother did what she thought best, but it wasn't right." His mother had doomed Bridget and her unborn child—

Mac's child—to an early death when Bridget died of fever. "I wonder if she knew the baby was mine."

Valiente snorted.

Mac had never been sure what his mother knew about Bridget's child—she hadn't let him confess. He wouldn't have married the girl, but he felt responsible for her, and he hadn't forgiven his mother for treating her so harshly.

He'd left Boston rather than admit his responsibility for Bridget's death—to himself or to anyone else. Then he rescued pregnant Jenny Calhoun to make up for his negligence with Bridget. "It took me most of the way to Oregon before I realized why I brought Jenny along," he confided to Valiente. "I thought it was because Pershing only wanted married men. But it was also guilt over Bridget."

The horse nuzzled Mac's pocket for sugar.

Another reason Mac had fled was to escape the life his father planned for him. The senior McDougall was a banker, and Mac's oldest brother followed in his footsteps. Mac's second brother was an attorney with a growing legal practice, which Mac's father urged Mac to join. Neither of his older brothers had rebelled against their father's plans, but Mac wanted something different.

He'd relished his freedom on the Oregon Trail. The men he'd led in the wagon company had recognized and followed his authority—unlike his father and older brothers, who never valued his abilities. Mac wanted to preserve the self-respect he'd gained on the trail and obtain his father's admiration as well.

The only home he knew was Boston. Was the law firm now his answer? If he didn't return to Boston, what would he do?

Mac fingered the baby bootie he'd found in his pocket the morning after he left Portland. He missed Jenny. And William. But if he'd stayed in Oregon, he wouldn't have been able to keep his hands off Jenny.

There was nowhere he wanted to be. Nowhere he belonged.

Chapter 4:   On the Farm

For three days Jenny stayed near the cabin, doing minimal chores and caring for William. She wanted to be there if Mac returned. Her mind spun with questions, but she only had the baby to talk to.

"What will I do if Mac comes back?" she asked her son as she nursed him. "What will I do if he doesn't?" She didn't know which fate she feared most—talking to Mac about why he'd kissed her or being alone on the claim without him.

She slept each night with her face nestled against Mac's pillow.

On Monday, three days after Mac's departure, Jenny's friend Esther Abercrombie arrived with her baby brother Jonah. "I thought you'd be in church yesterday," Esther said, hefting herself awkwardly out of her wagon. "First day without rain in three weeks." Esther arched her back, stomach extended in the late stages of pregnancy. "I can't stay long, but I had to get out of our cabin this morning while the weather's good. Daniel's clearing fields with his pa. Says it's about time to plant."

"William's teething," Jenny said. "I stayed home."

"No tea brewing?" Esther asked when she entered the cabin behind Jenny. "I thought Captain McDougall liked tea for breakfast."

"Mac's gone. I'll make some coffee."

"Where to?" Esther put Jonah down to crawl on the board floor.

"Back East."

Esther's eyes widened. "Back East? Why?"

"To see his family."

"Whatever will you do?"

"Tanner and Hatty will be back tomorrow. They've been working on Mrs. Purcell's house in town. I'll be all right." If she told Esther she'd be all right, then she would be.

"But you'll be alone for what—two years?" Esther said. "By the time he reaches Boston, then returns here? What if he left you with child?"

Jenny felt herself blush. "Oh, no—I can't be. Not . . . not with William still so young."

"Never can tell," Esther said. "Pa left Ma to go through her confinements when he was in the Army, so I suppose you'd manage. I surely hope I don't have another soon after this one. A newborn and Jonah will be enough for a bit."

"How much longer do you have—a month?" Jenny asked.

"Probably a little longer. First babies are usually late."

"You let me know when you want Hatty Tanner to come stay with you. And if you want me to keep Jonah then."

"Won't you need Hatty without Mac here?"

"I'll be all right," Jenny said again, as much to convince herself as Esther.

Jenny was worn out after Esther's visit. Caring for William and the farm animals was tiring enough, without having to keep a smile on her face when she felt so miserable. She went to bed as soon as she'd nursed William after supper.

Sometime in the dark night, she woke up startled. A noise from the barnyard had awakened her. She hadn't identified the sound in her sleep, but something prowled outside. Poulette whinnied in fear—that sound she recognized.

A chicken squawked, then came a throaty yowl. A mountain lion. Her spine prickled as she recognized the fearsome scream she'd heard during the wagon train days the year before. This cat sounded right outside her door.

Jenny wanted to hide her head under the pillow, but Poulette neighed again. She had to protect her beloved mare and the other animals. She crept out of bed, thrust bare feet into her shoes, and took the loaded shotgun down from above the cabin door.

Making as much noise as she could, Jenny opened the door and yelled, "Get away, panther."

Another feline scream sounded in the yard, filling her with terror, though she saw nothing. She raised the gun and shot in the direction of the howling lion.

One more caterwaul, from farther off in the woods. Then silence.

She was afraid to go to the barn, and Poulette didn't neigh again, so Jenny went back into the cabin and latched the door. She sat shivering in her rocking chair until dawn, shotgun reloaded and in her hands.

But the animal did not return.

In the morning Jenny went to the barn to do the chores, rushing across the yard with her shotgun raised. Large cat tracks were stamped in the mud in front of the barn door. Poulette was restless, but there was no sign of the panther other than the paw prints.

She kept the shotgun beside her in the cabin all day.

The Tanners—Clarence, Hatty, and their son Otis—returned to the farm that afternoon. By the time they drove up in their wagon, Jenny could almost smile.

The Tanners had been in the wagon train with Mac and Jenny, but could not buy land in Oregon because they were Negroes. They lived on Mac's property in a one-room shanty, smaller even than the cabin Mac built for Jenny. In exchange for their lodging, Tanner cleared fields for crops, and Hatty helped Jenny with housework and with William.

"What for Captain McDougall's gone?" Tanner asked when Jenny told them Mac had left. "He ain't got no call to leave. Not without tellin' us."

Hatty simply shook her head.

"You know he planned to go back to Boston this spring," Jenny said, though she agreed with Tanner. "That's why he wanted you on our claim. To help me."

Tanner pursed his lips. "It ain't right, him leavin' you."

"A panther was prowling around last night," Jenny said. She showed Tanner the tracks.

"You done good, Miz Jenny. No harm done. But you keep a gun with you when you's outside."

That night Jenny wrote:

Tuesday, March 7ᵗʰ—A panther tried to attack the farm last night, causing me a fright. I expected Mac to go. Why does it feel so wrong?

The following Sunday was a fine spring day, the sky bright after a cleansing rain two days earlier. Jenny took William into Oregon City for church. She couldn't continue to hide on her farm, or her friends would think she and Mac had parted on bad terms.

Mrs. Tuller bustled over to Jenny after the service, her doctor husband in tow. "Esther tells me Captain McDougall is gone," Mrs. Tuller said. The Tullers were the only people in the wagon company who knew Mac and Jenny had not been married.

"Yes." Jenny clutched William closer and hid her face in his blanket.

"You should have married him when he asked last fall," Doc Tuller said.

"I didn't want to marry him." Jenny sighed. "And he didn't want to marry me either. Not really. You made him ask. It wasn't right for either of us."

Marriage might have solved Jenny's trouble and given William a name. But it would have tied Mac down when he planned to go home to Boston. Jenny didn't want to interfere with his future.

Besides, she didn't think she would ever marry. Her stomach clenched every time she remembered the brutes raping her in Missouri. William was the result of that violation, and she cherished her son. But she wondered if she could ever stand to have a man touch her.

Chapter 5:   San Francisco

In late March Mac's ship reached San Francisco Bay after pitching and rolling its way down the coast. The crew maneuvered the barque between Point Reyes and the rocky Farallon Islands into the bay.

The harbor was stunning—calm, blue water edged with white beaches. Above the beaches granite cliffs rose, and beyond the cliffs stood rolling brown hills greening with the first growth of spring. Mac stood on deck with the captain as the ship sailed through the mouth of the Golden Gate. They passed the Presidio with the American flag flying high.

"Army took over from Mexico in forty-six," the captain said, pointing at the flag. "We'll drop anchor, then ferry the cargo to the wharf." He gestured at the port ahead of them. "Need to stay here several days. We'll be taking on more freight and repairing sails for the next leg to Panama. You might want to take a room on shore. Get your horse off the ship awhile."

Mac couldn't see much of the town from the ship's deck, but it didn't look any bigger than Oregon City. "How long can I take deciding whether to continue on board?"

"Until I sell your cabin to another bidder."

"Where's the best place to stay?"

The captain shrugged. "Ain't nowhere fancy. A couple of saloons with rooms for travelers. You'll find the customs a tad different than American settlements or even English posts like Fort Vancouver."

"Why's that?" Mac asked.

"City started under Mexican rule. Built up around the Papist mission. U.S. military captured it in forty-six, like I said. Old Uncle Sam will win the war soon, I'm sure. Them Mexicans can't fight a kitten."

While the crew anchored the barque and lowered the sails, Mac sat on deck and wrote in his journal:

> *March 27, 1848. More than three weeks at sea. We arrived in San Francisco today. I've made no more decisions about my future than when I left Oregon.*

After Valiente was transferred to the wharf, Mac mounted the spirited horse. Valiente pranced and danced, and Mac decided to give him a run. He spurred the stallion into the hills. From the heights west of town, Mac looked down on the grubby settlement. Most of San Francisco's buildings were as rudimentary as those in Portland—small huts of rough boards or adobe—though a few wooden houses dotted the streets.

Across the Golden Gate to the north, Mac saw a lovely cove with whaling vessels moored off shore. Cattle—at least the dark spots looked like cattle—grazed in the hills above the cove.

A calmer Valiente walked back into town. Mac found a livery and boarded the horse, then sought a room for himself. He walked down the street on legs still shaky from being on board the ship for so long, despite his long ride in the afternoon.

Music and laughter from one roughhewn building identified it as a saloon. He entered and found men clustered around a newspaper posted on the wall. Most of the men were armed, like the emigrants along the trail the year before. Weapons didn't worry Mac—he had his own six-shooter strapped to his hip, and he could use it effectively. He'd proven that.

"Gold! At New Helvetia. Where Sutter has his fort. Found it while building a mill." An unshaven fellow with greasy hair poked at the paper with his finger.

"Can't be gold." A second speaker paused to lift a mug to his lips. "Ain't nothing in those hills but grass."

"Says it's gold. Right here in *The California Star*. Published Saturday." The first man stabbed his finger at the page again. "Says there's lots of it. *The Californian* had a story 'bout gold last week."

"Don't matter," said a third man. "New Helvetia's a long ways away. Don't help us none."

"Let me see." Mac elbowed his way in until he could read the article. It was a small blurb, a paragraph mentioning gold flakes found at New

Helvetia. "Where's New Helvetia?" he asked.

"South fork of the American River. More'n hunnert and fifty miles from here. Need to go south to San Jose to get around the bay."

The discovery was too far away to interest Mac. He sat at a table and ordered beefsteak and whiskey. After his food and drink arrived, a young woman in a red taffeta dress with tattered black lace pulled up a chair and sat beside him. "Buy me a drink?" she asked.

Mac glanced at her, then nodded at the bartender. The man brought a glass and bottle to the table, setting them down without comment.

The woman poured for herself and topped off Mac's glass. "In town for long?" she asked.

"No."

"I hope you're here for the night at least." She ran her hand up Mac's arm, an obvious invitation in her lilting voice.

Studying her more closely, Mac considered her offer. She had dark hair, sad chocolate eyes, and rouged lips turned down just a little at the corners. Maybe Spanish, he speculated, as he sipped his whiskey. Attractive now, but her looks wouldn't last. Still, a romp might shake his restlessness.

"What's your name?" he asked.

"Consuela." Yes, she was Spanish.

Jenny was prettier, Mac thought, with sapphire eyes and brown hair that gleamed gold in the sun. But this woman's eyes showed the same weariness Jenny's had when Mac first met her. He remembered Jenny's tears the night he left.

"Sorry," Mac said. "I'll buy you the bottle if you want, but that's it." He couldn't take up with this woman, not after his drunken groping of Jenny. Not after what had happened with Bridget. Women had only led to trouble for him. "How long you been in San Francisco?"

Consuela lifted a pretty shoulder. "A while. My husband died and left me alone."

"Is that how you ended up here?" His gesture encompassed the saloon, her dress, her invitation.

She nodded with a rueful smile.

Mac took a coin from his pocket. "Take this." He didn't know why he felt compelled to help her. Maybe because she reminded him of Jenny. But helping Consuela wouldn't do a damn thing for Jenny. He didn't need to rescue another woman. He didn't need more trouble. He needed to find his own place in the world.

Consuela took the coin. *"Gracias."* She lifted the bottle from the table as she walked away.

Mac awoke the next morning to the sound of pounding on his door. "Mister, I gotta talk to you," a man bellowed.

Bleary-eyed at the early hour after drinking through the evening, Mac stumbled to the door and opened it.

"I hear you got a horse. I want to buy it," a bearded man demanded.

"He's not for sale," Mac said, pushing to shut the door.

The man wedged his foot inside the room. "I'll pay top dollar."

"Why do you need my horse?" Mac said.

The man's voice dropped to a whisper as he looked around furtively. "Gold."

"He's not for sale," Mac repeated and shoved the man away.

Mac would have to move Valiente back to the ship before someone stole the stallion. He dressed quickly and went downstairs. Men already filled the saloon, talking about gold at Sutter's Mill. He recognized one of the ship's crewmen in the crowd.

After splitting a biscuit and slapping bacon between its halves, Mac headed to the stables, chewing as he went. He saddled Valiente and rode to the wharf, where the ship captain paced in a dither.

"My men have deserted," the captain said. "Blinded by the talk of gold. I can't sail without a crew. Even one of my mates left."

"Do you mean you can't leave San Francisco?"

"It'll take me time to round up more men," the captain said.

Over the next two days, rumors about the gold discovery grew. Mac took Valiente out riding or stayed with the horse in the stables. He checked with the ship captain daily, but the captain couldn't find any experienced men. He wouldn't be sailing any time soon.

March 30, 1848. I might as well travel overland. There are no berths to be had to Panama. I shall see for myself whether the reports of gold are true, then follow the trails east. I have plenty of time to reach Boston before winter.

Chapter 6:   Wet Spring in Oregon

Jenny half-expected Mac to write. If he sent her a letter while he was still in the West, she might receive news from him soon. She went into Oregon City twice a week to check for mail, but nothing arrived.

Jenny and the Tanners made do in the weeks after Mac left. When she needed provisions, she bought on credit, like most of the emigrants did their first year in Oregon. She hadn't used any of Mac's gold coins yet. She hoped to scrape by on credit until harvest in the fall.

Dreary skies dumped rain almost daily during the latter half of March. Some days it even snowed. "Can't git the blamed crops planted till the weather gits better," Clarence Tanner complained.

Tanner had helped Mac clear the first fields for crops through the winter. They'd used Tanner's mules and a plow Mac bought in Oregon City. Now it was time to plant spring wheat. With Mac gone, Tanner had only his young son Otis for help. Hatty Tanner worked with Jenny in the house and yard and helped their other neighbors as well.

"It's time to git the wheat in the ground," Tanner said. "But it's too wet. And too early for vegetables. Leastways, it would be in the States. I ain't got a clue what to do in this infernal rain."

"We'll plant when we can," Jenny said. She had no idea what else to say.

Jenny wrote in her journal:

> *Saturday, April 1ˢᵗ—I feel so lost. I thought Mac would tell me how to farm before he returned to Boston. Even with Tanner's help, I*

don't know what to do. I suppose Mac was no farmer either, and I did watch Papa manage our land in Missouri. I will have to do the best I can.

Rain continued almost daily until mid-April. On Tuesday, April 11, the skies finally brightened and the air turned warm. With clear skies, Jenny's mood lifted. Her survival—and William's—was up to her. She'd vowed the autumn before, on the steep slopes of the Cascades with her newborn baby in her arms, to stay alive for her son.

On this fine spring morning, she believed she could not only survive but thrive in Oregon. With the help of friends, she would somehow manage. She'd keep the claim going—after all, it was Mac's land, and she would maintain the farm in good condition to give back to him, if he ever returned.

In the meantime, it would be her home and William's.

Taking advantage of the fine weather, Jenny bundled the baby into a sling, saddled Poulette, and rode to Esther's cabin.

"There's a Ladies Meeting in town tomorrow afternoon," Esther said as they sat with their mending. William and Jonah crawled on the floor beside the women. "Won't you go with me?"

"How did you hear about it?" Jenny asked.

"Mother Abercrombie," Esther said, referring to her mother-in-law. "She's become bosom friends with several of the prominent wives in town. Ever since Mr.—Captain—Abercrombie returned from leading the militia. He insists I call him 'Captain' now. Or 'Father Abercrombie.'"

Samuel Abercrombie had vied to lead the wagon train to Oregon, but the other emigrants chose Mac instead. When a militia was formed to seek out the Cayuse Indians who killed the Whitmans, Abercrombie insisted on leading a unit. Jenny was surprised Mac volunteered to serve under Captain Abercrombie's command—the two men had not had a liking for each other along the trail.

"Won't you be uncomfortable riding in a wagon, then sitting in a meeting?" Jenny asked Esther. "Your time is so near."

Her friend laughed. "You endured worse on the trail. I have to keep

Mother Abercrombie happy. Her other daughter-in-law Louisa can do no wrong, or so it seems. Won't you come? It'll be so tedious without you."

"If Hatty can mind William, I will. What will you do with Jonah?"

Esther shrugged. "Ask Hatty to keep him, too, please."

Hatty was willing to care for the babies, so on Wednesday, Jenny and Esther left in Jenny's wagon, picked up Esther's mother- and sister-in-law, and drove to Oregon City.

Before the Ladies Meeting turned to business, the women gossiped about families. "Mac went back East this year," Jenny said. "Did anyone hear of him passing through town?"

"You've had no word of him?" one lady asked, with a raised eyebrow.

"No, ma'am."

"It must be hard to have your husband away. He'll be gone most of two years, won't he?"

Jenny nodded. The absence of any news probably meant Mac left Oregon immediately, but she had no way of knowing for sure. He should have sent word, she fumed. Regardless how they parted, it wasn't right for him to tell her nothing.

The purpose of the meeting was to gather clothes for the militia fighting the Cayuse. "Five hundred of our brave men are after the savages," Mrs. Abercrombie announced. "Now that Captain Abercrombie's company is home, we must support the new troops."

"How will we find provisions for so many?" another woman asked, and the discussion droned on.

The battles were far up the Columbia River around Fort Walla Walla. Still, Jenny listened in trepidation, afraid the fighting would approach Oregon City and her cabin. She worried, even with the Tanners on the claim. Rampaging men were worse than panthers. She had felt safer when Mac was with her.

After she returned home and put William to bed, Jenny wrote:

> Wednesday, April 12ᵗʰ—No one at the Ladies Meeting had news of Mac. I am grateful to have a home for William and myself. But only men can file land claims, so the farm is in Mac's name. I wish he would write.

As she wrote, it occurred to Jenny she might not have a legal right to stay on the claim. Doc and Mrs. Tuller were the only ones who knew her plight. She would have to talk to Doc about the land.

Despite Jenny's worry, the press of the planting season kept her from visiting Doc Tuller. The weather stayed warm, and Tanner planted all the cleared land. She and Hatty helped him as much as they could. He plowed, while the women and young Otis sowed behind him.

Jenny fried or boiled meat and baked bread in the mornings. She put William in a sling and carried food out to the fields at noon. While Hatty spelled her husband at the plow, Tanner ate. They kept the mules working from dawn until dusk.

Normal household chores did not stop while they sowed the last wheat and began on the corn. On the Monday after the Ladies Meeting, Jenny hung laundry outside in the sunshine to dry. She dragged the buffalo robe Mac had bought for her at Fort Laramie into the yard, then put William on it to play while she worked. The seven-month-old kept crawling off the robe, and she stopped to nudge him out of the dirt.

As Jenny paused to stretch her back, Esther's eleven-year-old twin brothers ran into the yard. "Miz Jenny," one boy cried. "Esther's having her baby. She's at our place. She was helping Pa with laundry. We need Miz Hatty."

"Where's Doc Tuller?" Jenny asked.

"Rachel went to get him."

"Hatty," Jenny called toward the barn. "It's Esther's time. She's at Captain Pershing's."

Hatty rushed out of the barn, wiping her hands on her apron. "You be all right if I leave to help her?"

Jenny nodded. "I'll fix dinner for Tanner and Otis, then bring William over after noon. You go now."

"I'll git Esther to her home, if there's time," Hatty said. "You stop at her place first, afore you head to her pa's."

When the wash had dried and the dinner dishes were put away, Jenny saddled her mare Poulette, bundled William into a sling across her chest, and set out on the mile ride to Esther and Daniel Abercrombie's cabin.

27

Their land shared a boundary with Jenny's. Esther and Daniel had married at Independence Rock the summer before. And now Esther was having a baby.

Jenny urged Poulette into a trot. William had grown almost too big for the sling, but she couldn't handle the mare with the baby loose on the saddle. So she wedged the sling between her belly and the saddle horn and clasped him tight.

She shouted when she arrived at Esther's cabin. Daniel came out and helped Jenny and William down.

"I'll put your mare in the barn," he said.

"How's Esther?" Jenny asked.

"Long time ahead yet, according to Mrs. Tuller." A worried expression replaced Daniel's usual smile.

"Where's Doc?"

"Accident. Couple of men crushed by a falling tree." Daniel shook his head. "Don't know if he'll get here."

Jenny patted Daniel's arm. "With Hatty and Mrs. Tuller here, Esther will be fine." She tried to sound reassuring, but anything could happen during childbirth.

She entered the cabin, built just like her own—a single large room, with a loft over the back half. Esther lay on the bed in the corner, moaning as a contraction gripped her. Hatty bustled from fireplace to bed, carrying a pan of water and towels. Mrs. Tuller sat on a stool beside the bed, wiping Esther's brow.

"How's she doing?" Jenny whispered, fearful for her friend. Jenny's labor with William had been hard. She would have died without Mac there to encourage her.

"Fine, fine," the doctor's wife said. "First babies take a long time. Like William."

"Have you eaten?" Jenny asked Mrs. Tuller. She put William down in a corner with a toy. "Where's Jonah?"

"I sent him home with the twins," Mrs. Tuller said. "Rachel's old enough to mind him for the night." Rachel was Esther's thirteen-year-old sister, and the oldest Pershing girl at home, now that Esther had married. Their mother had died along the trail to Oregon after giving birth to Jonah.

Mrs. Pershing had seemed strict and unfriendly toward Jenny at the time, but Jenny later realized Esther's mother had mothered her, too. In fact, Mrs. Pershing had been a better mother than Jenny's own had been. Jenny missed Mrs. Pershing almost as much as the Pershing family did.

Esther groaned with another contraction.

Jenny winced in sympathy. "I'll make supper," she said. She found flour and made flapjacks. She fed everyone and tried to keep William quiet, while Hatty and Mrs. Tuller attended Esther.

By twilight Esther's moans had risen to wails. William fussed and rubbed his eyes. "You go on home, dear," Mrs. Tuller told Jenny. "She'll be at it for hours yet."

"I'll stay, Miz Jenny," Hatty said. "If I ain't home by morning, you come on back after breakfast."

Jenny rode through the forest, tall evergreens blanketing the path in shadow despite the full moon. She startled at every snap of a tree branch and rustle of leaves, worried about being alone in the dark. A wild cat screamed in the night, and she feared it was the one that had prowled around her barn. The ride to her cabin seemed to take twice as long as during daylight. When she reached home she sighed in relief.

Tanner took the mare from her. "I built a fire for you," he said. "All ready to light."

Jenny smiled her thanks. "See you in the morning," she said as she carried William inside.

Monday, April 17th—Esther's child is coming. May she be as happy as I have been with William.

I still need to talk to Doc about the claim.

In the morning Jenny heard Tanner chopping wood and went outside. "Is Hatty back?" she asked.

"No, Miz Jenny."

"Would you please saddle Poulette? I'll ride to Esther's after breakfast."

She nursed William and fed him thin porridge, then fried bacon quickly and added a slice of bread and honey to plates for Tanner, Otis, and herself. After she washed dishes, she and William rode back to Esther's claim.

As she slid off Poulette clutching William, she heard a newborn cry.

She tethered Poulette to a post and hurried inside.

"It's a girl," Daniel said, grinning down at the bundle he cradled in his arms. "Born at dawn."

"Did Doc make it here?" Jenny asked, hoping she could talk to him.

"Yes, but he and his wife left right after the baby came. Only Hatty's here now," Daniel said.

Jenny shifted William to her hip and peeked in the bundle Daniel held. "Look, William," she said to her fussing son. The wide-eyed newborn sucked her fist. "What will you call her?" she asked Daniel.

"Cordelia," Esther said from the bed. "After Ma."

"How wonderful," Jenny said. "Your mother would have loved her granddaughter."

Esther's eyes welled with tears. "I'm so happy," she whispered when Jenny hugged her. "But I miss Ma so much."

Chapter 7: To the Gold Fields

Mac spent several days in San Francisco buying food, ammunition, a tent and other necessities, and a pack mule to carry it all. On April 3, he left for Sutter's Fort, riding Valiente and leading the mule. According to tradesmen in San Francisco, the fort was the closest settlement to the mill where gold had been found.

He traveled through vast Mexican ranches along the marshy southern shore of the bay, then north to the Sacramento River delta. The trail along the Sacramento to the American River was smooth, the grassy riverbanks spongy with spring runoff. Swift waters ran cobalt below an azure sky. Oaks and cottonwoods hung over the trail, shading it from warm spring sun.

Mac encountered dozens of men heading toward Sutter's Fort, solitary or in small groups, most traveling as he did on horseback. A few drove wagons, causing Mac to remember his long journey of the year before. Now, without Jenny's company, loneliness enveloped him.

After eight days of travel, Mac arrived at Sutter's Fort. He found a two-story adobe building with high walls and guard towers at the corners, much like the Army and Hudson's Bay forts along the Oregon Trail. Not much of a settlement, but about what he expected. Inside the stockade, gold seekers carrying heavy packs thronged the fort.

Although only a few weeks had passed since news of the gold find reached San Francisco, men already gathered to seek their fortunes. Johann Sutter, proprietor of the fort, had commissioned a sawmill for lumber and a gristmill for grain not far away, but Mac heard little about those endeavors. All talk was of gold.

"Sutter claims all the land around his mill," a grizzled mountain man said. "Thirty-five miles in all directions. 'Tain't fair for one man to take title to all that land."

"His men found the gold," another man said.

"I hear 'tweren't Sutter's men at all," the first man said. "'Twere them damn fool Mormons. They was working on the mill and found the gold."

Mac didn't care who'd found the gold. He wondered how hard it would be to dig up a nugget himself. He asked the clerk behind the counter in the fort's store, "What do I need to find gold?"

The man glared behind a bushy beard. "Now why would I tell you? I'm heading to the fields myself tomorrow."

"You're still a clerk today. What'll you sell me?"

"Need a tin pan. I have a few left. What else you want?"

"Hard tack and dried meat. How will I know gold when I see it?"

The man snorted. "Greenhorn, ain't you?" His tone grew friendlier. The clerk must have decided Mac wasn't a threat. "Here's a sample." He handed Mac two rocks—a small yellowish stone which yielded when Mac pushed on an edge, and another shinier, harder piece.

"This is it?" Mac asked, handing the rocks back.

"When you see quartz on the ground—the flinty rock—it's a sign gold's nearby."

Mac nodded. "I know quartz."

"But you want the gold." The clerk bounced the soft yellow rock in his hand. "Wash sand and gravel to find flakes of it. That's what the tin pan's for." The man grinned. "One big nugget. That's all I want. Make my fortune."

Mac had always had money, but he'd never earned any himself. He'd tapped funds in a family trust for his trip to Europe in forty-six and his frontier journey in forty-seven. "Think I'll give it a shot for a few days. I can't stay long—I'm heading back East. What's the best route through the mountains?"

"You searching for gold or traveling?"

"Maybe both."

"You need to get to the Humboldt River. From there the trail to Fort Bridger is well-marked. But afore the Humboldt, you gotta cross the Forty Mile Desert."

"How do I get there?"

"There's a big lake 'bout ninety miles from here. Northeast. Truckee

River's ten miles north of it. Follow the Truckee to its source, then cross the desert."

"Any maps?"

The clerk scratched his chin. "Captain Frémont mapped the area for the Army in forty-four. I don't have a copy, but let me see if I got anything might help." He went into a storeroom and came back with a paper. "All's I got's this sketch. Won't let you take it, but you can copy it."

Mac sat on a stool at the counter and drew the rough map into his journal. It wasn't much guidance to head into mountainous terrain, not like Frémont's careful Oregon Trail maps that Mac's wagon company had used. He remembered shaking his head with his wagon captain, Franklin Pershing, when they'd encountered another company of emigrants using a handwritten sketch to travel to California.

That evening he wrote:

April 11, 1848. Leaving Fort Sutter tomorrow to see what the gold fields are like. Would Father respect me if I found gold? It's dirty work, but it would be my own. If I reach St. Louis before winter, I can be in Boston by year-end. I passed my 27ᵗʰ birthday en route to the fort.

The next morning Mac rode out of the fort and up the south fork of the American. He would need to cross to the north fork to find the Truckee. But the gold was on the south fork, so he would start there. Some men passed Mac, and he passed others. He rode along hilltop ridges and splashed through creek valleys.

As he traveled farther from the fort, Mac encountered fewer men. By the time he reached the base of the mountains, he was alone. When he chanced upon a rocky creek with sandy banks, he turned Valiente upstream to the north and made camp for the night.

In the morning he awoke to the sun rising bright behind the mountains and warm air. "Why not?" he said, grinning as he spoke to Valiente and the mule. "You'd rather graze than move on, wouldn't you? I might even find a nugget."

He sloshed his tin pan in the swift, gurgling water all morning and watched for specks of gold. Nothing.

After a quick midday meal, Mac packed up camp and rode farther upstream. Finding another good campsite just before sunset, he stopped for the night. The next day he panned for gold again. Still no luck. But then, he hadn't seen any quartz, so he must not be near gold.

The third day out of Sutter's Fort, Mac left the sandy creek and crossed a ridge to another valley. The next mountain stream he encountered had gravel banks, and he stopped when he saw stones glinting in the riverbed.

Mac swirled his pan in the water and found a few shiny flakes. He tapped them into a small leather pouch.

April 15, 1848. Found gold flakes. Are they real or fool's gold? I'll stay awhile.

Days passed while Mac panned on the isolated stream. He didn't see a soul for more than a week. He ate from his provisions and occasionally shot small game, but stayed near his camp on the mountain creek. Every day he found more specks of what he thought was gold.

Boston could wait. He relished the silence of prospecting, enjoying the solitude, warm sun and cold water, the burble of the creek. No demands on his time, no responsibility to anyone but himself.

His sack of gold flakes filled slowly, but the rhythm of the panning gave him time to think. Why had he hurt Jenny? he asked himself repeatedly.

They'd traveled together, pretending to be husband and wife for six months. He started out as a greenhorn, but became leader of the wagon company by the time they reached Oregon Territory. Those were good months, he realized now.

They'd had their share of tribulations. Jenny nursed Mac back to health when he lay near death from cholera. He helped her through childbirth and built her a home in Oregon. Through it all, they worked together as closely as any married couple.

But he never touched her in lust. Not until that last night. He had other regrets in life, but his actions that final night plagued his conscience as much as any other sin he'd committed. Mac had suppressed his attraction to Jenny while they traveled, but in the proximity of their cabin, he found her desirable—pretty and gentle, kind and caring. Still, she was a shattered fourteen-year-old girl when they met, disgraced by rape and pregnancy, and over a decade younger than he was. She'd rejected his proposal of marriage, saying she didn't want him, or any man. So he left her alone.

Until that last night, when in his drunkenness his restraint deserted him.

Now Mac saw Jenny's face reflected in the water he panned from the creek. He shook his pan to the rhythm of the words, "Why did I hurt her? Why did I desert her? How will she fare? How can I make amends?"

The answer came to him while he sifted dirt and sand in the frigid water—he would fake his death to free Jenny from their lie.

He would wait until he left the West and was well on his way home, so no word of his subterfuge would reach Oregon. He would find someone to write Jenny describing his death. He couldn't tell her of the plan—not if he wanted her to react as if it were real—but he could tell her he would set her free.

In the evening Mac took out quill and ink and tore a page from his journal. By the light of his campfire he wrote:

> *April 23, 1848*
> *Dear Jenny,*
>
> *No words can express sufficient remorse for my actions the night I left. I will find a way to free you from being bound to me by appearances. You and William can keep my name, and you will be at liberty to pursue a full life in Oregon. You can have the land—I have no need of it.*
>
> *I hope someday you are able to accept a man worthy of you. I am not that man, much as I regret to admit it. Zeke Pershing is a good man who cares for you.*
>> *Respectfully,*
>> *Caleb McDougall*

Mac reread the letter. Did he really want Jenny to consider Zeke? He swallowed hard. She needed someone. If Mac wasn't going back to Oregon, Zeke was a good choice.

Mac stared at the stars and made his plans. Since no fortune was to be found in the creek, he would return to Sutter's Fort to post the letter. Then head for Truckee and the route to Boston. Whether he wanted it or not, it was the only future he could see for himself.

"Soon Jenny will be free of me," Mac told Valiente, then turned over in his bedroll to sleep.

He awoke the next morning to a crisp spring day, sunshine peeking over the hills above him. The mountains would be lush when he climbed them—ripe with new grass and spotted with wildflowers. He filled his canteen with water still icy with snowmelt and breathed in the clean air. A fish splashed in the creek, and an otter slid into the water downstream.

One more day, he decided. This was too lovely a spring day to spend packing. Tomorrow he would return to Sutter's Fort.

Mac dipped his pan in the swift creek and swirled it gently. When the sediment settled, he glanced at the pan as he was about to dump the remaining grit. A lumpy stone the size of a walnut lay in the bottom. The worn rock was buttery yellow, veined with streaks of black. It glowed in the sun and bent when he pushed on a rough edge.

A nugget. A gold nugget.

He whooped a loud "Ya-hoo!" and danced in the frigid stream.

Chapter 8: Wanderlust

Sunday, April 23ʳᵈ—Easter. I have not heard from Mac. The Tanners and I work from dawn to dusk planting fields. I still have not talked to Doc about my rights to the land.

The land was fecund after the wet winter. Seeds spouted quickly, and soon the sown fields were green. But there was no respite from the toil, which left Jenny with blistered fingers and aching muscles every evening.

The Pershing twins ran into Jenny's yard the following Tuesday afternoon, a week after Cordelia's birth. It was a fine spring afternoon after several days of rain, with a brilliant blue sky and singing birds. "Miz Jenny," one boy cried, "Pa's having a party tomorrow night. Joel's leaving Thursday for California."

Joel, the second Pershing son, had talked about leaving for California ever since they arrived in Oregon last autumn. Some men simply couldn't remain in one place. Joel's father, Captain Franklin Pershing, had spent his career moving about with the Army. He'd left his family behind until he formed the wagon company that brought them all to Oregon.

"What shall I bring?" Jenny asked the boys.

They shrugged. "No matter. Esther said bring what you have."

It was too early for wild berries, and the garden wasn't bearing yet. Wednesday morning, Jenny made custard pie, using cream from the cow she shared with Esther, eggs from her hens, and sweet syrup boiled from the bigleaf maple trees in the woods on her claim. Jenny had never encountered syrup from trees when she'd lived in New Orleans and Missouri—Hatty Tanner had taught her how to make it.

"Looks mighty fine," Hatty said, when Jenny removed the baked pie from the side of the fireplace. "I got venison stew from the deer Clarence shot yesterday. It were tryin' to git in the garden."

In midafternoon Jenny bundled William in a blanket. After Tanner hitched his mules to the wagon, they all climbed in for the ride to the Pershing farm. Captain Franklin Pershing and seven of his nine of his children—all except Esther and the baby Jonah whom Esther was raising—lived in a house on Captain Pershing's land. Franklin Pershing and his twenty-one-year-old son Zeke had each filed a claim for 640 acres of land, the most they could claim, and they'd cleared a portion of both parcels to plant.

Joel, at nineteen, was old enough to file his own claim, but he said he didn't want to farm. He'd helped his father and Zeke build the house and barn and clear the fields through the winter and spring.

"What will Captain Pershing and Zeke do without Joel?" Jenny asked Tanner.

"'Spect they'll manage," Tanner said. "I'll help 'em. And those twins is growin' fast."

"Can you handle our place and help them, too?" Jenny asked.

"Do what I can. Don't you worry. We'll keep your place goin' till Captain McDougall gits back."

Only the Tullers knew Mac would probably never return. She could hardly admit it to herself, and she couldn't tell her friends without letting on she wasn't Mac's wife.

They arrived at the Pershing farm, and Zeke helped Jenny out of the wagon. "You're looking purty, Miz Jenny," he said with an easy grin.

"Thank you, Zeke." She smiled back at him, then reached up to take William from Hatty.

Esther Abercrombie and her sister Rachel Pershing supervised the placement of food on a makeshift table of rough planks laid on top of tree stumps. The Pershing twins and their younger siblings raced around, shooing off flies. Jenny and Hatty squeezed the custard pie and venison stew between other dishes.

"Jenny."

She turned and saw the doctor's wife. "How are you, Mrs. Tuller?"

"Come talk with me, dear." The older woman smiled at her.

Jenny let Mrs. Tuller draw her to a corner of the yard. "Any word from

Captain McDougall?" Mrs. Tuller asked after admiring how William had grown.

"No, ma'am."

"What are you going to do without him?"

"We're fine," Jenny said. "Tanner's minding the fields."

"That can't last."

"Why not?"

"Doc hears the legislature wants to run Negroes out of Oregon."

"There are other Negroes in Oregon City. One led a whole wagon train of them here a few years back."

Mrs. Tuller shook her head. "They could all be forced out. How long can Tanner keep his family here if he might be jailed?"

Jenny panicked at the thought of living alone on the claim with William. "Well, maybe Zeke can help me."

Mrs. Tuller looked skeptical. "Zeke has his own farm. And his father's. Besides, what would it look like for Zeke to spend so much time with you? Everyone thinks you're married to Captain McDougall. You can't manage the farm alone with a baby, and you can't rely on Zeke Pershing."

Jenny still wanted to talk to Doc about her rights to Mac's claim, but Mrs. Tuller did not seem to be of a mind to help. Jenny raised her chin. "Thank you for your concern," she said. "I'll figure out what to do if the Tanners leave." She turned away from Mrs. Tuller as Esther approached from the food table.

"Come, Jenny," Esther said, taking Jenny's arm. "Pa's about to give Joel a farewell speech."

In the middle of the yard, Joel and the rest of the Pershing children stood beside their father. Captain Pershing raised a bottle of whiskey.

Jenny gasped. "You're letting him drink?" she whispered to Esther. Captain Pershing had lost command of the wagon train because of his drunkenness after his wife died. Jenny knew his children tried to keep him from liquor, but he found it at the most inconvenient times.

Esther shrugged. "Zeke's supposed to watch Pa today."

"My son Joel is leaving," Captain Pershing began. He sounded maudlin, but not drunk. "He's like me—got the wanderlust in him. Bound for California. I'll miss him like I miss his ma." He tipped the bottle at Joel, then held it to his mouth for a long gulp.

"All right, Pa," Zeke said, taking the flask. "Let's pass it around." He took a sip and passed it to another man. Then he walked over to Esther and

Jenny. "We'll see if that slows him down. Though I reckon he'll be drunk by dark."

"Can't you stop him?" Jenny whispered.

Zeke shook his head. "No, but the bouts are less frequent. He ain't been on a bender since the Abercrombie barn raising." Zeke grinned. "We all had too much that night."

"Yes," Jenny said, remembering the feel of Mac's arms around her—first sweet, then demanding. And then he was gone.

"The music's starting," Zeke said. "You care to dance with me, Miz Jenny?"

Mrs. Tuller frowned at her from across the yard. But Zeke was her friend. Jenny turned to him. "All right. If I can find Rachel to take William."

Chapter 9:   Uncertainty and Change

It was the end of April before Jenny talked to Doc Tuller. She and the Tanners were in Oregon City for Sunday services, and afterward she pulled Doc aside. She greeted him, then asked, "Doc, if Mac never returns, can I keep his claim?"

"You don't expect him to come back, do you?" Doc's bushy eyebrows knit together in a frown. "You told him you wouldn't marry him."

Doc and Mrs. Tuller never let her forget their advice. "I couldn't. You know that."

"It would have been best for you and William."

She wished they wouldn't keep harping on the matter—it was too late to change her mind, even if she wanted to. "What rights do I have now?"

Doc shrugged. "As his wife, you might have something, but as it is, you probably don't. McDougall filed the claim in his name. Women can't claim land. It's his responsibility to improve it."

"If I make the improvements, can't I stay on the farm?"

"I don't know, girl. I doubt the legislature ever contemplated a situation as unlikely as yours."

"What if I were a widow? Surely they don't throw widows off their husband's claims."

"But you're not," Doc said. "And won't be, since you didn't marry. And I've heard the inheritance laws ain't set here in Oregon yet. Don't know what would happen."

Jenny clutched Doc's arm. "The land is all William and I have. Would you see what you can find out?"

Doc nodded. "It'll take some time. I can't be too direct. You don't want gossip, do you?"

Jenny shook her head, biting her lip.

That night she wrote:

> *Sunday, April 30ᵗʰ—Doc doesn't think I have any rights to the land, though he will inquire.*
>
> *Maybe I should have married Mac last fall, if only for William's sake. But I couldn't. And now I might be left with nothing.*

In the days after Joel left, the weather turned wet and cold. The green fields turned yellow. "Never seen so much rain," Tanner told Jenny. "Wheat's drowndin' in the fields. Don't know what it'll do to our crop come summer."

William seemed to grow bigger and heavier before her eyes. Every week he outgrew more clothes. Sometimes Jenny wondered which of her attackers had fathered her son. When she did, she turned her mind instead to how much the baby looked like her papa. Blue eyes, hair a shade lighter than her own, and a sweet smile—except when he was teething and cranky. William was hers, and no one else's.

Besides her land rights and the rain, Jenny had another worry—what would she do if the Tanners left? She didn't ask either Tanner or Hatty what their plans were, and they said nothing to her. Maybe Mrs. Tuller was wrong. Maybe they would stay.

By mid-May Jenny could no longer tote William around and do her chores at the same time. She frequently found herself taking him to Esther's, or inviting Esther with Cordelia and Jonah to her cabin, so they could share caring for the three babies as they worked. At ten months, Jonah wasn't walking yet, but he could crawl anywhere and needed constant supervision. William, at eight months, scooted after Jonah wherever the older baby went.

One morning Esther arrived in her wagon with both children—Jonah tied into the wagon bed with a rope around his waist, and Cordelia asleep in a sling across Esther's chest. Jenny hurried to lift Jonah down and saw Esther in tears, her mouth a thin angry line.

"What's wrong?" Jenny asked, while Tanner tied Esther's horse to the fencepost.

"Pa," Esther said, wiping her face.

"Was he . . . ?" Jenny didn't want to ask if Captain Pershing had been drinking again.

"He's getting married."

"Married? To whom?" Captain Pershing had been devastated by the loss of his wife, who'd died of childbirth fever after Jonah was born.

"Mrs. Purcell." Esther flopped down in Jenny's rocking chair and rocked Cordelia furiously.

Jenny put Jonah on the floor with William and handed him a straw doll. "Mrs. Purcell? But why?"

"I don't know," Esther sobbed. "He and Zeke came over after supper last night. Pa told me then."

"What did Zeke say?"

"Nothing. Not a word. All Pa said was the younger children needed a mother. They're getting married in Oregon City in two weeks." Esther dried her eyes with Cordelia's blanket. "I've been doing all I can to help Pa since Ma died."

Jenny knelt beside Esther. "Of course you have. You've been like a mother to Jonah."

"No one can take Ma's place. How can he do this?"

"Your papa's a man, Esther. He needs someone to help. The housework and children are too much for Rachel."

"But Mrs. Purcell's bringing three children of her own."

"Maybe that's why she's marrying him," Jenny said. "She's lived in town all winter in a ramshackle house even Tanner could hardly make sound. A widow can't do much to earn her keep. Her children need a father as much as your papa needs a wife." The Purcells had been in the same wagon train, and Mr. Purcell had drowned on the Big Vermilion River, when he tried to save his youngest child. The boy lived, but the father died—the first of many deaths along the trail.

"It ain't even been a year since Ma died." Esther sounded angry, but Jenny thought she was mostly sad.

"Oregon's different, Esther. We've seen girls of twelve, even younger, married to men in their forties. Men have been hanging around Rachel all winter. It'll be better to have a grown woman in the house."

"No one can take Ma's place," Esther said again.

After Esther left, Jenny wrote,

Saturday, May 20ᵗʰ—Captain Pershing is marrying Mrs. Purcell, and Esther doesn't like it. Her mother was a dear woman, whose death was a great loss to us all. But poor Mrs. Purcell suffered tragedy as well. Maybe some good can come from both families' grief.

Two weeks later, on Sunday, June 4, 1848, the Pershings and many of their friends from the wagon company drove into Oregon City to the Methodist church, where Franklin Pershing and Amanda Purcell were united in matrimony. Esther and Rachel cried—remembering their mother, Jenny supposed. And maybe wondering how their family would stay together. Zeke stood beside his father looking grim.

At a supper after the wedding at the Pershing home, Jenny asked Zeke, "How will everyone fit into this house?" It was bigger than Jenny's cabin, but still only three rooms downstairs with a loft above the back two rooms.

Zeke shrugged. "I built a room in the barn on my claim. I'm moving there. Let my three younger brothers and little Henry Purcell have the loft here. The four girls will share a downstairs room. By winter, I'll build my own cabin."

"Do you wish you'd gone to California with Joel?"

Zeke shook his head. "I've had enough travel. I don't have the wanderlust, like Joel. I'll keep farming. Oregon has good land." He smiled down at Jenny. "What about you? Do you wish you'd gone back East with Mac?"

"No," Jenny said. "There's nothing there for me."

Except Mac, she thought. Except Mac.

Chapter 10:   Gold Fever

As soon as he held his first nugget, Mac abandoned all thought of leaving the creek. A fortune might be his after all. From dawn until dark he sloshed silt into his tin pan looking for more color. He stopped briefly at midday to eat. Day after day he found flakes and several small nuggets. The glint of gold in the water reminded him of Jenny's hair in sunlight.

Panning for gold exhausted his body, but did not fill his mind. Valiente, the mule, and the chirping birds in the trees were his only company. The physical exertion and peaceful surroundings provided little distraction from memories—of his placid but lonely childhood, of his carefree days at Harvard, of his wagon trip along the trail.

Of Jenny.

As he panned, Mac relived each day of his trip from Boston to Oregon. After he'd cajoled Jenny into going with him, he'd watched her change. She'd started as a scared girl afraid of every river crossing. She'd grown into a young woman able to climb mountains carrying her newborn child until she collapsed from exhaustion.

William was everything to Jenny—Mac had seen that. While she was in labor, she badgered Mac into agreeing to care for the baby if she died. After William was born, she rejected Mac—and all men—saying she would be William's only parent. Then Mac betrayed her trust.

When he kissed her, he'd tasted her sweetness. She felt soft and desirable in his arms. He wanted more of her—then and now—but he needed to let her go. Still, he couldn't bring himself to return to Sutter's Fort and send his letter to Jenny.

So he remained on the creek, searching for gold. His sack of flakes and nuggets filled. By firelight one evening he wrote in his journal:

May 18, 1848. I have panned this creek for three weeks now. My back and legs ache from stooping, my fingers are wrinkled from the icy water. I estimate I've found around ten pounds of gold, but I don't know how pure it is. I will stay until my supplies run out.

Mac fished the creek for the trout he could see in the clear mountain water. Sometimes he left camp to hunt, killing a deer one morning. The meat lasted several days, wrapped in oilcloth and stored in the cold water. But by early June his flour and cornmeal were gone. He had brought only enough to travel to Fort Bridger.

June 2, 1848. I am out of flour. Fort Bridger is a good month away by horseback. I must return to Sutter's Fort to replenish provisions. I'll sell the gold I've found. And post my letter to Jenny.

The next morning Mac packed his camp and headed south to Sutter's Fort, retracing the route he'd traveled in April, though moving more quickly.

Along the way he encountered many more men than on his earlier trek. Like Mac, they panned streams and dug in rocks. They eyed him suspiciously as he made his way along the valleys and ridges in the warm early summer air. He didn't stop near anyone's camp, not wanting trouble, and kept his rifle handy in case anyone approached him. Thieves might not be after the gold yet, but they would arrive soon, he was sure.

Mac camped a short distance from Sutter's Fort on Sunday night. On Monday morning, when he neared the fort, he was amazed how much settlement had sprung up in the few weeks of his absence. There were ten or more bustling stores outside the fort, most of them advertising assayer services on crudely carved signs.

He rode through the stockade gate into the fort. After tying Valiente and the mule to a rail, he entered the general store he'd patronized in April. The clerk he'd talked to then was gone. An old man now served customers crowding into the premises. Mac wandered the store looking at provisions until the man was available.

"Lot of customers today," Mac said.

"Lot of customers every day." The old storekeeper smiled a toothless grin. "I hear tell San Francisco's plum cleared out. Nobody left. Every able-bodied man wants gold. I'd be out prospecting, too, if my rheumatism weren't so bad."

"Are all these men finding gold?"

"Some are, some ain't." The old man shrugged. "Them that's lucky do." He grinned at Mac again. "You been lucky?"

"I found something. Who's the best assayer around?" Mac asked. He'd have to judge for himself whether he was being cheated, but he might as well get a recommendation.

Eying Mac, the clerk rubbed his whiskery chin, then leaned over the counter. "I'd take mine to Nate's, if I was you," he whispered. "His place is right outside the fort. He'll give you fair weight."

"How do I file a claim for the land where I found it, if I decide to go back?"

The old man hooted. "Ain't no way to file no claim. Not in California. Closest land office is in Oregon City. Squatters' rights is all we got. Men'll mostly let you alone while you're prospecting, but they'll steal from you if you leave. Steal any equipment left behind, too."

Mac walked Valiente and his mule to Nate's store and took his bag of nuggets and flakes inside. The first nugget he'd found was the largest, but he had several marble-sized and pea-sized rocks as well. He thought they were nearly pure gold, but he didn't know for sure.

"You Nate?" he asked a neatly dressed gray-haired man with an eyeshade. The man resembled Mac's last tutor, his favorite instructor. Mac had spent more time with Mr. Sanders than with his parents. Now Mac brushed a speck of dust off his trousers, wanting to make as good an impression on the clerk as he had on his tutor.

The man nodded. "Nathan Peabody. What can I do for you?" He sounded educated, enunciating clearly.

Mac plunked his bag down on the assayer's counter. "How much is it worth?" He eyed Nate while the man sifted through the bag's contents.

Nate put his loupe to a nugget, then squinted at Mac. "Good color," he said. "Where'd you find it?"

"Creek toward the north fork of the American."

"Where exactly?"

Mac shrugged. No sense letting others know where he'd found gold. "How much?"

Nate turned back to the nuggets, weighed them, poked at the gold with a thin pick. "I'm offering eighteen dollars for an ounce of pure gold. My best guess is yours averages ninety percent pure. So I'll give you sixteen-twenty an ounce."

Ninety percent pure. He'd found real gold. And it was worth real money—the first he'd ever earned. Mac couldn't help grinning.

Then he wondered how the assayer made his calculations. "How do you get to eighteen dollars an ounce?" he asked.

"Gold's worth twenty-sixty-seven at the mint," Nate said. "But I have expenses. Transportation to the East, mostly."

"How do you know it's ninety percent pure?"

Nate grinned, rubbing his clean-shaven chin. "There's the art in it, son. I've been buying and selling gold since I was your age. Worked in a jeweler's store in New York, then as an assayer in Georgia." Nate looked Mac straight in the eye, like his tutor Sanders had done.

Mac scratched his head. "How much total?"

"Nuggets weigh eleven pounds and two ounces. One hundred seventy-eight ounces." Nate multiplied the weight by his price on a scrap of paper. "Comes to just shy of twenty-nine hundred dollars. I'll buy the lot for that right now," he said. "Or you can get another bid. Someone else might go higher. Or lower."

Nate sounded like he knew what he was talking about, and Mac had no reason to doubt the man's honesty. Plus he had no knowledge of his own to use for negotiating. He'd mostly been prospecting for the adventure and to keep from having to decide on his future. Though he'd like to earn a fortune to impress his father.

He scrutinized the assayer, then shrugged. He might as well sell to Nate. "Do I set up an account with you?"

"You can." Nate nodded.

"What about the flakes?"

"Most men keep their gold dust. It's as good as coins around here. Every store has a scale. But watch when they weigh your dust. No fingers near the scale."

They came to terms on what Mac would retain and what he'd put on account. Then it occurred to Mac he could send money to Jenny. "Can I send my gold to Oregon?"

"I can give you coins to ship," Nate said. "Or a letter of credit. I charge five percent to issue the letter. Can't say who'll honor the letter in Oregon, nor how it would be discounted. There aren't any banks or express companies in California yet. Assayers and shopkeepers are your only options."

"No bank in Oregon City either," Mac said. He thought a moment. Moving money was hard in the West, but maybe Abernethy's store would give Jenny credit. Mac asked for a letter of credit instructing Abernethy to add five hundred dollars to Jenny's account. The funds might not reach her, but at least he would try. It took five years to prove a claim, and one hundred dollars per year would allow Jenny and William to manage until then.

As he ate that night Mac pondered what to do next. His earnings from the gold would finance his trip home, but they weren't a fortune. Not enough for independence from his family.

If he left for Boston now, he could still make it before winter struck hard. He'd be home for Christmas. Then he remembered his last Christmas at home in 1846, when he'd learned his mother had thrown Bridget out on the street.

Mac didn't want to return to Boston. Nothing there for him but his parents' snobbery and a stultifying law practice with his brother. He wasn't ready to settle into the life awaiting him in Boston. He wanted his freedom.

Maybe he didn't have to return to Boston. At least, not yet.

He knew where to find gold. He could work the stream he'd found for the rest of the summer. Travel east through Panama in the fall, or spend the winter in California. Time enough for Boston next year.

Mac pulled out the letter he'd written to Jenny and added:

> *P.S. June 5, 1848. Since starting this letter, I have found gold, and will likely stay in California this year, returning to Boston next spring. The enclosed letter of credit should keep you and William until the land claim is proven. As I wrote above, the land is yours. C. McD.*

The next morning Mac sealed the letter of credit in his letter to Jenny, and posted it.

On his way out of Sutter's Fort he bought food, a shovel, and sacks to hold the additional gold he hoped to find.

Chapter 11:   Partners

"Mac." A voice called his name as he rode Valiente down the muddy street out of Sutter's Fort, leading his pack mule behind him. "Mac McDougall."

He turned. Joel Pershing trotted toward him on horseback, also leading a mule. Joel would know how Jenny was. "Joel, what are you doing here?" Mac exclaimed in surprise. "When'd you leave Oregon? How's Jenny? And William?"

"They was fine when I left six weeks ago," Joel said. "I'm here for the gold. I was on the Siskiyou Trail, when I heard rumors of gold lying on the ground everywhere 'round here. I'd planned on going to San Francisco, but decided to come straight to the gold fields. Search for some color myself. What're you doing here? Thought you was headed for Boston."

"I've been prospecting," Mac said. "You said Jenny was well when you left her?"

Joel waved vaguely. "She's fine. I hear mountains east of here supposed to be rich."

"Yes." Mac squinted. Joel had been a reliable scout on the trail to Oregon, though surlier than his older brother Zeke. Mac thought he could trust him. "I found gold to the northeast," Mac said. "It's a good site, more creek to pan than I can handle by myself. I could use a partner."

"I don't have any money. Can't buy in."

"Nothing to buy. Land's free." Mac shrugged. "I'll keep the gold I've found so far. We'll share going forward. We can each stake a claim, then work together. You can buy me out if you want when I leave for the East."

"What about provisions?" Joel asked.

"I stocked up." Mac gestured at the mule behind Valiente. "Bought

51

enough food for a few weeks. With two of us, we can take time to hunt and fish. And it'll be easier to travel back to the fort for supplies."

"I wrote Pa last night, so he'll know I made it this far. I'm ready." Joel grinned.

The two men started the two-day trek to the creek where Mac had found gold. Joel asked Mac countless questions, some of which Mac couldn't answer. "I'm a greenhorn still," he said. "Just lucky so far."

Mac probed for details about Jenny and William, but Joel couldn't tell him much.

When they reached the valley and stream where Mac had panned before, Joel looked around. "Purty land," he said.

"It's full of gold. High quality, the assayer told me."

They set up camp, and Mac showed Joel where he'd found the first nugget. "Biggest rock came from here. But I found smaller ones up and down the stream. And lots of flakes."

"Have you staked out a claim?" Joel asked.

Mac shook his head. "Didn't decide to stay until I was at Sutter's Fort. But now I've decided to keep prospecting through the fall. Go back to Boston next year."

"What about Miz Jenny?" Joel asked.

Mac's stomach tightened. He would have to confess to Joel, or the younger man wouldn't believe why Mac had left Jenny behind. "We weren't married. I have no reason to return to Oregon."

Joel's jaw dropped. "Weren't married? But what about the baby?"

"Not mine."

Staring at Mac, Joel took off his hat and scratched his head.

"You can't let on to anyone in Oregon," Mac pleaded. "I don't want Jenny hurt. She's been through enough." But he didn't explain further. There were limits to what he would tell Joel.

"No one else knows?"

"The Tullers do."

Joel shook his head. "A woman is trouble enough when she's your wife. Don't know why you'd take one on otherwise."

"Jenny needed help. And a home. There wasn't anything for her in Missouri." Mac hoped that summary would satisfy Joel. And he hoped he hadn't made a huge mistake in telling Joel as much as he had.

"You seemed plenty sweet on her. And did all right by her baby, too."

Mac lifted a shoulder silently.

"And now you've left her." Joel frowned. "Does Zeke know?"

"No." Mac sighed. "Not unless Jenny told him."

"She hadn't when I left Oregon," Joel said. "Or he'd marry her right quick."

Mac swallowed a burst of anger. After all, that's what he wanted, wasn't it? He'd told Jenny to marry Zeke himself.

"Damnedest thing I ever heard," Joel said, shaking his head and frowning again.

That evening across the fire from Joel, Mac wrote:

> *June 7, 1848. Back on the creek where I found the gold. Joel Pershing has joined me. I told him the truth about Jenny, and now I fear he will let it slip. I've never worked with a partner before.*

Mac and Joel staked out their ground the day after they arrived at the creek. "I'll claim this stretch where I found my nugget," Mac said, pointing at the stream. "You can go upriver or down."

"Does it matter?" Joel asked.

"Hell if I know," Mac said with a shrug.

"Then I'll go upstream."

They pounded sharpened tree limbs into the ground and piled rocks around them. Each man claimed about thirty feet of creek bed and from the water back to the ridge behind them.

"We'll build a shelter on my claim," Mac said. "Graze the horses and mules on the meadow back of yours."

A few days later, Mac assessed their partnership:

> *June 15, 1848. Working with Joel feels like traveling on the trail last year. He was a taciturn but amiable companion then, and he remains the same.*

Mac showed Joel how to pan for gold in the water and explained how he shoveled dirt from the nearby shore into piles for panning. They dug in the sand and gravel along the banks from dawn until twilight. With two of them working, they scooped big holes in the creek and pockmarked the dry land above the water looking for nuggets. In the evenings they cooked, talked of the dust and nuggets they'd found during the day, and planned their diggings for the day ahead.

"Sure wish we could get title to the land," Joel said. "Ain't it strange we left Oregon City, and that's the only place to file a California land claim?"

Some days one partner went hunting in the morning, leaving the other man panning alone, rifle at hand.

Yet despite their easy camaraderie, the relationship between the men changed from the year before in the wagon company. "You ain't boss now, Mac," Joel snarled one day when Mac directed him where to pan. "We're partners."

Joel seemed like only a lad—at nineteen, he was several years younger than Mac's twenty-seven. But Mac supposed he had a point. As wagon captain, Mac had given orders to Joel and the other scouts. But here in California, they'd agreed—share and share alike on the gold they found. Although they'd staked two claims, they worked the land together.

So to keep the peace, Mac tried to make requests of Joel rather than issue orders.

Summer days in California, even in the mountains, were almost always warm and bright. The water was cold on their hands and legs as they panned, but the sun beat on their backs all day.

They built a rough shed of pine planks on the ridge above the creek where a meadow opened to the sky. Wildflowers sprinkled the grasses around the shed, breezes whispered through tall pines, and the creek babbled without end.

The small shack held their belongings and provided a place to sleep during the rare rains. It was about ten feet square, with wood bunks on one wall and shelves on another. A rude door and no windows. No stove or fireplace, so they cooked outside. They spent little time in the shed and usually slept under the stars.

The hill country was beautiful—as pretty as any place Mac had seen in his travels. But the work was backbreaking. Stooping and shoveling all day, cold feet and scorched heads. Perhaps working at a desk all day had some advantages, he thought one night as he crawled into his bedroll.

After a few weeks Joel made a trip back to Sutter's Fort for supplies and to have their findings assayed and deposited. On the evening after Joel left, Mac wrote:

> *July 2, 1848. Joel is headed to the fort, and I am alone on our claim. He is good company, but I wonder how long our partnership will last. Which of us will tire of this work first and when?*

Chapter 12:   Fourth of July

Monday, July 3rd—Tomorrow is the Fourth of July celebration in town. Last year we were at Independence Rock. I climbed its steep slope with Mac, and Esther married Daniel.

Jenny put away her journal and slipped into bed, hugging Mac's pillow. She smiled, remembering how Mac's strong hand grasped hers to help her up the side of Independence Rock. She'd been swollen with child and awkward on her feet, but she'd felt safe with him.

This year on July 4, Jenny and the Tanners drove into Oregon City for a picnic and parade. They met Esther and Daniel and sat with Daniel's parents and the rest of the Abercrombies.

Jenny kept quiet around Daniel's father, Samuel Abercrombie. The man had constantly interfered with the leaders of the wagon train to Oregon—first Captain Pershing and then Mac. Mr. Abercrombie had even taken a portion of the travelers off on his own for several weeks, because he didn't want to follow Mac to Whitman Mission.

But after the two groups reunited, while they traveled the treacherous Barlow Road around Mt. Hood, Abercrombie saved Mac's life. On Laurel Hill near the summit, only Abercrombie's strength stopped a wagon from careening down the mountain and crushing Mac. After that, Mac and Abercrombie developed a cautious truce. So now Jenny tried to remember Mr. Abercrombie's fortitude.

"Why aren't you sitting with your family?" Jenny whispered to Esther, when Mr. Abercrombie left to join the militiamen marching in the parade.

His volunteer unit had received a citation for bravery for their campaign against the Cayuse.

"Don't like being around her," Esther responded, with a jerk of her head across the field toward her father and his new wife Amanda. "She's crammed all her things into his house. 'Tweren't big enough for all the young'uns before. Her girls are squeezed in the bedroom with Rachel and Ruth, and her boy is up in the loft with the twins and Noah."

"What does Zeke say?" Jenny asked.

"He don't talk about it. Stays on his own claim as much as he can. He's building a cabin for himself to have ready by fall."

"Have you heard from Joel?"

"Not a word." Esther sighed, shifting Cordelia on her lap. "He should be in California by now."

After the parade, the captain of the Oregon militia congratulated the volunteer troops. The Honorable Columbia Lancaster, a judge, and Peter Burnett, a member of the legislature, gave orations. A twelve-pound cannon offered a series of salutes to the nation, to the Declaration of Independence, to Oregon, and to the brave soldiers. The big gun sounded over and over. Samuel Abercrombie stood in formation and puffed up his chest the entire time.

"Hear tell there's gold in California," Abercrombie said when he returned to the picnic blanket. "Brig docked in Astoria two days ago. Its captain bought up all the supplies he could, until men at the stores ferreted out of him why he wanted so many picks and pans."

Esther clapped her hands. "Joel! Maybe he'll find gold."

Excited speculation about Californian gold continued through the afternoon, many men ready to pull up stakes and head south.

Zeke came over later to greet Esther and Jenny. "What do you think about the news of gold?" Jenny asked him.

He shook his head. "Need to hear more."

"You're still not tempted to follow Joel to California?" Jenny smiled.

"Nope. Farming's steady. This is only a rumor. No telling whether there's really any gold. Or how much. I'll keep clearing fields and planting crops." Zeke tipped his hat to Jenny and Esther and left.

"Wouldn't it be wonderful if Joel found gold." Esther sighed. "He could help us all. I'm so tired of living in dirt."

"Our cabins are nicer than the wagons last year," Jenny said.

"But we knew that would end. Now we don't have nothing but more of

57

the same to look forward to. Don't you get tired of housework and chores and tending babies?"

Jenny lifted her face to the sun. The summer air was pleasant, unlike the humidity of Missouri or Louisiana. Oregon was primitive, but it was beautiful. "At least I have my own place. A home for William and me."

"Any word from Captain McDougall?"

"No." Jenny was past being angry at Mac now. She'd decided she would never hear from him again—he'd been gone for four months without word. She didn't know how she would explain his absence to Esther and the others when he didn't return next year. But she would put that worry off as long as possible.

Then the niggling fear rose again that she wouldn't be able to keep the claim. She needed to find out what Doc had learned.

On a clear day the following week, Jenny rode Poulette to the Tuller farm. Poulette would foal in a few weeks, but Tanner assured Jenny she could still ride the mare.

"Jenny, what a nice surprise," Mrs. Tuller said. "Where's William?"

"I left him with Hatty," Jenny said. "Is Doc around?"

Mrs. Tuller frowned. "Is something wrong?"

"I need to ask him about my land."

"He'll be here soon for dinner. Come in and sit a spell."

Jenny tied Poulette in the barnyard and entered the cabin. Mrs. Tuller sat in the rocking chair she'd brought all the way from Illinois and took out her knitting. Jenny sat on a stool beside her.

"Now what's this about?" Mrs. Tuller asked.

"I started worrying about whether I can stay on the claim, now Mac is gone. I asked Doc to find out what he could about my rights."

"You and Captain McDougall should have married." Mrs. Tuller clucked and shook her head. "It wasn't right for you to stay with him otherwise."

"You know why I didn't."

Mrs. Tuller stared at Jenny over her knitting needles. "Did I ever tell you Doc and I only met twice afore we were married?"

Jenny shook her head.

"And we've been together nigh on forty years. Marriage isn't about poems and spooning. It's about working together through good times and bad. You had your bad times early, but you and Captain McDougall got on well."

"He didn't love me," Jenny said. But as she spoke, she remembered Mac's hands and mouth on her that last evening. Whether he'd loved her or not, he'd wanted her. His roughness had surprised her, but it was Mac. She should have let him take her. She owed him everything. It wouldn't have been like the men in Missouri.

"A man and woman can come to care for each other." Mrs. Tuller frowned at Jenny. "He never made any advances?"

Jenny looked at the floor and shook her head. She wouldn't tell Mrs. Tuller about the last night. That was between her and Mac.

Doc came into the cabin. "What's for dinner, Elizabeth?" he asked as he washed his hands in a bowl by the door.

"Jenny's come for a visit, Doc," Mrs. Tuller said. "She'll share our stew."

Doc smiled at Jenny. He was often gruff, but today his smile was kind.

"I wanted to know what you'd found out about the land claim laws," Jenny said. "What do I have to do to prove up the claim? Can I keep the farm without Mac?"

Doc's smile turned to a glare under his thick eyebrows. "Shouldn't you have talked to McDougall before he left?"

"He didn't tell me he was leaving."

Doc and Mrs. Tuller looked at each other. "Was there a problem, dear?" Mrs. Tuller asked, surprise in her voice. "We thought he left awful sudden."

"It was sudden," Jenny said. "I thought he'd write. But he hasn't."

"Did he leave you any money?" Doc's voice was sharp.

Jenny nodded. "Some gold coins. I don't want to use them, if I don't have to."

"He ain't coming back, girl." Doc said, his glare deepening. "You don't have any hold on him."

Jenny scowled back at the doctor, her chin in the air. "I know, sir. But I'll have his money and land ready for him if he does. Or I'll send the money to him in Boston. I can take care of William and myself. But I need to know what claim I have to the land."

"Well, you're a plucky one, that's for sure," Doc said. He pushed his chair back from the table, then continued, "Law gives each grown man the right to claim six hundred and forty acres. Any combination of meadow and woodlands."

"And Mac claimed his six forty." Jenny knew that much.

"That's what McDougall and the rest of us all took. He chose a prime piece—good farmland and woodlands right with it. Unlike the older Abercrombie son, who took his farm and woods in separate parcels." Doc eyed Jenny. "Old Samuel now thinks his son got a bad deal."

Jenny didn't care what Samuel Abercrombie or his son Douglass thought. "What do I have to do to prove the claim?"

"McDougall staked out the land and recorded the claim in Oregon City. Next step was to build a house or barn or enclose the fields to improve it. You have a cabin and a barn and crops, so you have improvements."

"That's it?" Jenny asked. "Then it's mine?"

Doc shook his head. "Ain't quite so easy. Man needs to live on the land within a year of filing the claim, or pay five dollars."

"Mac lived here till February."

"So he did. But he can't be away more'n two years, unless he pays five dollars a year to the recorder of deeds."

"Then I have to pay five dollars a year to keep the land?" She could do that, Jenny thought.

"Maybe, but your case ain't clear." Doc frowned, his eyebrows meeting over his nose. "Everyone thinks you're his wife. Is that good enough for the government?" He shrugged. "You ain't his wife, so someone could challenge your title, if they ever find out. You'd better pray Samuel Abercrombie don't find out you weren't married. Or that McDougall gets some sense in his head and high-tails it back here, but that ain't likely to happen."

"And when Mac is gone more than two years?" Jenny said. As the Tullers said, Mac had no reason to return.

"Don't know. Wait'll that time comes."

Chapter 13: Another Partner

Mac worked alone on the gold claim for several days while Joel was at Sutter's Fort. "Weren't but two hundred dollars in the flakes we found," Joel reported when he returned. "A lot of money on the trail to Oregon, but it ain't much here."

"You sell it?" Mac asked.

"Yep. There's a lot more stores and assayers around the fort now, but I went to that Nate fellow, like you said. Had him split it on our accounts."

"My first find must have been beginner's luck," Mac said. "You want to keep panning or should we move on?"

"Ain't got nothing better to do," Joel said. "I'm still seeking a fortune." The two partners found gold flakes every day, but they hadn't panned any large nuggets like Mac had found before Joel arrived.

Mac wanted his own fortune also. He had an image of returning to Boston able to do as he pleased, free of his family. In the meantime, he appreciated the unscheduled hours and even the hard physical labor that had him falling gratefully into his bedroll each night. "Guess I can stay awhile as well," he told Joel.

Other prospectors found their way into the valley. Mac told Joel, "Keep your rifle nearby. In case we see trouble."

Joel curled his lip. "I told you, you ain't wagon captain no more."

"We don't know these men," Mac said. "We could be ambushed."

"I ain't questioning the need for caution," Joel said. "But there ain't no call for you to order me around."

Mac made a show of checking his own gun each morning and evening, but he didn't raise the matter again with Joel. He also walked along the ridge above the creek each day, searching to see if other men worked claims nearby. Some men stopped on the creek for a day or two, but most moved on. Over time, more prospectors staked claims in the valley, but none near Mac and Joel.

One day in mid-July, a small man with a scraggly white beard and battered black top hat staked out land upstream of Joel's claim. The old man paced on bandy legs along the riverbank and eyed Mac and Joel while he dug near the water. But he stayed on his own territory.

The day after the bandy-legged fellow appeared, Joel found his first pea-sized nugget and bellowed for Mac to come see.

"Hush," Mac hissed after racing over to Joel. "Do you want the whole valley to know what you've found?"

The old man upstream walked over. "Name's Huntington," he said. "Jeremiah Huntington. Find somethin'?"

Mac introduced himself and Joel. "Where you from?" Mac asked, shaking hands with Huntington.

"Mined in Georgia. Up near Dahlonega. Didn't get there till the govmint was givin' away Cherokee land in thirty-two."

"Find any gold in Georgia?" Joel asked.

"Only enough to spend," Huntington said, spitting on the ground. "Strike petered out. So I come to California. Worked down south. That was in forty-six. Come north when I heard they's found gold at Sutter's Mill. This time, I aim to strike it rich. Sounds like you boys are havin' some luck."

"Found a few flakes." Mac didn't give any details. No reason to tell Huntington he'd found a large nugget of nearly pure gold on the land and Joel had just found a smaller nugget.

"You try sluicin'?" Huntington hawked up phlegm and spat again.

Mac and Joel shook their heads. "What's sluicing?" Mac asked.

"Wood box to run water and gravel through." Huntington squinted at the burbling stream in front of them. "Creek's plenty fast enough. I'm aimin' to try. If there's color in these parts, I'll find it."

"If we're finding gold with pans, why bother with sluices?" Joel wiped his forehead with a filthy handkerchief.

"Move more dirt." Huntington peered at the hills above the water. "Not much wood this side of the creek, but plenty of pines on the hills across. Enough for sluices."

"Will you show us how?" Mac asked.

Huntington cocked an eyebrow at the two younger men. "Sluices work best with more'n one man. You help me, and I'll help you," he said. "I got know-how. You got brawn. Partners?" He put out his hand.

Mac wondered about the fellow. He seemed loose-lipped and cantankerous. But the three men shook on the deal.

July 26, 1848. Seems I am putting down stakes in California. I now have two partners in the gold claim. I can trust Joel, but what of Huntington? Still, we need his experience.

Both Boston and Oregon seem very far away.

Mac fingered the worn baby bootie in his bag when he put his journal away. He wasn't likely to hear more about Jenny and William, not until Joel heard from his family. It was time to let them go.

Chapter 14:   Letter From Home

Wednesday, August 2ⁿᵈ—Today is warm. Harvest has begun. Tanner is mowing hay today and will be reaping wheat and oats soon. I am out of flour and must go to Oregon City.

Hatty and Jenny usually worked with Tanner in the fields now, but Jenny couldn't wait for her own grain to be milled. She would have to buy the high-priced flour at Abernethy's store. She also needed cotton yardage to make more clothes for William. At eleven months, he'd outgrown the shirts she'd made before he was born.

Jenny harnessed Poulette to the wagon and started for Oregon City. Hatty Tanner and Otis rode with her, and Hatty held William. They picked up Esther and her babies on her way to Oregon City. When the group arrived at the general store, they learned mail had been delivered to another store down the street.

"I'll go ask if we have any letters," Esther volunteered. "Joel said he'd write when he got to San Francisco." She took Cordelia with her.

While Esther was gone, Jenny browsed the dry goods. "Not much selection," she commented, seeing only two bolts of calico on the shelves.

"Everything's going to California," Mr. Hamilton, the store clerk, said. "Ships stop there, don't bother coming north. We can't get supplies."

"Any fresh food?" Jenny asked.

"Got some fruit from the Sandwich Islands. One ship came to Astoria to load up on wood for California. Every store in Oregon's bidding on the

64

little bit that comes our way."

Jenny picked over the fruit, but almost everything was soft after the long ocean voyage. She'd make do with berries. The balance she owed at Abernethy's store was growing, though she should be able to buy on credit through harvest.

"I'll only take the cornmeal. And two yards of blue cotton and two more of brown," she told Hamilton.

While the clerk added the purchases to her account, she turned to Hatty. "Good thing our wheat is almost to the mill. Until then, we'll eat cornbread. I hope Tanner can catch some fish or take time off from the fields to hunt."

"I'll fish, Miz Jenny," Otis said with a grin.

"You going to pay down your account soon?" Hamilton asked. "Your balance is getting mighty high,"

"It was paid off in early March, Mr. Hamilton," Jenny said. "Most folks aren't settling with you until the crops come in."

"You ain't given anything since your husband left in early March," he told her. "When's he coming back?"

Jenny forced a smile at the man. "I'll pay after harvest, like everyone else." She could use Mac's coins if she had to, but she didn't want to settle her balance if the store wasn't making others pay.

Hamilton lifted a skeptical eyebrow.

Esther returned, holding Cordelia in the crook of one arm and waving letters in her other hand. "Jenny, there's a letter for you and one for Pa."

Jenny's heart leapt. Had Mac finally written? She wanted to know how he was and what he was doing.

Esther prattled on, "Pa's must be from Joel. I can't wait to hear what he's written. Is yours from Captain McDougall? I barely knew it was for you—till I remembered your name is really Geneviève and your maiden name was Calhoun. But why wouldn't the Captain address it to Geneviève McDougall?"

Jenny took the letter Esther handed her. "Geneviève Calhoun, Oregon City," the perfect script read.

Jenny shook her head. "It's my mother's writing."

"Your mother," Esther sighed. "You must be so glad to hear from her. How I wish I could get a letter from my ma."

"I wrote her from Whitman Mission when William was born. This is the first letter I've had from her since I left Missouri." Jenny hadn't seen her mother since the day she ran away with Mac. Her mother, at the time expecting a child herself after her second marriage, had blamed Jenny for becoming *enceinte*, thinking Jenny had taken up with a neighbor boy. What had her mother's reaction been to learning she had a grandson?

Jenny waited until she was home to open the letter. It was dated in March, four months earlier.

Chère Geneviève,

I received your letter last week via a steamship from Nouvelle Orléans. I am pleased you have a son and I know your cher papa smiles down from heaven to know you named your son William after him.

I, too, was delivered of a son, born on May 29, 1847. I named him Jacques after my father, though Mr. Peterson calls him Jack. Jacques is a fine, strong baby, and looks very like his father.

Mr. Peterson manages the farm well, and with the tobacco and corn crops and the income from his tavern, we prosper. It is a shame you cannot have the advantage of Mr. Peterson's business faculties. How different he is from your papa! Mr. Peterson may not be an educated man, but he is well suited for life in Missouri.

I cannot imagine the rigors of your journey West, nor the bleak conditions of your life in Oregon Territory. You did not mention your husband in your letter, but I hope you have the protection of a strong man, as I do.

The circumstances of your leaving were unfortunate, but I pray you are happy now, where you and your son can live without the opprobrium you would have faced in Missouri.

Letitia sends her regards to you and your

child.

Affectionately, ta mère,
Hortense Peterson

Jenny shivered when she finished the letter. Her mother did not know Jenny had been raped, nor that Bart Peterson was one of the rapists. He might have fathered William as well as Jacques. Jenny did not want Mr. Peterson nor his business faculties in her life. She was better off alone than in Peterson's household.

Her mother had always lived in a world of her own concoction—a world that ignored ugliness and squalor. Hortense had been raised on a wealthy plantation in Louisiana and had tried to maintain the same lifestyle on the farm in Missouri. She'd tried to ignore her first husband's illness, leaving his care to Jenny and their slave Letitia. After Jenny's father died, Mama quickly married Bart Peterson, not seeing—or overlooking—how Peterson leered at Jenny and touched her whenever she passed him in the hall. Jenny had never understood why her mother married the man.

It was clear her mother did not want Jenny to return to Missouri. Mama expressed no desire to see either Jenny or her grandson. No matter, Jenny thought. Her life was in Oregon, and she would never again have to deal with Bart Peterson.

She put the letter on the mantel. She would answer it later—the parts she could answer. She could not tell her mother about a husband who did not exist.

The next morning Esther walked over to Jenny's cabin with Cordelia. "Rachel's minding Jonah," she said. "I left him with Pa and Mother Amanda last night."

"Mother Amanda?" Jenny asked. "Is that what you're calling Mrs. Purcell—I mean, Mrs. Pershing?"

Esther grimaced. "You see the problem? I can't call her 'ma,' like her brood does. Nor 'Mrs. Pershing,' though I suppose everyone else will."

"I have a hard time calling her 'Mrs. Pershing,' too," Jenny said, shaking her head. "I'll always remember your mama fondly."

"What did your ma say in her letter?"

Jenny shrugged. "Was glad to know I had a baby boy. She had one, too. Named him Jacques."

"That's all?"

"She fears our life in Oregon is harsh."

Esther laughed. "It's dirty and the work is hard, and we don't have nice houses like in the States. But at least the land is good. Daniel was telling me this morning the wheat's taller than what he grew back East. I just wish the stores had more calico. I've had to cut down Noah's threadbare shirts for Jonah and Cordelia."

"Was your papa's letter from Joel?" Jenny asked.

"Yes, indeed. From Sutter's Fort. He never made it to San Francisco. He was on his way to the gold fields when he mailed it. Says the fort was full of prospectors, all seeking gold dust and nuggets. Wouldn't it be wonderful if he found gold?"

Jenny smiled. Esther would always hope for more in life.

That evening after supper, Jenny sat at her table with paper, ink, and quill, an oil lamp lit in front of her. Hatty washed the dishes by the fireplace, and Otis played with William on the floor.

But she paused before she wrote. When she'd written her mother from Whitman Mission, she'd only told her mother Mac was the wagon captain. Now she didn't know what to say. She couldn't tell her mother she and Mac had not married. She couldn't tell her mother Mac had left her. There was little she cared to tell her mother, though she wished desperately for someone to know her story.

But not even Esther or the Tanners knew. Only Doc and Mrs. Tuller.

With a deep sigh, Jenny began writing:

> *August 3, 1848*
> *Chère Maman,*
>
> *I congratulate you on your son Jacques, and hope he is as much a joy to you as William is to me. William is crawling and pulls himself up on the table legs. He is almost eleven months old and will be walking soon.*

He looks more and more like Papa every day. He babbles to himself. I think he tries to say "Mama" to me, though that may be my imagination.

The wheat harvest from our first year's planting has just begun, with corn to follow. A Negro man named Tanner works the fields with his boy Otis, and his wife helps me cook and clean. All my neighbors from our wagon train are nearby, and we often work together.

I'm sure by the time you receive this letter you will have learned gold has been found in California. It is all one hears about in Oregon. Many of our men have left to prospect. But I am happy in my little house with William and the Tanners.

May God be with you,

Your daughter,

Geneviève

Jenny sealed the letter and set it aside to mail on her next trip to Oregon City. Writing her mother such a formal letter—one omitting all mention of Mac—seemed to sever the possibility of returning to her past life. It felt like leaving Missouri all over again.

Chapter 15:   Sluicing and Selling

At Huntington's direction, Mac and Joel cut tall pines growing on the plateau above the valley. They built small rockers to use in the water and sawed longer timbers into pieces to build sluice boxes. Soon boxes lined the creek bed along their three claims. Most of the sluices were only about ten feet long and could be moved from place to place in the stream.

Each box had riffles every foot or so along its length—these wooden slats acted as dams to stop the gravel that settled out of the rushing water. The riffles filled with sediment, which the men scooped out to search for gold flakes and nuggets.

They diverted creek water into the top of the box, then scooped dirt into the sluice to be rolled downhill by the current, leaving gold flakes behind. It was faster than panning, but required more hauling and shoveling of dirt. There was no end of dirt and gravel to fill the boxes and no end of water from the fast-moving creek.

They built two long boxes reaching from the top of the hillside to the stream. To work these sluices, they channeled snow melt running down ravines on their claims into the boxes. When that water dried up, they used their pack mules to haul water to the top.

"These boxes'll work better come spring," Huntington said. "When the water runs fast."

Mac grunted as he shoveled dirt into a sluice. "If we're still here in the spring."

"They's more gold in the gulches," Huntington said. "Easier to find flakes in the creek, but most of the nuggets'll be up high. We need these sluices."

As the summer days passed, the three prospectors worked their sluices.

They toiled in the ravines in the mornings and evenings, and saved the labor in the cool river for the heat of midday.

By dusk each day, Mac's bones ached, and he wondered if the wealth they were slowly accumulating was worth the labor. Mounds of discarded gravel tailings and muck near the sluices created an ugly mess. The claim no longer seemed one of the lovelier places he'd been.

Occasionally a miner or two passed on horseback, and more men staked claims in their valley. But only once did anyone stop to share their campfire. On a hot evening in mid-August, two men rode up and dismounted. One, a slim dandy with shifty eyes under a beaver hat, introduced himself as Tobias Jones. His companion—who gave his name only as "Smith"—looked like a boxer who won his fights through meanness.

"Finding much color?" Jones asked, as the men fried fish and johnny cakes over a campfire.

"You bet we are," Huntington crowed, drawing on a pint of whiskey. "Best damn creek I ever seen."

"Damned hard work," Joel said, his eyes narrowing at Huntington. "Ain't sure it's worth it." Now he'd found gold, Joel was as tight-lipped as Mac.

Huntington clapped Joel on the back. "You keep doin' what I tell you, boy," he said. "We'll be rich."

Mac seethed at Huntington's loose mouth. He'd make them a prime target for thieves if he didn't keep quiet. "We won't know what we found until we have our dust assayed," Mac said. "I do wonder if prospecting is worth the trouble."

"Then you won't mind if we stake out a claim upstream," Jones said, flashing white teeth beneath his black mustache and beaver hat.

Smith hadn't said a word, other than his name.

"Can't stop you," Huntington said. "But don't dam the creek. Can't run our sluices if we ain't got water to put through 'em."

By the campfire after Smith and Jones left, Mac wrote:

August 15, 1848. The valley is filling with other

prospectors. Most men keep to themselves, but two rogues stopped by this evening. I have little reason to think them shifty, but I did not trust either one.

By late summer when the run-off from the mountains ebbed, the sluices in the ravines depended on infrequent rains to wash away the lighter grit and sand from the gold. The men spent more time in the creek. The arduous work yielded a growing cache of gold flakes and small nuggets, and Mac worried more about theft.

"We could pump water up the hills," Huntington said as they sat by the campfire after supper one night. "Use the mules and horses to drive a wheel. Git more water up top than the beasts can carry."

"But we're finding flakes every day in the stream," Joel said. "Why bother to build a pump?"

Huntington shrugged. "We can always build it later. With the sluices we got, we's probably findin' about a thousand dollars a week in dust. I'd bet on it."

"No need to bet," Mac said. "I'll start for Sutter's Fort tomorrow. Hate to store too much gold here. Someone might rob us."

"Think I'll go, too," Joel said. "I'd like a few nights in a decent bed."

"You be all right by yourself?" Mac asked Huntington. He wasn't sure which was more dangerous—to be alone on the claim or to ride alone to the fort.

Huntington grinned. "I spent more nights alone than you've had days on the earth," he replied. "More nights with women, too. You young'uns go sow your wild oats. Think the whores found their way to the fort yet?"

Mac's face must have shown his surprise at Huntington's ribald comment, because the old man guffawed and continued, "Now, boys, if they's men with money, whores ain't never far behind."

August 25, 1848. Joel and I head to Sutter's Fort tomorrow, leaving Huntington to fend for himself.

Mac and Joel set off early in the morning, each leading a mule laden with bags of gold. They'd divided their findings to reduce the risk of losing everything if one man was robbed.

"If someone jumps us, we'll ride in opposite directions," Joel said. "Meet up at the fort, if we survive."

Mac wasn't sure he liked the idea of separating, but he didn't want to contradict Joel. He'd do what he thought best if the situation arose.

On the two-day trip to the fort, Mac saw men everywhere along all the creeks and in the hills. Their valley was quiet compared to the streams closer to the fort. Everyone was mining, with pans, rockers, and sluices. Small stores now dotted the trail to the fort, stores which hadn't been there the last time Mac made the trip.

"Should we stop here?" Joel asked as they passed one store.

"We don't know these folks," Mac said. "I trust the assayer outside Sutter's Fort. Nate. Didn't you like him? Besides, you want that soft bed, don't you?"

Joel grinned, and they rode on.

Sutter's Fort and its environs bustled with even more people than on Mac's last visit. Tent camps had risen like mushrooms all around the fort. Mostly men, but a few women, cooked on fires, while a few children ran between the canvas tents. Horses and mules stood staked near camp, cropping what little grass remained in the dusty meadows. Mac smelled fried meat and horse dung, bringing back memories of camps along the Oregon Trail.

"Doesn't look like there'll be much room in the fort," Mac said. "Let's talk to Nate, then see what we can find for room and board."

Joel grunted, and they tied their horses outside Nate's store.

Nate weighed their gold. "Two thousand dollars. A lot more than what Pershing here brought in last time," he said, nodding at Joel. "How long it take you to gather this?"

"A month," Mac replied.

"Huntington was off," Joel said. "He said we'd taken in a thousand a week."

The assayer laughed. "There's so much gold in the fort now, prices are down. Back East you'd probably get twice as much."

Mac and Joel sold their gold and added to their accounts at the store. They also set up an account for Huntington. Nate showed them their entries in his ledger and gave them receipts. "A lot of dishonest storekeepers around here these days," Nate cautioned. "Only do business with men you trust." He named two general stores in the fort. "Tell them I sent you. They'll treat you right."

"What about the stores setting up along the trail, closer to the gold fields?" Mac asked.

Nate shrugged. "If you trade there, make sure you see their books. Some are good men, some aren't."

"That's the truth anywhere," Joel said. "Any rooms to be had nearby?"

"You might get lucky," Nate said. "A new saloon recently opened next door—the Golden Nugget. It has the best food in these parts. Cleanest whores, too."

Joel gave a hoot and slapped Mac on the back. "Huntington was right. Let's go."

Mac and Joel left the assayer's office. The bar and dining room of the Golden Nugget were crowded and noisy when they entered. At Mac's inquiry, the proprietor responded, "Got one room left, one bed. You two want it?"

"Fine," Joel said.

They dropped their now empty gold sacks and their saddlebags in the room, then ate supper when a table became available. After they ate, they sat with a bottle of whiskey between them.

"*Buenas noches*," a soft voice behind Mac said. "Remember me?"

He turned. It was the Mexican girl from the San Francisco saloon. "Consuela, is it?"

She smiled, placing her hand on his shoulder. "You do remember."

"Why did you leave San Francisco?" he asked.

She lifted one bare shoulder. "The men are here now."

Joel ogled Consuela. "I'm Joel Pershing," he said. "Traveled with Mac to Oregon last year. We're partners on a gold claim now."

"Partners," Consuela said. "You should drink to your partnership." And she poured them each another whiskey, before moving on to another group of men.

"How'd you meet her?" Joel asked.

Mac shrugged. "In San Francisco. Just like tonight, she poured me a drink and asked me to buy her one."

"You take her upstairs?"

Mac shook his head.

"You taking her upstairs tonight?"

"Not planning to," Mac said.

"Mind if I do?" Joel asked.

"That's up to the lady," Mac said, sipping his drink.

Joel left his chair and approached Consuela.

Mac sat at the table with his whiskey and watched them walk up the stairs. Consuela was pretty, not yet haggard from drink and abuse, with sad eyes like Jenny's. He couldn't take up with a woman who reminded him of Jenny.

He considered a buxom blonde named Ethel with a loud laugh. She looked nothing like Jenny. But he didn't want to be the kind of man who used one woman when he wanted another.

Chapter 16:   Gunfight

Mac and Joel purchased food, nails, and ammunition at one of the stores Nate had recommended, then steered their horses and mules out of the fort and toward their claim. On the first evening after leaving the fort, they made camp by a small stream and started a fire. The woods around them rustled in the autumn wind.

As they finished eating, a tree branch cracked. "Think a raccoon wants to share our supper?" Joel asked, nodding in the direction of the sound.

"I hope that's all it is," Mac said. "There was a man on the trail this afternoon. Kept an even distance behind us. When we stopped, he stopped. We might be in for trouble."

"We're rid of our gold now. No reason for anyone to follow us."

"Unless they want to know where we found gold and are tracking us back to our claim. Or maybe they want the horses." Mac stood up. "I think we should stand guard tonight."

Joel snorted. "Still trying to be trail boss, ain't you?"

Mac didn't want to argue. "I'll take the first watch." He picked up his gun and moved away from the fire into the shadows. "I'll wake you later."

Mac sat quietly while Joel slept. Maybe he was being overly cautious. They didn't have anything except food to steal. And two horses and the mules. But whoever was following hadn't approached them to share a camp for the night. Maybe the man was merely a loner, not a thief. Still, a little vigilance couldn't hurt.

Mac woke Joel shortly after midnight. Joel grudgingly sat guard. Mac slept lightly and awoke at first light. "Might as well head out," he said. "We'll be back to the claim about midday if we start now."

They traveled quickly. Mac kept an eye out for other men on the trail, but saw no sign of followers.

Mac and Joel arrived at their mining shack not long after noon. Huntington came running out of a ravine. "Found a new lode. A pure vein and nuggets a-plenty," Huntington shouted. "Up this here gully." He gestured back toward the ravine he'd just exited.

A shot rang out from behind Mac. Huntington's hat blew off his head. The old man dropped to the ground and rolled behind a clump of trees.

"Take cover," Mac yelled. He jumped off Valiente, grabbed his rifle, and ducked behind a large rock.

Joel hid behind a boulder near Mac. "You were right," he said. "We *were* followed. But I never saw 'em today."

More shots sounded across the clearing. Bullets twanged into rocks and chips flew. Valiente, Joel's gelding, and the mules still laden with provisions bolted into the woods.

Then the clearing went quiet, but Mac knew the bandits were still there. He thought there were three attackers, but he wasn't positive. "Can you see anything?" he whispered.

Joel shook his head.

It felt like forever, but could only have been a minute or two before Mac saw a hat poke out from behind a tree. It looked like the beaver hat their recent foppish visitor had worn.

A rifle barrel followed the hat. Mac aimed right beneath the gun barrel and took his shot.

A man cried out, then toppled to the ground near the tree.

Mac quickly reloaded his gun rifle as a volley of shots sounded. Gunsmoke rose from behind two trees—only two attackers left, he assumed.

"I'm going around behind 'em," Joel said in a low voice. "Cover me."

"Stay down," Mac hissed. He stuck his rifle out over the rock, raised his head slightly, and aimed near a tree where he thought the shots came from.

Huntington stood up and yelled, firing his pistol. In response, a shadow moved in the trees. Mac took another shot.

A man screamed. The rustle of feet followed by thundering hooves sounded through the brush. A horse whinnied, and a man on horseback hurtled through the trees. Another man scrambled away, firing back toward them, until Mac heard a second horse gallop off.

Joel appeared at the edge of the clearing beside the first man Mac had shot. "He's dead," he said in disgust. "Other two got away. No telling who they were."

"Dead?" Mac's throat went dry. "I killed him?" He looked down at the body. "It's our visitor from a few weeks back. There's his beaver hat." It was lying on the ground beside the dead dandy.

Huntington ran up beside Mac and Joel. "You done some fine shootin', boys." He clapped Mac on the back.

Mac's gut lurched, and he barely kept his breakfast down.

"I knew you'd be good pardners," Huntington continued. "McDougall, you shot him square in the chest. He went down like a felled tree."

"Either of you remember his name? Jones, was it?" Mac asked. "Tobias?"

Joel and Huntington shook their heads. "Don't matter, now he's dead," Joel said.

Mac looked through the man's pockets. No letters, not even a lock of braided hair. "We'd best bury him," he said.

"Wonder who his pals were," Joel said. "One was a big fellow. Might have been the surly bastard with this 'un when he was here before." He tapped the body with his foot. "Smith, was it?"

Mac and Joel went after their horses and mules. When they returned with their animals, the three partners dug a grave at the side of the clearing away from their shed. As they hacked through the tree roots and rocky ground, Huntington recounted the battle over and over. Before they moved the body, Huntington removed the dead man's boots and clapped the beaver hat on his own head. "Too bad you shot up his vest," Huntington said. "It's a nice brocade."

"What are you doing?" Mac asked, pausing to lean on his shovel and wipe his forehead.

"Haven't been in a gunfight since thirty-six." Huntington chortled and held up the boots. "These'll make a nice trophy. Bring us luck, for sure."

Mac still felt queasy when they lowered the body into the ground. Luck? He'd killed a man.

He'd been in skirmishes as a soldier in the Oregon militia, but he was only sure of killing one man before—on the day he'd met Jenny in Arrow Rock, Missouri. He and Valiente had ridden into town and stopped at the tavern Jenny's stepfather owned. Two men harassed Jenny as she cleared the table after dinner. When Mac tried to stop them, one pulled a gun. Mac shot then in self-defense, just like today, but it didn't make the killing any easier.

The partners kept watch all night, in case the remaining bandits returned. After Mac climbed in his bedroll, he couldn't sleep. He lay wide-eyed, worrying again whether he'd done the right thing taking Jenny away from her home. She needed to leave Arrow Rock, but he'd brought her all the way to Oregon, only to abandon her. He wondered how she was doing on the farm.

"Joel?" Mac called in the dark.

"Huh?" Joel grunted.

"Have you heard from your family?"

"Nope. Sent another letter to Pa from Sutter's, telling him to write me care of the fort. They ain't known where to write before. Did you write Miz Jenny?"

"No."

The next morning Mac was up early. He sat beside the stream with a mug of coffee and his journal.

> *September 1, 1848. I killed a man yesterday in a fight over our claim. He attacked us, but this killing was no easier than my first. Gold takes plenty out of a man, from both body and soul.*

After the gunfight, the three partners kept their rifles beside them while they worked. But there was no more trouble.

"I wonder who the two men what run off were," Huntington mused. "You ain't seen 'em at the fort?"

"Not to notice," Mac said. He wished Huntington would let the matter drop. He'd been justified in defending himself, his partners, and their claim, but Mac still didn't like having killed the dandified thief.

Huntington coughed and spat. "Wonder why they picked on us."

"Maybe because you yelled about finding a new lode," Mac replied.

Chapter 17:   Another Letter

All through August Jenny's vegetable garden yielded abundant corn, peas, cucumbers, and beans, and the chickens and cow provided eggs and milk. Tanner and Otis kept her supplied with meat and fish in addition to handling the farm work.

Poulette was due to foal any day. Jenny loved the mare, which Mac had bought for her at Fort Laramie the year before.

"Keep her close to the barn," Tanner told Jenny. "Call me in from the fields if she starts pacing."

Tanner wanted to harvest the wheat as quickly as possible. "Weather here ain't like the States," he told Jenny on the morning of August 24. "Had our first frost last night. Need to git the grain in."

Jenny was grateful the weather stayed clear for most of the following two weeks. They all worked feverishly to reap the wheat. Tanner did the brunt of the work, aided occasionally by Zeke.

Hatty and Otis helped the men bundle the sheaves and load the shucked wheat into bags and into the wagon. They were too busy to accompany Jenny into Oregon City, but she needed dry goods. Zeke had brought his team to her claim that day, so she hitched Tanner's mules to the wagon for a trip into town. She and William stopped at Esther's cabin to pick up Esther and her children.

"I can't manage both babies and an armful of packages, too," Esther said. "Let's take Rachel." So they stopped at Captain Pershing's farm for Rachel. The wagon was full before they left for Oregon City.

In town, Rachel took Jonah and William off to play on the green. Esther kept Cordelia on her lap while Jenny drove the wagon toward the stores.

New emigrants from the East already camped in Abernethy Green to the

80

north of town. "Early arrivals," Esther said. "We didn't get here till mid-October last year. Remember how wonderful it was to see the town?"

"I remember Mr. Foster's farm. The dinner they fed us." Jenny smiled, recalling the taste of the savory vegetables—the first fresh peas and carrots they'd had in months. "And the dance here in town on the green." She felt Mac's arms around her again as they had waltzed that night.

"The dance." Esther's voice was dreamy. "Daniel and I danced till midnight." Then her tone sharpened. "And Pa danced with Mrs. Purcell, too—I mean Mother Amanda. I should have seen it coming."

"Nothing you can do about it now," Jenny said.

"She's expecting."

"Already?" Jenny was surprised. But then, she and Esther both had become pregnant easily.

"She didn't waste any time. She don't need another child, and Pa for sure don't."

They tied Tanner's mules to the rail, climbed out of the wagon, and entered Abernethy's store. As they made their purchases, the clerk told them, "Been another mail delivery. Best check at the postal office."

Jenny and Esther thanked him, put their bundles in the wagon, and walked down the street to the store that handled mail.

"What's your papa going to do about school for the children?" Jenny asked Esther as they passed the schoolhouse.

"He says town's too far to take 'em every day." Esther sighed. "But the children need schooling. Ma taught us all to read, excepting Noah who was too young. But last winter they didn't learn nothing. Just sat in the cabin or played outside in the mud. I can't teach 'em—I'm too busy with Cordelia and Jonah and my housework."

"What about your stepmother?"

"She has too much cooking and washing, too, she says. I'll give her this much—she's a hard worker, and she keeps Pa from drinking. But she has the baby coming. And she don't know any more book learning than I do."

"I could hold a school," Jenny said. "I read most of the books in Papa's library. History and Shakespeare. I know French and English grammar and literature, though Papa had only just started me on Latin when he died. I can do arithmetic, but not algebra."

"How'd you have time for so much studying?"

"It was easy, until Papa became ill. I could make time this winter to teach. I have Hatty to help with the house. And my cabin is closer than town for your brothers and sisters."

"Would you really open a school?" Esther beamed and took Jenny's arm. "Could you handle all the children?"

"How many would there be?" Jenny thought out loud. "Rachel, if she's not too old. Jonathan, David, Ruth, and Noah. The three Purcell children. And Otis."

"Otis?" Esther said. "You'd teach a Negro with the other children?"

"He can sound out his letters. I've heard him. Letitia, our slave back home, could read. I couldn't leave Otis out when his parents are helping me. But I don't have books, other than a Bible."

"We brought some books in our wagons last year," Esther said. "And the Abercrombies have a few. Maybe Daniel's nieces would come, too."

Jenny's heart sank at this, because it meant more ties with Daniel's father, Samuel Abercrombie—the man who had caused so much dissension along the trail. But she couldn't exclude his grandchildren from her school because she didn't like him. "Talk to your folks," she said. "I'll talk to the Tanners about Otis and about making some benches for the children to sit on. My cabin would be crowded, but I think I can manage."

"How would we pay you?" Esther asked.

Jenny shrugged. "We'll work out something. Talk to your papa."

At the mail delivery counter, Jenny found another letter waiting for her, this one addressed to Geneviève McDougall. Her heart leapt—it looked like Mac's handwriting. It was all she could do not to tear the letter open right away, but she wanted to be alone when she read it.

"Is it from Captain McDougall?" Esther asked.

"I think so," Jenny said.

"Are you saving it for yourself?" Esther teased, a grin on her face.

Jenny nodded, unable to return Esther's smile.

That evening she fidgeted during supper with the Tanners, wanting to see what Mac had said. As soon as they left for their cabin, Jenny eagerly broke the seal on the letter. A paper folded inside floated to the floor. She picked it up—a financial document of some type—and set it aside to examine after she read Mac's letter. Her hands shook as she read.

California! Mac had stayed in California. He was only weeks away from her, not months or a year. He was mining gold. But he offered no hope he would return to Oregon—he still planned to go to Boston. Jenny stifled a sob.

Jenny reread the letter, more slowly this time. Mac apologized for his advances the night he left. She remembered his arms around her, and again she wished she had responded. It wouldn't have been so bad. If Mac needed her, she should have yielded. Maybe then he wouldn't have left.

He wrote he would find a way to free her. How would he do that?

Jenny sniffed when she read Mac's comment about Zeke. Zeke *was* a good man. But he wasn't Mac. She'd told Mac she didn't want any man. She wondered again whether she should have married him when he'd asked. Now she'd have to live without him—as she'd done for many months already.

He wrote the land was hers. Could he give her the land in a letter? She would need to talk to Doc again.

The paper Mac had enclosed was a letter of credit, whatever that was— more money, Mac wrote. Jenny should take it to the store and see what the storekeeper would do. But she didn't want Mac's money. However unreasonable it was, she wanted Mac—any way she could have him.

After William was in bed for the night, Jenny wrote in her journal:

> *September 2nd—Finally, a letter from Mac— from California. Much closer than Boston, but he does not say he will return.*
>
> *I have offered to teach school to children on nearby farms. Perhaps I can earn my living without Mac's money, even if I lose the land.*

"What did Captain McDougall say?" Esther asked when Jenny visited the following week.

"He's in California. Prospecting. He's staying there before heading to Boston."

"California—will he see Joel?"

"I don't know," Jenny said. "California's a big place, I think."

"But he'll be gone even longer," Esther said. "How will you manage?"

Jenny shrugged. "I have the farm and soon the school."

"It's worse'n when Pa was in the Army leaving Ma and us young'uns alone." Esther sighed. "What else did he say?"

"Only private things," Jenny said. She had hidden Mac's letter under the floorboard in the loft with his money. She hadn't told anyone what Mac had written, nor had she talked to Doc yet about the letter of credit or the land.

Jenny made a small berry tart for William for his first birthday. She and the Tanners clapped and sang. The little boy grinned at everyone paying attention to him.

In the evening Jenny wrote:

> *Saturday, September 16ᵗʰ—It is William's birthday. Last week he started walking, though he clutches my finger for safety. He is such a joy. I would not have my son, and I might have died myself, if not for Mac.*

Chapter 18:   Starting School

Poulette had a little black colt, a small replica of Mac's stallion Valiente, except for a cluster of white spots on his rump. Jenny named the colt Chanticleer, after the rooster in the French stories she'd heard growing up. But Otis Tanner called him "Shanty," a nickname which soon stuck. Poulette and Shanty roamed peacefully in the paddock, and Tanner used his mules to help with harvest.

While September ran into October and summer turned to full autumn, Jenny toiled in the fields with Tanner and Hatty to bring in the last of the corn and potatoes and mow another crop of hay before winter. The skies stayed clear, though mornings and evenings were crisp and cool.

Jenny's hands grew calluses on top of calluses, and her back ached from stooping to gather the sheaves of corn that Tanner and Hatty cut. She and Hatty spent time preserving vegetables as well.

"I hate to see you working so hard, Miz Jenny," Zeke Pershing said when he came to help one day at the end of September.

"Can't be avoided," Jenny replied. "I'm not working as hard as Tanner or Hatty."

"They're used to it. You should be sewing and cooking in the house."

Jenny laughed. "That's work, too. Putting up beans isn't much easier than digging potatoes. And chasing after William, now he's walking? There's plenty of drudgery for everyone in Oregon."

"Are you going to the harvest dance next week?" Zeke asked.

"Haven't decided," Jenny said. "Not much reason to go. Not without Mac. And I have William."

"You hear from Mac?" Zeke asked, scratching his forehead.

"Just the one letter." Jenny was as close-lipped with Zeke about what

85

Mac had said as she'd been with Esther. She certainly wasn't going to tell anyone Mac wanted her to take up with Zeke.

"Well, I'll look for you at the dance," Zeke said.

But when the night for the harvest celebration arrived, on Saturday, October 7, Jenny and William stayed home. She told the Tanners to take the wagon into town, but they didn't go either.

Jenny spent the evening in her small cabin. She needed to mend a shirt for William and start the lesson plans for her school, but instead she stared into the firelight, remembering again when she and Mac had waltzed on Abernethy Green.

Before she went to bed she wrote:

> *Saturday, October 7th—Wednesday was my 16th birthday. I was too busy to take any note of it. I start teaching school in a week. It is such a responsibility to form young minds, and I have no experience and few materials.*

Jenny's students ranged in age from Rachel Pershing, who'd just turned fourteen, down to Noah Pershing and Henry Purcell at five. She had eleven students—five Pershings (Rachel, Jonathan, David, Ruth, and Noah), three Purcells (Sarah, Nettie, and Henry), the two Abercrombie granddaughters (Annabelle and Rose), and Otis Tanner. Some of the children could read well, but Noah, Henry, and Otis knew only a few simple words.

Jenny had two primers, three Bibles, and one book of Greek mythology. Amanda Pershing also gave her three torn and dog-eared issues of *Godey's Lady's Book* which had somehow made it across the prairie and mountains. Jenny longed for the wall of books in her father's library. The children shared four small slates. When the weather was dry, they scratched their arithmetic lessons in the dirt outside.

But by late October, the rain came regularly, and the yard between the house and barn stayed muddy. The children tracked in dirt every time they entered the cabin.

Jenny's school began in midmorning, stopped briefly for a noon meal of food the children brought in pails, then resumed. She ended classes in midafternoon, so her students could reach their homes before time to help with supper and chores.

Despite the shorter days and cooling weather, the children were lively and made Jenny laugh, even as she told them to sit still on the benches crammed into her cabin. Hatty worked around them, humming as she cooked and washed. William toddled everywhere, until one of the girls took him on her lap.

Jenny's schooling had started with a French governess who taught her to read on her father's plantation in Louisiana. Then she attended a convent school in New Orleans until the money ran out. After her father went bankrupt and they moved to Missouri, her only lessons were in her father's library. She sat in a chair beside his desk studying at his direction, while he worked on farm accounts or read his Latin and Greek texts. He taught her the words she couldn't sound out.

Teaching the boisterous Oregon children was a far cry from quiet studies with her father.

> *Saturday, October 28ᵗʰ—I have finished my second week of teaching. The little ones fidget, but are a delight. I do not know what to do with the older pupils. The Pershing twins do not want to study, and the Purcell and Abercrombie girls giggle all day. I am tired when two o'clock comes and I send them home.*

The next day Jenny and William drove into Oregon City for church. After the service, Samuel Abercrombie and his wife strode over while Jenny stood talking to Doc and Mrs. Tuller.

"I hear you admonished my granddaughter Annabelle at school yesterday," Mr. Abercrombie said. His wife hung on his arm meekly.

"She and Sarah Purcell whispered and distracted the other pupils," Jenny said, lifting William into her arms. Her throat tightened, though she smiled at Mr. Abercrombie as she spoke. She didn't want to explain herself to the older man. He was bound to take his granddaughter's part. On the trail he'd thought he and his kin were right about everything.

"Way I hear it, the Purcell girl started it," Mr. Abercrombie said, thumbs under his suspenders and a glare on his face.

"Now, Samuel—" Mrs. Abercrombie began.

"No 'now Samuel' about it," he shouted, still glowering at Jenny. "I want my kin treated right, or we'll take the girls out of that school of yourn. And our books, too."

"Your Annabelle's the problem," Amanda Pershing said, bustling over from the church doorway. Captain Pershing lagged behind her. "Franklin, you tell him. My poor Sarah is bullied every day by the Abercrombie chit."

Captain Pershing grunted.

"I should have known you'd hide ahind your new wife's skirts, Pershing," Abercrombie sneered. "Can't control her any more'n you could the wagons last year."

William started to cry. Jenny tried to comfort him, but her son hid his face in her shoulder and wailed.

"Let poor Jenny get her school going before you start judging her," Mrs. Tuller said, patting William's arm.

"She's teaching that little Negro boy next to my granddaughters, too," Abercrombie said. "'Tain't right."

"Otis ain't harming anyone," Mrs. Tuller said. "He's a good child."

"I'll be watching." Abercrombie wagged his finger in Jenny's face. "Don't you treat my grandchildren harsh, just because McDougall and I had our differences."

Chapter 19:   The New Lode

Mac had little time to brood about killing the thieving dandy or to worry about the man's companions who'd escaped. Huntington's boast proved true—he'd found a rich new lode of gold. A narrow vein of pure color ran down the side of the ravine, from its floor to higher than Mac could reach.

"We ain't seen it 'cause of the gravel and dirt coverin' it," Huntington said when he showed the vein to Mac and Joel. "I saw a glint and scraped at it, and there she was."

"Any idea how far back into the hill it goes?" Mac asked.

"Nope," the old prospector said, pushing the dead man's beaver hat back on his forehead. "I seen these veins go deep underground, and I seen 'em peter out in inches. We'll have to dig. Findin' the nuggets at the bottom of the gulch is easier. We'll start there."

So the men built another sluice for the ravine and diverted a rivulet of runoff water to flow through it. They shoveled gravel from the bottom of the ravine into the sluice and picked out the nuggets and flakes they gleaned. New mounds of tailings rose at the bottom of the gully.

Into the autumn the three men spent most of each day shoveling dirt. When the water in the ravine dried up and the sluice became useless, they carried buckets of gravel from the lode to pour through sluices near the stream. The golden hues of changing aspen leaves barely registered in Mac's mind. His hours were spent mining, with only occasional breaks to hunt.

"This is the easy part," Huntington said.

"Should've built us a pump," Joel complained. "Carrying rock is hard work."

"Might oughta build it this winter," Huntington said. "When it's too cold to stand in the water. Afore the snow melts in the spring it'll be ready."

Winter. Mac had delayed his return to Boston too long this year. He'd have to spend the winter in California. And all three partners would have to stay on the claim to protect it from thieves. They buried their sacks of gold near the cabin until they could take the color to Nate, but Mac worried they would be attacked again.

That evening Mac rolled his aching shoulders and wrote by firelight:

> *October 11, 1848. Our gold findings grow. I will soon have enough to be independent of my family— from pulling $500/week out of the ground, we are now making $5000/week, and the lode yields more every day. Will my fortune impress Father? At the moment, riches do me little good. I am trapped through the winter with two men who bicker constantly, their sole virtue that they work hard. And I am still uncertain of what comes next in my life.*

As Mac stowed his journal in his saddlebag, he fingered the little gray bootie he kept with him. He needed to write his parents to let them know his plans. He also needed to execute his plan to free Jenny, but how could he fake his death while he was still mining with Joel?

The three prospectors decided to work the lode as long as weather permitted. Most of October was clear, though mornings started brisk. The yellow aspen leaves shimmered in the sunshine, then fell and coated the ground.

Joel made another trip to Sutter's Fort to purchase supplies and deposit some of their gold. Mac or Joel went hunting when the men needed meat. But two men stayed to guard their claim at all times.

On several occasions when he rode the hills, Mac thought he saw the big man Smith who had accompanied the dandy to their claim prior to the gunfight. He wondered if Smith had been one of their attackers. He still had no idea who the third man was.

"Maybe we should find another partner," Mac said. "Then we could send two men to the fort while two stay here."

Joel snorted. "Who else can we trust? We're lucky Huntington turned out all right. I don't want to chance it again."

Joel grinned as he spoke to soften his comment, but Huntington took umbrage anyway. "You're lucky?" the old man said. "I'm the one took the chance. I ain't knowed neither of you afore we shook hands. And all you two brung is strong backs. You don't know squat about minin'."

"The only thing you do know is mining," Joel said, now frowning at Huntington. "Listening to your tall tales is worse'n listening to my pa when he's drunk."

Remembering Captain Pershing's binges on the trail led Mac to think of times with Jenny. He needed to stop worrying about her, to let her move on, and he needed to do it soon. Meanwhile, he responded to Joel and Huntington with a shrug, "I can't make you take on another partner. But we're wearing ourselves out with this new lode. There's more than enough gold for another man."

"Speak for yourself," Joel said. "You come from money back East. I'm aiming to get enough to live in luxury. And help my family out back in Oregon."

"What you know about luxury, boy?" Huntington guffawed. "All you know is the whores at the fort. That ain't luxury, that's scratchin' an itch."

Mac tried to ignore his partners when they squabbled. Joel had been a good scout on the trail, almost taciturn when they rode together for hours on end. But Huntington brought out the worst in the younger man. The two argued daily, and neither man offered Mac the comradeship he yearned for.

Jenny had been such a peaceful companion. He wished she were there in the mining shanty to greet him when he came back filthy and cold after digging in dirt and water all day. He imagined her hands scrubbing his back in a hot bath. It had never happened, but he could dream. He did dream, despite his resolve to put her in the past.

In late October Mac and his partners started to build a scaffold to reach the high end of the vein of gold, which rose many feet above Mac's head on the side of the ravine. They still didn't know how far back behind the surface the lode extended—all their digging through the autumn had not revealed the end of it.

They felled trees and lashed the trunks together to build rickety ladders and platforms twenty to thirty feet above the ground. The endeavor took several days before Huntington judged it stable enough to climb.

"I ain't got a head for heights," Huntington said when he started up the ladder the next morning. "Ain't never liked this part of minin'. Give me a pan or sluice any day. Keep my feet on the ground."

"You're the lightest man here," Joel said. "Those platforms might not hold me or Mac."

"So I'm the one what oughta get killt in a fall?" Huntington glared down at Joel while he continued to climb. His foot slipped, and the old prospector tumbled to the ground. "My leg!" he screamed.

Mac and Joel rushed over. Huntington's foot was twisted under him, the beaver hat several yards away.

"Let me see," Mac said. He felt the older man's ankle inside his boot. "It's swelling. Can you move it?"

Huntington turned his leg back and forth and the ankle turned with it.

"It might only be sprained," Mac said. "Let's take you to the shack and get the boot off."

"Maybe there's no real harm," Joel said. "You can rest it a day or two and be back to work."

Mac and Joel helped Huntington hobble to his bunk. In the end, Mac had to cut Huntington's boot off. "I'm afraid it's a loss," he said.

"You see," Huntington cackled. "They was a reason I kept that damn claim jumper's boots."

Huntington's foot and ankle turned black and blue. "It's broke, for sure," he said that night when Mac and Joel returned to the cabin to find him groaning in pain.

Mac wrapped the foot tightly. Joel made a crutch from a green tree limb, complaining the whole time he whittled the wood, "Old coot shoulda been more careful."

October 25, 1848. Huntington has broken his ankle and will be laid up for weeks.

As Mac predicted, Huntington limped along for several weeks, leaning on the crutch and issuing orders to the two younger men. Mac and Joel shored up the ladders and platforms to bear more weight, but still climbed carefully until they were sure the scaffolds were secure. Soon they were both shimmying up the makeshift ladders to dig into the vein of gold in the ravine.

After Huntington adapted to the crutch, they left him to pan in the stream as best he could. The weather turned colder, and Huntington could tolerate less and less time each day in the frigid water.

"Least you could do is make our supper," Joel complained one evening. Mac and Joel had returned to the shack to find Huntington shivering on his bunk under a blanket, no fire started for cooking.

"I ain't feelin' good," Huntington said. "Spent all day in the ice-cold creek."

"We need to set up a winter camp," Mac said. "Buy provisions and expand this hut, so we can hole up in some comfort. We can't leave the claim unguarded."

Later he took out his journal and wrote:

November 7, 1848. Winter will be here soon, and we must prepare. Huntington cannot travel, so it is up to Joel and me.

Chapter 20:   Back to the Fort

Two days after he declared they should prepare for winter, Mac set out for Sutter's Fort carrying more of their gold. He left Joel and Huntington arguing over how to add a room onto the shack to store food and other supplies.

Mac hated the idea of the three of them sharing such close quarters through the winter. Even with a small storeroom added on one side of the shanty, their three bunks lined the walls, and a table and chairs filled the cramped room. In the cold winter months, all food preparation and meals would have to take place in the cabin. The small fireplace barely kept them warm. They'd be lucky if they didn't murder each other or burn the place down.

Still on Mac's mind were the letters he needed to write—one to his parents and the other to Jenny. He should update his parents on his plans. They expected him back in Boston by Christmas. It was now too late for a letter to reach them before year-end.

He had no idea how to write Jenny. He didn't want to lie to her about his death, but he didn't know how else to end their friends' illusion she was his wife. Either she would have to confess they'd lived a lie for a year—which would destroy her reputation—or he would have to appear to have died so she could marry in truth. But he wasn't sure he could trust Joel not to tell his family that Mac was still in California.

When Mac reached the fort, he bought enough food for winter, blankets, and other necessities. Then he hired an Indian with a mule to accompany him back to the claim the next day to carry everything.

His purchases complete, Mac went to Nate's assaying office to sell their gold. The old assayer raised an eyebrow at the full bags of nuggets and

94

flakes. "You boys have had some luck. Thought so when Pershing brought the last bags to sell. He spent pretty freely that night on drinking and whoring. And gambled a good portion of his takings away as well."

Mac was surprised—Joel hadn't owned up to gambling. But Joel was a grown man and had a right to learn his own lessons. "We found a vein on our claim," Mac told Nate. "Don't know how big it is. We'll keep working as best we can through winter."

Nate grinned. "Maybe you should buy me dinner to celebrate."

"I was going to suggest that myself," Mac responded. The old gentleman still reminded him of his tutor—Nate had been educated and trained in New York City and was as well-spoken as Mac.

They settled down to their meal in the Golden Nugget. Nate seemed troubled, so Mac asked, "Something on your mind?"

"My granddaughter."

"I didn't know you had a granddaughter," Mac said. He'd never asked Nate about family. "You married?"

"Long time ago. Married my childhood sweetheart. We were very young." Nate sighed. "Younger than you are now. We had a little girl."

"Where are your wife and daughter now?"

"My wife died giving birth. I left the baby with my sister. Couldn't see myself raising a daughter alone. So I left her and followed the gold. I haven't been back to New York since."

So much tragedy hidden in families. Mac would never have guessed Nate's story from the man's calm demeanor. "You haven't seen your child since she was a baby?"

Nate shook his head. "Never."

Mac had always assumed he'd have children someday. But he didn't want to father any until he could spend time with them. He wouldn't leave his children to be raised by nannies and tutors, as he had been. He wanted children he could care for like Jenny did William—her son was obviously the center of her world. "Did you stay in touch with your daughter?"

"My sister wrote me often, and later my girl did also. My daughter married a young man when she was eighteen. I never met her husband. They had a baby—my granddaughter Susan. My daughter and her husband both died of diphtheria, leaving my sister to raise Susan."

More tragedy. "I'm sorry," Mac said.

"My poor sister—she never married, but raised two generations of my offspring." Nate raised his whiskey glass and drank a finger's worth. Then he continued, "I recently received a letter from Susan. My sister died, leaving Susan alone. She's coming to California."

"When?" Mac asked, surprised. There weren't many women from the East in California yet.

"As soon as she sells my sister's belongings, she's traveling here." Nate took another swallow and frowned at Mac. "What am I going to do with a granddaughter? She's twenty-two, a school teacher, and never been west of the Catskills."

One of the whores across the room laughed raucously. She dropped her shawl revealing most of a plump breast. Several men at the bar shouted their appreciation. "California isn't much of a place for a well-bred woman." Mac grinned at the thought of how the schoolmarms he'd known in Boston would react to such a brazen display.

"It certainly isn't." Nate downed the rest of his whiskey. "What about you? Haven't you left any women behind you?"

"I suppose," Mac said, turning his glass around in his hand. "I traveled to Oregon with a young woman. Jenny. But she didn't want to marry."

"You wanted to marry her?"

Mac shrugged. "It seemed appropriate to offer at the time. Jenny had a troubled past. She wasn't ready to marry."

"I'm sorry, son. Seems we all have sorrows behind us." Nate's words echoed what Mac had thought earlier. "Time for this old man to turn in," Nate said, and he rose from the table.

After Nate left, Mac took a closer look at the men at the bar. The largest man was familiar—Mac had seen that misshapen nose before. It was Smith, the dead dandy's companion, the one who looked like a boxer. Mac crossed the room to the bar. "You following me?" he asked Smith.

Smith's eyes narrowed as he frowned at Mac. "Who wants to know?"

"I do. You've been hanging around ever since your partner Jones died when you attacked my claim," Mac said.

"Never had no partner." But Smith didn't deny the attack.

"If I see you around our claim again," Mac said, "I'll shoot you like I did Jones." Mac hadn't wanted to kill Jones, but he'd kill again if Smith or anyone else harassed them.

Smith sneered, shrugged, and turned away without comment.

All the rooms at the saloon were taken, so Mac spent a cold night under a tarp beside a campfire. He wrote his parents, decided to delay writing

Jenny, then took out his journal:

> *November 10, 1848. I can't prove it, but the man calling himself Smith is following me. Most likely a thief who wants our claim. I think he tried to rob us earlier.*

Chapter 21: School Days

Teaching kept Jenny so busy she couldn't help Clarence and Hatty Tanner plant the winter wheat crop.

"We didn't git the fields plowed in time last year," Tanner told her over supper one evening in late October. "But this year I aim to plant more winter wheat than spring. It'll even out our work next summer. Might try some oats and barley, too."

Jenny simply nodded, then turned her mind back to her lesson plans. She'd discovered how difficult it was to keep the older children occupied for an entire day. She had few books to give them to read and little paper to dole out on which they could write essays. She gave them arithmetic problems and lectured them each day about geography and horticulture and the science she knew, but she thought her time best spent teaching the younger children to write and do their sums.

> *Wednesday, November 8th—Papa moved a roomful of books from Louisiana to Missouri, and I spent so many happy hours reading with him. I wish I had his books. I wish Papa were still alive.*

Jenny had read whatever took her fancy from her father's library. He helped her pronounce and comprehend the words she didn't know. And every day he taught her mathematics and science and geography—just like she was trying to do now.

Until his illness. Then all her lessons ended. Still, she'd been fortunate to have as much education as she'd had.

And from her mother she'd learned fluent French. But she didn't think the emigrant children needed to speak French—not until they could read and write English well.

Jenny asked the Tullers to save her the newspapers they purchased in town. She bought the paper when she could go to town, but Doc Tuller went to Oregon City more frequently than she did.

The *Oregon Spectator* put out an edition every other Thursday. She knew an issue was scheduled for November 9, and she itched to visit the Tullers over the weekend to get their copy. But the skies poured rain until Monday.

Right after Jenny sent the children home Monday afternoon, she saddled Poulette, bundled up William, and set off for the Tullers' homestead.

"Jenny," Mrs. Tuller said, coming out of her cabin. "What brings you out so late? Will you stay for supper?"

"Have you and Doc read your *Spectator* yet?" Jenny asked, handing William down to Mrs. Tuller. "I am desperate for new reading material for my students."

Mrs. Tuller clucked. "Doc almost burned it last night, but I told him he should keep it for you. There's news of the Mexican War treaty in this week's paper."

Jenny sighed. "The children will find it dry reading, but perhaps we can learn history and government. I have to find lessons where I can."

"There are some funny stories, too. One about an Irish man and a snake. And an article about temperance. Surely you can make do." When they were inside, Mrs. Tuller handed the paper to Jenny.

"Oh, an article about a telescope," Jenny exclaimed. "I've never seen one, but Papa told me about them. The lens brings the stars close enough to touch, he said. And another piece about farming—the boys will like that."

"How are the Abercrombie girls doing?" Mrs. Tuller asked. "Any more trouble?" She turned to William. "Would you like a biscuit and honey, dear?"

The toddler grinned and reached out his arms so the older woman would pick him up.

"Annabelle is a trial," Jenny said, shaking her head. "She doesn't mind me and stirs up her sister and the Purcell girls, and even little Ruthie. They all giggle and gossip. Rachel is the only one I can trust. I often ask her to work with the primer children, while I teach the older students."

"You should talk with her parents," Mrs. Tuller said with a firm nod.

"Mr. Abercrombie doesn't like me as it is."

"Samuel is her grandfather. It's up to Douglass and Louisa to govern their daughter."

"You know how timid Douglass is," Jenny said. "And Louisa is almost as silly as her daughters." She sighed. "But you're right."

On Tuesday morning Jenny gave the newspaper to the older children. She told them to each read a paragraph out loud, then pass it to the next student to read. As she worked with her younger pupils, she heard the older boys and girls droning on and on about the Mexican War treaty.

After about thirty minutes, the Pershing twins snickered.

Jonathan read in a loud voice, "Hu wee! Hu wee! A big copperhead black rattlesnake, eleven feet long, crawled up my trousers, and is tying himself in a double-bow-knot round my body!"

Then David piped up, "Jayzus! Oh, howly Vargin! Oh, Saint Patrick!"

All the children laughed and giggled.

"What is causing the commotion?" Jenny asked.

"It's the story, Miz Jenny," Jonathan said, his eyes twinkling despite his attempt to sound innocent. "We was just reading the story in the paper."

"We were," Jenny corrected him, as she took the paper and read where the boy pointed.

"David took the Lord's name in vain," Annabelle Abercrombie said solemnly, though she'd been one of the loudest gigglers. "Are you going to wash his mouth out with soap or give him a licking?"

Jenny read the story—David had in fact quoted the newspaper. The story was a parody of Irish speech and Catholic practices, including references to the Lord and the Virgin Mary. Prejudice against the Irish was strong most places in the States, though Jenny had known few Irish anywhere she'd lived.

She swallowed hard. How would she explain this to the children? And to their parents? "It's my fault," she began. "I should have read the paper thoroughly before I assigned it to you to read. This story makes fun of the Irish, as well as blaspheming. Both are wrong, and you shouldn't be reading it."

"But Miz Jenny, David swore," Annabelle insisted.

"He did. It's my fault, so I won't punish him this time," Jenny said. "But if there are more stories you have questions about, I expect you to bring them to my attention immediately." She sighed. "For now, skip that story and read about telescopes."

After supper she wrote:

Tuesday, November 14ᵗʰ—The children read an inappropriate article in the paper today. I'm sure I will hear from Mr. Abercrombie as a result. How I wish I had proper books for my students.

As Jenny had anticipated, the next morning Samuel Abercrombie drove his granddaughters to school in his wagon. He strode into her cabin with the girls behind him. "I hear those Pershing boys were cussing with my grandchildren there, and you ain't done a thing about it."

"Mr. Abercrombie, the boys were reading a story in the *Oregon Spectator*. I didn't read it first, which I should have done. Shall we step outside to discuss this?" Jenny didn't want her other students to hear Mr. Abercrombie berating her.

"I knew you was too young and flighty to teach. I've half a mind to pull the girls out of your school. Have Louisa teach them."

"I'm sorry, Mr. Abercrombie. I'll go see Douglass and Louisa after class today and apologize to them."

"Watch your step, girl." He shook his finger in her face.

When classes were finished, Jenny asked Rachel to stay with William while she rode Poulette to Douglass's claim. He was away, but she spoke with Louisa Abercrombie. Annabelle and her sister Rose stood smugly beside their mother.

Jenny explained what had happened and apologized again.

"La," Louisa said. "Father Abercrombie was very upset when Annabelle told him about those rowdy Pershing twins. He wants me to teach the girls, but Lord knows I have enough to do already."

"I'm sorry, Louisa," Jenny said.

"Please make sure it don't happen again. Or Father Abercrombie will make us take them out of school for certain. And I couldn't abide spending my days teaching, not with all the housework as well."

"Your girls should focus more on their schooling," Jenny said. But after her apology, she didn't think Louisa would take her seriously. "Annabelle in particular likes to talk with the other girls."

"Well, now, children need to be sociable. You just tell them to talk quietly." Louisa turned back to her fire. "The girls and I need to fix supper now."

As she mounted Poulette to leave, Jenny saw Annabelle smirking in the doorway. "She gave us an essay to write tonight, Mama," the girl complained.

"Help me shell the peas," Louisa said. "You can do your schoolwork later."

Chapter 22:   Mining Code

Mac and the Indian he'd hired and their heavily laden mules kept to a quick pace while returning to the gold claim. When they reached it, the men unloaded supplies and stashed them in the cabin in piles as high as the low ceiling. Mac paid the Indian and sent him on his way.

On a cold mid-November evening a few days later, the three partners sat by their campfire cooking. "Time we set some rules for this valley," Huntington announced. "Whilst you boys been diggin', I been talkin' with other men settlin' in these parts. Been some squabbles over claim boundaries and such."

"Have you seen that bastard Smith snooping around again?" Mac asked. "I was in the ravine all day. I didn't see or hear anyone. But he followed me to the fort."

"Ain't seen him this week. Like I said, we need rules. Winter's comin'. Men'll be leavin' their claims. They need to know what rights they got come spring. Everyone from Bible thumpers to drunkards 'round here. Someone's got to make 'em toe the mark." Huntington coughed and spat toward the fire.

"Only law we've needed so far is a gun," Joel said, stabbing a piece of venison with his knife. "But I heard tell at the fort some miners are writing their own rules. Makes sense to me."

"What do you suggest?" Mac said to Huntington. "Have you seen this done elsewhere?"

Huntington nodded. "Call a palaver. We meet to decide what rules we want. You're the man knows the law. You write 'em down."

Mac thought a moment. Even if the miners didn't follow the rules after they were in place, it couldn't hurt to have a code of sorts. Most of the men in the valley seemed reasonable. Only Smith had been a problem thus far—and whoever the third accomplice was who'd accompanied Smith and Jones when they attacked the claim.

With rules in place, Mac would feel more secure about leaving just one partner on their claim—at least he would if the prospectors in the valley all agreed to protect each other's claims.

He nodded to Huntington. "Ride around the valley tomorrow. Tell the prospectors we'll meet here on Sunday afternoon."

Then he took out his journal and wrote:

November 16, 1848. What would Father say now? I will be scrivener for the miners in our valley. I hope the men prove to be sensible. But I fear desire for gold may warp the minds of some.

The following Sunday afternoon about thirty men converged on their claim. Mac recognized most of them, though Smith was one of the few names he knew. His first order of business was to take a roll call.

"Why we need to set rules?" a tall, scrawny man with a long dark beard asked. His name was Duncan. "Doin' fine all summer."

"How big is your claim?" Huntington asked. "How many men workin' it?"

"We doin' all right," Duncan said. "You three got more land'n my group."

"I'm workin' the top of the ridge," another man—Fitzgibbons—said. "Ain't got no water, but what I carry in a bucket to drink and wash in. How do I get water rights?"

Duncan spat. "Shoulda got here sooner. First come, first claim."

Before more arguments could develop, Mac raised his hand. "All right," he said. "Here's what I know. There are no laws governing us, because California has no government other than the U.S. Army at the moment. But if we agree on our own rules, we'll be safer."

Smith sat on a log apart from the rest of the men, whittling a stick into shreds with a large knife. His lip curled into a sneer.

"Have we all staked our claims?" Mac asked.

The men nodded.

"Any disputes over the current stakes?"

The men shook their heads. "We worked 'em out 'mongst ourselves," one man said.

"They's still unclaimed land in this valley," Huntington said. "But we's all abidin' by the stakes what's been pounded into the ground already."

"Then shall we agree each prospector can mine the land he and his partners have staked? And we'll stay off each other's claims?" When the men nodded, Mac dipped his quill in the ink bottle and began writing.

"What about when we leave to git supplies?" Duncan asked, scratching his skinny chest. "I suspect men been wanderin' onto my land when I'm gone." He looked at Smith as he spoke.

"Will we watch each other's land? Keep intruders off?" Mac asked. That, of course, was his primary concern.

"For how long?" Smith asked. "We gonna let some go off to the whorehouses all winter? Let 'em come back free and easy, while others guard their claims?"

"Thirty days." Joel said. "Let a man be gone thirty days. Any longer, the claim's fair game."

Another miner—Gabhart—nodded, "Month is plenty of time to get to San Francisco, lose our gold, and come back."

"Month is fine," an older man in a vest and top hat said. Mac wasn't sure of the man's name. "If a miner leaves his tools on his land, we ain't gonna disturb it for a month."

Mac wrote it down.

The men debated until dusk. They agreed on one claim per man, though they permitted partnerships, and they agreed to limit future claim sizes to the largest existing claim—thirty feet of creek bed, back to the top of the ridge, which was roughly fifty feet from the water. Mac, Joel, and Huntington together had around eighty feet along the creek, and most of the ravine where the big lode was located fell within their stakes.

"Fair enough," Huntington said. "Thirty feet is plenty to dig a hole on, see whether there's color on the claim. Man can't work more'n one hole at a time."

"I'm goin' out tomorrow to expand my claim," Gabhart said.

"What about partners?" Mac asked. "Some of us have been using rockers and sluices. Those are best worked by teams of men."

"Men can work together," Huntington said. "That's always been the rule

105

'mongst prospectors. Don't see why men can't join their claims."

"But we're agreed," Joel said, "if a man pulls out, after a month the land is free again. What about selling claims to others?"

"Man can't hold more'n one claim. We just said so," the old man in the vest said.

"But a man ought to be able to sell what he has," Joel protested. "Not have to open it up to anyone."

"Shall we list our claims?" Mac asked. "I'll keep the roster of men and what diggings they've claimed."

"No Negroes or Mexicans or Chinese," Duncan said. "Only Americans. If a man can't vote in the States, he don't deserve no California gold."

"But let's be clear on the selling," Joel said. "If a man wants to leave his claim, he oughta be able to get something for it—sell it to a man he trusts."

Mac thought Joel must be remembering his offer to sell his claim to Joel when he left. "That all right?" he asked the group.

"Why not?" Fitzgibbons said. "We's only tryin' to keep others from squattin', not to do a man out of work he's done on his own."

"So sales and partnerships are fine, as long as they're recorded on my books," Mac said. When he received the assent he wanted, he continued, "And we're agreed we'll back each other against any squatters?"

The men nodded. "Just let a man try," Huntington said. "We'll string him up."

"We need a man to serve as magistrate," Joel said. "They call 'em *alcades* in California. I guess that's you, Mac."

"Why him?" Smith asked.

"He's a lawyer," Joel said. "Been wagon captain, too. Kept order then."

Smith cocked an eyebrow, but didn't say anything. Mac was elected *alcade*.

After the meeting, Mac wrote up the rules the men had agreed on:

> *This valley is subject to the following laws by which our claims are to be governed:*
>
> > *1. No person shall hold more than one claim by location.*

2. *No claim shall exceed thirty feet along the creek, nor farther back than the ridge line.*
3. *Every claim not registered with the alcade within ten days after being staked shall be deemed open and subject to claim by another.*
4. *All sales and transfers of claims shall be registered with the alcade.*
5. *Each claim shall be worked at least one day during every thirty or shall be deemed open and unclaimed. Except that in the case of a company or partners holding two or more claims, it will be sufficient to work one of their claims one day during every thirty.*

Signed, this 19th day of November, 1848.

Caleb McDougall, Alcade

He wrote out a copy, then placed the original in an oilskin bag with his journal, and nailed the copy to a tree near the dead dandy's grave.

"Well, that oughta do us, least till the govmint gits involved," Huntington said, as he watched Mac post the rules.

Chapter 23:   Winter in Oregon

The Oregon weather turned dank in mid-November. The Saturday after Jenny met with Louisa Abercrombie, a hailstorm struck. She had just let the children out of class at midday and hoped they all arrived home safely before the tempest hit. She tethered William to the table leg so he wouldn't burn himself in the fireplace, then rushed out to move Poulette and Shanty into the barn.

Jenny smiled, remembering when Valiente had stuck his head in the wagon during a hailstorm on the prairie. She seemed to find reminders every day of her time with Mac.

The late autumn days and nights turned monotonous. Jenny spent dreary days with her students followed by quiet evenings alone with William or sometimes with the Tanners. While Jenny prepared lessons for the following day, Hatty sewed, and Tanner cleaned and repaired his tools. Otis and William played on the buffalo skin rug on the floor.

Tanner labored on Jenny's land and on the claims of other families from their wagon train. Once the fall harvest was finished and the next year's winter wheat crop planted, the emigrant farmers cleared more fields to plant in the spring. Stores in Oregon City were full of talk of increased demand for food in both Oregon and California.

Tanner also built a small smithy on the road passing Jenny's claim. Men straggled in and out with horses to be shod. There weren't many skilled farriers and blacksmiths in Oregon, and Tanner was in high demand.

Though Tanner couldn't own land in Oregon, he and Hatty more than earned their keep on Jenny's farm. Jenny suspected Tanner was amassing a healthy credit in his own account at the stores in Oregon City.

Jenny had paid down her account at Abernethy's after the harvest, and still kept the letter of credit from Mac hidden. She worried she would have to buy staples through the winter—her students' families brought her eggs and meat, but they couldn't supply everything she and William needed.

"Everything all right?" Zeke asked her one morning in December. At least once a week he drove the Pershing and Purcell children from Captain Pershing's farm to Jenny's house for school, saving them the long walk.

"Fine," she said. "The children are doing splendidly in their lessons. I can hardly keep ahead of them. How's your farm?"

"I'm hoping the apple trees I planted this fall don't freeze," he said. "They won't bear for a few years, but the trees folks put in last year grew fast. Apples'll ship well to California."

"Still no notion to go to California yourself?" Jenny asked.

Zeke shook his head. "Joel can do the wandering. I'll stay here."

"I heard three families at church on Sunday say they're leaving for California in the spring," Jenny said. "They think they'll find gold."

"So many of our fine elected representatives have left, there ain't even a quorum for the legislative session." Zeke snorted. "Damn fools get elected, then don't do their job. Pardon my language."

Jenny laughed. "With all the men traipsing through Tanner's smithy, I hear plenty of cursing. I have to remind the men I have children here."

"You be careful, Miz Jenny," Zeke said. "That's one reason I stop by your place. I don't like all those men passing your farm to the smithy. They're worse'n mountain lions."

"It's a good living for Tanner," Jenny said. "I can't tell him to stop."

"You got too much traffic through your land," Zeke argued. "It ain't right with McDougall gone."

Zeke had always watched out for her, Jenny thought. A good man, like Mac had written. "I'm fine as long as Tanner's here," she said.

"You be careful, Miz Jenny," Zeke said. "No telling what some of these ruffians might do."

Jenny knew what ruffians could do. She hugged William closer. "I'm careful," she said.

After supper, while she put William to bed, Jenny thought of the December afternoon two years earlier when the two Johnson men and her stepfather had raped her. Those memories came less frequently now, but the conversation with Zeke brought them to mind.

William smiled up at her sleepily and stuck his thumb in his mouth. She couldn't regret having him. Motherhood was difficult, the hardest task she'd ever had, but she loved her son with all her being.

No one but the Tullers and Mac knew the truth of William's conception. The Tullers thought she should have wed Mac despite her past, but Mac had understood her reluctance.

Still, after two years, was it time to move on? To think about marriage and more children? Not all men were bad. Mac and Zeke were two fine men. But how could she wed anyone when her friends thought she already was married?

On December 18, a half-inch of ice coated the road past Jenny's farm. None of her students made it to school, so she and Hatty spent the morning making bread.

Jenny could tell Hatty was expecting a child, but the other woman hadn't said anything. While they baked, Jenny asked, "Are you feeling all right?"

Hatty stretched her back, then said, "Good as I can be, Miz Jenny." She put a hand over her mouth, but Jenny saw Hatty's lip quiver.

"What's the matter, Hatty?"

"Just rememberin' my baby Homer."

The Tanners' younger son Homer had died on the trail to Oregon from the cholera that killed so many. Even Mac, strong as he was, had almost died of it. While tending Mac during his illness, Jenny realized he depended on her as much as she relied on him. She learned something of her own strength nursing him back to health and coping with the challenges of wagon travel.

"Poor Homer," Jenny said to Hatty now. "We lost so many along the way."

"That's a fact, ma'am. And who knows what will come next?"

Jenny looked at Hatty in surprise. "What's worrying you, Hatty? We have a good home now."

"Ain't you heard, Miz Jenny? They gonna expel any Negroes stayin' in

Oregon."

"That can't be true. Men drive a day's journey for Tanner's smithing and carpentering."

"It's the law. They gonna run off any of us who stay more'n two years in Oregon. Clarence and me, we been here over a year now."

"I'll talk to Doc Tuller," Jenny said. "He'll know what to do."

The ice melted through the morning, though a trace of snow fell in early afternoon. Nevertheless, Jenny set out for the Tullers' farm, leaving William with Hatty and Otis.

She greeted the Tullers, then said to Doc, "Hatty says Negroes can't stay in Oregon."

Doc snorted. "Buffoons in the legislature—passing laws they have no intention of enforcing. Then they hightail it to California. Yes, that's the law. Been the law since forty-five, I'm told. Before then, law said they'd flog any Negroes who stayed in the territory. But there ain't been anyone expelled yet. I hear they planned to repeal the ridiculous law, but with the legislators gone this year, nothing's been done."

"Hatty's worried. She's in the family way again."

"I suspected so." Doc sighed. "Tanner's a good worker. No one'll touch him. They need his skills and labor too much."

"What if someone shows up on my land to take him?" Jenny couldn't help worrying. She would be alone if the Tanners left.

"Don't fret, Jenny," Mrs. Tuller said. "We'd all stand behind the Tanners. Most of us wouldn't have made it across the plains without him mending our wagons."

"Unless Samuel Abercrombie makes an issue of it," Doc said. "No telling what that stubborn cuss will do."

Doc's statement worried Jenny more. Mr. Abercrombie was unpredictable, and he'd complained about her teaching Otis with his granddaughters. If he didn't like something, he'd chew on the matter like a dog with a bone, just to cause trouble. "If the Tanners leave, I'll have no one to mind the farm."

More snow fell the next morning. Zeke stopped by Jenny's claim to let her know the Pershing and Purcell children would not be coming to school.

"Zeke." Jenny smiled when she opened the door to him. "Have you eaten? I have fresh biscuits and gravy."

The oldest Pershing son lived by himself on his claim now in a small cabin. Sometimes he ate with his father's household, but usually he kept to himself. "Mighty nice of you, Miz Jenny. I'd be obliged."

Jenny, William, the Tanners, and Zeke squeezed around the table in the cabin for breakfast. Zeke seemed to take up more room than any one man should. Mac was taller, but Zeke was broader.

After they ate, Hatty said, "Otis and I'll clean up, Miz Jenny. You go show Mr. Zeke how the foal's grown."

Jenny frowned at Hatty, but said nothing. She grabbed a wool shawl, and she and Zeke went outside. The snow had stopped, so they moved Poulette and Shanty from the barn to the paddock.

"I hear you're worried about being alone," Zeke said.

"How'd you hear that?" Jenny asked.

"Doc."

"I'm worried about the Tanners being forced out of Oregon."

"Won't happen, Doc says."

"Maybe not." Jenny hugged her shawl around her against the chill December air. She didn't want to think about coping without Tanner and Hatty. And Otis was a joy to teach.

"You know we'd all take care of you if the Tanners left," Zeke said.

Jenny smiled. "Thank you."

"I'd care for you." He stood close, but didn't touch her.

Jenny glanced at Zeke and shivered. "Thank you, Zeke," she said again. She would need all her friends if the Tanners left. But what did Zeke mean? Did he care for her like Esther and the Tullers did, or did he mean something more?

The next Monday was Christmas. Jenny wrote:

> Monday, December 25th—A quiet Christmas, William enjoyed Hatty's sweet fruitcake. I miss Mac and pray for him daily. But as 1848 ends, I know I am blessed with many friends. Zeke has been steadfast, as he has been since I met him.

Chapter 24:   Winter in California

Mac stretched out on his bunk in the small mining shack he shared with Joel and Huntington. The afternoon dragged on, Mac's thoughts revolving and colliding in his head. Christmas had passed, but they hadn't even wished each other a merry Christmas when the day arrived. Now the year had turned—January 1849.

The men had worked their claim into December, but then winter hit like a sledgehammer in midmonth, stopping almost all outdoor activity for days at a time. Heavy snows covered the hills above them. Rains flooded the American and Sacramento Rivers at lower elevations, and the mountain creeks were either frozen or treacherously swift. Travel was almost impossible. The miners worked when weather permitted, but spent many days confined to cabins and tents.

The hard labor of mining had kept Mac's questions at bay for many months, but in the winter doldrums he had nothing to occupy his time except to ponder what he wanted to do with the rest of his life.

He'd been away from Boston almost two years now, spending 1847 on the trip to Oregon and 1848 mining for gold. He'd been successful at both endeavors and now had a fortune in gold deposited with Nate. Yet he'd killed at least two men along the way—one in Missouri and the other on the gold claim. He couldn't have avoided the shootings, but the deaths still troubled him. The West was a dangerous land, and he wondered how much longer he should stay.

He thought earning a fortune might raise his standing with his father and brothers. But he wasn't sure if it would. His father might still press him to join his brother's law firm. Mac didn't need to earn a living with the riches he'd found, but his father might still push him.

He'd reconciled himself to leaving Jenny behind. But thoughts of her still meandered through his mind. He worried about how she managed the farm and how she coped with William.

He'd sent Jenny enough money to keep her and her son secure, but he needed to break off all ties with her. He planned to send Jenny word he'd died, and include a deed for the claim when he did so. But he still thought he should be on his way to the East when the letter left California, so no word would get back to Oregon that he was still alive. Therefore, he needed a plan for himself before he could release Jenny.

Joel and Huntington argued over a game of checkers by the fire. "You devil," Joel said, "you can't jump backward till you're kinged."

"That one's been kinged," Huntington replied. "We ain't got enough checkers to show all my kings."

Mac was slowly going mad listening to his partners. He sighed and wrote:

January 14, 1849. I am tired of this mining camp. I need to get to Sutter's Fort, if only for the diversion.

Then he threw his journal on his bunk and stood. "I'm going to the fort tomorrow if it doesn't snow tonight," he said. "They had a land auction scheduled. Think I'll see who bought the lots outside the fort."

"It's my turn," Joel said. "You went last time." Joel took every opportunity to ride to Sutter's Fort. Consuela was probably the reason—or gambling. Nate had said Joel was wasting his riches on wagers and women. But that wasn't Mac's concern.

Despite the mining code in the valley, the three partners tried to keep two men on their claim whenever possible. If Joel left, then Mac would have to wait.

"You boys fight it out," Huntington said, scratching his beard. "My bones is too old to leave the fire whilst snow is on the ground." Huntington had coughing spells every night. Mac wondered if the old man would live until spring.

Mac shrugged. It wasn't worth arguing about. "Suit yourself," he said to Joel. "But don't dawdle. I've still a mind to go when you get back, weather permitting."

Joel was gone a week. A week in which Mac listened to Huntington cough and complain and boast about his earlier mining escapades.

"You ever kill a man?" Mac asked Huntington one afternoon, mostly to keep the old prospector from telling him again about building a rocker from a rotten ash tree in Georgia.

"Oh, sure." Huntington leaned back in his chair. "We had a thievin' varmint wanderin' around our camp back in thirty-five. Some men thought a raccoon was stealin' our cornmeal, but I knew it was a man." He chuckled until he hacked up phlegm. "I set a trap. Rigged up a bag with a hole in the seam, so's when a body picked it up, the meal left a trail behind him. Led me right to his tent. I busted in, pistol in hand. He dove for his gun, and I plugged him full of lead. Got most of the cornmeal back, too."

"Didn't you feel bad about killing him?"

"Hell, no. He was a thief."

"Maybe he was hungry."

"So was I, Mac. So was I." Huntington guffawed. "He got what he deserved. And I got my cornmeal."

Huntington made it sound so easy. An eye for an eye. Mac didn't think justice was so simple—law school had shown him the complications.

"You ever marry?" he asked Huntington.

"Hell, no," Huntington said, in the same tone he'd used when talking about killing a man. "Women ain't worth gittin' tied to. One or two nights is the most a man needs 'em. I ain't never been set on any gal for more'n a week or two. 'Tain't worth the aggravation."

"Some women are mighty fine." Mac thought of Jenny's full lips in a shy smile when he said something nice to her. Of her breasts and hips in his hands.

"One might be fine, but so's another. Who you moonin' over?"

"No one in particular."

"Joel told me you was with some gal all the way from Missouri to Oregon," Huntington said. "But she weren't your wife. That true?"

"That story wasn't Joel's to tell."

"Must've been true." Huntington's laugh turned into a wheeze. "If you was sweet on her, why didn't you marry her?"

"I wasn't sweet on her. And she didn't want to marry me."

"Then you asked her?"

"She needed someone to take care of her."

"Now that's the foolishest reason I ever heard for a man to marry," Huntington said. "No man should marry 'cause a woman needs him. Only reason to marry is if you need her. And like I said, there's always another woman."

"I don't see you carrying on with any women at the moment," Mac said, bristling at Huntington's callousness.

"Don't git mad." Huntington coughed. "You want her, you go git her," he rasped. "All's I was doin' was tellin' you my philosophy."

"I'm going out for more firewood," Mac said. He shrugged into his coat, pushed his hat down on his head, and took the axe out to the woodpile, where he chopped for an hour.

He never went to Sutter's Fort in January. By the time Joel returned, Huntington was bedridden with fever, coughing incessantly, and Mac felt trapped.

He prayed for an early spring.

Chapter 25:   One Year Alone

Jenny woke to a frigid February morning. The fire across the room had died to embers. She shivered as she put another log on the coals and stirred until flickers of flame licked the wood.

William fussed when he awoke. He still slept in the cradle Mac and Tanner had made when they arrived in Oregon. Now the seventeen-month-old toddler filled it end to end. She would ask Tanner to make him a trundle bed, something her son could use until she felt comfortable allowing him to sleep alone in the loft. But the cradle reminded her of Mac every time she rubbed its polished maple. She wouldn't like putting it away.

> *Saturday, February 17ᵗʰ—Mac left me a year ago today. Sometimes it feels like yesterday. Sometimes I feel I've been alone forever. Our life on the trail seems like a dream.*

Jenny felt a lump in her throat as she put her diary away. She started breakfast, mixing cornmeal and milk with a little soda for flapjacks. Jenny tried to do most of the heavy housework, now that Hatty's pregnancy was well along. Jenny didn't know how they would manage the crops this year. Hatty had helped her husband almost every day the year before, but she wouldn't be able to do much planting with a new baby.

Jenny could try to hire a man to help Tanner. But most men had their own land to farm, like Zeke. Or they'd gone to California or planned to leave in the spring.

Hatty knocked and entered the cabin, Otis at her side. "Miz Jenny," she said, taking off her shawl. "I could have started the flapjacks."

"No matter," Jenny said. "Would you please wash William's face? Get him ready for breakfast."

Hatty lifted the toddler, a grunt escaping her as she did.

"Is your back bothering you?" Jenny asked.

"Some," Hatty said. "I'll be fine."

Jenny sighed. She wouldn't be able to count on Hatty's help much longer, though the Negro woman would never complain.

Jenny's school had done well through the winter. She would have to close it in a few more weeks, so the children could help their families with spring planting. The Pershings and Abercrombies had paid her in kind or with credit on her account at the Abernethy store in Oregon City. She was well fixed through spring, but she worried about next winter already, hoping she would have a bountiful harvest in the fall.

She hadn't spent much of Mac's money. The coins were there if she needed them, but she didn't think of them as her money. They were Mac's, and she wanted to replenish what she had spent, so she could return them to him someday—somehow. And the letter of credit remained hidden in the loft with the money.

A few days later the Abercrombie girls brought a gold coin to class with them. "Look what Grandfather Samuel gave us," Annabelle said. "A beaver coin."

"What is that?" Jenny asked.

"New money made here in Oregon. By the government," the girl told her, pointing to the etching of a beaver on one side. "Grandfather says it come from the gold in California."

"Came," Jenny corrected.

The other children all wanted to touch the beaver coin. Jenny wondered if the money Mac had left her would be worth less if coins were being minted in Oregon.

When she saw Doc after church the following Sunday, she pulled him away so she could speak to him. Mrs. Tuller followed.

Doc was upset because the *Oregon Spectator* would no longer be printed. "The only printer up and left for California," he fumed. "Won't be no way to learn the news."

"Now, Doc," Mrs. Tuller said. "The publisher says he's looking for another printer."

"It'll be a month of Sundays afore he finds anyone. Every able-bodied man is headed to California, so it seems."

"Doc," Jenny interjected, "the Abercrombie girls brought a new coin to school. Minted here in Oregon, they said."

Doc shook his head. "Legislature don't know what it's doing. No more'n the newspaper does. Those coins were only made for a few weeks. They ain't legal. Only the federal government can make money. Says so in the Constitution."

"So what will happen with the beaver coins?" Jenny asked.

"Well, they're still gold, so they're worth something," Doc said. "But no different than gold flakes, if you ask me."

"Mac left me some gold coins," Jenny said. "Are they worth anything?"

"U.S. coins?" Doc asked.

Jenny nodded. "Double eagles."

"They're good tender," Doc said. "Mind you keep 'em hidden. You don't want nothing stolen. But here's some more news for you."

"What's that?" Jenny asked.

"The last issue of the *Spectator* published a new law about land claims." Doc held up the newspaper. "Right here on page three. Says land claims are part of a man's personal property after he dies. Widows can reside on the land while they're alive and don't remarry. Of course, you ain't a widow. Nor a wife neither."

"What happens if a woman remarries?" Jenny asked. She had no plans to marry—and couldn't remarry—but she should know what the law was.

"Then the land passes as her dead husband's personal property. To his heirs." Doc frowned at her. "But if anyone finds out you ain't married to McDougall and William ain't his son, you'll likely lose the land. Without a wife or heir, all McDougall's rights in the claim are gone."

Jenny swallowed a pang of fear. "I'll farm until that happens."

"You need to come to grips with McDougall being gone."

Doc was right. But every time Jenny thought of never seeing him again, she panicked. "Maybe I should have married him," she said.

Mrs. Tuller sighed. "The two of you got along well, and could have made a good marriage, Jenny. Love would have come."

"Well, it's too late now," Doc said.

Jenny was silent. It wasn't love she'd lacked, but courage. Could she have lived with a man after being raped? She hadn't thought so when Mac asked her. Now she couldn't bear the thought of being alone. Maybe she would have been happy married to Mac.

Zeke still came by Jenny's farm about once a week. He usually had some reason to talk to Tanner about the fields or shoeing a horse. But after he talked to Tanner, he sought out Jenny. Sometimes he stayed for a meal, sometimes he said he needed to get back to his claim.

"Have you heard from Mac, Miz Jenny?" he asked her one evening.

"Not since his letter months ago," Jenny said. Everyone knew Mac had written her—Esther made sure of that. All Jenny had told her friends was that Mac was staying in California awhile.

"Joel wrote Pa he was mining on a place two days outside Sutter's Fort. I wonder if he and Mac ever see each other."

Jenny laughed. "Wouldn't that be a fine thing? They both leave Oregon, only to run into each other in California. But Mac won't stay in California." Then she stopped herself. What more could she tell Zeke?

Zeke frowned, seeming puzzled. "When do you think he'll be back?"

Jenny shrugged. "I don't know. He said when he left he was going to Boston, but then he stopped in California. I don't know whether he'll go on to Boston or come back here."

"I never understood the way he treated you. He shouldn't have left you and William alone."

"He treated me fine."

"Mac never appreciated you. Must have seen too many fancies and fripperies in Boston to know what he had. I wouldn't leave my wife alone for so long, that's for sure."

Chapter 26: Civilization

February 17, 1849. The weather continues to confine me to our cramped cabin, though on a good day I can hunt, which gives me a few hours of peace and replenishes our meat. Not the life I expected when I left Oregon a year ago. One year ago today.

Mac's cabin fever mounted, while Huntington's cough lingered on. In late February the old prospector's health finally began to improve, and Mac felt comfortable leaving Joel and Huntington on the claim and traveling to Sutter's Fort.

The community around the fort had grown even more in the months since his last visit. A wood and canvas city had sprung up on the river delta, the nearby forest slaughtered for tent poles and boards. Shacks and shops dotted fields outside the fort walls. Muddy streets wide enough for wagons to pass ran between the buildings. Men pounded hammers and worked saws near the river—a cacophony of civilization. Pilings in the water marked what looked to be the outline of a bridge.

Mac stocked up on food and bought nails to build more sluices. He didn't have any gold to deposit with Nate, because the partners had done little digging since Joel's last trip to the fort. But he stopped in the assayer's store anyway.

"Good to see you, McDougall," Nate said, coming around the counter to shake Mac's hand.

"Place has changed since the last time I was here." Mac brushed dust off his hat, then waved it at the door. "Lots of new buildings."

"We call ourselves Sacramento City now," Nate said. "Army surveyed and laid out the streets in December. All the land between the American and Sacramento Rivers. Sutter sold a huge parcel of land outside the fort at auction in January. New stores are opening every day. Only thing holding us back is the flooding."

"I'd heard about the auction. Also heard the American overran its banks at the Embarcadero. Did the water reach this far?" Mac asked.

Nate shook his head. "We're too far from the river. Folks with land along the American had trouble, though the river lots are now the ones most in demand. I was glad to be on higher ground. New miners flock into town daily."

"So early in the year?" Mac was surprised.

"These men traveled from South America, where summer's just ending. We'll be overrun with Spaniards and Mexicans soon. A steamship makes a regular run from Panama to San Francisco now. And a Post Office in San Francisco, too. Someone brought a bag of mail to the fort, so you might check before you leave town to see if there are any letters for you." Nate shook his head. "Susan wrote—she's on her way."

Mac recalled the assayer's concern over his granddaughter. "Is she traveling alone?"

Nate shrugged, but seemed troubled. "Her letter said other women also booked passage on the ship, but that's all I know. I have no idea when she'll arrive."

"I'm sure she'll be fine," Mac said. Not much he could say to reassure his friend.

Nate continued with more information, "Newspaper is planning to start publishing soon. *The Placer Times*."

"Civilization in California," Mac said, glad to shift the conversation to less personal matters.

Nate chuckled. "If you want to call it that. Most of the new arrivals are pretty rough characters. More than two thousand folks call Sacramento home now. There'll even be a bridge to span the American."

"I saw the construction as I rode in."

"Bridge should open this spring. Wide enough for wagons."

"How are the prices of gold holding up?" Mac asked.

"Sixteen dollars an ounce for dust," Nate said. "A storekeeper here—man named Mills—is planning to open a bank."

"Will a bank hurt your business?"

Nate shrugged. "Plenty of gold for everyone, I expect. The government might even open a U.S. Mint in San Francisco. Half a million dollars' worth of gold left port in one ship last November, headed for the mint in Philadelphia. But that's too much risk even for Uncle Sam."

Mac finished his business and went to the fort to ask for mail. "Nothin' for McDougall or Huntington," he was told. "But here's a letter for a Mr. Joel Pershing."

Mac took Joel's letter and headed for the Golden Nugget. He was tempted to break the letter's seal to see if it mentioned Jenny, but that would be wrong. So he'd stay close while Joel read it.

Mac wasn't surprised when Consuela joined him in the saloon when he ate. "Evening," he said.

"*Buenas noches.* Where is your high-spending friend Joel?"

"Still in camp. He didn't make this trip."

"So it is only you here this evening?"

"Only me." Mac said. "And I'm only interested in eating."

Consuela frowned at him. "Who is she, Mac?"

"Who?" He raised an eyebrow. No reason to tell Consuela his history with women—he didn't like to relive that history even in his own mind.

"The woman you think of."

Consuela sounded friendly, but Mac didn't want to recount his troubles. Not about Jenny. Not about Bridget. "Let's just say I haven't had much luck with women."

"Then there has been more than one woman in your life?"

Mac stared at his glass, avoiding her eyes. "You're working. You don't have time to hear my sorry tale."

"Someday you will tell me," Consuela smiled, touching his cheek. "'It's a pity, whoever she is, that she keeps you from enjoying life."

"Do you enjoy your life, Consuela?"

Her laugh was low and husky. "But I am not a handsome rich prospector like you. Enjoy your warm dinner, because your bed will be cold."

The next morning Mac bundled himself in his overcoat, loaded his supplies on the pack mule, and headed back to the gold claim. The journey was cold but uneventful, no sign of anyone following him.

When he arrived, he handed the letter to Joel, who opened it eagerly.

"It's from Esther," Joel said. "She had a baby girl. Named her Cordelia, after Ma."

"Does she mention anyone else?"

"Damn." Joel threw the page covered with Esther's small tight script to the ground.

"What's wrong?" Mac said, reaching for it. Had something happened to Jenny?

Joel grabbed the letter back before Mac could read it. "Pa's married."

"Married? To whom?" Mac waited for Joel to scan the words.

"Amanda Purcell," Joel said, groaning in disgust. "She and her three children have moved onto Pa's claim with him."

"Well, that's a surprise," Mac said. "Though both your father and Mrs. Purcell might relish the help of a spouse."

"Esther's beside herself. Hates the woman. And her kids."

"Why? Mrs. Purcell did the best she could after her husband drowned on the trail last year."

Joel shrugged. "Esther and Ma were close. Esther fretted at Ma's interference, especially when she and Daniel were courting, but she and Ma were thick as thieves against the rest of us."

"What about others from our company?" Mac asked, not wanting to mention Jenny. "Did Esther say anything else?"

"It's all about family. Zeke moved to his own claim. The young'uns are in school this fall. Miz Jenny's the teacher."

"Jenny's teaching?" Mac was surprised—had she run out of money? "What else does she say about Jenny?" He reached for the letter.

"That's it." Joel yielded the paper to Mac.

Mac read every word carefully, but Esther's letter didn't say anything more about Jenny.

Chapter 27:   Sorrow

Frantic knocks on the cabin door woke Jenny one early March morning, shortly before dawn. She grabbed her shawl and cracked open the latch. Otis stood outside, tears streaming down his dark cheeks.

"Miz Jenny, it's Ma," the boy said. "The baby's comin'."

"I'll go for Doc Tuller," Jenny said, already turning away from the door. Hatty's baby wasn't due for another two months.

"Too late." Otis pulled on her sleeve. "It's comin' now. Pa says he needs you."

"Wait," Jenny said. "You stay with William, once I'm dressed." She didn't want to face what would likely happen to Hatty's baby, but there was no one else to help. She shut the door and pulled on her clothes in a hurry. Then she shooed Otis inside—"Stay here until I get back"—and ran to the Tanners' cabin.

Hatty was wailing in the bed.

"Baby won't wait," Tanner murmured. "Hatty just woke up an hour ago, and she's pushin' already."

"It's too soon," Jenny said.

"No matter," Tanner said. "This baby's birthin' now." He sat beside his wife, like Mac had sat beside Jenny when William was born.

Hatty moaned. Jenny grabbed her hand. "Hold on, Hatty. You'll meet your baby in a little bit."

When Hatty groaned again, Tanner said, "Head's here. Push, Hatty, push." Hatty's hand squeezed Jenny's until it hurt. Jenny mopped Hatty's forehead when she relaxed.

"Another big one, Hatty," Tanner urged.

Hatty screamed once, and Tanner held up a tiny, slippery infant. "It's a girl," he whispered. "A daughter." His voice broke.

"Why ain't she cryin'?" Hatty asked, trying to push herself up.

"Stay down, Hatty," Jenny said. "Let Tanner clean her up."

Tanner took the baby to the washbowl and wiped her with a soft towel, while Jenny helped Hatty deliver the afterbirth.

Silence weighted the air. Tanner slapped the baby's back. More silence. "She ain't breathin'," Tanner said. "I can't wake her up."

He tapped the baby's chest, then thumped it hard. Still silence.

"My baby," Hatty keened when the silence became deafening and Jenny couldn't bear it any longer. She remembered Hatty's cries when her boy Homer had died of cholera. This baby was supposed to make up for that loss, though nothing could replace a child who died. Either child. Tears filled Jenny's eyes.

Tanner handed the baby's body, wrapped tightly in a worn blanket, to his wife. "'Tweren't meant to be, Hatty," he said, dropping to his knees beside the bed. "I'm sorry," he whispered. They sobbed together.

Jenny stole out of the cabin and went back to her own home, pausing to wipe her cheeks before she opened the door.

Otis looked up at her with big brown eyes. "Ma?" he asked.

Jenny sat on her bed and pulled the boy beside her into a hug. "Your mama's fine," she said. "But your baby sister died."

He nodded. "Like Homer."

"Yes," Jenny said. "Like Homer. Do you want to see your mama?"

Otis nodded again.

Jenny gathered up William, still asleep. She nestled her warm, healthy son close to her face, then took Otis's hand and led him across the yard to his home.

Inside the small cabin, Tanner held a saw to the cradle he'd made for the baby. "Takin' the rockers off," he said, his voice cracking. "Need the wood for a coffin."

The next afternoon, after Jenny's students had left for the day, a small group gathered on Jenny's farm to bury the baby. Doc and Mrs. Tuller came, along with Esther and Daniel Abercrombie, and Franklin and Amanda Pershing and their brood, including Zeke. Daniel and Tanner had dug a small grave in a meadow behind the cabins, away from the creek.

"Will you say a prayer, Captain?" Tanner asked Pershing.

The former wagon captain nodded somberly. "Naked came I out of my mother's womb," he began. Jenny remembered so many prayers beside fresh graves along the trail west. When Pershing finished, Jenny lifted her voice in song, trying to praise the Lord despite the sorrow she felt:

> Yea, when this flesh and heart shall fail,
> And mortal life shall cease,
> I shall possess, within the veil,
> A life of joy and peace.

The baby, whom Hatty named Jenny—"if you don't mind, Miz Jenny"—was laid to rest. Jenny hoped the poor child's existence now was full of joy and peace. That evening she sobbed while writing:

Wednesday, March 7ᵗʰ—We buried the Tanners' infant daughter today. She never drew a breath.

Jenny's farm was a somber place in the days after the baby's funeral. Tanner spent every day in the fields planting spring wheat, no matter what the weather. When he finished the wheat, he cleared another acre and planted oats on the new field. He said little in the evenings over supper.

Hatty recovered slowly. She went back to cooking and cleaning within days, but she didn't speak unless spoken to. Even Otis couldn't make her smile.

Jenny closed her school term a few days after Hatty's stillbirth. Most of the children were needed to help their families plant the fields.

Monday, March 12ᵗʰ—William and I are alone with the Tanners. No more school until after autumn harvest. Otis joined his father in the fields today, working from sunup until twilight.

After Governor Joseph Lane arrived in Oregon City, Jenny and the Tanners went to hear his first speech. The governor spoke from the balcony of Rose Farm, owned by William Holmes and his wife. Jenny looked wistfully at the roses Mrs. Holmes had grown from seedlings brought from the East. She hoped one day her home would look so grand.

"First governor of the U.S. Territory," Samuel Abercrombie told them all at the gathering in town. "Fresh off the ship from San Francisco to take his post in Oregon City. First thing he's going to do is make them damn Cayuse who killed the Whitmans surrender. Time those heathen were hung."

"'Bout time we had a governor," Franklin Pershing said. "Been three years since the United States gained control of the territory. Took the Whitman Massacre for the President to act."

"We done all right on our own," Doc Tuller said. "Sometimes the best government's the least government. Fools who say they're representing us just pass laws that hurt folks. Like the damn bill to get rid of Negroes."

"Now, Doc," Mrs. Tuller admonished. "There's ladies present."

"Will Governor Lane keep that law?" Jenny asked. She still worried the Tanners would leave her farm.

"Sure hope he does," Abercrombie said. "Most of 'em don't do a lick of work."

"How can you say that, Pa?" Daniel Abercrombie asked. "Tanner rebuilt most of our wagons two and three times over when we traveled in forty-seven."

"Some of 'em are all right, I suppose," his father said. "But mark my words, we'll end up like the Southern states if we don't set limits. We don't want Oregon to become a slave state, and they ain't smart enough to manage their own property."

Jenny didn't speak up among the men, but Otis Tanner learned his letters as fast as Noah Pershing. And he studied harder than Mr. Abercrombie's granddaughters.

As March continued, rain fell almost every day. Tanner and his son worked outside until they were drenched. Often Hatty worked with them, though Jenny tried to find excuses to keep Hatty in the cabin with her.

"It's no good, Miz Jenny," Tanner told her in the barn one evening at the end of March. "Hatty ain't happy. She ain't never been happy in Oregon. She ain't been happy since Homer died. We should never have left the States."

"She'll come out of it. Give her time," Jenny said. "It's only been a few weeks."

Tanner shook his head. "We gotta leave. I'll git your fields planted this spring, like I said I would. Then we's goin' to California. Need to leave this gray, sad place behind us. Oregon don't want us anyways."

"You don't have to leave, Tanner. Doc Tuller and Captain Pershing will vouch for you. No Negroes have been whipped yet, and no one's been thrown out of the territory either. No matter what the law says."

"Ain't that, Miz Jenny. Leastways, not all of it. Hatty ain't happy. I need to find her a home where she's happy."

Chapter 28:   Trouble on the Claim

After reading the letter Joel received from Esther, Mac worried about Jenny. He'd left her with plenty of money, then sent more with Nate's letter of credit. She shouldn't have to teach. Wasn't Tanner working the farm for her? Surely the Tullers and the Pershings watched out for her.

As March days in the mountains lengthened, Mac alternated between barking orders at Joel and Huntington and working in morose silence on the far side of the claim away from his partners.

"We need to dig out the gold vein whilst the snow melt's runnin'," Huntington told Mac and Joel one morning over breakfast. "Use the water whilst we can. In the summer it'll drop to a trickle again. Dry diggin's are twice as hard to work."

"But we're still finding flakes and nuggets on the ravine floor," Joel said. "That's easier."

"Sure, it's easy," Huntington said, propping his boots up on the table in their shack. "Save the easy work for later. Tomorrow we build another sluice and start on the pump we been talkin' 'bout." He described in detail how the water would flow from one sluice to another.

Mac grunted at the older man's schemes. Huntington could no longer tote or lift much. His cough hadn't improved with the warming weather. But he was still able to shoot off his mouth, and Mac's responses were surly.

"You still moonin' over that gal of yours?" Huntington asked.

Joel glanced at Mac, a lopsided grin on his face.

"I'm not mooning," Mac said through his teeth. "But I don't need to be told twenty times how to build a sluice. We've been doing this for almost a year now."

130

"Sorry to waste my wisdom on your sour mug," Huntington said. He slammed his feet to the floor and stalked out of the shack.

"Now you done it," Joel said to Mac. "Huntington's a pain in the ass, but he knows more'n we do about mining."

Mac snorted. "I found plenty of gold before he happened along. We have so much now, I don't know how we'll ever spend it. Yet he's dreaming of more. He'd be better off taking care of his health."

"Speak for yourself, Mac," Joel said. "You had plenty of wealth before you came to California. And you hardly spend a nickel in town. Why are you still here if you hate it so much?"

"Nothing else to do. At least I'm not wasting my money on whores and gambling. How much have you lost, anyway?"

Joel's face turned grim.

The men worked all day without talking, hammers pounding. Each stroke took a little of Mac's anger away, but he still had plenty left when dusk fell.

As they collected their tools at the end of the day, Joel asked Mac, "You thinking of leaving? Going back to Oregon?"

"No." Mac worried about Jenny, but he had no future with her. He had no future anywhere.

"Well, then, you going to Boston?"

"Don't know."

"When you going to make up your mind?" Joel asked, stretching and pushing his hat back on his forehead.

"Maybe when the gold runs out. Maybe never."

"Sounds like you don't know what you want." Joel shook his head and strode off.

Cooped up in the shanty with his partners that evening, Mac wrote:

March 14, 1849. I must make plans soon. All the gold in the world won't help me to decide my future. If not Boston, where?

He couldn't answer his own question and slammed the journal shut in disgust.

The rest of March passed in a blur of activity. Prospectors streamed into the valley where the three men had their claim. Whites. Mexicans. Indians. All apparently intent on finding gold. Mac thought he saw the roughneck Smith riding along the ridge above their claim.

"Gotta watch them Indians," Huntington said. "They'll take a man's scalp for a few flakes of gold."

"We traveled from Missouri to Oregon in forty-seven without any problems," Mac said. "And I've heard Indians don't place much value on gold."

"Californian tribes are meaner. As bad as Pawnee," Huntington argued.

"The Pawnee didn't cause us any trouble," Mac said.

Joel leaned on his shovel. "Could be our company was too big for 'em to fight."

"Whose side are you on?" Mac wiped the sweat off his brow with his sleeve.

"Didn't know we was taking sides," Joel said. "Seems you're a might tetchy these days."

Mac, Joel, and Huntington kept their guns nearby while they worked. Every morning they walked the boundaries of their claim, making sure the corner stakes were still there. Despite the code the miners in their valley had adopted, Mac worried about claim-jumpers. They'd already been attacked once—and he still suspected Smith of that attack.

"We shouldn't leave our land unattended," he told Joel and Huntington. "Maybe we should bring in more partners."

"More partners?" Huntington said. "Means less gold for us."

Joel pointed a finger at Mac. "He don't want the money. He's rich already."

"I've worked as hard at prospecting as you have," Mac said. "But I haven't frittered my takings away."

Joel's eyes narrowed. "My money—I'll spend it how I please."

"We'll all get more gold faster with more hands working," Mac said, ignoring Joel's response. "And we'll have more guns. I've seen Smith riding in the hills."

"Well, we scared him off before, though my druthers are not to meet him again." Joel stood with his hands on his hips, frowning at Mac. "You said you'd sell out to me when you left. You backing away from that now?"

"No. I'll sell when I'm ready to go," Mac said. "I'm not ready yet."

"Don't know why you're stayin'," Huntington said. "You been itchy since the first warm day. If I was you, I'd go into town, find me a whore for the night."

"You're not me, Huntington."

Joel grinned. "I'll take the offer. I'll ride to Sacramento tomorrow. Leave afore sunrise, so's I won't be followed."

"You're likely to come back diseased," Mac grumbled.

Huntington chortled. "Y'all is both young fools," he said.

Mac spent the evening writing letters, then noted in his journal:

March 29, 1849. I have written letters to my parents and to Jenny for Joel to mail. I asked Jenny why she's teaching school. It will be months before I hear back—if she responds at all. If I'm here to receive the letter.

Joel didn't leave as early as he'd planned. At sunrise the next morning, a band of ten Indians rode into their camp. The natives were scrawny and unkempt, dressed in a mix of leather and cotton clothing, much like the tribes Mac had encountered on the Plains. The leader wore a silver and turquoise necklace.

"Buy tent," the leader said.

Mac shook his head. "No tent for sale."

"Trade deerskins for tent," the Indian insisted. Another Indian shifted his rifle so it pointed toward Mac.

"We don't need skins." Mac folded his arms and kept shaking his head.

"Only thing those damn savages understand is buckshot," Huntington muttered behind Mac.

"Don't set 'em off," Joel said. "There's too many of 'em." But out of the corner of his eye, Mac saw Joel's hand move toward his gun belt.

"We need to give them something," Mac murmured. "What do we have?"

"Got a pickax with a cracked handle," Huntington said. "Think that'll do?"

"Go get it," Mac said to Huntington, though his eyes remained focused on the natives. "Give you ax for deerskins," he said to the leader. "Two skins." He held up two fingers.

Huntington returned with the ax, its handle bound with cloth to hold it together. He handed it to the Indian chief.

The man fingered the handle and hefted the ax head. "One skin."

Mac nodded.

The chief motioned for one of his braves to hand over a deerskin. Joel took it, and the Indians rode off.

"They'll be back," Huntington said. "Steal our good tools. Maybe scalp us."

"That's why we need more men working with us." Mac gestured at the mining code, still hanging where he'd tacked it in November. "Despite our rules, our neighbors didn't show up to defend us today."

"We managed the Indians fine," Joel argued. "Only gave 'em a tool we don't need."

"Maybe you shouldn't go to town." Huntington said. "Wait awhile."

Joel argued he wanted to go, and Mac wanted his letters mailed. So despite Huntington's protests, Joel left for Sutter's Fort in the afternoon, his mule laden with more gold to deposit with Nate.

"If you see anyone you think looks like a good worker," Mac said when he handed Joel his letters to post, "bring him back with you."

"We don't need more partners," Joel said.

Mac shrugged. "Then we're likely to see more trouble."

Chapter 29:   Murderer's Bar

After almost a week's absence, Joel returned from Sutter's Fort without any new miners to work with them. "Don't need anyone," he told Mac, just like he had before he left for the fort. "We're purty good shots. I didn't see anyone I wanted to trust."

"I hope you're right," Mac said. "But there are only three of us."

April 5, 1849. I cannot force Joel and Huntington to take on more partners. But every week more men crawl through the hills seeking riches. Some prefer violence to hard labor.

I turn twenty-eight today. How long will it be before I decide my future?

The weather warmed. By late April the men could sit comfortably in the evenings around a campfire outside their shack. Sometimes miners from nearby claims in the valley joined them, though Mac kept his pistol handy even among faces he knew.

One night another prospector from Oregon named Eberman joined them as they passed a bottle of raw whiskey around. "Indians been killin' whites not far from here," Eberman said.

"How do you know the killers are Indians?" Mac asked. His wagon train hadn't had much trouble with Indians when they traveled west. Still, he remembered the braves who'd come to their claim a few weeks earlier.

"Bodies was found all carved up and charred," Eberman said, then paused to belch. "One man burned at the stake. Only a savage would do that. And the murderers left the gold. Must've been Indians—whites or Mexicans would've taken the color."

"I'd a thunk Indians would steal it, too," Huntington interjected.

Eberman shook his head. "Most of the tribes don't care about gold. Folks is callin' the creek where it happened 'Murderer's Bar' now."

"How many were killed?" Joel asked.

"Four. This time. Last time it was three. Rascals took clothes and tents that time, but again left the gold. We're outfittin' a posse to go after 'em. Men from these parts, mostly Oregonians. You boys want in?"

"We need to stay here. Guard our claim," Mac said. The Oregon militia seeking the Whitmans' killers had searched for weeks without success. He didn't want to leave the gold claim for long.

"I'll go," Joel volunteered. "You and Huntington can stay."

"Why don't y'all both go?" Huntington said. "Need to catch the varmints what's murderin' folks. I'll stay. If I was ten years younger, I'd trade places with you. But my bunk is softer'n the ground." He coughed.

"No one'll bother your claim if'n you're with our posse," Eberman said. "Men stayin' behind in this valley have agreed to look out for each other till the Indian scourge is gone. You're from Oregon, ain't ya?"

Joel nodded. "Mac and I came out in forty-seven."

"You sure it's Indians?" Mac asked again. He didn't like the idea of leaving Huntington alone on the claim. But he could always leave the posse if it stayed away too long.

"Sure as shootin'," Eberman said.

"Which tribe?" Mac asked. He knew very little about the Californian tribes and wondered how much Eberman knew.

"They're all the same." Eberman shrugged. "Some valley Indians who been workin' for white folks in the gold fields say it's the mountain tribes. So the posse is headed into the mountains with some valley tribe guides."

The next morning Mac and Joel rode with Eberman and found the posse gathered under the direction of a Captain O'Brien. Mac was surprised to see Smith in the group, and he eyed the large man suspiciously.

"What's he doing here?" Mac asked Eberman.

Eberman shrugged. "Don't know. Someone else must have rounded him up. You know him?"

"I think he attacked our claim last fall. We killed his partner. Though he denies any involvement." Mac had been uneasy about this posse from the start. Smith's inclusion made him feel worse.

The group headed out in the direction the valley Indians pointed, but after two days of searching saw no sign of other tribes. "Must not be the mountain tribes. Must be these thievin' valley Indians after all," Eberman said.

Mac was sure they were on a wild goose chase. He worried about Huntington, alone on the claim. He thought about leaving the posse and returning to their mine.

O'Brien led the men south toward Coloma, near Sutter's Mill, then announced the posse would look for the valley tribe's camp. After half a day's searching, they found the camp twenty miles from Coloma at the mouth of Weaver Creek.

"These must be the killers," O'Brien said. "We need to attack." He motioned the posse to follow him.

"Where's the evidence?" Mac asked.

"We'll find it when we capture the camp," O'Brien answered. "Just ride like the devil and shoot any Indian you see."

It wasn't much of a plan, Mac thought. The Oregon militia he'd ridden with had been much better organized, even with Samuel Abercrombie leading the unit. "Should we split into two? Flank them?" he asked.

"Hell, ain't no need for strategy. They ain't expectin' us," O'Brien said. "And we got more guns."

Mac wanted to question the commander further, but stayed quiet. He hadn't appreciated interference as leader of the wagon train. O'Brien was leading this posse, and Mac decided not to object.

At O'Brien's signal, the posse charged into the Indian camp, every man shooting as fast as he could.

Heart pounding, Mac fired at a couple of Indians, one of whom dropped to the ground. As best as he could tell, none of the Indians shot back. When he didn't see any Indians with guns, Mac stopped shooting, sickened by the slaughter.

It wasn't long before O'Brien gave the signal to cease fire. The posse surrounded the Indian camp and counted bodies.

"Twenty-six dead," Smith told O'Brien, kicking one of the bodies. "Six men surrendered. Plus women and children." The Indian women wept loudly among the bodies.

"Why you shoot us?" one Indian man asked. He knelt on the ground, hands in the air.

"You killed our men," O'Brien said.

"White *Californos* pay us to kill," an Indian woman said. Another woman nodded. "Oregon men steal. Give bad goods in trade. But *Californos* pay us."

"Hell," Eberman muttered from behind Mac. "Them Californians don't give fair trade to the Indians neither. Us Oregonians is just better at negotiatin'."

"Californians are only mad we're undercutting 'em," another posse member said with a grin.

So the attacks were motivated by disputes between two groups of whites, Mac thought with revulsion. He remembered the cracked ax handle he'd traded for the deerskin the month before. All he'd wanted was to get the Indians to leave the claim. Had his trade been part of the unfair dealings that led to the killings at Murderer's Bar?

He'd probably killed another man today, though there was no way to know for certain whether his bullet had felled the Indian he'd seen drop. He wanted no more part in this posse.

"Tie 'em up," O'Brien told his men, gesturing at the surviving Indians. "We'll take 'em to Coloma."

"But they weren't the leaders," Mac protested. It wasn't right for these Indians to die, when white men put them up to it. "What about the white Californians who encouraged them?"

"We'll go after them next," O'Brien said.

So far, Mac had only killed in self-defense or battle. He didn't want any role in punishing these Indians—not if the white men went free. "Come on, Joel. This isn't our fight anymore. Never was."

Joel shook his head.

"But these men weren't guilty."

"I'm staying," Joel said.

"Well, I'm not." Mac spun Valiente around and rode away.

Mac arrived back at the claim the next day. "Was there any trouble?" he asked Huntington.

"Someone nosin' around in the trees one night," Huntington said. "Never got a look at him. I shot into the woods, and he headed away.

Could it have been your friend Smith?"

Mac shook his head. "Smith was part of the posse."

"So what happened?" Huntington demanded every gruesome detail of the battle, which Mac recounted in disgust.

"You left before O'Brien strung 'em up?" Huntington hooted. "Why, a good hangin's hard to beat for entertainment."

"I don't need that kind of entertainment," Mac said.

"What kind you like then?" Huntington asked. "No women? No hangin's? You'll take good whiskey, but ain't you got any other vices?"

After supper Mac lounged in his bunk and wrote:

April 30, 1849. More killing over gold, this time the posse killed a group of unarmed Indians who may or may not have killed whites. And to my regret, I was a part of it.

Mac and Huntington worked the claim for a week before Joel returned.

"Did ya string 'em up?" Huntington shouted when Joel rode into camp.

Joel shook his head somberly. "No hangings, but they're dead. We took 'em into Coloma, where O'Brien got into an argument with a sawmill overseer. The overseer was who put the tribe up to killing prospectors— he'd ordered one of the Indians working in the mill to hire the valley tribe to kill the Oregonian prospectors. When we brought in the prisoners, the overseer tried to take 'em and let 'em go."

"What happened?" Huntington asked.

"O'Brien kept hold of his prisoners. After a time, he let the women and children free. Then he ran the six Indian men and the mill overseer out of town. But when they ran off, O'Brien ordered our posse to shoot 'em like deer."

Huntington wheezed. "Mowed 'em down, eh?"

"Only two Indians made it to the river. One got shot in the water, and the last was killed as he ran up the far bank."

"Wish I'd seen it," Huntington said, shaking his head with a grin. "Ain't seen nothin' like that since a lynchin' back in Georgia."

Mac's stomach lurched at Joel's description and Huntington's response.

"We don't need any part of Indian conflicts," he said. "Should have stayed out of it from the start."

Joel nodded with a grimace. "They may be Indians, but they didn't deserve what happened," he said. "Even folks in Coloma think O'Brien was too harsh. Now they fear an Indian uprising."

"What happened to Smith?" Mac asked.

Joel shrugged. "He was one of the men shooting at the Indians near the river. Then he rode off. Don't know where he went."

"He didn't follow you back to this valley?"

"I didn't see him," Joel said.

As Mac swung his pick and ran water through the sluices, he thought about what mining had become. When he'd started the year before, it had been an adventure in a pristine wilderness, a treasure hunt like those of childhood birthday parties. Now? With so many miners? The quest had warped into violence.

Gold had brought him wealth, which in turn gave him independence from his father. But he'd earned enough. He didn't need to toil any longer. He didn't need to battle men like Smith and O'Brien, nor to incur guilt killing helpless Indians.

Should he pull out? Turn his claim over to Joel, as he'd promised? Then what? He had no place in Oregon. So return to Boston? Maybe it was time.

The confines of a law office still didn't appeal to him after the freedom of trail and mountains. But he didn't want more carnage on his conscience. He'd been partially responsible for the Indians' deaths in Coloma, even though he'd left before it happened. Maybe if he'd stood firmer before the attack on the village, taken charge as he had of the wagon train, he could have lessened the tragedy.

Spring was still young. He could leave for Boston and be there by fall.

Chapter 30:   Letter from Mac

One morning in early April, Jenny, Esther, and Hatty Tanner worked on a quilt in Jenny's cabin—a gift for Hatty to take to California. Jenny tried not to argue with the Tanners while they prepared to leave. "You know you don't have to go," was all she said to Hatty.

"Yes, Miz Jenny," Hatty said. "But it's for the best. Folks don't want our kind here in Oregon. We need to be where hard workers is wanted. California's boomin' with the gold fields."

"Oregon needs good laborers, too," Jenny said. Still, though it pained her to see the Tanners leave, she knew Hatty had to move on. Some memories were too much to bear—like the memories of Missouri Jenny had fled.

Tanner continued to spend long hours in Jenny's fields, clearing more land and sowing the rest of the spring crops. He and Zeke scattered grain seed and tended the fruit trees they'd planted last fall.

"You'll have apples and cherries and peaches in a few years," Tanner told her when he stopped by her cabin while the women sewed on the quilt.

"I've always loved peach jam," Jenny said. "Most of our land in Missouri was in tobacco, but we had a few fruit trees. Letitia made pies and jams." She sighed. "I'll miss Hatty's help."

"Miz Tuller make good jam," Hatty said. "And Miz Pershing. They can teach you."

Jenny was growing accustomed to calling Amanda Purcell "Mrs. Pershing."

Esther sniffed at Hatty's mention of her stepmother. "Cooking's about all she does," Esther said. "That and birthing babies." Amanda Pershing had given birth to a baby boy, Franklin, Jr., the week before. "I'm expecting again, too." She sighed.

"How wonderful." Jenny rose to hug her friend.

Esther closed her eyes and shook her head. "Cordelia ain't even had her first birthday yet, and I'll have another baby in six months. She'll still be in diapers, and maybe Jonah, too. Ma always told me a woman couldn't get in the family way again while nursing. Guess that's just an old wives' tale."

"Don't you want another baby?" Jenny asked.

"Part of me does. I know I'll love this one, too. But I already have my hands full with Cordelia and Jonah."

"What's Daniel say?"

"Says he wants a boy this time." Esther snorted. "Not much I can do 'bout that."

"Can't your papa and Mrs. Pershing take Jonah?" Jenny asked.

"She's got Franklin now." Esther's lips turned down. "I don't want her raising Ma's baby—Jonah's all I have left of Ma. And Pa's house is too crowded already."

Jenny reached out to touch Esther's hand on the quilting frame. "Well, then, we'll all have to help you. Now, Hatty, don't you wish you were staying?"

But Hatty's eyes had filled at the mention of Esther's pregnancy, and Jenny said no more.

Tuesday, April 10ᵗʰ—Esther and Hatty have both known such sorrow. It makes me glad sometimes for my life, however lonely I am. At least William and I are healthy and safe.

As she put her journal away, Jenny thought about her own sorrows. She was better off in Oregon than in Missouri, and she vowed to bear her loneliness without grumbling. There was no one she could talk to anyway, no one who knew how much she missed Mac. Even the Tullers thought she'd put him in the past.

Planting continued throughout April—wheat and oats and barley and corn. While Tanner and Otis worked in the fields, Hatty and Jenny seeded a large garden—potatoes and corn, beans and carrots and cucumbers.

William started talking, just a word or two at a time, then new words every day. It awed Jenny to see how quickly her son grew, physically and mentally. Such a bright little boy had come from such a terrible beginning.

Zeke stopped by Jenny's cabin one morning late in April. "I'm headed out to the fields to plant with Tanner," he said. "I was in town yesterday and picked up this letter for you." He handed it to her.

The handwriting was Mac's. "Thank you, Zeke," she said, putting the letter in her apron pocket.

Zeke didn't move to leave. He eyed her apron, but she wouldn't open Mac's letter with him watching. Though she was eager to read it, she had no idea what Mac would say and wanted to be alone when she read it. "Would you like some coffee?" she asked.

"Thank you, Miz Jenny."

They made small talk and watched William play on the floor while Zeke sipped his coffee. Jenny busied herself with some mending.

Zeke finally stood to leave. "I'd best go help Tanner before the rain comes."

"Thank you for bringing the letter." Jenny smiled at Zeke, fingering the paper in her pocket.

After he left, Jenny broke the seal on the letter. It had been written only a month earlier—it was almost as if Mac were with her.

March 29, 1849

Dear Jenny,

I am mining gold with Joel Pershing and a man named Jeremiah Huntington from Georgia. We have found good color on our claim. California has its share of thieves and men who prefer to make their money on the backs of others, but we have chased off the scalawags that have come our way.

I hope all is well with you and William. Esther told Joel you were teaching school. Are you out of funds? I hope you are spending the coins I left—I gave them to you to use. With the Tanners on the claim, I trust you are well cared for and the farm prospers. In a few years, the claim will be proved, and the land will be yours.

As I wrote before, I will let you know when I leave for Boston. It will likely be at the end of summer, when I turn over the gold claim to Joel.

Your servant,

Caleb McDougall

P.S. You can write me in Sacramento.

My, how news traveled, Jenny thought. From Esther to Joel to Mac. He knew what she was doing, which warmed her heart. He would probably hear of the Tanners leaving and Zeke working her farm. How would Mac react to that news? She didn't think it would bring him back to Oregon, but maybe he would write again.

He'd told her where to write to him. Now she needed to figure out what to say.

After supper, when the Tanners had returned to their cabin and William was asleep, Jenny took out her ink bottle and quill. She spread out a piece of the finer paper she saved for her more advanced students to use for their compositions.

Then she hesitated. What should she tell Mac? He would likely hear more news through Joel, so she should tell him about her life before he heard it through the Pershings.

April 30, 1849
Dear Mac,

Her salutation seemed too informal. But "Mr. McDougall" was too distant, and she'd never thought of him as "Caleb." "Mac" would have to do.

I received your letter of March 29. It must have come straight from California to Oregon by ship, because it arrived so quickly. Zeke delivered it from town today.

William and I are well, thank you. I taught school this past winter because the children need to learn, and I have more education than Esther or any of our other friends, except for the Tullers.

I have spent very few of your coins. . . .

Did she sound too ungrateful?

. . . I know you meant for me to use them if William and I were in need, but by the grace of God, the crops and my teaching have provided for our livelihood, and I intend to replace what I have spent.

She would have to tell him about the Tanners—surely he would hear of their departure.

When Tanner and Zeke finish the planting, the Tanners are leaving for California to seek more opportunity. Perhaps you will see them. I shall miss them terribly. Hatty was delivered of a stillborn girl and remains deeply distraught. After losing Homer two years ago, this new bereavement is more than she can bear. I am so blessed William is healthy.

Our other friends are well. Captain Pershing married Amanda Purcell, as perhaps you learned from Joel. Esther and Daniel anticipate another child. Dr. and Mrs. Tuller are kind to me, as always. I ask Dr. Tuller's advice about staying on the claim and proving it up. Even the Abercrombies are good neighbors, and their granddaughters were among my pupils.

I wish you well in your prospecting, and a safe journey to Boston.

How should she close the letter? "Affectionately"? "Your servant," like Mac had written? She would leave it at . . .

Jenny

Chapter 31: Good-Byes

By early May the planting was done, including the vegetable garden. The Tanners began to pack their wagon. "Packin' ain't as bad as when we left Arkansas," Hatty told Jenny. "We ain't got so much stuff this time."

"You need a man to farm for you," Tanner said. "Mr. Zeke says he'll do it for a share of the crops. He can git his younger brothers to help."

"I'm not sure that's a good idea," Jenny said. "People used to talk about Zeke and me."

"That was two years ago, Miz Jenny," Hatty said. "You got a baby now. Captain McDougall will be back this year. You'll see."

Jenny clenched her teeth to keep from crying. Only she and the Tullers knew Mac would not be back. Like his first letter, his second also had made no mention of returning to Oregon.

"I wish you'd stay," she told Hatty wistfully. "I've enjoyed having you with me. Otis has been good for William." She watched the boys play in the yard. Her son, now almost twenty months old, toddled after Otis and mimicked everything the older boy did. "William will miss him."

Hatty sighed when she looked at William. Jenny knew every small child reminded Hatty of the baby girl she'd lost. Jenny hoped Hatty would find happiness in California, but wondered if she could be happy anywhere after seeing two children dead.

"You still planning to set up a blacksmith's shop in California?" Jenny asked Tanner.

"Horses and mules always needs shoes," Tanner said. "And they's building everywhere in California, I hear. I'll find work."

"Who'll shoe our horses here?" Jenny asked.

"You git Mr. Zeke to find you a good smith," Tanner said. "Shop's

147

here. Needs some tools, 'cause I'm taking what the wagon'll hold. But someone can make use of the fire pit and tables."

"But you be sure you hire someone respectable," Hatty said. "Someone to handle the men a smithy brings."

Jenny didn't relish the idea of strangers on her farm, though it would be better to have another man around besides Zeke. She'd hated the gossip of their fellow emigrants on the wagon journey when Zeke helped her. Zeke was her friend, but she didn't want the gossip starting again. Not without Mac here to protect her from speculation.

Jenny held a supper party on the second Sunday in May. The Tanners were pulling out the next morning. Many of the families who had traveled in their wagon company came—all the Pershings and Purcells, Samuel Abercrombie and his family, Daniel and Esther Abercrombie, and Doc and Mrs. Tuller.

Samuel Abercrombie muttered to his wife it was a "damn good thing" the Tanners were leaving. "Don't need their kind in school with our granddaughters."

Jenny glared at him but said nothing.

"How long will the journey take?" Doc asked Tanner.

"Two or three months, I 'spect."

"Not so bad as our trek in forty-seven."

"No, sir." Tanner shook his head. "But they's plenty of mountains twixt here and there. Hope there ain't no snow left in 'em."

Zeke had been on Jenny's claim frequently in the last few weeks to talk to Tanner and help with Jenny's crops. "I'll be by on Tuesday," Zeke told her now. "After the Tanners have left."

"Thank you, Zeke," Jenny said, tears welling in her eyes. "I'll be lonely without them."

"You and William will do fine," Zeke said, patting her arm.

"Maybe Rachel could come stay with you. Or Ruth," Amanda Pershing said. "Heaven knows we have more'n enough bodies 'round our house."

"Maybe," Jenny said. "Give me a few days to see how William and I do on our own." She'd always liked Esther's younger sister Rachel. At fourteen, Rachel seemed weighed down by the responsibility of caring for her younger siblings and stepsiblings. She'd missed many days during the school term, staying home to help her stepmother with sick children and housework. Jenny was surprised Mrs. Pershing offered to let Rachel move.

The next morning at dawn, the Tanners loaded their last belongings into the wagon and hitched up their mules. Jenny and William stood in the barnyard and waved while the Tanners pulled out.

"Where Otis?" William asked when they could no longer see the wagon.

"Otis is gone," Jenny said. For William's sake, she tried to keep her voice from quavering. "Let's go find some eggs." She took William's hand and led him to the chicken coop.

But the Tanners' departure left a silence that William's squeals and the chickens' squawks couldn't fill.

Monday, May 14ᵗʰ—The day was quiet with only William and me.

Jenny went to bed early that night and cuddled the pillow she'd taken from Mac's bed over a year before. She swallowed the lump in her throat. She truly was alone now.

Zeke knocked on Jenny's door on Tuesday shortly after breakfast. "I'm working your crops today, Miz Jenny. Brought my mules. You need anything, you come get me."

She nodded. "Shall I bring dinner to you, or do you want to come to the cabin?"

"Why don't I come to the house? Then I can do any chores you need doing 'round the barn."

"I can care for Poulette and the colt," she said. "And the chickens."

"You let me know if you need any lifting or carrying," Zeke said. "Tanner told me to be sure you didn't overwork yourself."

Jenny smiled and shook her head.

"You need some mules to pull the plow, now Tanner took his," Zeke told her. "Poulette needs to stay with her colt still, and I can't always bring my team. Man at church last Sunday had a nice pair for sale. He'd trade for your colt when he's ready to leave his dam, I think."

"I can't sell Shanty." Jenny thought of Valiente and Mac every time she saw the colt.

"You have money?"

Jenny nodded. She'd use Mac's coins rather than give up the colt. "How much?"

"Forty dollars for the pair."

Jenny went up to the loft and came back with two double eagles. She handed them to Zeke. "Buy the mules." She'd worry later about how to replace the money.

He stuffed the coins in his pocket. "I'll see the man and bring the pair over next week. And Mother Amanda"—that seemed to be what all the Pershing children called their stepmother—"said to come talk to her about Rachel."

"Do you think it's a good idea for Rachel to live with me?" Jenny asked. "I'd appreciate her company, but I don't want her to feel obliged."

Zeke sighed. "You ain't the one making her leave. She don't feel comfortable with Mother Amanda. Rachel thinks she favors her own daughters. Ruthie fits in with them all right, but Rachel don't feel she has a place at home anymore. It's a shame, after all Rachel did for Pa and the young'uns after Ma died. Esther took Jonah, but Rachel kept the rest of our family going."

"I'll talk to Captain and Mrs. Pershing."

"Rachel talked about living with Esther. But staying with you might be better. Esther don't have any extra room in her house."

"Esther'll have three children to care for soon," Jenny said. "You sure Rachel can't be more help there?"

Zeke shrugged. "Talk to Pa and Esther. But I think you'd be doing Rachel a favor."

Jenny started with Esther. "What do you think about Rachel coming to live with William and me?"

Esther clutched Jenny's arm, eyes wide and a smile on her face. "Would you take her? She's so unhappy at home."

"You don't want her with you?"

"Maybe when the baby comes. But till Daniel adds on to our cabin, I don't have room. Not with Daniel and me—" Esther stopped, blushing. "Well, you know. It's bad enough having Jonah and Cordelia around, but Rachel's a grown girl. I'm so tired by nightfall, but when Daniel comes to bed—" Esther stopped again. She sighed. "I'll probably be expecting babies for the next thirty years."

Once again, Jenny felt the chasm between her experience with men and Esther's. "I'll talk to your papa about Rachel," she said.

When Jenny went to visit the Pershings, Mrs. Pershing was ready to pack a bag for Rachel on the spot. Captain Pershing just nodded sadly.

"What do you think, Rachel?" Jenny asked. "You'd sleep in the loft. It'll be hot up there this summer."

"But I'd have a bed to myself." The girl smiled. "I'd be happy to come stay with you, Miz Jenny."

"Then you'll have to stop calling me 'Miz Jenny.'" Jenny smiled back. "You'll be helping me, but we'll be friends. Call me 'Jenny.'"

Rachel's grin grew brighter. "I'll come over with Zeke on Thursday."

On Thursday Rachel brought a small bundle of clothing wrapped in a quilt. She leapt out of Zeke's wagon. "Here I am."

Chapter 32:   Letters from Boston

Mac, Joel, and Huntington mined their claim as the spring weather warmed. The lode still produced, but they weren't finding as much color as they had the year before.

"Got the easy pickin's last year," Huntington said. "Now it's hard work."

"Been finding a fair amount," Joel said. "I ain't ready to pack it in."

"No one said we'd pack it in." Huntington wiped his brow and coughed. "I'm out here slavin' in the sun, ain't I?"

Mac listened to his partners bicker, which they did every day. Huntington couldn't work as fast or as long as he had the summer before. He still gave orders, acting as if he knew more than the younger men.

Joel resented the older man's bossiness. "He ain't doing much work," Joel complained to Mac. "How come he gets to tell us what to do? We're old hands now."

Mac was content to let Huntington's demands flow over him and then work as he pleased. He shrugged. "Doesn't hurt to let him talk."

"Hurts my ears plenty," Joel grumbled.

Mac wondered how long it would be before Joel stormed off to Sacramento to see Consuela. Joel found an excuse to leave the claim every few weeks—sometimes to buy supplies, sometimes to deposit their gold, sometimes he gave no reason at all for leaving.

Mac didn't really mind. He didn't like Huntington's chattering, but he tolerated the old man's company better than Joel did.

In mid-May Joel returned from the fort with mail. "From Boston," Joel said, handing two letters to Mac.

Mac looked at the handwritten addresses. One was his father's dark,

152

heavy scrawl, the other his mother's finer, more even script.

He took them into the cabin, poured himself a glass of whiskey, and sat at the small rickety table. Then he broke the seal on his father's letter. It had been written months ago.

> *December 12, 1848*
> *Dear Son,*
>
> *I had hoped to see you in person by now. If you plan to take the place in your brother's law firm that he has been saving for you, you must return to Boston forthwith. His good favor cannot last forever. The legal work amasses and his clients demand prompt attention.*
>
> *I could forgive your desire for the adventure of traveling our frontier, which was your plan when you left home almost two years ago. However, I fail to see the lure of farming or prospecting, dirty occupations both. Now that you have seen the West and the grubby work men must do to cultivate a new land, I trust you understand your good fortune in receiving an education and funds to keep you from such endeavors. The successful men in life are not those who work with their hands, but with their minds. It is time you took your place among those who prosper.*
>
> *I shall expect you by the autumn.*
>
> > *Your father,*
> > *Andrew McDougall*

Mac pictured his father sitting at his large oak desk with the leather inset, pince-nez perched on his nose, forcing ink onto paper with a heavy hand pushing the quill, and his jowls reddening when his emotions rose. The ink would blot more with every line, as demonstrated by the splotches in the missive Mac held.

Mac shook his head and laid the letter on the table. His father had no conception of the fortunes being pulled from the ground in California. Mac had earned enough in a year to be comfortable for the rest of his life, if he prudently invested what he had made thus far. He no longer needed to rely on his family's holdings in Boston.

He sighed and picked up his mother's letter. What would she add to his father's command for Mac to return? She would have written at her delicate Chippendale writing table in the morning room, sun streaming in large windows to brighten upholstered furniture and a mahogany tea cart, her skirts enveloping the straight wood chair where she sat.

Mac opened his mother's letter.

> *December 13, 1848*
> *My dearest Caleb,*
>
> *Your father tells me he will post a letter to you this morning and begs me to send a note also. I hardly know what to say, it has been so long since you left us.*
>
> *We had hoped to have you home well before Christmas, and instead we must wait another year for your return. Your brothers and their families miss you terribly—their daughters have grown into quite the young ladies. No sons yet, which your father regrets, though the girls are lovely companions for me. I pray you to settle down with a wife upon your return and provide me with more grandchildren to spoil.*
>
> *I was horrified to learn you had cholera on the plains last year and hope you have fully recovered your health. So many people never regain their strength after a serious illness. You were fortunate to have a doctor in your company, and I'm sure his care was a blessing for you.*
>
> *I could scarcely believe it when I read of your mining adventure. Of course, we learned earlier this month of the great gold fields in California, but to think you have been a part of it all. My son, a treasure hunter!*

Still, it must be a dreadful occupation to spend your days digging in the dirt. I pray you will tire of it soon and return to us by next Christmas, as your father requests.
With all my love,
Mother

Mac tilted the chair back and plunked his boot heels on the table. His mother would be appalled if she saw him.

Return to Boston? He would be crawling into a coffin. He'd fled Boston when his mother discharged his lover Bridget, which resulted in the early deaths of both Bridget and Mac's unborn child. If he returned, his mother would parade every well-bred maiden she could find beneath his nose, like cattle at the market. She would manage his home life, while his father interfered in his work. The independence he'd savored for the past two years would be lost.

So should he continue to prospect in an increasingly crowded and violent valley? He might be killed. All his money wouldn't help him then.

What if he returned to Oregon? No, he had to break all ties with Jenny. Besides, a life of farming was no easier than prospecting, though a tad tamer. He'd made at least one decision—there was nothing for him in Oregon.

Mac was taciturn all evening, lost in internal debate.

May 17, 1849. I will not keep mining much longer. But what comes next? Is Boston my only option?

Joel and Huntington teased him about letters from lost loves in Boston. He told them the letters were from his parents.

"Man don't go into a funk over a letter from his mama," Huntington said. "Must be some gal you left back home."

Mac quit defending himself.

The next morning he saddled Valiente. "I'm riding to Sacramento," he said.

"I just got back. We don't need nothing." Joel said.

"I have to go to town." Mac had to get away by himself. Away from the claim and away from his partners. If he could get away from his thoughts, he might find some peace.

He took three days instead of the usual two to ride to Sacramento. He stayed clear of other prospectors along the trail and ate by himself, taking time to catch fish in the streams for meals. He thought about his future, but made no decisions. He'd relished leading the wagon train, though the responsibility had weighed on him. Where could he find a similar purpose in a place to call his own?

When he arrived in Sacramento, he went to Nate's store.

"Joel Pershing was here recently with a deposit," the assayer said. "You boys must be doing well if you have another already. Though he lost half his earnings in the saloon in just two evenings."

Mac wasn't surprised Joel was gambling, but he didn't want to gossip with Nate about Joel. "No deposit this time. Just wanted to see something other than dirt and rocks."

Nate chuckled. "Got cabin fever, do you? It's long past winter. Your mine should be keeping you busy."

Mac shook his head. "I'm tired of digging. Don't want to go back East. Don't know what I want."

"You're too old for such ambivalence, young man. Time to settle down."

Mac smiled—Nate sounded again like his old tutor. And his parents. "That's what my father said. And my mother."

"And you're too old to be listening to your parents. Need to make your own way in this world."

"I can't figure out what that is, Nate. But I know I don't want to kill Indians for sport."

"You heard about that?" Nate pulled at his neatly trimmed mustache. "Bad situation."

"Joel and I rode with the posse. I left, but Joel went back to Coloma with them. He saw it all."

"Maybe you ought to open a store. More men find wealth in merchanting than in the gold fields. And more certainty. Folks need to spend money to outfit themselves. Find yourself a lot here in town and open a shop."

"Maybe," Mac said with a shrug.

"My granddaughter Susan should arrive soon," Nate said. "I've been thinking about selling this place, if she doesn't like life in Sacramento. I have a good trade in mining hardware and dry goods in addition to assaying now." He grinned. "I try to help the miners spend the gold they deposit with me. So they don't take it to the brothels and gambling halls like young Pershing."

"Have you heard from your granddaughter?" Mac had almost forgotten their conversation about her. "It's been months since you mentioned her."

Nate shook his head. "No, but I expect her any time."

"Ships come from Panama more frequently now," Mac said. "But they're full of eager prospectors. She might have had trouble finding passage." Mac hoped nothing had happened to the young woman, but he didn't say so—Nate was knowledgeable enough to worry on his own.

"Anyway," Nate said, "I'd be willing to sell this store to you, if you want to quit mining. You're smart and you're honest. And you have the gold to buy me out." The older man winked. "I can take money from you as easily as from a new prospector."

"I'm not sure storekeeping is for me."

"Think on it, son. I'm not going anywhere right now. As I said, I have to wait for Susan."

Chapter 33: The Beast and the Beauty

Mac left for his claim the day after he talked to Nate, traveling more quickly on the return trip than he had on the way to Sacramento. The weather was hot and humid along the American River, but cooled as he climbed into the hills. Soon he rode along sparkling mountain streams instead of the placid American.

On his second day out, as Mac approached the valley where he and his partners mined, he spotted Smith riding the ridge above him.

He'd had enough of the man following him. Mac turned Valiente up the hill and stopped within hailing distance. "What're you looking for?" he called.

Smith rode over, halting his horse about ten paces from Valiente. The man's ugly face hadn't improved in the months since Mac had seen him. "Been prospecting. Like every other man around here."

"Have you staked a claim yet?" Mac asked.

"No reason I should tell you."

Mac shrugged. "Why do you keep following me?"

"You sought me out this time. How come you high-tailed it away from the posse afore we was done?"

"Done murdering Indians, you mean?" Mac knew he was letting the scoundrel get to him, but the aftermath of Murderer's Bar still upset him. According to Joel, Smith had been one of the men most eager to go after the Indians, and the brute had reveled in the slaughter at Coloma.

Smith grinned. "Call it what you like. Need more of that kind of killing. And ain't no reason to limit it to Indians."

"Where's your partner?" Mac still wanted to know who had attacked their claim with Smith and Jones the summer before.

"I told you, I ain't got no partner."

"I suppose if you were teamed up with anyone, you'd have ambushed us again," Mac said. "I'm warning you—stay away. If you step foot on our claim, my partners and I—we won't hesitate to shoot."

Mac arrived at the claim and told Joel and Huntington of his encounter with Smith.

"He ain't bothered us in a year now," Joel said. "Without men to back him up, he's all bluster. I seen that when we was in the posse together."

"Don't go into conniptions over that bully," Huntington advised Mac. "We's more'n a match for the likes of him."

But for days Mac kept his rifle handy and a watchful eye on the hills above their claim.

He wrote one evening:

May 30, 1849. The valleys are more crowded this year than last, though the emigrants from the East have yet to arrive. Soon the hills will swarm with more men than they can support. The thrill of mining is gone. Perhaps Father is right—it may be time to sell out.

A week later on Thursday evening, a boy rode into the partners' camp with a message from Nate to Mac. "She's here, Mr. McDougall," the boy said. "Mr. Peabody wants you to come meet his granddaughter."

Mac sent the lad into the cabin to get a meal from Huntington, then read the note the boy had handed him:

Mac,

I would appreciate your return to Sacramento at your earliest convenience. Susan arrived in San Francisco on the Panama *on the 4ᵗʰ of this month, and took the ferry to Sacramento on the 5ᵗʰ.*

*I have lost all ability to charm a young lady, if I ever
had such, and I require your assistance.*
Nathan Peabody

"Damn." Mac liked Nate, but the man was presuming. After two years away from Boston, he didn't trust his own ability to charm a lady. And he didn't have any desire to entertain a young chit from New York.

"What's wrong?" Joel asked. He dropped the load of tools he carried in a heap beside the cabin.

"Nate wants me to meet his granddaughter."

"The one from New York?" Joel asked with a grin.

"I think she's the only one he has," Mac said.

"What's the problem?"

"I just returned from Sacramento."

"I could go," Joel said, still grinning.

"You?" Mac knew Nate didn't have much liking for Joel. "I don't think she's your kind of woman."

"You mean, she ain't a whore?" Joel's smile grew wider.

"That's what I mean." Mac grimaced. "I'll leave with the messenger boy in the morning."

Mac and the boy made the trip to Sacramento in a day and a half, reaching Nate's shop around noon on June 9.

"Am I glad to see you," Nate said, pumping Mac's hand.

"Where's your granddaughter?" Mac asked.

"I put her up in the hotel nearby," Nate said. "My rooms aren't good enough for her, nor is the Golden Nugget." He sighed. "You'll see when you meet her. But we have to get you cleaned up first. Did you bring a suit?"

A suit? There was no reason to wear a suit in Sacramento. "No."

"You go to the bathhouse. I'll bring clothes around for you."

"Nate—"

"You'll want to make a good impression on her."

Mac gave up. He could afford a bath and a suit of clothes.

He'd finished with a bath and a shave, when Nate arrived with his new clothes. They fit reasonably well, considering they weren't tailored. The wool was decent, the waistcoat a pale blue silk. He'd seen worse.

Mac dressed, then walked with Nate to the hotel lobby. Nate sent a clerk upstairs to find his granddaughter. A few minutes later, a fine lady glided down the staircase, and Mac understood why Nate had fussed.

She was beautiful. Blonde hair, brilliant blue eyes, diamond ear bobs, and a dark gray dress that made her creamy skin even paler. A fine figure, which her small waist emphasized, top and bottom.

Mac swallowed.

"Grandfather," she said, kissing the old man on the cheek.

"Susan, my dear," Nate said. "I want you to meet Caleb McDougall. The Boston lawyer I've been telling you about. Mac, this is my granddaughter, Susan Abbott."

Mac bowed over the slim fingers she extended toward him. "At your service, Miss Abbott."

Chapter 34:   A Man Around

As May turned into June, Jenny and Rachel settled into a routine. In the morning Rachel tended to chores in the barn and chicken coop while Jenny dressed William, fixed breakfast, and started a stew or soup for the midday meal. Then they tilled the garden or labored in the fields. Except on Mondays, which they devoted to laundry.

Zeke worked Jenny's farm two days a week. After the Tanners left, she'd agreed to share her crops with Zeke in exchange for his labor. With the new mule team he'd bought for her, he mowed the hayfield or cleared more land. Sometimes he brought his younger twin brothers to help, and they all hoed weeds in the grain fields.

Each day, Jenny fed whoever was on her claim a noon dinner. Then they all worked outside again until time for a quick supper, washing up, and the evening care of the animals.

After supper Jenny and Rachel sewed and read. Jenny borrowed every book she could from her neighbors, and soon Rachel could read as fluently as Jenny. Jenny hoped Rachel would assist her teaching school in the autumn.

They went to church in Oregon City on Sundays. All the men could talk about on Sunday, June 3, after services was the election to be held the next day. Governor Lane had scheduled a vote to select representatives to the new Territorial Legislature.

"First time I can vote," Zeke said. "I'm twenty-two now. I weren't old enough back East. Now I'm a landowner in Oregon."

"'Bout time we had a legislature approved in Washington. Governor Lane's overdue for calling it," Samuel Abercrombie said, hooking his thumbs in his suspenders. "Congress set it up last year, but the governor ain't done nothing till now."

"Don't we still use the laws from the old legislature?" Jenny asked.

Most of the men ignored her, but Doc Tuller replied, "We have a real governor now, one appointed by the President. Good thing he's set an election to replace those fools who left for California. Governor Lane has approved the statutes on the books, but we need a legislature to conjure up new laws. Particularly after the Whitman Massacre. Militia needs more funds to keep seeking the savages who killed the missionaries."

"Be fair to the governor," Daniel said. "He only arrived in March."

The men's conversation flowed around Jenny, all about land laws and slavery and taxation. She listened while she and other women served the church picnic. She thought she understood most of what the men said.

"Too bad McDougall ain't here," Doc Tuller said. "He'd be a fine representative. Got the legal training."

"Did purty well as captain, too," Daniel said. His father frowned at him, and Jenny thought again of the clashes between Mac and Samuel Abercrombie over which of them should lead the wagon company. Mac hadn't sought to become captain, but stepped up when elected. He'd been a good commander, though it meant he'd spent less time with her. That's when Zeke started helping her more.

Zeke and Mac had been friends on the trail. Yet Zeke, though physically strong and a good scout, had seemed a boy compared to Mac, who had more education and experience in the world.

Now Jenny watched Zeke participate in the men's political discussion, as confident as one of the Abercrombies or Doc. He would be a good husband for some woman. Then she remembered Mac had suggested she marry Zeke. Mac had said he'd see to it she was free to marry. How could he, unless they told their story or he died?

Her heart twisted at the thought of either option. She didn't want to tell their story, and she certainly didn't want Mac to die. She wanted him to return. She wanted to work with him like she had along the way to Oregon. She knew Mac would never come back to Oregon, but that's what she wanted.

Sunday, June 3rd—Rachel is good company, but I miss Mac. I wish we could have continued like in those first months after we arrived. I was happy then.

Later in the week, after the hubbub of the election was over, Zeke stopped by Jenny's cabin before heading into the fields. Though it was now June, the morning was misty with low clouds.

"Not a pretty day to be outside," Jenny said, handing him a mug of coffee. Behind Zeke, she saw the twins petting Shanty and Poulette in the paddock.

Zeke shrugged. "Soon it'll be so warm we'll be begging for rain. Where's Rachel?"

"Gathering eggs," Jenny said. "The hens are laying well now. I'll cook some for your dinner, shall I?"

"Only if they're hard boiled so I can eat in the fields. I want to plant another acre of corn today. It's late, but I just cleared the ground last week."

"Don't we have enough land cleared?" Jenny asked. "I sold plenty from the farm last year."

Zeke laughed. "You can always sell more," he said. "Mills will buy all the wheat and corn folks can grow. Don't you want to get rich off the gold miners in California?"

"I suppose." She wanted to survive on what the farm produced. But she didn't need to be rich—only safe and secure.

"Besides, you never know what the weather'll bring. Farming's a fickle business."

At noon Jenny and Rachel took William and a basket filled with hard boiled eggs, bread, slices of fried ham, and ginger water out to Zeke and the twins. They spread a picnic on a blanket by the stream that formed the boundary between Jenny's claim and Esther's. The morning mist had lifted, and warm sun shone through the trees, dappling the blanket where they sat in the shade.

After they ate, Rachel stood up and said, "May I go visit Esther? I'll be back shortly."

Jenny shooed her on. Jonathan and David ran after her, leaving Jenny and William with Zeke.

"I wish she would treat me like a friend, not her mother or employer,"

Jenny said, watching Rachel and the boys wade the stream. "She's only two years younger than me."

"She's a timid one, our Rachel. Got lost in the middle of the passel of young'uns. Caught behind Esther, who talked over poor Rachel all the time."

"I like having her with me." Jenny smiled. "She's good company."

"You need a man around the place, Miz Jenny."

"Now, if Rachel's not to call me 'Miz Jenny,' then you shouldn't either." Jenny hid her pink cheeks by picking up William and fussing over him. He was a chunky toddler now and squirmed when she tried to hold him.

"This year's crop of emigrants'll arrive soon," Zeke said. "Ain't as many as last year yet, but there'll still be a lot of strange men around. Been some mountain lion and wolf sightings also. I'd feel better if you and Rachel had someone here who can use a gun."

"I can shoot," Jenny argued. She'd shot a man in Missouri and didn't regret it. "And you're here several days a week."

"Not at night."

"I don't have room for you. And it wouldn't be proper, you living here." She blushed again.

Zeke sighed. "With Rachel here, no one would say anything. I could sleep in the Tanners' cabin."

"What about your farm?"

"I'm there enough. I can prove up my claim."

"I'll think about it," Jenny said. She didn't know why she was uncomfortable with the notion of Zeke living on her farm. She was already cooking for him many days. Would it matter if he moved into the Tanners' cabin? It would be nice to have a man here if another panther prowled around the barn like last year.

What would Mac say if he returned? He wouldn't return, but what if?

"Have you heard from Mac?" Zeke asked, as if he'd heard her thoughts.

She shook her head. "Not since the letter you brought me in April."

"When do you expect him back?"

Jenny shrugged. "When he's done prospecting, I suppose." She hadn't told Zeke what Mac had written about not coming back. "Unless he goes on to Boston, like he'd planned."

Zeke swore under his breath, but Jenny heard him. "Doesn't he know you and William need taking care of?"

"William and I are fine," Jenny said, sticking her chin in the air. "Mac wouldn't like you saying such things. I don't need you living on the claim. Rachel's all the company I need."

Zeke stood and stalked off to the plow and mules. "Thanks for the dinner, Miz Jenny."

Jenny swallowed her anxiety as she watched him go.

Chapter 35:   The President's Emissary

In mid-June in the heat of the day, a man in a dark suit and silk cravat rode into the partners' camp, accompanied by two soldiers in uniform. Mac paused in his work, as did Joel and Huntington nearby.

"I'm Thomas Butler King," the man said, tipping his stovepipe hat toward them. "I have traveled from Washington at the behest of President Taylor. I'm here to tell you General Bennett Riley has called a constitutional convention for California in September."

Joel mopped his brow with a dirty bandanna. "What's that to us?"

"There will be an election in August for delegates to the convention," King continued. "As the personal emissary of the President, I'm encouraging you to vote for delegates from this district."

"Ain't never voted before," Huntington declared. "Why should I start now?"

"Isn't Riley a military governor?" Mac asked. "How can he call a civil election?"

King ignored Huntington and answered Mac. "California has been a U.S. territory since early in 1847. But Congress still hasn't seen fit to appoint a territorial governor or approve any territorial laws. General Riley is the only authority in California at this time. Might I trouble you fine gentlemen for a drink of water?"

Joel handed King his canteen.

With a flourish, King pulled a white handkerchief edged in lace from his pocket, wiped the mouth of the canteen, and took a drink. Then he handed the container back to Joel with a nod. "Confidentially, gentlemen," he said, "President Taylor wants California to become a state, and a free state at that."

Huntington spat, then muttered, "Damn Yankees."

King continued, "Indeed, in the past year this region has grown in power and wealth, as if by magic, thanks to the discovery of gold, which you good men wrest from the ground. Our President sees no need for the interim step of a territorial government. Still, whether to seek statehood or continue as a territory will be one of the first orders of business at the convention."

"Why should we leave off minin' to listen to politicians palaver?" Huntington said. "I'll be stayin' right where I am. On my claim."

"And you, sir?" King looked at Mac. "Your question shows you to be an educated man."

"When is the vote?"

"August first. I beseech you to encourage the civic-minded men of this region to participate in creating the next state in our great Union." King tipped his hat again. "Good day."

As Mac and his partners watched King and the soldiers ride off, Joel said to Mac. "You know more'n we do 'bout what's legal. Where to put the 'whereases' and 'wherefores.' You should go to this convention."

Mac shook his head. "I've never been involved in politics. Don't know that I have a mind to start." But he remembered his father's letter calling mining a dirty business.

Later in the day Joel caught Mac alone and urged again, "You oughta sign up to be a part of the law-making. The man's right, even if he is a pompous prick. California's gonna be a state someday. Don't you want to help make that happen?"

"Who'd work the claim with you?" Mac asked. "Huntington's not much good this year. And you didn't want any other partners."

Joel shrugged. "We ain't finding so much gold now. Maybe I'll pack it in myself. Though don't know what else I might do. Move on, maybe."

"Where?"

"Don't matter. Stake another claim somewhere. You ain't deciding anything any time fast—I don't have decide now, do I?"

"No," Mac said. "And I don't either. Let's see what the election brings."

After his conversation with Joel, Mac had a hard time concentrating on his digging. His father had commanded him to return to Boston by Christmas. He would have to leave soon if he wanted to travel overland. But ships now routinely sailed between San Francisco and Panama—he could wait to leave in August if he went by sea. Maybe even early September.

June 15, 1849. There will be a vote on delegates to a Constitutional Convention on August 1. I shall stay for the vote, but then I must decide my future. Should I participate in Californian politics or not?

Mac stopped writing to think. Would his father see any value if he worked on a new government for California? His father respected many Massachusetts politicians. But California? Andrew McDougall had never thought much of the West. What profit would he see in forming the new state?

If Mac wasn't going back to Boston, he owed it to his parents to let them know before Christmas when they expected him. He started composing a letter in his head, but couldn't decide whether to declare he'd stay in California for the convention or not.

"What you mulling over, boy?" Huntington asked Mac that evening. "You ain't been worth a piss all day."

"He's trying to decide whether to be a prospector or a politician," Joel said with a grin.

Huntington grunted. "Politicians are all jackanapes. Can't trust any of 'em."

"I'm tired of mining," Mac said.

"Hell, boy, I'm tired of minin', too," Huntington said. "But we been doin' purty well at it. If'n you're ready to hang it up, find yourself a good woman and live off your earnings. I'm too old to git a woman, so I'll keep diggin' till I drop. But you're a good looker still."

A good woman. Now where would Mac find a woman he could care for? Not in the saloons of California, like Joel did. There were hardly any women one could call "good" in California. If it was a woman he wanted, he should probably go back to Boston. Mac thought of Susan Abbott's trim figure floating down the hotel staircase. More women like her would come to California.

Then he remembered Jenny's small hand pushing a strand of sun-lightened brown hair out of her face as she smiled at him. He couldn't help smiling to himself in response.

Mac and Joel learned from the July 7 issue of the *Placer Times*, a new weekly paper published in Sacramento and passed from claim to claim in the mining country, that their valley was in the Sutter's Fort precinct for the August election. They would need to make another trip to the fort to vote.

Huntington refused to leave the claim. "I ain't never voted afore. Don't see no need to start."

"Will you be all right alone?" Mac asked. "Any thieves around here aren't likely to stop stealing while we vote."

"I can keep myself alive till y'all return," Huntington said. "If I can't shoot 'em, I'll hide in the woods."

Mac shook his head at Huntington's bravado. "We need to think about how to keep our mine going," he told his partners. "I'm not staying on the claim past August. I've decided that much. Huntington, you've been coughing all year. You should take your money and settle down where you're comfortable."

Huntington's face reddened above his gray beard. "You can't put me out to pasture, boy. I'm fit enough to work."

"You're the only one who wants to leave, Mac," Joel said. "So leave. We'll fend for ourselves."

"Mining is becoming more complicated," Mac said. "There aren't many sites where placer mines can still extract color. The new longer sluices require large companies of men to operate. You could hire some greenhorns to help after I'm gone. Men are starting to arrive from the East."

"They all want to make their own fortunes," Huntington said. "Like you boys did last year."

"You could hire Indians," Mac said. "Diggers. They're likely to leave when the weather shifts, but some of them are honest."

"I ain't spending my time watching over no Indians," Joel said. "We'll make do on our own."

Mac couldn't make his partners take on more help. But as he continued to shake the rocker in the stream running along their claim, he worried what would happen to Joel and Huntington after he left.

It was no surprise Huntington's health suffered, though he'd improved some in the summer heat. The men spent days standing in rushing water and laboring in the hot sun. They shoveled heavy sand and gravel into sluices and pushed the rocker arm for hours at a time. They ate bread and salt pork traded at the fort. They could see salmon jumping in the stream they stood in, but rarely took time to fish or hunt. Mac's mouth watered as he remembered wide-ranging hunts along the trail to Oregon and fresh venison.

Auld lang syne. He would never have thought he'd recall the trek to Oregon with fondness. In retrospect, it had been the best six months of his life.

Chapter 36:   Summer's Heat

Jenny and Rachel hoed the fields one hot morning in late June. They left William on the edge of the tilled land under a shade tree. Jenny kept an eye on the toddler, who now ran more than he walked. Zeke worked his own farm that day.

"There's too much for you and me to do, with Zeke here only part of the time," Rachel said, flopping down beside William for the noon break.

"We'll have to ask at church again whether anyone knows of a reliable man," Jenny said. "I can't hire just anyone to live on the farm." She and Rachel had the same conversation almost every day. Men weren't plentiful in Oregon this year. Maybe autumn would bring new emigrants wanting work. Unless all the able-bodied men were lured to California.

"Try to find a young handsome man." Rachel grinned. "Ain't no reason we can't have someone fine to look at."

Jenny frowned. "You know people would talk. Two young women alone with someone like that? That's why I won't let Zeke stay here."

"You're married. No one would think anything."

"Mac's gone. People would think plenty." Jenny shook her head. "We're better off with an older man. An experienced hand. But there aren't any men around who don't want their own farms. Not when land is free for the taking. And not when there's gold in California."

"Well, I hope we find someone before harvest." Rachel stretched out on her back. William tickled her nose with a piece of grass until she pulled the boy down beside her. "Zeke can't bring all the crops in with only the twins and us to help."

Jenny smiled at her son and her friend. It had worked out well to have Rachel living with William and her.

Saturday, June 30ᵗʰ —I shall ask Dr. Tuller again whether he knows of anyone willing to hire on as a farmhand. Rachel and I must have someone to help with the heavy labor. But I shudder to think of a stranger living with us.

The next morning after the church service, Jenny looked for Doc Tuller, but Samuel Abercrombie stopped her before she found the doctor.

"I want to buy a part of your claim off you," Mr. Abercrombie said. "The strip of meadow near the stream by Daniel's place. Don't know why you had young Pershing clear a field there. It'd be better as pasture, with the water nearby."

"I'm not planning to sell any of the land, Mr. Abercrombie. Can I even sell it until it's proven up?"

"You don't know what you're doing, girl," he said, shaking his finger in her face. "Without McDougall here, you're at the mercy of Zeke Pershing and any other man trying to take advantage of you."

She saw Doc and waved him over. "Mr. Abercrombie says Zeke is taking advantage of me," she told Doc. "He's offering to buy the part of my land next to Esther and Daniel."

Doc's face turned red and he glowered. "Abercrombie, you keep your nose out of where it don't belong. Jenny's doing a fine job on her claim, and young Zeke's been a better neighbor than most of us to her."

"I wonder why," Abercrombie said with a leering grin.

Jenny gasped. The rumors would start again, like on the wagon train. "I'm not selling any land to you, Mr. Abercrombie." She pulled Doc's arm. "Could I have a word, please, Doc?"

When they moved away from Abercrombie, Jenny asked Doc if he knew anyone who wanted farm work.

He shook his head. "You should marry Zeke Pershing," he said. "That would solve your problems."

Marry Zeke? Jenny wasn't even sure she wanted a man living on her farm. "No, Doc. I don't want to marry." She shook her head. "And Zeke won't ask me. Not while he thinks I'm married. I'm not in love with him. Plus, I'd lose Mac's claim."

Doc frowned. "Sounds like you been giving the matter some thought. Mrs. Tuller and I could talk to Zeke, tell him you weren't married."

Jenny stared across the churchyard, silent. Had she thought about marrying Zeke? Only when she remembered Mac telling her to.

"McDougall's not coming back." Doc's voice was gentler than his face. "You had your chance with him."

Jenny swallowed hard. "He didn't want me." But he *had* wanted her that last night. She sighed. "And I didn't want him." She hadn't wanted Mac then, she thought, but would she take him now?

Jenny didn't take William to Oregon City for the Fourth of July picnic this year. It was too hot. Although Oregon was cooler than Missouri or Louisiana, Jenny sweltered in the evenings in her closed cabin. She felt sorry for Rachel, who slept in the loft above, trapped in the heat left over from the day.

"We should put a window in the loft," Jenny said one evening in mid-July, when the two young women latched the door for the night, closing in the heat. "Downstairs window doesn't open, but maybe we could get one for the loft that does. Then we could move some air through the cabin."

"Windows are so dear," Rachel said. "You can't afford it."

Jenny sighed. "Mac left me a little money." She hated to spend Mac's coins on frivolities like windows, but she didn't want Rachel suffering. She would ask Zeke how much a window pane would cost, and how hard it would be to put in a window in the loft to open and close.

Zeke examined the loft the next day. "It could be done," he said. "But I ain't seen any glass panes in the stores recently. Be better to try to fill the chinks in the walls afore winter comes, now Rachel's sleeping up here. Cold's a bigger problem than heat."

Jenny thought of Mac sleeping in the loft through their winter together. He'd never complained, but he must have been cold.

"We'll make a mud paste," Rachel said. "Start on it as soon we can."

One more thing for Jenny to worry about. Along with how to finish the harvest.

Jenny didn't ask again about men needing work. Doc and Zeke were the only men she trusted, and they hadn't been able to help.

The women set out their offerings at a church picnic the next Sunday. Jenny and Rachel brought blackberry jam from the first picking of the season. Her fruit trees had years to go before they would bear, but berries were plentiful in the wild. Even William had helped pick the plump juicy treats. He'd sampled the berries as he picked, and Jenny had to scrub his face, hands, and clothes to remove the stains.

"This year's emigrants are starting to arrive from the East," Amanda Pershing said. "Captain heard it in town. They're early to have made the overland trek by July. Took us till October."

"No one here with wagons yet. Only men riding horseback. And fewer men than last year," Mrs. Tuller said. "Way I hear it, most folks took the trail to California. Not like in forty-seven when we came."

"But some families want the land. No free farmland in California." Mrs. Pershing laid out a meat pie.

"Wonder how Joel's doing," Esther said as she placed her cornbread beside Jenny's jam. "Ain't heard from him but twice." By now Esther's back swayed from the weight of pregnancy. Cordelia, now fourteen months old, toddled at Esther's feet, clutching her skirts for support.

"You'd think they'd write more, Joel and Captain McDougall," Mrs. Pershing said, fanning herself against the heat. "There's monthly mail service between Astoria and San Francisco now."

Jenny listened to the chatter around her rise and fall like buzzing insects in the summer air. Maybe she should write Mac again and ask him about his plans.

"That your jam, Miz Jenny?" Zeke asked.

She smiled. "Try it with Esther's cornbread," she said.

"Too hot for cornbread," Zeke said. "Just a slice of that loaf." He pointed, and Jenny slathered her jam on bread for him.

"I put up a sign in the stores asking for help," he said. "We might find a man down on his luck after traveling from the East."

"I thought the stores gave folks credit," Jenny said. "At least enough to get through their first winter."

"Some do. But the American stores ain't so generous as Hudson's Bay was." Zeke shook his head as he chewed. "John McLaughlin managed Fort Vancouver well for Hudson's Bay. Too bad he's gone now."

Jenny handed Zeke another slice of bread with jam. "He was very helpful to our wagon train."

"If I find a hired hand for you, can you pay?" Zeke asked, raising an eyebrow. "You can offer a share in the harvest, like you offered me, but some men might want cash wages."

Jenny nodded slowly. It seemed there was a need for money every time she turned around. "I have money from Mac. I'll use it if I have to, but I'll want to replace it after harvest."

Zeke chuckled. "If it's Mac's money, it's yours. You're his wife. He'd want you to have the help. Keep the farm going till he returns."

"I suppose," Jenny said. "But I want to show I can take care of myself and William."

Zeke looked at her quizzically.

Chapter 37: Letting Go

July 29, 1849. Joel and I leave tomorrow to vote. The election is in two days.

Mac and Joel headed to Sacramento to vote for delegates to the upcoming Constitutional Convention. They were to vote at the fort, and they decided to lodge at the Golden Nugget nearby. When they arrived in town on the evening of July 31, men and horses milled about, but the streets weren't any more crowded than on Mac's last visit. None of the conversations Mac overheard concerned the election.

"Surprised ain't more men here to vote," Joel said.

"Voting is less important than gold to many men," Mac replied. He remembered election days in Boston. Politicians' cronies dragged men from saloons in the hours right before the polls closed, but most men ignored the voting completely.

"You still seeing her when you're in Sacramento?" Mac asked Joel, nodding at Consuela, after they took a room at the Golden Nugget and sat at the bar.

Joel shrugged. "If she's available. Or one of the other girls."

"So you're not partial to Consuela?"

Joel signaled the bartender. "One whore's as good as another."

Mac frowned. "What would your mother say if she heard you?"

"Ma's dead. What she don't know don't hurt her."

"Then you don't think the dead are watching over us?" Mac wasn't sure he subscribed to that notion either, but he certainly didn't approve of Joel's cavalier attitude toward women—an approach which had only brought Mac trouble.

"Don't preach at me," Joel said.

"Have it your way," Mac replied, as Consuela joined them. Her smile seemed sad. "Something wrong?" Mac asked her.

"You haven't heard?" Consuela responded. "About Juanita?"

"Who's Juanita?" Mac asked.

"One of the other girls," Joel said. "Where is she?"

"*Muerta*," Consuela said. "Hung." She leaned on the bar next to Joel.

"Hung?" Joel looked surprised. "What'd she do?"

"Stabbed a man. So they say." Consuela sighed. "The *hombre* died, but he deserved it."

"What'd he do?" Mac sipped the whiskey the bartender put in front of him.

"Tried to rape her."

Joel snorted. "How can a whore get raped?"

Consuela jerked away from the bar, her eyes flashing. "It's one thing to sell yourself by choice. It's another to be taken by force."

Mac swallowed hard, thinking of Jenny. No woman deserved to be raped. He was still ashamed of pawing at her that last night at the cabin. "Shut your trap, Joel," he said. "The lady's right."

Joel left to amuse himself at the card tables. While Mac continued drinking alone at the bar, he made his decision. He'd been putting it off, but he had to let Jenny go. Now that he'd decided to quit mining, it was time to send her evidence of his death. She hadn't responded after he wrote her in late March—she must not care that he had left.

He asked the bartender to find him paper, quill, and ink. His first step was to draft a deed giving his Oregon land claim to Jenny. He wasn't sure if he could give away the claim before it was proven, but a deed would at least declare his intention. It would give Jenny an argument the land was hers.

When he finished his legal drafting, he pulled Consuela aside. "Can you write?" he asked.

"Yes. But my English spelling is not so good."

"I'll tell you how to spell, if you'll write a letter for me. Can we go someplace private?"

"My room." She looked around at the busy saloon. "You'll have to pay for my time."

Mac nodded. "Let's go."

Consuela's room was small, but neat. A bed, a table with a chair beside it, and a washbowl on a stand peeking out from behind a wood lattice screen. Pegs on the wall held a few flashy dresses and a robe.

Consuela gestured at the bed and sat at the table.

Mac took off his coat, sat on the bed, and handed her the writing materials.

She smoothed out the paper and dipped the quill in the ink. "I'm ready."

"Dear Señora McDougall," Mac began.

"You're married?" Consuela stared at him in surprise.

"Just write."

Mac dictated, with Consuela asking occasionally how to spell a word. When they finished, she handed him the letter to read:

July 31, 1849

Dear Señora McDougall,

I regret to inform you that your husband, Caleb McDougall, died here in Sacramento. He took fever a few days ago and left this earth yesterday. I nursed him at the end, and his last words were of you and your son.

Señor McDougall left his mining claim to his partner Joel Pershing. Your husband's dying wish was for you to have his land in Oregon. A deed he signed during his illness is enclosed.

My deepest sympathies on your loss.

Respectfully,

Consuela Montenegro

"Thank you," Mac said. He put the letter in his pocket, flipped a gold coin on the bed, and strode down the stairs to the bar.

"Where's Pershing?" he asked the bartender.

"Upstairs." The man jerked his head. "With one of the girls."

While he waited for Joel, Mac drank more than he had since the night he left Jenny.

Mac awoke with a throbbing head, sprawled face down on a soft bed. He lifted his head and the walls whirled around him. When the spinning stopped, he recognized Consuela's room. She sat on a chair beside the bed.

"Tell me about your wife," she said.

"What?" He didn't have a wife.

"Why are you writing her a letter that says you are dead?"

A letter? Ah, yes. The letter to Jenny. "She's not my wife." Mac buried his face in the sheets again.

"*Por qué* . . . ?" She sounded puzzled.

"People in Oregon think we're married. I have to set them straight. I have to make her free of me."

"Why do people think you are married?" She rose and moved across the room to open the curtain.

Mac rolled over onto his back and moaned, placing his arm over his eyes to shield them from the bright morning sun streaming in the window.

"What harm will it do to tell me?" Consuela placed a cool cloth on his forehead.

He mumbled his thanks and sighed. "It's a long story."

Consuela shrugged. "I have nothing to do until the saloon opens at noon. What's her name?"

"Jenny." Mac's voice croaked.

Consuela sat beside him and waited.

"She"—Mac couldn't say her name again—"was expecting a child. Only fourteen years old. She needed help. We couldn't travel to Oregon unless we were married. So we said we were. It got out of hand."

"What do you mean?"

"We arrived in Oregon, then there wasn't a way to leave her."

"Did you want to leave her?"

Mac shrugged. "She didn't want me. I filed a land claim. Built her a house, so she'd have a place to live. I couldn't just abandon her."

"Did you love her?" Consuela's voice sounded sad, even in Mac's pounding head.

"I don't know. I cared for her. She did her part when we were together."

"Why didn't you marry her?"

"I said, she didn't want me. Neither of us wanted to marry." Mac tried sitting up. He didn't want to continue this conversation.

"Did she have her baby?"

Mac nodded, falling back on the bed. "A boy."

"Where was the baby's father?"

"She'd been raped. By several men."

Consuela's breath hissed in. "And yesterday I told you Juanita's story."

Mac sat up, too angry to care about his head. "Jenny isn't a whore." Then he remembered Consuela's profession. "Sorry. I'm sure you didn't have a choice. But I couldn't let Jenny—"

"You didn't want Jenny to become like me."

"I didn't know you."

"But you didn't want Jenny to be forced into prostitution."

"I didn't know what would happen to her."

"Why did you take her to Oregon?"

He shrugged. "She needed to go somewhere. That's where I was headed."

Consuela shook her head. "Dangerous trip for a pregnant woman. Yet she went with you?"

"She had nowhere else to go."

Consuela laughed, a short, harsh sound. "You wouldn't let her prostitute herself, but you took her on a journey that could have killed her?"

"Perhaps it was foolish."

"And now you will tell her you are dead."

"We didn't end well."

"Ahh," Consuela said. "This is maybe the true story." She sat still, waiting, it seemed, for Mac to speak again.

He picked at a blister on his palm, ashamed to look at Consuela. "I scared her. The last night I was there. I wanted her."

"She is pretty?"

Mac couldn't help smiling. "Yes."

"Prettier than me?"

Mac looked at her then, assessing. Yes, Consuela was pretty. "Her eyes are sad like yours. But blue."

"Her hair?"

"Light brown. It turns gold in the sun."

Consuela smiled. "You do love her." Her voice was gentle.

"Maybe."

"Then how can you tell her you are dead?"

"She can't want me. Not after how I behaved."

"Shouldn't that be her choice?"

"I'm no good for her. Just like Bridget."

"Bridget?"

"A girl back in Boston. She died, after I left her alone."

"Did you love this Bridget, too?"

Mac sighed. "No. But she was carrying my child."

Consuela raised an eyebrow. "You surprise me, Señor McDougall. Never would I have guessed such troubles in your life. You have been the gentleman in California, never touching the girls. I cannot believe you treated Jenny or Bridget any differently."

Mac was silent. He had nothing more to say. The truth was, he'd hurt the women he touched. His actions had led to Bridget's death. He'd taken Jenny away from her home.

Consuela knelt by the bed and brushed his hair out of his eyes. "When will you forgive yourself, Mac? When will you seek happiness for yourself?"

Mac stood up then, though his stomach roiled. He couldn't take any more preaching. "How much do I owe you for the night?"

Consuela shook her head, her mouth a thin line.

Mac dropped another gold piece on the table. "I need to find Joel." And he headed out to vote. As he walked, he thrust his hand in his pocket, slipping his fingers past the bootie he kept with him always, to take hold of the letter to Jenny.

He mailed it on his way to vote.

Chapter 38: Old Friends and New Endeavors

After they voted, Mac told Joel about the letter he'd had Consuela write Jenny. "It says I'm dead. And I've deeded my Oregon land to her. You can't let on I'm still here when you write your family."

"I don't know why you're going to all this trouble if you and Miz Jenny ain't really married. Giving her your land?" Joel shook his head. "Ain't no reason for it."

"I owe her something. She was a good companion along the trail."

"Then you're going back to Boston?"

"Nowhere else to go."

"You could keep mining," Joel said. "If I don't tell, no one in Oregon will know you're still in the West."

"I'm tired of mining," Mac said. "I have enough gold to be comfortable the rest of my life."

The men stayed in Sacramento two days after the election while Mac drafted a contract assigning Joel his portion of their mine. "It's only you and Huntington now," Mac said. He and Joel sat in the Golden Nugget signing papers in late afternoon on August 3. "I still think you ought to hire on more men."

Joel shrugged. "Don't like working with folks I don't know." Joel pushed back from the table. "Hear tell a man named Brannan is building a big hotel in Sacramento down by the river. Think I'll stay there next time I go for provisions. Beds'll be softer than here at the Golden Nugget, most likely."

"Seems your bed's been soft enough," Mac said, nodding at Consuela.

"She ain't been so friendly this week," Joel said. "Ain't friendly to you neither. What'd you do to her? Besides make her write that letter."

183

"Nothing," Mac said.

"Must've been something," Joel insisted. "She ain't even looking at you."

"It was nothing," Mac repeated.

Joel's voice boomed as he chortled, "Did you finally screw her? You was upstairs with her all night."

Men at other tables stared at them. "Quiet down, Joel," Mac murmured. "No need to tell the whole saloon our business."

One of the men staring was a balding man in a black suit, starched collar, and string tie. When Mac frowned at him, the man stood and walked over to their table. "Where you fellows from?" he asked, holding out his hand to Mac.

"Mining claim a couple days northwest of here," Mac replied. "Caleb McDougall." He stood to shake the man's hand. Joel rose also.

"Lansford Hastings," the man said. "Haven't I seen you men here before?"

"Could be," Joel said. "We come to town regular for provisions."

"Hastings," Mac said. "Not the Hastings who wrote the emigrants' guide?" The guidebook had been well-known in Boston, though it proved deadly for some emigrants to California—the Donner party in particular. The Donner company had been trapped in snow through the winter of 1846-47, and many of the poor souls had starved. Others survived only by eating their animals and leather harnesses—and possibly the bodies of their fellow travelers. If Mac had known of their plight before he left Boston, he might not have been so eager to make the perilous journey.

"The very one," Hastings said. "Did you read it?"

"I certainly did," Mac said. "Our company followed Frémont's maps, but your story, sir, was my original inspiration to see the West. We traveled to Oregon originally, not California. I'm from Boston."

Hastings smiled. "I was born in Ohio. Went to Oregon myself in forty-two. Since then, I've been in Alta California, went back East, then back to California. I have a law practice, and now I aim to go to Monterey as a delegate to the convention."

"Mac's a lawyer, too," Joel said. "I've been telling him to go to Monterey, have his say about the laws in these parts. He's tired of prospecting. Too dirty for him." Joel grinned at Mac. "Says he's going back to Boston."

"Now, Joel, I never said prospecting was too dirty."

"You should join me, McDougall," Hastings said. "If you want to be a part of California politics, now's the time. This territory will grow faster than we can imagine. Those men who are here first will reap the riches. We'll be a state before you know it."

Hastings sounded like Mac's father. Still, it might be interesting to help establish a new government. "I'll think about it, sir," he said.

"Monterey, first of September. If you come, look me up. I'll put you to work. Lawyer work. You'll keep your hands clean." Hastings gave a slight bow and left the saloon.

Soon after Hastings left, Mac stood. "I'm having dinner with Nate and his granddaughter," he told Joel. "Would you like to join us?"

Joel shook his head. "Nate don't like me. And maybe with you gone, Consuela will treat me more kindly. I ain't asking her to tell anyone I'm dead." He winked. "I got lots of life in me yet."

Mac met Nate and Susan in the lobby of their hotel near Fort Sutter, and they went to a restaurant on the ground floor of a gaming hall right outside the fort. "We need to find a more suitable place to live," Susan said, as Mac seated her at the table. "The hotel is full of ruffians and drunkards. It's no more than a saloon."

"I've offered to buy us a house in town," Nate said. "Though the hotel offers better lodgings than most have in Sacramento. Most men are living in tents, as are many families. Not enough houses for folks who haven't already made their fortunes. I've even told Susan I'd take her to San Francisco."

"But if we move, who would run your store?" Susan asked. "You need a man of business to help you."

"Can't find a knowledgeable man I trust in these parts," Nate said. "Unless you want the job, Mac?"

Mac shook his head. "Don't give me another option. Joel thinks I should go to Monterey to the Constitutional Convention. And I've about decided to head back to Boston."

"Monterey," Susan exclaimed. "Why, Mrs. Frémont wrote me she is there now. I traveled with her and her daughter from Panama City. She and

I became close acquaintances on the boat. She was horribly ill with a fever she acquired in the tropics, and I helped tend her daughter. After many weeks she recovered, but was still only slightly improved when we set sail for San Francisco."

"Who is Mrs. Frémont?" Mac asked.

"Captain John Frémont's wife. Senator Thomas Benton's daughter. Surely you've heard of Captain Frémont."

"I have indeed," Mac said. "His guide book and maps saved our wagon company many times on the way to Oregon. He's in Monterey?"

"For the convention, I suppose," Susan said.

What harm could it do to spend time in Monterey? Mac thought. He had an offer of employment from Lansford Hastings, and he could meet his hero, John Frémont.

The next morning Mac told Joel of his change in plans. He wanted to return to the claim one last time before riding to Monterey.

"Ain't no way to persuade you to keep digging?" Joel asked.

Mac shook his head. "Time for me to move on."

As they rode away from Sacramento, a voice called out from the camp of travelers outside town, "Captain McDougall! Joel Pershing!"

Mac peered around and recognized the dark-skinned man running toward him. "Tanner," he shouted. "What are you doing here?"

"Brought my family to California," Tanner said. "For the gold."

"Where's Jenny?" Mac asked.

"On your claim, of course," Tanner said.

"You left her alone?" Mac's throat went dry at the thought of Jenny struggling to provide for herself and William. He'd thought the Tanners were with Jenny when he'd sent the letter from Consuela. How would Jenny cope alone?

"I couldn't stay in Oregon, Captain," Tanner said, shaking his head. "Weren't nothin' there for colored folks like us."

Hatty came up beside her husband, smiling. "Captain McDougall, it's right nice to see you."

"How was Jenny when you left?" Mac asked. "And William?"

"They was fine, Captain. Mr. Zeke was tendin' the farm for her. No need to worry 'bout Miz Jenny nor your boy."

Despite Tanner's assurances, Mac panicked inside. He hadn't feared for Jenny's safety when the Tanners stayed on the claim with her—Mac trusted them, which is why he'd asked them to live on his land, knowing that he would leave after one winter in Oregon.

He still shouldn't worry, he told himself. Zeke would watch out for her. That was what he wanted—for Jenny and Zeke to marry once Jenny received word of his death. That's why he'd had Consuela write Jenny. Wasn't it? But he'd never meant her to be alone.

Talk between Joel and the Tanners swirled around him. "Mac," Joel said. "You ain't listening. How 'bout we take the Tanners to our claim? Tanner can work for me and Huntington, since you're leaving."

"You leavin'?" Tanner sounded surprised. "Thought California was the land of milk and honey. Where you goin'? Back to Oregon?"

"Mac don't know what he's doing," Joel said in disgust. "One day it's Boston, the next Monterey. There's a government convention next month. What do you say, Mac? Let's take the Tanners to the claim. I'd be comfortable working with Tanner."

Mac shrugged. "That all right with you, Tanner?" he asked. "It's rough work."

Tanner chuckled. "No rougher than Oregon, I 'spect. Can our wagon make it through?"

"What about Huntington?" Mac asked Joel.

"I'll deal with that old coot." Joel grinned. "I'd like to see him try to squabble with Hatty." He turned to Tanner. "Is your wagon ready for more hills?"

The men walked around the wagon. "It's in good repair," Mac said. "Your mules should be able to pull it. Trail's not as bad as Barlow Road, and a lot shorter."

The expanded party set out for the mining valley. It took four days in the hot August sun to move the wagon through the hills to the claim. On the evening of the second night of travel, after ruminating while the group struggled to maneuver the wagon on the trail, Mac wrote:

August 6, 1849. I sold Joel my claim, and good riddance. He and Tanner can mine with Huntington's guidance while I go to the convention, where I hope to learn something. Perhaps I'll hear more of Jenny later through Joel. If she marries Zeke, I won't need to worry about her.

When they arrived at the diggings, the Tanners professed themselves pleased with the land. Otis immediately splashed into the stream looking for fish.

"I'll build us a little cabin on the ridge afore winter," Tanner said. "We can live in the wagon till then. We's used to it."

"My tools are here. Joel can outfit you with what you need," Mac said. "I'm only taking what Valiente can carry. Give you my pack mule, too."

"You ain't changed your mind, now Tanner's here?" Joel asked.

Mac shook his head. If anything, he was more set on leaving. The Tanners' presence was a constant reminder that Jenny was alone. "Might as well see how a constitution is written. I'll look up Hastings, like he offered. And perhaps I will meet John Frémont."

"I knew it." Joel chuckled. "You're a politician at heart."

Mac made his way back to Sacramento, down the Sacramento River, across the bay by ferry to San Francisco, and along El Camino Real—the King's Highway—to Monterey. In San Francisco, he posted a letter to his parents:

August 25, 1849

Dear Mother and Father,

I have an opportunity to participate in the Constitutional Convention for California this autumn, and have decided to remain here for the winter. I regret that I will not return to Boston to be with you this Christmas, as you had requested.

I have been offered a position with Mr. Lansford

Hastings, Esq., from Ohio, who has made his livelihood in California for many years. He is an inspiration to those of us who love the West. I am eager to try my talents at constructing the government for a new Territory, which quite possibly will become our nation's next State.

I shall think of you frequently this winter, and I will write of my plans for next spring. Please convey my disappointment to my brothers and their families at our continued separation, but I believe I can be of the greatest service to society by remaining in California for another season.

> *Affectionately,*
> *Your son, Caleb*

Chapter 39:   Hired Hand

On a Monday morning early in August, Jenny heard hoof beats and looked up from her washtub in the yard. A strange man on horseback trotted up the road toward the cabin.

Jenny and William were alone. Rachel had gone to visit Esther. Jenny's rifle was inside—she couldn't get to it before the man reached her. She rushed to pick up William, who played in the dirt beside her.

The man stopped his horse at the edge of the yard. "Beg pardon, ma'am," he said, touching his hat. It was a battered broad-brimmed hat like many cavalry soldiers wore.

Jenny waited, holding William close. She wished Zeke were there.

"Hear tell you need help on your farm, with harvest 'bout to start." The man removed his hat. He was older than Zeke or Mac, but younger than Captain Pershing or Samuel Abercrombie. Maybe in his mid-thirties. His pockmarked face was creased around the eyes, and his hair was neatly trimmed.

"Who told you that?" Jenny asked.

"Doctor by the name of Tuller. He treated me for frostbite."

"What's your name?" Jenny clutched William more tightly.

The toddler in Jenny's arms squirmed and fussed. "Lemme go, Mama."

"Robert O'Neil, ma'am. From Kentucky originally. My folks farmed there. I grew up in the fields. I ain't afraid of hard work."

"How'd you get to Oregon?"

"With the First Mounted Rifles. Got to Oregon City last month. Now I've mustered out and need work."

"Why'd you leave the Army?" The man seemed polite and clean, but Jenny was suspicious of any stranger.

"Ma'am, if you'd been on the trip we took 'round Mount Hood, you'd muster out, too. Came through Barlow Road in June. Got caught in heavy snows, even in midsummer. Lost most of our horses. Some men lost toes to frostbite. Doc Tuller done good—I still got all mine. My term was up along the way, and I told my sergeant I was gittin' out soon as I could."

Jenny remembered the wagon trip on Barlow Road—the worst stretch of the whole trail between Missouri and Oregon City. She softened a little. "And now you need work," she said.

"Yes, ma'am. I want to git to California, but I ain't got money for provisions."

Doc must have trusted the man, or he wouldn't have mentioned her to O'Neil. But Jenny needed to be sure before she hired the ex-soldier. "I want to talk to Doc Tuller before I decide. If you muck out the stable, I'll give you dinner."

O'Neil dismounted and led his horse into the paddock. He nodded at Poulette and Shanty grazing inside the fence. "Nice Indian mare," he said. "But the colt'll be the better horse when he's growed."

Jenny smiled. The man recognized good horseflesh. "His sire was an Andalusian owned by m-my husband." It was hard to lie about Mac, even to a stranger. "Shanty's black like his papa. But with his mama's spots." She started toward the barn to get Poulette's saddle. "I'll go see Doc now."

"Lemme saddle her, ma'am." O'Neil said. He brought the tack from the barn and saddled the mare as Jenny watched. "Can I hold the boy for you while you mount?" he asked.

Jenny glanced at him warily, but handed her son over. William grinned at the man and patted his rough face. After she mounted, O'Neil sat William on her lap, and Jenny rode toward the Tuller claim.

When she arrived, she found Doc boiling his medical instruments in a large pot. "Morning, Doc," she said, when he helped her and William off Poulette. "Did you send a Robert O'Neil my way?"

"O'Neil." Doc said, scratching his beard. "Ah, yes—the soldier from Fort Leavenworth. They had a nasty time of it on Barlow Road. Remember our trip?"

"Yes." Jenny had just birthed William before their wagon train ascended the mountain pass. The road was rough, the weather foul. She was ill and became exhausted carrying her newborn son up the mountain. But she and William made it to the top.

"He seems an honest man. You wanted help." Doc used tongs to remove

191

some of the instruments from the pot.

"I was afraid to hire him without talking to you. And to Zeke."

Doc Tuller scowled at Jenny. "You need a farmhand. He's the only man who's wanted the job."

"Did you talk to his sergeant?" Jenny asked.

"Of course. And the lieutenant. They both gave O'Neil strong references. A good soldier, they said. Responsible. Does what he's told."

"Mr. O'Neil says he's going to California. He won't stay long."

The doctor shrugged. "He'll stay through harvest, because you won't pay him till you've sold your crops to the mill. That's all you need for the time being." Doc turned to her, hands on hips. "He's the best man you're going to find, Jenny."

Jenny frowned, worrying whether to take O'Neil on. She had to consider William's and Rachel's safety as well as her own. She left the Tullers' claim and returned home.

As Jenny rode into the clearing outside her cabin, she saw Zeke standing next to the barnyard paddock with his rifle drawn. Robert O'Neil stood in the barn doorway, hands in the air facing Zeke. Rachel sat on Zeke's horse at the edge of the yard nearest Jenny.

"Found him in the barn," Zeke shouted at Jenny. "Says he's going to work for you."

Jenny trotted over on Poulette. "It's all right, Zeke. Doc sent him."

Zeke lowered his rifle, but didn't put it back in the scabbard. "Who is he?"

"Name's O'Neil," the former soldier said. "Robert O'Neil. Lookin' for work." He slowly dropped his hands to his sides.

"Doc talked to his sergeant and lieutenant," Jenny said. "They say he's all right."

"Who might you be?" O'Neil said to Zeke.

"Zeke Pershing. I'm tending Miz McDougall's land."

"That's right." Jenny rode to Zeke's side. "If you take the job, you'll work for Zeke in the fields," she told O'Neil. "He's in charge."

"Do you need me or not?" O'Neil asked Zeke. "I farmed in Kentucky. If you won't have me, I'll hire on with someone else. I gotta work."

Zeke turned to Jenny, at last putting his gun away. "You all right with him being here?"

She nodded. "Doc says he's a good soldier. I'm fine with hiring him, if you are."

Zeke looked at Rachel. "How 'bout you?"

Rachel looked at Jenny, then at O'Neil. "If Jenny is."

"Who's she?" O'Neil asked, nodding at Rachel.

"My sister," Zeke said, glaring at O'Neil. "You'll answer to me if either of these ladies is harmed." He gestured for Rachel to ride forward, then lifted her off the saddle when she reached him. "Put these horses away," he said to O'Neil as he turned to help Jenny and William down. "You'll sleep in the barn."

Monday, August 6ᵗʰ—I've hired a man, Robert O'Neil, whom Dr. Tuller recommended. I hope I have not made a mistake.

Despite Jenny's initial fears, O'Neil was as responsible as his sergeant had said. And he was quiet. She never heard him approaching. More than once, he startled her coming up behind her in the yard or barn. "Land sakes," she cried one morning when she opened the cabin door to throw out a bucket of water and found him right outside.

"Sorry, ma'am," O'Neil said. "I'm used to sneaking up on Indians. I'll try not to scare you." He started whistling whenever he came near the cabin.

Wednesday, August 22ᵗʰ—Mr. O'Neil has become indispensable. He totes our water, has chopped logs until the woodpile is as tall as I am, and does all the outside chores except gathering eggs—all this, while working from breakfast until supper in the fields.

The wheat harvest occupied everyone's time. The winter wheat planted the previous autumn had been ready to reap and thresh at the end of July. The spring wheat was ripe in mid-August, so field work continued throughout the month.

Zeke spent most of the hot August days on Jenny's land. She had to ask him how he was managing his own farm. "Take Mr. O'Neil to help you," she offered. "It's only right you use him, too, since you're spending so much time here."

"I'm here to watch out for you and Rachel," Zeke said. "O'Neil seems all right, but we don't know him. I took him to meet Pa. Pa said he talked like a good Army man."

"That means a lot coming from Captain Pershing," Jenny said, smiling.

"Pa still said not to trust him. Particularly 'round a young girl like Rachel."

As O'Neil made himself useful, both in the fields and around the cabin, Jenny relaxed in his presence. Although Jenny grew comfortable with the man, Rachel remained tongue-tied whenever O'Neil was nearby. The girl did her chores in silence and skittered away from him whenever she could.

"Don't you like Mr. O'Neil?" Jenny asked Rachel on an afternoon at the end of August, as they sewed together at Esther's cabin. William and Jonah played with wooden blocks on the floor, and Cornelia toddled beside them.

Rachel blushed. "I like him fine enough. I just don't know what to say to him."

"Treat him like one of your brothers," Jenny suggested. "Like Zeke or Joel."

Rachel's eyes widened, and she shook her head. "I can't."

Esther chuckled. "Mr. O'Neil's better looking than Zeke or Joel." Jenny didn't agree, but she didn't argue. Esther continued, "Even with his pockmarks and weathered face. Not exactly handsome, but he has a kind smile."

"He's handsome enough," Rachel said. She stabbed her needle into the skirt she was hemming.

"You're not sweet on him, are you?" Esther said, giggling.

Rachel's cheeks turned from pink to red. "He's awful old."

"Stranger things have happened than falling in love with an older man," Esther teased her sister.

Esther and Jenny couldn't get Rachel to say anything more about O'Neil.

Chapter 40:   At the Convention

Mac reached Monterey on Monday, September 3. General Bennet Riley, military governor of California since April 1849, had organized the meeting of delegates in the old Spanish colony.

Mac found Lansford Hastings at the largest hotel in town.

"Caleb McDougall," Hastings shouted. "Just the man I'd hoped to see. The convention sessions started today, and I need a clerk. You ready?"

Shaking Hastings's hand, Mac said, "Yes, sir. I haven't done any legal work in over three years, but I expect I can handle it."

Hastings clapped him on the back. "Good man. Do you have a room?"

"Not yet. And I should buy another suit."

"Let's find you a bed here in the hotel. I want you close by."

The hotel clerk assigned Mac to share a room with William Shannon. Shannon was an attorney a few years older than Mac, a delegate to the convention representing Coloma. Mac and Shannon had met before in Sacramento.

After finding a tailor who promised to have a suit altered to fit by the next morning, Mac dined with Hastings and Shannon.

"I hate to be immodest," Hastings said, "but the group of men gathered for this convention is as talented as any governing group assembled since the federal Constitution was written in Philadelphia."

Shannon nodded. "Not only lawyers like ourselves, but also ranchers, merchants, surveyors, and military officers. Men born throughout the United States, and in Europe, and a few men native to Spanish California. Despite my birth in Ireland, County Mayo, here I am—a delegate to the formation of a new state."

Mac smiled to himself. His father would have no confidence in a man

195

from County Mayo. British nobility might influence Andrew McDougall, but otherwise it would take a Cabot or Lodge born and bred in Boston to impress the man.

Hastings puffed on his cigar. "We've decided to pursue statehood," he informed Mac. "No reason for California to remain a territory."

"Doesn't Congress have to decide whether we merit statehood?" Mac asked.

"President Taylor is on our side. California will be a state." Shannon flashed a wide grin. "Our job is merely to create the institutions to support it."

"We're starting with a blank slate," Hastings added. "We can design the government to suit our aspirations."

"Most men now in California are miners," Mac said. "Are any of the delegates prospectors?"

"I represent a mining district," Shannon said. "And I own a claim. You're a miner also, though you are not a delegate. Surely men like us can do right by our fellow prospectors."

"But the future of California isn't in the mines. It's in the land." Hastings seemed very sure of himself.

"The men I know are all after gold." Mac eyed Hastings while lighting his own cigar.

"Well, then, sir, you counsel me if I don't remember the needs of the miners." Hastings moved on to other topics, apparently bored with the discussion of prospectors.

September 5, 1849. I am settling into my role as clerk. Much of the work is tedious. I attend debates, take notes, then compare my notes with the official record of the Secretary of the Convention.

Mac went to the committee meetings Hastings told him to attend. The first debate he witnessed dealt with which state constitution to use as a model for California. The debate ended when Hastings pronounced, "There is but one Constitution containing the wisdom of the ages laid down by our founders. That, my good friends, is the Constitution of the United States.

We must use that great instrument as our guide."

As the days passed, Mac became more interested in the issues discussed among the delegates. The largest argument was over slavery. The delegates came from both slave-holding and free states—both factions knew their decisions would affect the balance of power in the States.

"I never knew any colored men in either Ireland or New York," Shannon told Mac. "But I saw the deplorable conditions in which slaves were kept in Rio de Janeiro when we sailed around the Horn to California. No one deserves such treatment."

"As a Northerner, I agree," Mac said. "I've known many Negroes who managed their freedom as well as most white men. We had a free Negro couple with us on our overland trip in forty-seven. Tanner was as handy with tools as any man I have known. He saved many a wagon along the way. He's here in California now."

On September 10, a week after the sessions started, Shannon launched the debate on slavery. He moved to include a section in California's Constitution reading, "Neither slavery nor involuntary servitude, unless for the punishment of crimes, shall ever be tolerated in the State."

Morton McCarver, a pro-slavery delegate, tried to amend Shannon's language with an addition, "Nor shall the introduction of free Negroes, under indentures or otherwise, be allowed."

The arguments raged. Ultimately, Shannon's motion passed without McCarver's amendment. But the Negro question came up repeatedly during the remaining weeks of the convention, in one form or another.

Late on Wednesday, September 12, Mac returned to the hotel to find a note from Mrs. John C. Frémont. She invited him to a soirée at the Frémont home in Monterey the following evening.

"So Captain Frémont has arrived," he said to William Shannon as they climbed the stairs to their room.

"Oh, yes. He's one of the delegates. His wife recently came to California and has joined him in Monterey."

"I wonder why I was invited to their gathering. I haven't met either of them." Mac's copy of Frémont's report to Congress about Oregon was dog-eared and torn. He and Captain Pershing had referred to it almost daily on the trail. If Mac had any hero other than his grandfather, it was John Frémont. He was eager to meet the great explorer.

"Who knows? Jessie Benton Frémont is quite a hostess. She will probably invite every delegate and clerk to some event through the course of the convention."

Once in his room, Mac quickly penned an acceptance to Mrs. Frémont and gave the hotel's messenger boy a coin to deliver it the next morning.

At the appointed time, Mac walked to the Frémonts' comfortable suite in an old Mexican building the Army had appropriated. He was ushered into a drawing room that would rival his parents' in Boston.

When his name was announced, a lovely, dark-haired woman walked toward him. "Mr. McDougall," she said, "I am Jessie Frémont. I had the pleasure of meeting an acquaintance of yours on my travels from the States earlier in the year. Miss Susan Abbott? She is visiting me and encouraged me to include you this evening."

Behind Mrs. Frémont Mac caught sight of Susan Abbott's blonde curls. He bowed to Mrs. Frémont. "Delighted, ma'am."

Mac met other delegates and their assistants at the gathering, including his hero John Frémont. He managed not to stammer when he told the captain how valuable his report had been to their wagon company.

"My report?" Frémont laughed. "It bears my name. But I confess my wife wrote much of it. You must tell her how much it helped you."

"Do not confuse the young man, John," Mrs. Frémont said, taking her husband's arm. "You were the one who traveled across our nation. I simply took your words and made them more readable." She turned to Mac. "And the maps, Mr. McDougall? Were they helpful."

"We could not have survived in the wilderness without them," he said.

"Charles Preuss, a German cartographer, was with us." Frémont chuckled. "An excellent mapmaker, but a very fussy man. And particular in his diet."

"John," Mrs. Frémont admonished. "You said the man was a genius."

"Only with maps, my dear. Only with maps." The captain patted his wife's hand, then said to Mac, "I understand you are clerking for Lansford Hastings."

"Yes, sir."

"Another of our explorers of the West." Something in Frémont's tone made Mac wonder what the man thought of Hastings.

"Now, John." Mrs. Frémont seemed to be cautioning her husband.

"The man is a charlatan, Jessie," Frémont said. "I do not mean to denigrate your employer's ability as a lawyer, Mr. McDougall, and he is an able politician. But he sent emigrants on a route to California that killed many of them. You've heard of the Donner party?"

"Yes, sir."

"No more need be said." Frémont's tone was harsh.

"Have you spoken with Miss Abbott yet?" Mrs. Frémont asked Mac, clearly intending to change the subject. "You must renew your acquaintance." She led him to a corner where Susan Abbott held court among several young delegates and clerks.

"Miss Abbott," Mac said with a bow. "I understand I have you to thank for my invitation this evening." Mac hadn't been in the East for over two years, but he assumed her pale green dress was the height of fashion. The silk and lace were finer than the gray frock she'd worn when they dined with her grandfather in Sacramento.

"Why, Grandfather told me you'd decided to attend the convention." She held out her hand. Mac took it and bowed. "I knew then I must accept Mrs. Frémont's invitation to visit. She was kind to extend it to me so we could refresh our acquaintance from the voyage."

"I am delighted to be here," Mac said. "I have known of Captain Frémont's exploits since before I went to Oregon. He is an intrepid surveyor."

"And his wife a courageous woman." Susan smiled. "An example for women hoping to civilize the West."

"Is that your intent, Miss Abbott? To civilize the West?"

"If not before I arrived, then certainly now," she replied. "You cannot deny the roughnecks of Sacramento and the gold fields need taming. Gamblers and drunkards on every corner. Why, even here in Monterey some of the delegates are less than refined."

Mac refrained from asking whether she thought him one of them.

Chapter 41:   Continuing the Debates

To Mac's surprise, Hastings proposed that the California Constitution abolish the death penalty for crimes.

"The time is fast approaching," Hastings asserted, "when a prohibition on the punishment of death shall be engrafted into the laws of all the states of this great nation. No individual has the right to take human life, except in self-defense. And this principle applies equally to the government."

The argument caused Mac to think. He'd taken lives during his time in the West, starting when he defended Jenny in Missouri, again when men had attacked his claim, and probably during the fight with the Indians after Murderer's Bar. He pondered the matter in his journal:

> *September 16, 1849. I have always assumed that "an eye for an eye" is the punishment God desires our justice system to mete out. But the debate this week has caused me to question my assumption. I acted to defend myself and others, except on the ill-fated posse. Still, the deaths sit uneasily on my conscience.*

Ultimately, the delegates rejected Hastings's motion. Through his cigar smoke that evening, Hastings told Mac mournfully, "The nation isn't ready."

The convention delegates also discussed the establishment of banks.

Mac's father had firmly believed state-chartered banks improved the development of commerce. But many delegates argued that banks—indeed all corporate associations—were evil institutions they should ban.

After heated discussion, the majority agreed to permit associations for the deposit of silver and gold. But they refused to permit those associations to issue any notes or paper that would circulate as money.

When Mac wrote in his journal, he thought of the difficulty he'd had sending funds to Jenny in Oregon. The proposed limitations would not make transferring assets in the West any easier.

> *September 17, 1849. I suppose there is merit to the argument that banking fosters speculation, and I suppose it makes sense to limit the creation of specie to the government. But without easy transfer of funds from one source to another, how will commerce grow? And how will men in the West care for families they have left behind?*

Mac received another invitation from the Frémonts, this time for a supper on September 18.

"Miss Abbott seems to have taken a shine to you," Shannon remarked with a grin. "Do you fancy her?"

Susan Abbott was the type of woman his mother would want him to marry. Attractive, educated, able to mingle in society—Mother would not be able to find fault with Miss Abbott. "She probably doesn't know many people here, and I am a friend of her grandfather's. Mrs. Frémont is simply being kind to invite me."

"Well, if Miss Abbott didn't like you, she could certainly tell Mrs. Frémont not to include you. Be careful the young lady doesn't think more of your attentions than you intend."

Mac kept Shannon's caution in mind, but enjoyed the evening thoroughly.

"Why don't you call me 'Susan'?" she said as they talked in the parlor after the meal. "You're such a good friend of Grandfather's."

"Then you must call me 'Mac,'" he said with a smile.

"Oh, that's so informal. Might I call you 'Caleb'?"

"Only my mother calls me that," Mac replied, remembering Jenny's lips pursing as she pronounced his name, "Mac." Now he bowed to Susan, "But as you wish."

Another debate concerned which men in California should have the right to vote. The delegates presumed Negroes would not vote, and the discussion centered on men of Mexican descent.

Hastings rose to declare, "The Treaty of Hildalgo ended our war with Mexico. It demands we recognize the property and rights of the former citizens of Mexico, regardless of their color. If we violate the stipulations of this treaty, we violate the Constitution of the United States. Every man who was a citizen of Mexico is a citizen now of California."

"Just because a man is a citizen doesn't mean California has to permit him to vote," a delegate from Monterey stated.

The plenary sessions and committee meetings, on issue after issue, lasted from morning until late in the evenings. Mac had to decline the next invitation he received from the Frémonts. The evening sessions were conducted over dinner, followed by drinks and cigars. Mac limited his intake of whiskey when he was required to take notes. But a good cigar was a pleasant end to a busy day.

The Negro issue was complicated by boundary questions. How much of the territory east of the Sierra Nevada should be included in the new state? Should California claim the Salt Lake region where the Mormons had settled? Should California be split into a northern free state and a southern slave state?

Hastings was appointed to the committee to determine the boundaries, and William Shannon was also influential on that issue. Shannon proposed that California encompass most of the Sierra Nevada range, but not the Mormon territory, and the delegates ultimately adopted his suggestion.

In the end, the committee created a large single state from north to south, with no expectation that any portion of California would permit the ownership of slaves. If this proposal were adopted, California would be the first state south of the latitude 36°30' to prohibit slavery—a line held inviolate since the Missouri Compromise of 1820.

Even after the question of slavery was resolved, arguments about admitting Negroes to California continued through September. Most delegates from the mining districts adamantly opposed permitting Negroes—free or slave—into their territory. On the other side of the issue, the representatives from San Francisco and San Jose supported citizenship for all men, regardless of color.

"We cannot tolerate the enslavement of those of darker skin," Shannon fumed to Mac one evening. "And it is equally repugnant to ban them from our state."

"I'm not the man you need to convince," Mac said, thinking of the Tanners. They'd left Oregon because they weren't wanted—would they now be forced out of California?

Shannon sipped his cognac, then continued his tirade. "It's nonsense to assume Southern plantation owners would dump their slaves in California, as some delegates say."

Mac laughed. "I'm not arguing with you. Save your breath for the debate."

But the next day in another heated session, a delegate representing Stockton argued, "Even in the absence of slavery, I cast my vote in favor of prohibiting the Negro race from coming amongst us. The Almighty created the Negro to serve the white race, as the instinctive feeling of the Negro is obedience to the white man. If we wish all mankind to be free, then we must not bring the lowest in contact with the highest, or one will rule and the other must serve."

"He's a doctor from Ohio," Shannon whispered to Mac. "But he has spent his adult life in Louisiana—a Southerner by sympathy." Then Shannon stood to argue the points he'd made to Mac the evening before.

One faction of delegates wanted to defer the question to the future legislature. The man who had earlier attempted to amend Shannon's proposal against slavery, Morton McCarver, threw down another gauntlet. "Let us resolve," he said, "that the first legislature elected after this Constitution is adopted must pass laws to prohibit the immigration and settling of Negroes into this state and further prohibit owners of slaves from bringing them into California for the purpose of freeing them."

"There's the rub," Hastings murmured to Mac as they listened to the debate. "No one wants newly freed slaves in the state. They have no skills or resources with which to prosper and will be a drain on the public coffers."

"Many Negroes are quite skilled," Mac said, thinking again of Tanner.

In the end, McCarver's proposal was successful, and the question of admitting Negroes into California was left for the future legislature. The delegates' cavalier abdication of their responsibility appalled Mac. He wrote late one night:

September 25, 1849. If these men of supposedly great education and experience can't—or won't—make difficult decisions, why did they volunteer to serve as delegates?

Chapter 42: Harvest

The harvest kept everyone on Jenny's farm busy. Zeke came almost every day, usually with new instructions for O'Neil. Zeke showed his suspicions about the hired hand, but O'Neil didn't complain when Zeke interfered.

"We'll finish the wheat harvest today," O'Neil reported to Jenny on September 10. "Zeke and his twin brothers will be here to help by midday. We'll git the last of it to the mill by evening. Then we'll start on the barley and oats."

"Rachel and I can help, too," Jenny said. "We've finished putting up the vegetables."

"Don't you rush your work, Miz Jenny. Zeke and I can handle it." O'Neil had taken to calling her "Miz Jenny," like the younger Pershing children. Zeke now made a point of calling her "Jenny." "Next week I'll scythe the meadow for hay. Git a cuttin' done afore the corn's ready to reap."

"You've been a prayer answered, Mr. O'Neil." Jenny smiled at him. Rachel still blushed when the man was around, but Jenny now relied on him. William doted on O'Neil, demanding piggyback rides in the evenings after supper.

When Zeke and the twins arrived midmorning, Zeke asked Jenny, "Why weren't you at church yesterday?"

"William had a fever. He's still croupy."

"We should be able to hire some day laborers to finish the harvest, if we need more men. Several prospectors have returned from California. Seems finding gold is harder than they expected. The nuggets ain't just lying on the ground." Zeke sounded smug. "I could've told them farming is more dependable."

"Any word from Joel?" Jenny asked. She really wanted to know whether anyone coming back from California had seen Mac, but Zeke would most likely have asked about his brother.

"Nope. I asked whether we had mail when I was in town last week. I'd hoped Esther or Pa might have a letter from Joel, but nothing yet." Zeke squinted at her as he answered her unasked question. "And nothing for you from Mac either."

Jenny sighed. "We'll hear soon enough, I expect." While she and Rachel packed a basket of cold dinner for the men and boys and carried it to the fields, she wondered where Mac was—still prospecting, or on his way to Boston.

The next week O'Neil and Zeke mowed the hayfield with sickles, while the twins raked the cut grass behind them and piled it in the wagon. Jenny and Rachel brought them dinner and ginger beer each noon and helped with the raking. Even William followed behind the mowers, placing stray stalks in a basket to take back to Shanty.

When the heat grew to be too much, they rested beneath the trees and ate.

"You teaching school again this winter, Jenny?" Zeke asked on their last afternoon working in the meadow.

Jonathan and David groaned at his question.

"I plan to." She smiled at the twins. "You boys did fine last year. This year I'm expecting you to parse sentences." The twelve-year-olds groaned again.

"New families from the States are arriving," Zeke said. "Maybe some of them will settle nearby and want their young'uns to go to school also."

Jenny nodded. "I could teach a few more children. Might need another bench or two if I have more students."

While Rachel gathered eggs in the barn that evening, O'Neil said quietly to Jenny, "I'll build your benches if you teach me to read and write. Never had the chance to learn as a boy. I can write my name, but that's it."

Jenny suspected O'Neil didn't like confessing his lack of schooling and had waited to catch her alone to ask the question. "We'll start tonight." She smiled at him. "You've been such a help, it's the least I can do." She found a primer and gave it to O'Neil. "I'll need this for the children when school starts," she said. "But you can use it now. Sit by the fire, and I'll listen to you read."

Before she doused the lamp that evening, Jenny wrote:

> Saturday, September 15th—I forget how fortunate I have been to have received an education, though I do not use it much except when teaching. Mr. O'Neil, who is a fine man, never had the opportunity to learn to read. What he missed! And how I miss having many books around me now.
>
> Tomorrow is William's second birthday. I am so thankful to have him. I am too busy to bake a cake—we will celebrate next week.

The following Tuesday, after Jenny had her receipt from the mill for her wheat harvest, she went to Abernethy's store in Oregon City. She paid Zeke and O'Neil with a portion of her wheat, first crediting her account at the store, and then asking the clerk to transfer credit to the men's accounts. In the absence of much coinage, farmers and townsfolk alike bartered grain as their primary instrument of exchange in Oregon.

As Jenny submitted her grain receipts to the clerk, she smiled in satisfaction at the summer's yield. With Zeke's and O'Neil's assistance, she'd managed the farm without Mac or the Tanners. She'd had to spend some of Mac's coins on the mules and on sundry other items, but she'd made it through another harvest.

Jenny stocked up on supplies, needing not only flour and sugar for a cake for William, but dry goods and cloth as well.

"Glad to see you paid down your balance," the clerk Hamilton told her when he tallied her purchases. "Don't go building it back up too fast now, you hear?"

Jenny seethed at his patronizing tone. The man hadn't talked to any men like that, nor to the wives whose husbands were at home. But she would need the store's credit again through the winter, so she held her tongue.

"You cashing out, Mr. O'Neil?" she asked when she gave him his accounting. "Or would you like to stay here for the winter? I'd be obliged if you did. And we can continue to work on your reading."

"Ain't no reason to leave till spring," he said. "I'll winter here. Do your chores, if'n you'll give me meals. And I appreciate the lessons. Come spring, I'll see what the news from California is, then decide what to do."

As Jenny wrote in her journal before bed, her doubt whether she could keep the farm resurfaced.

Tuesday, September 18th—How long will Zeke and Mr. O'Neil continue to work my land? I may need to find another hired hand. Or will I have to forfeit the claim when Mac has been away two years? I need to talk to Doc again.

On Wednesday, she baked a cake, killed a chicken, and made a belated birthday dinner for William. Rachel, O'Neil, Zeke, and the twins joined them, and she thanked the men and boys for their harvest work.

She kept her fears to herself.

Each evening Jenny helped O'Neil read the primer. He was hesitant at first, but as September days waned, he began to improve.

He hadn't wanted his lessons in Rachel's presence, but Jenny convinced him the cabin was too small for her to tutor him privately. After supper, Rachel washed the dishes. Jenny dried them and looked over O'Neil's shoulder to assist him as he sounded out words he did not know. Some evenings the women switched places, and Rachel assisted O'Neil. The younger girl grew more comfortable with the hired hand, smiling in encouragement when he figured out a new word on his own.

On the last Saturday in September, Oregon City held a harvest celebration. Some farmers were still reaping their crops, but winter would come soon, and most of the hard work of summer was behind them. Unlike the year before, Jenny decided to attend.

When Jenny saw Doc at the celebration, she pulled him aside to ask him about the land laws. "You told me when Mac left he couldn't be gone more than two years, or I'd lose the land. Is that still the law?"

"If a man's not on his land, he can pay a tax instead," Doc said. "It's five dollars. Do you have the money?"

Jenny nodded. "I'll find the money, if that's all I need to do."

Doc shook his head, but said only, "Let me ask around. McDougall left in February of forty-eight? You have a few months yet."

New emigrants joined the established farmers for the harvest feast. Jenny and William shared their meal with a family named Bingham from Illinois. The Binghams had three school-aged children, as well as a daughter named Meg, who was two years old, like William. Esther and her family also sat near Jenny, Esther now heavily swollen with her second child. The older children ran in the meadow, and the toddlers played together on a blanket while the adults talked.

"Most of our company turned south at the Parting of the Ways," Mrs. Bingham told Jenny. "They were all after gold. But Mr. Bingham and I wanted to farm. And now that I see Oregon men returning from California, I know we were right."

"The land here is good," Daniel Abercrombie said. "Fertile, with plenty of rain."

"Jenny's husband and my brother are still in California," Esther said. "We haven't heard from them since spring. That's the hardest part—not knowing."

"Surely they will send word," Mrs. Bingham said. "They wouldn't be so cruel as to leave you in ignorance of their fate. Perhaps I can understand a brother not writing, but a husband . . . ." Her words trailed off.

If Jenny had been Mac's wife, she would have been hurt by the woman's insinuation Mac didn't care about her. As it was, she had no right to expect anything from him. But she still hoped for some word of how he was doing.

Chapter 43:   Debating Next Steps

By the end of September 1849, the last provisions of the California Constitution emerged from the debates. A small committee wrote the final text, which was then translated into Spanish, so that the document would have two official versions. The resulting Constitution was read to the delegates, passed, and signed in early October. Lansford Hastings was not a part of the final drafting committee, and there was little for Mac to do.

He wrote one evening:

> *October 4, 1949. I spend my days wondering how to occupy my time this winter. Would it still be possible to catch a ship to Panama and reach Boston in the spring?*

Susan Abbott remained with the Frémonts through the end of the convention, and Mac spent several evenings with them. He and Captain John Frémont sat at the table after the meal drinking port, and Mac listened to his hero's tales of traveling the West.

When Mac first tried to coax him into telling stories, Frémont said, "You've read my report. What more can I tell you?"

"I'm glad of the opportunity to hear it unfiltered from the source," Mac responded.

So the great explorer indulged Mac's interest.

"And what of young Miss Abbott?" Frémont said late one evening in the last days of the convention. "My wife and I have developed quite an affection for her. Do you share our sentiments? In the absence of her grandfather, I must ask."

"Miss Abbott is charming," Mac said, raising his glass. "To the ladies. Shall we join them?" He swallowed the last of his port.

In the parlor Mac found himself sitting beside Susan while the Frémonts discussed plans to return to San Francisco.

"And you, Caleb, what are your plans?" Susan asked.

Mac shrugged. "I suppose I will head back to Boston. I've sold my share in the mine to Joel Pershing. There's nothing to keep me in California."

"Nothing?" Susan smiled at him from under lowered eyelids. "Grandfather has offered you his store. You're not interested? He and I have decided to set up house in San Francisco. Captain Frémont and Grandfather both believe its harbor will make it the largest city in California. Perhaps as big as Boston or New York."

"I'm considering the store," Mac said. "But I don't see myself remaining in California."

"Why not?"

Jenny's face popped into Mac's mind. Susan knew nothing of Jenny, so he simply said, "I suppose I feel I must go home someday." But where was home?

As Mac sat ruminating one evening in the hotel's saloon, William Shannon joined him. "What's next for you?" Shannon asked as he signaled the bartender for a whiskey.

Everyone asked him the same thing. "That's what I'm trying to decide," Mac said, raising his finger for another glass also. "And you?"

"I've been elected judge in the criminal court in Sacramento." Shannon said. "I'm returning there tomorrow. We should have dinner when we're both back."

"If I'm there," Mac said.

"Where else would you be?"

"Boston. Maybe it's time."

"You haven't seemed eager to leave California this past month." Shannon lit a cigar.

"My family is in Boston. My brother's law practice." Mac sighed. "But

I have no desire to go. And no desire to shackle myself in a law office."

"You sold your interest in your mine, didn't you?"

Mac grinned as his second drink arrived. "I've come to enjoy the comforts of Monterey—clean sheets, good whiskey, and cigars. Makes a man's day easy. Much easier than mining."

"And Susan Abbott is here." Shannon's smile was almost a leer.

"And Miss Abbott is here." Mac sipped his drink.

"If you like comfort, maybe you're cut out for life as a lawyer after all," Shannon said. "You could join me. I aim to practice law in addition to my judicial duties."

"I'll think about it." Mac liked Shannon, but he felt too restless to look forward to sitting at a desk all day.

Lansford Hastings joined the two younger men. "Governor Riley's set a vote of the people on November 13 to accept the Constitution," Hastings said. "He wants to hold the election before the rainy season begins. We could use men canvassing the territory to encourage voters to approve the document. McDougall, why don't you return to Sacramento and help out?"

Mac shrugged. "Why not?" It would put off his decision for another month. Maybe through the winter—by November it might be too late to leave for Boston.

"We'll be electing the first legislature at the same time," Hastings continued. "You could run for office."

Mac shook his head. "No. I won't run for a seat. I don't want to tie myself down for years in California. But I'll spend a month in Sacramento campaigning for the Constitution. I can attest to the good intentions of the delegates."

"Well, most of them." Hastings raised a humorous eyebrow and puffed his cigar.

After Hastings had drunk his fill and gone to bed, Mac and Shannon continued talking and drinking. Shannon brought up Susan Abbott again. "If you stay in California, will you see her again?"

"Her grandfather is a good friend, so I suppose I shall."

"She's going to expect you to declare. Or her grandfather will."

"Declare?" Mac knew what Shannon meant, but he wondered how far his friend would push the discussion about Susan.

"Don't be obtuse, Mac. You're smarter than that. She'll expect you to marry her."

"I haven't given any thought to marrying her."

"Well, you'd better. You can't toy with her like the looser women in California. Maybe you've been away from the East too long. Proper young women expect an offer of marriage from men who spend time with them."

Mac downed his whiskey. "I'm going to bed." He recalled Consuela telling him his bed would be cold.

Chapter 44:   Smallpox

Jenny started her new school term the Monday after the harvest celebration. The older Bingham children joined her students from the prior year. She asked Rachel to assist with the younger children. "You've done well working with Mr. O'Neil on his reading," she told Rachel. "The little ones will be much easier."

William was still too young for school and played on the buffalo skin beside the students' benches. Jenny or Rachel had to stop their teaching frequently to care for him when he grew bored.

A few days later Rachel seemed distracted. "What's wrong?" Jenny asked.

"I'm worried about Esther," Rachel said. "Her baby's coming any time, and she gets so tired caring for Jonah and Cordelia."

Jenny shook her head. "Can't your papa take Jonah awhile? It's too much for Esther."

"Mother Amanda refuses because of her baby Franklin. She says she has too many to tend already. May I go stay with Esther?"

"Of course," Jenny said. "It's selfish of me to keep you here when Esther needs you."

"They don't have much room, but I'll live there till her baby's born." Rachel twisted her apron in her hands. "What about the school? Maybe I can come help one or two days a week till Esther's confinement."

"I'll manage if I have to," Jenny said.

That night she wrote:

Thursday, October 4ᵗʰ—For Esther's sake, I must let Rachel go. I will miss her company dearly. She has become a good friend and such a help with school, house, and William.

Today is my 17th birthday. I doubt anyone in Oregon even knows.

The following Sunday morning William complained, "Mama, I'm hot."

Jenny felt his forehead—burning. O'Neil brought her a bucket of water, and she removed William's shirt and wiped his chest and back with a soft rag. The toddler shivered and cried. "I hurt" was all he could tell his mother as he wept.

"There's smallpox around," O'Neil said quietly. "A company of this year's emigrants brought it with them. Lots of folks sick."

"Smallpox," Jenny whispered. She hugged William close. "You think he has smallpox?"

"One family it struck is the Binghams. Their baby's sick. You spent time with them at the picnic. Their older children been comin' to your school."

"My heavens!" Jenny said. "Go get Doc Tuller."

O'Neil set out at once. While she waited for Doc, Jenny fretted over William and continued to bathe him.

"My head hurts, Mama," William complained. He puked up the water she gave him to sip. Jenny nearly vomited herself in fear.

She tried not to let the toddler see how afraid she was, but she was close to tears when O'Neil and the doctor returned.

"Is it smallpox?" Jenny asked, crossing her arms as if she could ward off the response she dreaded.

Doc examined William's body, arms and legs, paying particular attention to his hands and feet. He listened to the boy's heart and felt his forehead. "Too soon to tell," he said. "Early symptoms are there—fever, vomiting, achiness. But no spots yet. That'll be the true sign."

"What do I do?" Jenny's knuckles turned white when she clutched the table where William sat for Doc's examination.

"Watch him. Keep him away from other people. Give him lots of water. Like you did for McDougall when he had cholera." Doc gathered his instruments. "You'll have to close your school till the boy's well. I'll stop by the Pershing farm on my way home. Jonathan and David can tell the rest of your students." Doc frowned at Jenny. "You ever had smallpox?"

She shook her head. "I don't think so. Mama never told me I did, and I don't remember it."

"If not, you're likely to get it now. It spreads fast, and you been around your pupils and William."

Jenny gulped and nodded.

"There's an innoculation in England, and it's used in the East," Doc said. "Some doctors swear by it, others think it causes more harm than good. But no matter, 'cause I ain't got any to give folks."

"I've had smallpox, Doc." O'Neil gestured at the marks on his face. "When I was a lad."

"Then you can help nurse the boy," Doc said. "Keep Jenny away as much as you can. Seems the closer someone is to the sick, the more likely they are to get the disease."

"I'll take care of my son," Jenny said, lifting her chin and clenching her jaw. She wouldn't abandon William, even if she became ill.

When Doc had packed his bag and washed his hands, she escorted him to the cabin door. "Could William die, Doc?" she whispered, tears running down her cheeks.

Doc patted her arm. "Don't worry about that yet. Most folks pull through. Keep water in him and watch the fever. But if it's smallpox, he's likely to end up scarred. You know that, don't you?"

"Just as long as I still have him," Jenny said. She would love William, scars and all. But she couldn't lose him.

When Rachel stopped by the next morning, Jenny wouldn't let her in the cabin. "I don't want you catching it," Jenny said. "Esther needs you. Any sign of her baby yet?"

Rachel shook her head. "This one's taking its time."

"Don't let Esther anywhere near here," Jenny pleaded. "She can't risk getting sick."

"I'll bring hot food every day, so's you don't have to cook," Rachel said. "I'll leave the pot outside, and Mr. O'Neil can bring it in."

Jenny's days and nights ran together. A few days after William came down with the fever, he developed red spots on his face and hands. Then spots sprang up on his stomach and back. The spots turned to blisters, which filled and burst, then scabbed.

Jenny hadn't nursed anyone seriously ill since Mac had had cholera at Ash Hollow along the trail. She'd felt so alone tending him then, surrounded by others in their company ministering to their own invalids. Doc Tuller had been there, but he rushed from tent to tent caring for all the patients. The same was true now. Doc traveled from cabin to cabin looking after people with smallpox. He only came to see William every two or three days.

O'Neil insisted on relieving Jenny of much of William's care. "The boy likes me, Miz Jenny," he said. "And you need your sleep." He sent her up to the loft to rest, while he watched William during the nights. During the days, he did the chores, started the corn harvest, and—Jenny hoped—caught a few hours' sleep in the barn. The man seemed tireless.

"You're doing what you can, Jenny," Doc Tuller told her during one visit. "The boy's fortunate. Not many pox on his face. Are you feeling all right?"

She nodded. "I don't seem to be getting sick."

"Are you sleeping?"

"Some, thanks to Mr. O'Neil. He works all day and watches William at night."

"And eating?"

Jenny nodded again. "Rachel brings over dishes from Esther. And I keep a pot of soup on the fire."

"The boy'll be better soon. If you stay well, you'll be back to teaching by the end of November."

"How are my students?" Jenny asked. "Have any of them . . . ?" She couldn't bear to ask if any had died.

"None of them dead yet, though some of my other patients have died," he said. "But the Binghams had it bad. All their children, especially young Meg. And one of the Abercrombie granddaughters."

Jenny gasped. "Those poor families."

"Don't open your school till all your students have been without scabs for two weeks," Doc said, packing his bag. "Seems to be passed along while the pox are open and scabbing. And don't let William scratch. Or his scars'll be worse, and he could get gangrene."

Jenny grabbed a moment to write that evening:

Monday, October 29th—Doc says William is improving, but not out of the woods yet. Some poor souls have died of this horrible disease, though none of my students. Some are marked for life. I pray my boy heals!

Jenny and O'Neil couldn't keep William from scratching. She tried distracting the two-year-old with blocks and other toys, but he was too fretful to play for long. If she read to him, he scratched. She put socks on his hands, but he pulled them off.

Some of his pox grew infected and turned an angry red, visibly pulsing with heat. William's fever raged again, and he became delirious, screaming about spiders in the corner.

"Too bad the boy's pa ain't here," O'Neil said one night. He held William while Jenny sponged her son with a damp cloth.

"What do you mean?" Jenny asked. Did he mean Mac, or had he heard something else about who William's father was?

"S-s-sorry, Miz Jenny," O'Neil stammered. "I shouldn't have spoke."

Jenny felt faint when she realized why O'Neil had brought up William's father. She sank to the floor beside William's bed. "You mean William might die? Without his father seeing him again?"

"I shouldn't have said nothin'."

"William will be fine. He has to be. He's all I have." Jenny pulled the wet rag from the bucket by William's bed and wrung it out. "We have to bring his fever down." She couldn't speak further for the lump in her throat.

She wished Mac were with her. He'd always given Jenny strength.

"Sweet Jesus, save my boy," Jenny sobbed as she bathed William in oatmeal to soothe his itchiness. Prayer and a loving hand were all she could offer him now.

Chapter 45:   Return to Sacramento

Mac rode Valiente back to Sacramento. The young town now almost filled the delta formed by the American and Sacramento Rivers. Mac heard the din of pounding hammers long before he saw the new construction.

After he reached the Golden Nugget and settled into a room, Mac discovered news of the delegates' work and the Constitution's terms had already spread. Most men seemed predisposed to accept what the convention had decided. They easily agreed to vote for approval of the Constitution.

Men seeking seats in the new legislature campaigned for votes throughout the region. John Sutter, son of the Sutter who had built the fort, was a candidate for governor. He'd been a convention delegate, but Mac had little interest in politicking for the man. He relished the process of making laws, not promoting the personalities of elected officials.

Mac rode out to the gold claim and found Clarence Tanner laboring with Joel and Huntington. "How's mining life?" he asked Tanner.

"Like anythin' else," Tanner replied. "Man gits out what he puts in."

"How's Hatty?"

"Doin' fine." Tanner smiled. "Leavin' Oregon was good for her. She's takin' in laundry from men in these parts. Earns as much gold dust with her hands in clean water as I take out of the dirty ground."

Huntington's cough had worsened in the cool autumn weather. "I 'spect this is my last winter," he told Mac.

"You mean you'll pack it in next spring? Quit mining?" Mac asked.

"Nope," Huntington replied. "I mean I'll be packed under the earth come spring."

Mac grimaced. He hadn't realized the old man was so ill. "Leave now and go to town. You have your gold to live on."

Huntington shook his head. "Minin' is what I know. I'll die with my boots on and my feet in the creek."

Mac pushed his hat back on his forehead. "Well, I'm not so stupid as to keep doing what's hurting me. I'm planning to winter in town. Come look me up if you change your mind."

After spending one night on the claim, Mac headed back to Sacramento. He went to the postal office and asked for his mail, receiving in return a letter from Oregon City—from Jenny. Had she seen the letter from Consuela yet? If so, why was she writing?

He opened the letter outside the postal office and sighed. It contained only old news—Jenny had explained why she was teaching and told him the Tanners were leaving. The letter was dated at the end of April—why had it taken so long to reach Sacramento? Or had he missed it before he went to Monterey?

If he'd known the Tanners were headed to California before he'd dictated the letter for Consuela to write, would it have made a difference? Mac didn't know. He'd planned all along to have someone write Jenny that he was dead. But he'd thought then that the Tanners were still with her.

That evening Mac sat alone in the Golden Nugget, drinking whiskey into the night. He worried about Jenny and wondered why he had nothing to look forward to in life.

Consuela ignored him until he was one of the few men still at a table. "You look lonely," she said, passing by his table with an open bottle. "Or angry."

"Not angry," Mac said. "Just don't have anywhere I need to be."

"Then you're lonely. And so you spend your time and money on whiskey." She filled his glass.

"Seems so."

"At least you're not a gambler like your young friend Joel. Takes longer to lose your money with drink." Consuela wiped the neck of the whiskey bottle. "Did you post the letter I wrote for you?"

Mac nodded.

"Still searching for what makes you happy?"

He didn't want to talk about himself. "What about you, Consuela?" he challenged. "Are you happy?"

Consuela looked up toward the chandelier, then turned back to Mac, tears glistening in her eyes. She shook her head.

"Then why do you stay here? Tanner's wife takes in laundry in the gold country. You could make your living another way."

"I'm with child," she whispered.

"What?" Mac tugged on her arm until she sat in the chair beside him. "When?"

"Come spring, I'll have a *niño*."

"Who's the father?"

Consuela stared at Mac. "I'm a whore. *Yo que se.*"

"Joel Pershing?"

"I doubt it." She lifted a shoulder. "Only *Dios* knows."

"What will you do?"

She shrugged. "Prospectors don't mind if a whore is pregnant."

"But how will you care for the baby?"

"Two of the other girls have *niños*."

"It's no place for a child."

"That's not your problem." Consuela rose and flounced away.

Mac seethed as if it were his problem. He thought of Bridget and his unborn child. Of Jenny and William. Of Consuela—now alone and pregnant. He finished his drink and headed to his room, where he paced and plotted. Then he pulled out his journal and wrote:

October 25, 1849. Consuela is expecting a child. I need to talk to Joel.

Early the next morning Mac rode out of town, pushing Valiente to a fast canter toward the mining claim. He shouldn't be angry about Consuela's situation—he'd done nothing to cause it. He'd atoned for his sin with Bridget by saving Jenny and then freeing her. Hadn't he?

If anyone he knew was responsible, it was Joel, and there was no way to know if Joel had fathered the child. So many times he'd told himself Joel would have to learn his own lessons. Well, it was time for Joel to face the consequences of his actions. Time for Joel to step up.

If Joel wouldn't take responsibility, Mac had no obligation to Consuela. Other than the obligation of friendship. Someone had to help Consuela and her child.

Mac's irritation grew with every mile he and Valiente traveled. He kept the horse moving with few rests. New snow was visible in the mountains as they approached the mining valley, but the trail they followed was clear. With no pack animal trailing behind, Mac arrived at the end of a single day of hard riding.

The evening sky was almost as dark as the hills above the valley when he dismounted. Only Hatty Tanner was outside, tending a kettle hung over a small campfire. "Hello, Hatty. Where's Joel?" Mac asked.

Hatty greeted him with a smile. "In the cabin with Huntington, I 'spect. I ain't seen him since supper."

"Thanks." Mac tied Valiente's reins to a tree and strode to the cabin. He threw open the door without knocking. "Joel," he said through his teeth. "Consuela's pregnant."

Joel looked up from the bunk where he sat whittling. "So?"

"It could be your child."

Joel frowned, thinking, then shook his head. "Nope. I ain't been with her in a while. I been seeing Ethel. Lot of men more likely to have knocked her up than me. Besides, what's it to you?"

"She can't raise a child in a whorehouse."

"Ain't you seen the other brats upstairs? She won't be the first."

"So you won't take responsibility for Consuela and the child?" Mac knew he wasn't handling this well. But he wanted Joel to be the man he hadn't been with Bridget. Or with Jenny.

"Damn it, Mac," Joel said, standing up. "Consuela's bastard ain't my concern. I told you—I ain't been with her in months, I don't think. Even if I had, she's a whore. Ain't no man the father. You sure you ain't been with her? Way you're acting—"

Mac lunged for Joel.

Huntington shoved an arm between them. Mac checked his fist before he struck the old man.

"Calm down, boys," Huntington said. "Y'all sit." Huntington pushed Mac into a chair, saying, "You can't make Joel do nothin' 'bout the brat. 'Tain't your concern neither."

That's what Mac had told himself, but he wasn't convinced it was true. He blew out a deep breath. "She needs help."

"She's a grown woman," Huntington said. "She's made her choices."

"But now there's a child."

"You made that clear," Huntington said. "Now sleep off your mad, and take yourself back to town in the mornin'. Unless you want to git back to minin'."

Mac shook his head and went outside to sleep by the Tanners' fire. In the light of the dying embers, he wrote:

October 27, 1849. Joel will not help. It is up to me.

The next day Mac headed back to Sacramento after eating the breakfast Hatty made him. He kept Valiente to a slower pace than the breakneck trip to the claim the day before. The autumn sky was clear, and the aspen leaves golden as the sunrise. But snow had fallen in the higher altitudes during the night.

Mac mulled over his options. He considered Consuela a friend—he couldn't abandon her. He needed to offer her an alternative to prostitution.

He arrived at noon on Monday and went directly to Nate's store. "Your offer to sell still good?" Mac asked the older man.

Nate continued weighing the gold sample in front of him. When he finished, he asked, "What's changed your mind?"

"Looking for something new. Something to tide me over until spring. Running your store will do."

"Ships are still sailing from San Francisco to Panama. And there's a steamship from here to San Francisco. You could be on your way to Boston in a week."

"I did enough lawyering in Monterey to last me awhile. Not ready to go back to Boston yet."

"The gold claim?"

"You know I sold my interest to Joel. They don't need me hanging around."

Nate squinted at Mac. "Minding the store isn't easy. And you'll need to learn to work the scales."

"I'm not looking for easy. I'm looking for busy."

"Does this have anything to do with Susan?" Nate asked.

"No."

"She's back from Monterey now. Told me you spent a lot of time with the Frémonts while she visited." Nate wiped off the counter.

"I enjoyed our conversations very much. Susan's a nice girl. But I'm only looking for something to do through the winter." Mac couldn't look Nate in the eye. He'd spoken the truth that buying the store had nothing to do with Susan. But he didn't want to explain his intentions to Nate. What he wanted was a place for Consuela, even though she'd made it clear she didn't need him. And he wanted a reason to delay going back to Boston.

"Just want a way to keep your mind off your troubles, huh?" Nate said with an eyebrow raised.

"Something like that."

Nate harrumphed. "What troubles do you have, son? You're young. You're rich. Most men don't have nearly the education or breeding you have."

"Will you sell me the store or not?"

"Sure, I'll sell you the store." Nate named a price, then frowned at Mac. "You draw up the papers. But I'll bet you five pounds of gold dust you'll want to sell it back in the spring."

"I'll bring you a contract in the morning." Mac slapped his hat on his head and left the shop.

Chapter 46:   Recovery and Loss

Jenny didn't allow Zeke in her cabin, because he'd never had smallpox, but he stopped by every few days. She thought he came mostly to watch O'Neil. On the last Tuesday of October, Zeke brought over a pot of stew from Rachel, who was still living with Esther and Daniel Abercrombie. Esther's household had remained free of smallpox.

"Esther had a boy last Saturday," Zeke said when he handed Jenny the stew. "Named him Samuel Franklin, after both grandfathers." Zeke sounded disgusted. "Why she had to saddle the child with Samuel Abercrombie's name is beyond me."

"I imagine Mr. Abercrombie is proud," Jenny said.

Zeke snorted. "I saw him at church on Sunday. Acted like he birthed the boy himself. It's his first grandson after three granddaughters—Douglass's two daughters and Esther's Cordelia."

Jenny laughed. "Well, let's hope he treats little Samuel better than he does everyone else. He's been a bully since we met him in Independence."

William slowly recuperated while the autumn days grew shorter and the rains began. He was left with two pox scars on his forehead, another on his cheek, a few on his hands and feet, and some on his belly. Jenny tried to keep him amused with finger games and stories, but the boy fussed constantly.

She and O'Neil continued to tend the boy. Doc told her to keep everyone else out of the cabin. Jenny prayed daily in thanksgiving that

William's life had been spared, but she grew weary with the isolation.

"Most folks are better now," Doc Tuller told her when he visited in early November. "Had five people die on me, but the rest survived. One boy went blind."

"So sad," Jenny murmured.

"And lots with scars. Your William is lucky his ain't too bad." Doc sighed. "Little Meg Bingham, she'll never be the same. And the older Abercrombie girl is left with a pocked face also."

"Those poor girls." Jenny shook her head.

"Old Samuel Abercrombie ain't taking it well." Doc frowned at her. "He's blaming you."

"Me?"

"I told him the pox came with one of the emigrant companies. Probably the Binghams' wagon train. He thinks his granddaughter got it at your school."

"What could I have done?"

"Nothing. No way to know till folks got sick."

"When can I reopen my school?"

Doc shrugged. "Should be safe by next Monday. Your pupils have all been well long enough. But don't let in any new children, unless they've been free of any sickness for at least two weeks."

"How's Esther? And her new son?" Jenny asked.

"Both healthy," Doc told her as he left.

After Doc gave her permission to leave her claim, Jenny went to Captain Pershing's home to ask the twins to go to all her pupils' homes and tell them school would start on Monday. Despite the boys' groans, they agreed.

She wrote by lamplight after William was in bed:

> *Thursday, November 8th—My school will reopen on Monday. I hope my students all return—lessons had barely started when William sickened. It will be difficult to manage without Rachel.*

During the first week after her school resumed, Jenny was so busy she had no chance to visit Esther. Her first trip into Oregon City in over a month took place on Sunday, November 18, when she and William went to church.

Esther's whole household was there—Esther, Daniel, and Rachel, as well as the three children, Jonah, Cordelia, and newborn Samuel. A crowd of Abercrombies and Pershings surrounded them, and it took Jenny fifteen minutes after the service to move close enough to whisper a word of congratulations.

Jenny stroked baby Samuel's cheek. "He's beautiful," she told Esther. "How are you managing?"

"Rachel is a gift from God," Esther said. "She minds Jonah and Cordelia, so I can nurse the baby. And she helps with the chores and cooking."

"Do you want her to stay with you?" Jenny asked, her heart sinking. She'd hoped Rachel would return to her cabin, but Esther had first claim on her sister.

Esther nodded. "For a while. We're cramped, but Daniel added a room onto our cabin. Rachel, Jonah, and Cordelia sleep there. How's William?"

Jenny gestured at her son, who ran around the churchyard with Jonah. "Much better. Some scars, but nothing like poor Meg Bingham." The little girl stood across the yard, her face covered in pockmarks. Her mother clutched the two-year-old tightly by the hand. "Mrs. Bingham won't let her go."

"She barely survived, Mrs. Tuller told me," Esther said. "Her ma is probably still afraid of losing her."

"Or of what others will say." Jenny shook her head. "People can be so unkind. Annabelle Abercrombie is scarred, too."

Esther sniffed. "Much as I don't like Father Abercrombie, I'm sorry for poor Annabelle. How will she ever catch a beau now?"

"At least they're all alive." Jenny loved William, pockmarks and all.

"Pa got a letter from Joel this week," Esther continued. "He's fine. Says Captain McDougall went to some political convention in Monterey. And sold his gold claim to Joel. Did you know that?"

"Mac is well?" Jenny asked eagerly.

"Joel didn't say he wasn't. Seems we hear more from Joel than you do from your husband. Oh!" Esther exclaimed. "Daniel picked up a letter for you in town yesterday. I have it in my pocket." She pulled it out and handed it to Jenny. "Who's it from?"

Jenny looked at it. "I don't recognize the handwriting."

"Daniel said it came on a ship from San Francisco. Do you think it's from Captain McDougall?"

"I don't know."

"Well, open it," Esther urged.

Jenny stared at the letter. If it was about Mac, she wanted to know right away. But why wouldn't he have written himself?

"I'll wait until I'm home," she told Esther.

The letter crinkled in Jenny's pocket all Sunday afternoon, but she didn't have time alone until after she fed O'Neil and William, washed the dishes, and put William to bed. The toddler was tired and cranky after the excitement of his first trip to town since his illness.

When at last Jenny sat alone in the lamplight, her hands shook as she broke the seal on the letter. A legal document fell to the ground. Jenny picked it up without looking at it and put it on the table.

The letter was from a Consuela Montenegro, Jenny saw, glancing at the signature. Who was she?

Dead!

Mac was dead!

Jenny shrieked once, then stifled her sobs to a low keening, not wanting to wake William. Her supper rose in her throat.

It couldn't be true, she thought. Mac couldn't be dead. He was so strong.

But cholera had almost killed him along the trail. And she'd almost lost William to smallpox. Illness or injury could fell anyone. And why would this Montenegro woman write her if Mac were *not* dead?

Still, according to the news Esther had from Joel, Mac had sold his gold claim and gone to a political convention. Had he done those things before his illness?

Or was Consuela Montenegro lying for some dreadful, dreadful reason?

Jenny read the letter again, not knowing what to believe. Then she looked at the document on the table—a deed to the Oregon land she lived on. Mac had given her the farm. She'd rather have Mac—alive and with her.

After Jenny went to bed, she couldn't keep her sobs silent. She muffled her face in Mac's pillow, hugging herself the way Mac never had.

Then it dawned on her—maybe the deed Mac had sent wasn't valid. Could she lose the land as well as Mac? She was a woman, only seventeen years old—could she hold title to the land? If Mac was dead and she couldn't own the land, what would happen to her and William?

Maybe she shouldn't tell anyone about the letter or the deed—keep the letter's contents secret. She would have to decide quickly, because Esther would certainly ask.

She had to think. She had to know more.

The only people she could talk to were the Tullers.

Monday afternoon was cold and rainy. A chill wind blew down the Willamette River valley. Jenny let her students leave after their morning classes, then approached O'Neil, who was chopping firewood. "Would you please watch William?" she asked. "I need to see Doc Tuller."

"You all right, Miz Jenny?" O'Neil said. "You look pale. And your eyes are red. You ain't looked good all day." Then he hemmed and hawed about not meaning anything bad by that, just hoping she was fit.

"I'm fine, Mr. O'Neil. Please keep William with you in the barn." And Jenny rode Poulette over to the Tuller claim.

"Doc ain't here," Mrs. Tuller said, when Jenny arrived. "He's out on calls. Don't know when he'll be back."

"It's Mac," Jenny said, tears flowing as she spoke.

"What's wrong, dear?" Mrs. Tuller asked. "Come sit down." Mrs. Tuller poured her a cup of tea, then sat with Jenny at the table.

Jenny pulled out the letter. "It says Mac is dead."

Mrs. Tuller gasped. "Dead? What happened?"

"You read it," Jenny said, handing Mrs. Tuller the letter.

"Fever. Brief illness. Dying wish. Consuela Montenegro." Mrs. Tuller looked up. "Who is she?"

"I don't know," Jenny wailed.

"You poor child."

"It can't be true," Jenny said, sobbing. "It can't be. Joel wrote Captain

Pershing Mac had been to Monterey. And sold his gold claim. Joel didn't say anything about Mac being ill. Maybe it's not true."

"Nobody would write such a wicked falsehood."

"I have to know the truth. I have to know what happened to Mac." Jenny stood and paced the room. "And I have to know about the land here. Mac deeded the land to me—is it any good?" She thrust the deed at Mrs. Tuller.

"Well, if Captain McDougall's dead, no one will question you marrying someone else. You don't need his land."

"I can't marry anyone else, not until I find out what happened to Mac. I loved him."

"Now's a fine time to realize that. If you'd married him two years ago, you wouldn't be in this pickle."

Jenny shook her head. "I wasn't ready then. I don't know if I'd marry him now. But I do love him, and I don't want him dead." She buried her face in her hands.

"We'll have to ask Doc what to do. You go on home. I'll send him over tomorrow."

Jenny had been too distraught to write the evening before. But when she arrived home, the first thing she did was to pull out her journal.

Monday, November 19—Some woman in California wrote to tell me Mac is dead—I pray it isn't true. It is too much to bear after almost losing William. I am desolate.

The rain continued on Tuesday, and Jenny's spirits matched the sodden skies. She could barely focus on the lessons she taught, and was thankful the Abercrombie and Bingham children had not come to class that day.

Late in the afternoon, after her few other students had gone home, the Tullers arrived at Jenny's claim in their wagon. O'Neil tied their horse to the paddock railing, then Jenny again sent William to the barn with the hired man.

"You got yourself in a fine fix, Jenny," Doc said, glowering, as they walked into the cabin. "You should have married McDougall when you could."

"Shhh," Jenny said, looking back to be sure O'Neil could not hear them. "Do you think it's true, what the letter says?" She gave it to him to read.

After reading, Doc said, "Why would this woman lie to you?" He shook his head. "But if you doubt, only thing you can do is write him. See if he responds. The man owes you the truth."

"If he's alive," Jenny whispered.

"Did you get a deed to the land, like this Montenegro woman said?"

Jenny nodded and handed Doc the paper. "It was sealed in with the letter. Does this make me the owner of the claim?"

"You write McDougall." Doc said. "Write Miss Montenegro and Joel Pershing also. Let's see what responses you get. In the meantime, don't say anything about this letter to anyone. I'll ask around about the deed."

Chapter 47: Storekeeping

Mac ceased canvassing for votes in support of the convention's work when he decided to buy Nate's store. Based on what he'd heard, the men in California were likely to adopt the Constitution by an overwhelming majority—his efforts weren't necessary. He spent the early part of November taking inventory with Nate, learning to weigh gold dust and test the purity of nuggets, and finalizing their agreement.

They signed the sales contract and shook hands on Friday, November 9, then Nate treated Mac and his granddaughter to dinner.

"Susan and I are off to San Francisco on tomorrow's steamship," Nate told Mac while they ate. "The trip is only nine hours now, so we'll be there by evening. We'll find hotel rooms to spend the winter in, maybe buy a house. While you toil here in the store."

Mac grinned. "You'll have me looking for ways to void our contract, if you keep touting the virtues of San Francisco."

Nate laughed and shook his head. "I've never been sure why you want the store. But I'm not complaining."

"Maybe it's a whim," Mac said, his face sobering. "Nothing else to do. Nowhere else to go."

"You'll visit us, won't you, Caleb?" Susan said, touching his hand. "We'll always welcome your company."

"If I can." Mac sipped his wine and smiled. "Your grandfather told me I'll be too busy."

After seeing Nate and Susan off at the Embarcadero the next morning, Mac went to the Golden Nugget to find Consuela. She was washing tables before the saloon opened. Her pregnancy was beginning to show, and she tried to hide it with looser dresses.

"I have a job for you," Mac told her. "I bought Nate Peabody's store and need a clerk."

Consuela stared at him. "I can't leave the saloon."

"Why not?"

"I've worked here over a year now. I have regular customers. And I'll have a child to raise. I need the money."

"Your customers will find other girls. You don't owe them anything. Have any of them stepped forward to help you?"

Consuela lifted her chin, looking for all the world like Jenny when she was stubborn. "I don't need their help."

"You need someone's help. I'm offering you mine."

Consuela stared at him. "Why?"

He shrugged. "You need a friend." He nodded toward her belly. "So does your child. As I said, I could use a clerk."

"I'll think about it." She turned to wipe off another table.

Mac found his days fuller than he'd thought possible. He kept busy from early morning until well into the evening serving customers and restocking inventory in the store. But he relished the responsibility.

He wrote one evening:

> *November 21, 1849. Running the store is harder than I thought. Assaying gold is the least of it. Assisting customers and keeping inventory on the shelves has me darting from task to task until I barely remember what I need to do next. Nothing gets done unless I do it. I did not lie in telling Consuela I need a clerk.*

Despite the challenges, Mac discovered he liked helping customers. He put his wagon train and prospecting experience to use. Many of the men who entered the store were greenhorns, just arriving after a long journey.

They asked countless questions. He sympathized with their weariness—was it only two years since he and Jenny had reached Oregon? Mac tried to show the newcomers the same patience Nate had shown him when they first met.

When his work was done, Mac went to the Golden Nugget for supper. He didn't renew his offer to Consuela, he merely watched her while he sipped his whiskey. He drank a single glass each night, then returned to his lonely quarters above the store.

One evening he signaled to Consuela to bring him a second whiskey. It was time to talk again.

"Another, Mac?" She smiled as she poured.

"You don't seem to have as many patrons as you used to," he said, taking the refilled glass from her.

She shrugged. "Business is slow."

"Mine isn't. I need you." She wouldn't leave the saloon if she thought his offer was charity. He'd have to convince her she'd be doing him a favor.

She raised her eyebrow. "Need me?"

"I'm too busy in the store to help everyone, restock my supplies, and assay the gold men bring me. I could really use your help."

Consuela stared at him. "This isn't the truth."

He took a swallow and shrugged. "You can believe me or not, but the truth is I need someone to serve customers."

"Will the customers let me serve them?"

He knew what she meant. "Most of them are new to town. They won't know you were a working girl. They're too grateful for any advice they can get. And for the credit I extend."

"In a few months I may have to stop working here," she admitted. "At least for a while."

"Come see me tomorrow. We'll talk." Mac downed the rest of his whiskey and left.

Midmorning the next day, Consuela appeared in Mac's store. "Tell me what you need," she said, smoothing her hands over her skirt. Her gesture emphasized the swell of her abdomen.

"I need a clerk," he said. "I'll continue to weigh the color and manage stock on the shelves."

"I can't live at the Golden Nugget if I'm not working there."

"You can have the room above the store. I'll take a room in the saloon."

She frowned. "That will cost you. Why would you do that?"

He shrugged. "I have money. I'm eating there most days anyway. It's no trouble, and they'll launder my clothes and bedding."

"And when my *niño* comes?"

"We'll worry about that in the spring." He looked at her. "Have you seen a doctor?"

Consuela shook her head. "The other girls know as much about birthing as doctors do."

"Will one of them come help you when your time comes?"

"I think so." Consuela did not sound worried about the birth.

Mac had stayed with Jenny when William was born. She'd been young and terrified, exhausted to the point of stupor by the time the baby came after a full day of labor. But maybe Consuela was stronger.

"I will give my notice at the saloon," Consuela said. "I will start here as soon as I can."

She was back in an hour with a small parcel of clothing. "They do not need me." Her voice caught when she spoke.

Mac wasn't surprised. Consuela had worked at the Golden Nugget since it opened. But the saloonkeeper showed no loyalty—he could easily replace a prostitute.

November 27, 1849. Consuela has accepted my offer of employment in the store.

Consuela was not a good store clerk. She tried hard, but her lilting Spanish accent and low-cut gowns put off the female customers. Mac gave her a shawl from his inventory. Most of the customers were men, and they flocked to her until they saw her blossoming belly. She lacked the knowledge of gunpowder and hacksaws they needed, and Mac ended up advising the miners himself.

Still, knowing Consuela's baby would not be born in a brothel eased

Mac's mind. When he traveled to San Francisco to purchase more goods, he was glad Consuela was there to watch the store. He taught her to handle a pistol and told her to keep it with her at all times.

And she cooked him his noon meal. She filled a pot on the fire in the kitchen each morning before the store opened, then stirred it between customers. Mac ate her savory *paellas* gratefully, though he continued to take his evening meal at the saloon with his whiskey.

"Well, this is cozy," Joel said when he came into Mac's store to deposit more gold. Consuela sang in the kitchen while Mac replenished bolts of cloth on the store shelves. "You shacking up with her now?"

"It's not like that," Mac said.

Joel looked at him skeptically. "Sure looks like it. Or is something wrong with you? First Miz Jenny. Now Consuela. You just look at the women and never touch?"

"It's not like that either," Mac said, tight-lipped. "They needed my help." He wondered again whether he'd atoned enough for Bridget's death. And for what he'd done to Jenny.

Joel laughed. "What about Miss Abbott? She don't need your help."

Mac grabbed Joel's shirt front. "No more talk from you. You're the one who should be watching over Consuela, not me."

"Take it easy," Joel said, shrugging Mac off. "I'm only here to sell you my gold and buy flour and lead for the winter."

"How's Huntington?" Mac asked as he hefted a bag of flour onto the counter.

"Coughing more with the cooler weather."

"Send him to town if he gets worse," Mac said. "He could stay in the back room here."

"You take in all the strays, don't you?" Joel said. "I doubt he'll come, but I'll tell him. He's too old for mining. Good thing Tanner's here now. He does the work of two Huntingtons."

Chapter 48:   Christmas Secrets

Shortly after she talked to Doc Tuller, Jenny penned a letter to send to Mac at Sutter's Fort.

> *November 22, 1949*
> *Dear Mac,*
> *I am in receipt of a letter from a woman named Consuela Montenegro, who wrote that you have passed to the next world. I pray what she wrote is not true and her words were a cruel jest. If you receive this, please reassure me as to your well-being.*
> *I want only your health and happiness. Whatever your sentiments and future intentions, I will accept them.*
> *But if you are able, I deeply desire your return. I want to see you again.*
> *My love,*
> *Jenny*

Jenny worded her letter carefully, but she could not keep from saying she wanted to see him. She had to ask him to return. Just once, she was going to let Mac know what she wanted. If he was alive to respond.

Nor could she leave off her closing, which she wrote in a mad dash, and sealed the letter before she reconsidered.

Then she wrote a letter to Consuela Montenegro.

November 22, 1849
Dear Miss Montenegro,
 I received your letter containing the devastating news that Caleb McDougall is dead. I must know the details of his passing. He was my dearest friend and companion, and I am distraught at losing him.
 I await your prompt reply. Thank you.
Yours respectfully,
Geneviève McDougall

She would use Mac's name for this purpose. She didn't know what claim the Montenegro woman had on Mac, but she, too, wanted to claim his affections, even if she had no legal right to his presence in her life.

And finally, Jenny wrote Joel Pershing:

November 22, 1849
Dear Joel,
 I have received word that Mac was ill and died. Please advise immediately if I should believe it.
 I hear also that he sold you his mining interest. I wish you good fortune in your prospecting.
 Your family and friends in Oregon are well.
Sincerely,
Jenny McDougall

Two days later, on Saturday, as soon as her students left, she drove to Oregon City to post the letters. She prayed they would reach California quickly and she would receive at least one response.

"Who was your letter last week from?" Esther asked on Sunday after church. "A friend of Mac's?"

"Yes." Jenny kept her tone neutral. If she said much more, her voice would tremble.

"What did it say?"

"Mac was ill." That much was true, though the letter had said far more.

"My stars! Is he all right?"

"I don't know," Jenny said, telling herself this was true also. "I wrote to ask if he was better."

"It must be hard to be so far apart. Daniel and I have our spats," Esther said, "but I am so fortunate to have him with me." She prattled on about an argument she'd had with Daniel over his dirty boots on a clean floor, then asked, "Anything in the letter about Joel? He ain't said much in his letters."

"No." The letter had said Mac left his gold mine to Joel. But Jenny didn't want to pass on information that might not be true.

When December came, the Oregon community planned for Christmas. Most of the settlers from earlier years—including Jenny—had a good harvest, and the new 1849 emigrants were busy building homes and clearing land. The Whitman Massacre was avenged, a new government in place, and the future looked bright. Life was not easy in a place of many scarcities and hardships, but most people had more opportunities than they'd had in the States.

Jenny bought yarn in Oregon City and knitted in the evenings—socks for William, mittens for Rachel, and a scarf for O'Neil. She baked pumpkin bread for Esther's family and made molasses and mint candies for the Pershings, Tullers, and Abercrombies. She taught the schoolchildren Christmas hymns and asked the older pupils to write compositions about their favorite Christmases back home.

"Back home," she caught herself saying to the children.

But home for all of them was in Oregon now. Jenny had no wish to return to Missouri and could not imagine living again through the perils she and Mac had faced on the trail west. Still, she often wondered how Mama and baby Jacques were faring in Missouri.

After church services each Sunday, Esther asked Jenny, "Have you heard any more from Captain McDougall?"

"No word yet," Jenny said. "I pray he has recovered." If Mac wrote he was not returning, or if she never heard another word from him, she could still use the letter from Consuela Montenegro as proof Mac was dead. She didn't have to say anything now.

Not knowing the truth made her stomach churn. She didn't like keeping secrets from Esther. Their friendship had been founded on a falsehood— the lie that Mac and Jenny were husband and wife—but now she had more lies she had to tell.

The Tullers also asked Jenny if she'd heard from Mac. With them, she simply shook her head.

Rachel divided her time between Esther's and Jenny's homes. "It's too crowded at Pa's," she told Jenny. "And too noisy at Esther's, with Jonah, Cordelia, and Samuel all crying. I want to help, but I like staying with you and William."

"You're welcome to live here," Jenny said. "I know Esther needs the help, so bring Jonah to visit, if you want. He and William play well together."

Jenny suspected Rachel wanted to spend time at her cabin partly because of O'Neil. Rachel no longer blushed when O'Neil was around. In fact, now O'Neil stammered in Rachel's presence.

"I don't know what to do," Esther whispered to Jenny on Sunday, December 9. She gestured at Rachel and O'Neil, who had walked to the Willamette Falls after church with a few other couples. "He's too old for her, but he's so nice. And he's better than the other farmers hanging around her—friends of Pa's and Mr. Abercrombie's. I don't like them half as much as Mr. O'Neil."

"Aren't there any young men after Rachel?" Jenny asked.

Esther shook her head. "Most grown men under thirty are still in California. You need to watch Mr. O'Neil when he's with Rachel on your place. I owe it to Ma to look after Rachel, like Ma did for me."

"She's turned fifteen now," Jenny said. "As old as you were when you married Daniel."

"I know." Esther sighed. "But she's still my little sister. I can't let anything bad happen to her."

Jenny wanted to reassure Esther that Rachel would be fine. But she and William were proof bad things could happen to young girls. "I'll watch her. And Mr. O'Neil," she told Esther.

So Jenny didn't let Rachel collect eggs in the barn while O'Neil mucked out the stalls. She made Rachel take William with her when the girl carried O'Neil's noon meal to him in the forest when he was felling trees. And she tried to keep Rachel near the cabin, so they could work together.

But on Friday morning Jenny saw Rachel stumble out of the barn with a foolish smile, her cheeks red. O'Neil followed behind Rachel, a grin on his lips.

"Are you all right, Rachel," Jenny asked. She followed as the girl hurried into the cabin.

"Fine," Rachel said. She dropped into Jenny's rocking chair, her whole face beaming. "Mr. O'Neil just asked me to marry him."

"Did he take advantage of you?" Jenny asked sharply. She sounded like old Mrs. Tuller or Rachel's dead mother, she knew.

"No, Miz Jenny," Rachel said. It had been months since Rachel had called Jenny "Miz." She must be flustered. Then the girl blushed. "He kissed me. But I let him."

"And he wants to marry you?"

"Yes." Rachel's eyes were dreamy.

"What did you tell him?"

"Yes." Rachel hugged herself. "He said he'd ask Pa before Christmas." She grabbed Jenny's arm. "Don't tell anyone till Robert's had a chance to ask."

So Rachel called him "Robert" now, Jenny thought. "Do you love him?" she asked.

Rachel nodded. "I think so. He's a sweet man."

"You're not doing this to have your own home, are you?" Jenny worried Rachel had wandered from place to place like a vagabond for so long she might just want to be settled.

"I do want my own home," Rachel sighed. "And my own babies. Like you and Esther have. But I wouldn't wed just anyone. Robert's a good man."

Jenny couldn't dispute that. "Yes," she said. "He is."

Friday, December 14—Mr. O'Neil wants to marry Rachel. I would miss them both dearly if they left. I should offer them the Tanners' cabin to live in.

The next afternoon Zeke appeared in Jenny's clearing unexpectedly. "Did you know about this?" he demanded.

She sat outside on a stool peeling potatoes to boil for supper. William was with her, picking up the peels to give to the chickens. "About what?" she asked.

"Rachel and O'Neil." Zeke dismounted and looked around the yard. "Where is he?"

"Hauling water," Jenny said. "I take it Mr. O'Neil asked Captain Pershing about marrying Rachel." She shooed William into the cabin, so he wouldn't hear Zeke shouting.

"Last night." Zeke looked angry. "You did know. He's way older'n I am. Older'n Mac, too. Must be almost forty."

"I thought you liked Mr. O'Neil."

"He's a good hand. But Rachel's only a girl."

"She's the same age Esther was when she married. About what I was when William was born. Who would you have her marry?"

"No one," Zeke said. His hands whipped the reins tight as he tied his horse to the paddock fence post. "Where is he?" he repeated when the horse was secure.

O'Neil walked into the yard with a full bucket of water in each hand. "Right here, Pershing," he said. "Somethin' on your mind?"

Zeke strode over until he was in O'Neil's face. "You," he snarled. "You and my sister."

"I'll treat her right," O'Neil said.

"Where you going to live? What you got to offer her?"

"I been over that with your pa," O'Neil said. "Miz Jenny said we could have the old Tanner cabin. It ain't much, but it's a place of our own. I can fix it up a bit. And I'll look for land nearby."

"You ain't hauling her off to California?"

O'Neil shook his head. "I've changed my mind. Oregon's good enough for me."

Some of Zeke's anger seemed to drain out of him. "You better treat her right," he said, shaking a finger in O'Neil's face. "Or you'll answer to me."

Zeke turned to Jenny, his mouth still grim. "If you was in on this, you'll answer to me, too." He untied his horse, mounted, and rode off.

"Why is Zeke upset?" Jenny whispered.

"He cares about his sister." O'Neil smiled. "And he just wants what I've found. A good woman to make his evenin's brighter."

Chapter 49:   Winter in Town

Mac's business slowed down in December when the weather grew cold and wet. Heavy winter rains had started in November and continued almost daily. The mines in the hills past Sacramento were too sodden to work— ground water rose in the pits as fast as prospectors dug them.

To get away from the tedium of the store and from Consuela's puttering in the kitchen, Mac took the steamship to San Francisco almost every week. The ticket cost thirty dollars each way, but the day-long trip was easier than riding eighty miles on Valiente in winter weather.

On one such trip, he sat under the boat's awning to avoid the cold rain and wrote:

> December 13, 1849. Winter in Sacramento is little better than last year, when I holed up in the shack with only Joel and Huntington for company. Men roam the town idly, waiting for the weather to let them dig, waiting for something to occupy their time. Consuela stays in the store, waiting for her baby. Trips to see Nate and Susan are my only respite from boredom.

Sacramento had not existed when Mac arrived in the spring of 1848. Now general mercantile stores the size of Mac's or larger and smaller specialty shops filled most of the lots in the commercial district between Sutter's Fort and the Embarcadero on the river. Houses, saloons, gambling halls, and even a theatre lined the broad streets. The town also boasted a magnificent hotel built by Sam Brannan, the newspaperman who had publicized the discovery of gold at Sutter's Mill.

The larger establishments were built of wood, but much of Sacramento remained a tent city. Some buildings were wood frames with canvas walls inside.

"How can the gold fields support so many businesses?" Consuela asked.

"Thousands of miners arrived in the area this year. They stop in Sacramento before they head to the gold fields. They all need food and tents and tools. Small towns in the hills must buy their supplies from somewhere. More money to be made in retailing than in mining, and it's easier work."

Consuela looked at him. "That's not why you bought the store, is it? You don't need more money, and you don't shy away from hard work."

"It's something to do." Mac shrugged. "If I go back to Boston, I'll do so on my own terms. The store adds to my fortune. I have enough now that I never need to join my brother's law firm."

"I thought you enjoyed working with Señor Hastings at the convention. You've told so many tales about the delegates."

"I did." Mac sighed. "But there are few opportunities to build a new state. Usually, practicing law is not very interesting."

Consuela smiled and shook her head. "When will you find your true calling, Mac?"

He frowned. Nothing called him, no matter how hard he searched. "And you? What is your calling?"

"Me, I work to survive. Only the rich can follow a dream."

"Soon you'll have your child. Maybe motherhood is your calling."

Nate asked Mac many of the same questions Consuela did. One evening they sat alone in a San Francisco tavern while Susan attended a Daughters of Temperance meeting. "You seem bored with storekeeping, Mac. What do you really want?"

Mac shrugged. "The store is fine. I won't hold it forever, but it'll keep me through the winter."

"I hear Consuela Montenegro, one of the Golden Nugget girls, is working for you."

"She's having a child."

"Is it your child?"

"No. But I don't want to see the baby born in a brothel."

"I haven't told Susan you have a soiled dove in the store, but maybe you should." Nate's fingers rubbed his glass, and he quirked an eyebrow at Mac. "What do you think Susan will say when she finds out?"

Aha, Mac thought. What William Shannon had predicted was coming to pass—Susan Abbott must envision him as a potential husband. He wondered what Susan and Nate had discussed.

He'd thought about Susan some evenings while he sipped his whiskey. He would have to ponder the idea more, knowing she considered him as well. Susan was a beautiful woman, educated and refined. He could take her to Boston, and his family would approve. Her grandfather was a good friend. He could do worse in choosing a wife.

And he had severed his ties with Jenny.

As the rains continued through December, the road to San Francisco grew muddier and the riverboat journey dangerous. Miners grumbled when Mac raised his prices for grain and tools to cover the increased costs of transportation.

"Six dollars for mule feed," one man exclaimed. "That'd buy me grain for my family for a year back East."

"I'm sorry," Mac said. "Goods are scarce, and freight costs from San Francisco keep increasing. Maybe prices will go down in the spring."

The mountain snows deepened, and prospectors holed up for the winter, fewer coming to town. When Joel and Huntington made a rare trip to Sacramento, they told Mac stories of miners defrauding one another.

"Heard a man boast about spikin' his claim with gold to sell it for a high price," Huntington said with a grin.

"How'd he do that?" Mac asked.

"Took some nuggets he'd found on another piece of land and spread 'em under a layer of dirt. Then he raked 'em up. Other men saw the gold, started biddin' on his land." Huntington chortled. "Now he's livin' high on the hog in San Francisco. Wish I'd thought of it." Huntington's laugh turned into a hacking cough.

"You wouldn't cheat a man," Mac said.

"Wouldn't I?" Huntington wheezed. "Ice is settlin' in my bones this year. I may take you up on your offer to move to town."

Mac looked at Joel. "If he leaves the claim, can you manage it?"

"Tanners are there. Hatty takes good care of us. Been eating as good as I ever did since Ma died. And Tanner can lift a lot more'n this old fool." Joel turned to Huntington. "You want me to buy you out? Mac here can write it up legal, then transfer the gold from my account to yours."

Huntington leaned back on his chair. "Maybe I should. Maybe I should." He coughed. "I always said I'd die with my boots in the creek. But maybe I'll change my mind."

"A lot of men talk 'bout leaving, going back wherever they come from," Joel said. "They know now prospecting ain't easy. They seen men die, from sickness and injuries. Some newcomers this year ain't got no shelter, or a tent at best. They sleep on the ground in the rain and snow." He shook his head. "Damn fools."

"But you're not ready to quit?" Mac asked.

"Nope." Joel took out a pouch of tobacco and rolled a cigarette. "Been drinking and gambling and whoring too much. I can buy out Huntington, but I ain't got enough set aside to last my lifetime yet."

"Consuela'll have her baby in a few months," Mac said.

Joel shrugged. "Ain't my problem. You made it yours."

The next morning Huntington told Mac, "I reckon I'll let young Pershing buy me out and stay in town. That still all right by you?"

Mac nodded. "We'll take care of your accounts today. You have enough to live in luxury if you want. Or if you help in the store, I'll let you have a cot in the back room."

Consuela looked at Mac. "And me?"

Mac blinked at her. He hadn't thought—maybe Consuela would be uncomfortable with Huntington on the premises. "You have the upstairs room. Do you mind if Huntington stays downstairs?"

"It's your store. You can take in as many vagabonds as you like." She turned away.

"Are you sure?" Mac asked, following her into the back room.

She lifted a shoulder while she stirred a steaming pot on the stove that smelled of peppers. "I will be safer at night with a man downstairs."

"Then why did you ask?"

Consuela turned to look at him, a hand on her belly. "Señor Huntington is another who is not your concern."

"Like you."

"Like me." She cradled her stomach more closely.

"He was my partner. Now he's old and ill."

"It is your money and your store." She shrugged again. "Do as you please."

"Why do you care what I do?" Mac asked. "You're reaping the benefit." She seemed to judge him, even when he was doing the right thing.

"When will you look to your own happiness, Mac? Perhaps you will find it too late." She smiled ruefully and turned to stir her pot.

By Christmas Huntington was established in the back room of the store. He still rasped and coughed—"It's the cold," he said—but he was a help. He carried wood and water, lifted bags of cornmeal and flour, and exchanged tall tales and boasts with the miners who came to trade. He was a better assistant than Consuela, though she continued to feed the two men, and made extra money selling dinners to other men staying in town.

Mac invited Joel and the Tanners to come to town for Christmas, but Joel declined for all of them. "We can't leave the claim, not all at once. I ain't had much interest in Christmas since I left home. Hatty'll cook something fine for us."

So a quiet group sat down to a beef roast Consuela prepared—just Mac, Consuela, and Huntington. After they ate, Mac read the Christmas story from the Bible, and Consuela sang a Spanish hymn. Mac didn't understand the words, but the tune haunted him. He remembered Jenny's clear voice singing "Amazing Grace" and other hymns at services along the trail, and in the church in Oregon City once they were settled.

"Why so sad, Mac?" Consuela asked, tears in her eyes.

"Thinking of home," Mac said, then realized the trail and Oregon, where his thoughts had led, were not his home. "And you? Why do you cry?"

"The same."

Chapter 50:   Wedding

On Tuesday, January 1, 1850, Rachel Pershing and Robert O'Neil were married at the Methodist church in Oregon City, not even three weeks after O'Neil had asked for her hand.

"No reason to wait," Rachel told Jenny. "This is what I want."

Despite the cold and rain, many friends made the trip into town for the ceremony—all the Pershings, all the Abercrombies, and the Tullers. New acquaintances like the Binghams were there also.

Captain Pershing gave Rachel away, and Esther and Daniel Abercrombie stood up with the couple. Jenny sat near the front of the small church with Doc and Mrs. Tuller. Esther dabbed her eyes when the minister spoke. Daniel leaned over and touched Esther's cheek, then handed her a handkerchief. He whispered something to Esther, who smiled back at him.

Jenny's throat tightened with tears as she watched Esther and Daniel. She missed Mac and the first Mrs. Pershing and the Tanners. Rachel's mother should be here to see her daughter wed. And Hatty would have loved this day as well.

Mac? She didn't know what he would have thought of Rachel and O'Neil—he hadn't approved of Daniel and Esther marrying. He'd said they were too young. And later Mac hadn't seemed eager to marry her, though he'd asked.

Jenny's heart jumped in her chest every time she thought of the letter she'd sent Mac in late November. She hadn't received any response yet. If he was alive, did he have her letter by now? Would he write back? Or would Consuela Montenegro or Joel write? Would she ever know the truth of what happened to Mac?

Across the church aisle from Jenny, Zeke looked grim. Jenny wondered what could be bothering him. She thought Zeke had accepted O'Neil as a husband for Rachel.

Zeke must have seen Jenny staring at him, because he turned her way and caught her eye with a frown. She blushed and looked down at the top of William's head. The toddler slept in her lap.

After the vows, Jenny congratulated Rachel and O'Neil, then found Esther. "Are you all right?" she asked her friend, who was still crying.

"Just thinking about Ma," Esther said, wiping her face again. "She would have been so happy to see Rachel married."

"So you've decided Mr. O'Neil will make Rachel a good husband?"

Esther nodded. "He'll be a good provider, and he's a kind man. Not everyone gets the romance me and Daniel had." She sighed. "And flowers and furbelows don't count for much when there's babies underfoot and meals to fix and clothes to mend."

"No," Jenny said. She didn't know much about romance, but she did know about babies and meals and mending.

"I don't know how Ma did it," Esther said. "So many young'uns, and Pa away with the Army for a year at a time."

"Your mama was a strong woman." But Jenny remembered how tired Mrs. Pershing had been while expecting Jonah, when they walked along the wagons each day.

"And yet, it's a fine thing to have someone hold you in the night." Esther sighed again, this time with a little smile. "At least Daniel and I have that, and now Rachel will, too."

Jenny remained silent.

"Don't you miss Captain McDougall?" Esther asked. "He's been gone nearly two years now. You've had no one to love since he left."

Jenny swallowed, incapable of saying anything for a moment. "Yes," she whispered when she could, "I miss him. But I have William. And my friends."

Esther shook her head. "It's not the same, and you know it."

But Jenny didn't really know. She'd never had a man hold her in the night. It sounded like a fine comfort. She wandered over to see Zeke, who stood by himself in a corner, glowering. "What's wrong, Zeke?" she asked.

"O'Neil and Rachel—they won't stay with you for long, you know." Zeke clenched his jaw.

"Has Mr. O'Neil said something to you?" Surely O'Neil would talk to her, if he planned to move away with Rachel.

"No. But you know he wants his own farm. No point in working for someone else when you can get your own land for free."

"He said he needed to build up credit before he could file a claim." Jenny's voice quavered. Zeke was right—Rachel and O'Neil would leave her soon.

"If I was you, I'd tell him to plant your crops early this spring." Zeke brushed his hat against his leg. "I'm busy tomorrow, but I'll see you Thursday."

The rain continued into Wednesday, and Jenny spent the day in her cabin with William. She'd canceled school until Thursday.

As far as she knew, Rachel and O'Neil were in their cabin, which Rachel and Jenny had scrubbed clean before the wedding. Only mice had lived in it since the Tanners left.

Wednesday, January 2ⁿᵈ—Rachel married Mr. O'Neil yesterday. I have not seen them yet today, though Mr. O'Neil had mucked out the barn before I collected eggs this morning. Soon I must make supper for William and me.

Jenny remembered the shivaree the wagon train had held for Esther and Daniel after their wedding, and Esther's smiling face the next morning. Esther wanted to talk about her first night with Daniel, but Jenny had no interest in giggling with her friend.

Jenny had nothing to laugh about, only the memory of being violated— the pain, the humiliation, the fear.

Then she thought of Mac's kiss. She'd felt warm in his arms, though shocked at his roughness, at the lack of control in a man who'd always seemed in complete command of himself.

What had Esther said? "Someone to hold you in the night." Jenny felt warm again, imagining Mac's arms around her. It would be nice to be held.

What if it were Zeke? The thought popped into her head. Along the trail, Zeke had jumped onto the wagon seat beside her when her horses shied on a river crossing. But she couldn't recall how it felt to have him sit beside to her. Not like she remembered Mac's arms.

That evening as Jenny fried bacon for supper, Rachel and O'Neil knocked on her door. Rachel offered a pan of cornbread. "M-may we join you?" the new bride stammered.

"I'll slice more bacon," Jenny said. "That and your bread should be plenty."

Conversation during the meal was stilted. O'Neil didn't say much, and William's chatter stopped while he stuffed his mouth with cornbread and butter. Jenny tried talking about the wedding ceremony and the gifts the couple had received. But Rachel blushed whenever Jenny mentioned the wedding. At least Rachel didn't seem inclined to giggle, like Esther had the day after she and Daniel had married.

After a long silence, O'Neil said, "Tomorrow I'll be choppin' wood on the south side of the claim."

And they spent the rest of the meal discussing the farm.

"Does Rachel seem happy?" Esther asked Jenny on Saturday afternoon, January 12, when they sat in Esther's home mending. Jenny's students had left at noon, and she'd taken William to visit Esther. Two-year-old Jonah and William teased twenty-one-month-old Cordelia. Baby Samuel slept on the bed in the corner.

"I think so," Jenny said, wrinkling her brow. "But she's so quiet."

"I know." Esther sighed. "Not like me. I always say what I think, but Rachel never lets on. I want her to be happy."

"Rachel's fine." Jenny smiled and touched Esther's arm. "She and I do chores together like always. We mostly cook together, though she and Mr. O'Neil have breakfast in their cabin now. Rachel would have come with me today, but Mr. O'Neil needed to go to town for supplies. She wanted to go with him."

"Which she can do till she's tied down by children." Esther grimaced. "Did you ever think, Jenny, we'd be old married women here in Oregon?"

Jenny laughed. "We're not old. I just turned seventeen in October, and you won't be eighteen until next month."

"I feel old." Tears came to Esther's eyes, and she wiped them away with the shirt she was stitching. "Three children under three. I love 'em all, but some days it's too much."

"Samuel's so little still. Only three months old. Is he even sleeping through the night?" Jenny asked.

Esther shook her head. "Not often."

"Well, no wonder you feel old. Why don't I take Jonah home with me this afternoon? He and William can play."

"No," Esther said. "Jonah keeps Cordelia busy. Till they start fighting. Then I want to scream. Daniel's gone from morning till suppertime. If he's not in our fields, he's working somewhere with his pa and brother. He's only home when he wants to eat or sleep. And then he doesn't want to sleep, if you know what I mean."

"Mmmm," Jenny said.

"How long are you going to wait for Captain McDougall, Jenny? What if he didn't recover after he was sick? Will you ever know?"

"What choice do I have? All I can do is wait." Jenny replied. But she did have a choice—she could show everyone the letter saying Mac was dead. She didn't want to do so until she learned the truth, whether from Mac or the Montenegro woman or Joel.

But Esther was right—how long could she wait?

Chapter 51:   Commerce and Culture

Rain poured as the new decade greeted Sacramento. The few old-timers in the area said it was the wettest winter California had ever seen.

Mac wrote:

> *January 7, 1850. I cannot tolerate the constant gray days. At least in Boston, crisp blue skies followed our heavy snows. Here, the rain drips day after day. Oregon was just as bad.*

The monotony of winter affected his store. Not many customers came in each day, and Consuela and Huntington had little to do. The two of them bickered over every trifling task—who should do it, how it should be done, when it should be finished—until Mac wanted to shout.

"I should have stayed on the claim," Mac told Huntington one morning. "Listening to you and Consuela gripe is worse than wintering with you and Joel."

"Nothin' to do but gripe," Huntington said, lighting his pipe.

"Can you put that thing out?" Consuela asked. "I have *náuseas*."

"Thought women only puked in the first few months of breedin'," Huntington said, puffing away.

Consuela shrugged. "For me, it comes again."

"Are you ill?" Mac asked. He worried about what they would do when Consuela's child arrived. She still had two or three months to go, he figured.

"No, but I do not like the smoke." Her arm went around her stomach as if to protect the child.

Huntington frowned at Consuela, but tapped out his pipe. "Man told me they's openin' a gold transport firm in San Francisco," he said to Mac. "You heard anythin' about it?"

"California needs a way to secure the gold, then ship it back East," Mac said. "Makes sense someone would try to make money moving the color to market."

"Will it hurt your business?" Huntington asked.

"Might. Or it might be a help, if I'm part of it. Maybe I'll look into getting a contract to haul gold from the mines and small towns around here to Sacramento." Mac thought a moment. "I'd need a small sturdy wagon, mules, and a driver and good rifleman."

"You're good with a gun. Killed that claim-jumpin' bastard right quick in forty-eight." Huntington stretched out his legs toward the fire.

"I'll go into San Francisco next week to talk with the owners of the shipping company. Give me an excuse to get away from you and Consuela." Mac grinned when he spoke, teasing his old partner.

January 10, 1850. The rain keeps me from San Francisco, but I aim to see if there is a role for me in building commerce. Mining is dirty work, storekeeping too confining. I yearn for the days on the trail, where I had both responsibility and action.

Mac delayed his trip to San Francisco for two weeks because of the continuing rain. "American's been over its banks for days now," a customer told Mac in mid-January. "All those new houses and stores ruined."

"And fire in San Francisco last month destroyed a lot of buildings there." Mac lifted a bag of flour onto the counter for the man. "Seems the Almighty doesn't want us building in the West."

"Not even the Almighty can stop a man chasin' gold," the customer replied. "Add the flour to my account, please." As he browsed the shelves, he added, "There's been another robbery in the camps."

"What happened?" Huntington asked from his stool behind the counter.

"Some fool from Ohio had a trunk of gold in his tent. More'n two thousand dollars. Trunk got stolen. Found it broke open 'bout a mile away. Empty."

"Did they find the thief?" Mac asked. His mind leapt to Smith, though he hadn't seen the man in months. He didn't know if Smith was still around. If the thief wasn't Smith, it was someone like him, no doubt.

"Found somebody. Had a trial, but couldn't pin it on him. Had to let him go. No tellin' who did it." The customer spat a stream of tobacco juice into a spittoon at the end of the counter. "Here I'm toilin' away, only findin' two dollars a day, and this fellow who struck it rich gets robbed. Man can't win."

By Tuesday, January 22, the flood receded enough to permit steamship travel between Sacramento and San Francisco, and Mac set out. When he arrived in San Francisco that evening, men talked about the fire in December and an earthquake on January 16. Newcomers from the East spoke of these disasters as proof they'd left all civilization behind. San Francisco businesses had already begun rebuilding, and sounds of hammers rang through the air.

Mac found Nate in a saloon. "I thought you and Susan were going to board at the Parker House," he said to the older man. "Somewhere better than a saloon. You might as well be in the Golden Nugget in Sacramento."

"Parker House is gone. Burned to the ground in the Christmas Eve fire," Nate responded. "San Francisco is growing too fast to be safe. The only rooms I could find were here. Susan is none too happy to be living in a saloon. Only leaves her room to attend her Daughters of Temperance meetings."

"Move back to Sacramento," Mac said, gesturing to the bartender for service. "You and Susan could put up in the hotel there. It might offend her delicate sensibilities less than this place," he said with a grin. "Though Huntington's living in the store now, so she'd likely see him on occasion."

"Is that old windbag staying with you?" Nate had never cottoned to Huntington. "He's as like to steal you blind as sell to your customers."

"He's taking it easy this winter." Mac nodded his head in thanks to the woman who placed a glass of whiskey in front of him. "But I'm glad to get some time away from him. Huntington and Consuela don't get along. They argue as much as he and Joel did."

"Well, I don't think adding Susan to those two would make our lives any easier." Nate shook his head with a smile. "We'll stay put in San Francisco. Maguire is building another hotel where the Parker House was. It'll be done in the spring."

"I'm planning to talk with the gold transport firm tomorrow. See if I can reach agreement to haul from the mines to Sacramento. Use my store as a transfer point."

"The transport company's warehouse burned, too," Nate said. "Everything burned. Even the brand new California Exchange. Man named Cornwall said he'd rebuild that gambling hall in two weeks. I didn't think he could, but it's open again. There's a musical there tonight to celebrate the grand reopening."

"Culture in San Francisco?" Mac grinned. "The town is growing fast."

Mac, Nate, and Susan attended the musical performance at the California Exchange. The orchestra was not of the caliber Mac had experienced in Boston, but it was the first music program he'd seen since leaving the East three years earlier, other than fiddles and guitars beside a campfire.

Susan wore one of the dresses he'd seen on her at the Frémonts' home in Monterey. She was stylish, but less flamboyant than many of the women at the musical. Mac suspected some of them were high-end prostitutes.

Susan seemed unaware of the women's likely profession, though surely she knew the Exchange was a gambling establishment. She frowned when she saw glasses of wine and whiskey in men's hands and exclaimed over the fine chandeliers and furniture. "Why, the only place I've seen this sumptuous in California was the Frémonts' residence in Monterey."

"There will soon be more refined venues, I'm sure, my dear," Nate said. "But for now, we must seek our amusements where we can." The older man's eyes twinkled at Mac over Susan's head.

At the intermission, Nate excused himself. "I find myself tiring early," he told Mac. "Can I trust you to see Susan safely back to our rooms?"

"Of course."

Susan watched her grandfather walk away. "I'm sorry," she said. "I think he planned this. I hope you don't mind."

"Are you really sorry?" Mac asked with a smile.

"No." She cocked her head and looked at Mac. "I enjoyed our conversations in Monterey."

"As did I." Mac offered her his arm to escort her back to their seats. She leaned into his shoulder through the second half of the program.

After the concert, when they reached the door to Susan's room at the saloon, Mac bowed over her hand. She stepped closer. "Surely you can offer a more friendly parting, Caleb."

He dipped his head and kissed her.

"That's more like it," she murmured against his lips.

Mac pulled her into a dark corner and kissed her more fully. He was in trouble now, he thought, sinking again to Susan's mouth.

Or maybe it wasn't trouble. He whistled when he left Susan smiling in her doorway.

The next morning Mac awoke early. Before breakfast he wrote:

> *January 24, 1850. They say one should see to business before pleasure, but I had my pleasure last night with Susan and Nate—perhaps more pleasure than I should have. Today, I must focus on business.*

After he ate, he walked to the transport warehouse—now relocated after the fire—and asked to see the man in charge, a Mr. Dunbar.

A portly man with a gold watch chain across his stomach came out of an office. The man frowned at first, but smiled when Mac described his family's background in Boston and the store he owned in Sacramento.

"Mr. McDougall," Dunbar said, "I took you for another rough prospector initially. But I see you have decided—as I have—that the easiest money to be made in California comes from taking advantage of other men's hard work."

"I've done my share of prospecting, sir," Mac responded. "I aim to give miners a fair deal and help them move their gold safely. I hear you are amassing gold in San Francisco to ship to the States. I thought I might haul it from the mining country to Sacramento for you."

Dunbar stroked his mustache. "For a percentage, I assume?"

Mac nodded. "I'm familiar with the hills beyond Sacramento, and I know the miners who patronize my store. I'm growing uncomfortable with the amount of gold I keep in the store. Too tempting for thieves."

"So you think I can take it off your hands?"

"I understand you have a large brick safe," Mac said. "Better equipped to hold the bags of dust and flakes than my premises in Sacramento."

"We'll take the gold, certainly," Dunbar responded, hooking his thumbs in his silk waistcoat pockets, "and give you good rates. Both you and I can profit."

They talked about schedules and weights and prices. When they had reached agreement, Dunbar asked Mac, "And what of your personal assets? Do you plan to keep them in California or send them back to Boston?"

"Here for now," Mac said. "But later in the year I will most likely move on. Then I'll need my gold transported."

"And were you one of our famous Forty-Niners come from the East last year?"

"No," Mac said. "I came from Oregon. I took a wagon train there in forty-seven, then to California in forty-eight."

"An educated man like you on such a hazardous journey? Whatever for?"

"Adventure," Mac said, grinning. "To see the West. Someday the land will be full of men like the prospectors you disdain."

"To be sure, to be sure." The man hastened to direct the conversation back to rates of exchange.

From Dunbar's warehouse, Mac went to inquire about mail. A new Post Office was under construction, but for now the postal service still operated out of cramped quarters uphill from the main square. Mac asked for any letters addressed to him at Sutter's Fort or Sacramento, figuring it would be quicker to get his mail now than to wait for delivery in Sacramento. The clerk rummaged in bags labeled for Sacramento and handed Mac two letters.

The handwriting on one letter was his father's. He put it in his pocket and frowned at the other letter. His breath hissed in when he saw it was from Jenny. Why had she written? Consuela had told her he was dead.

Mac moved to the side of the boardwalk and opened Jenny's letter. He groaned in frustration as he read. She hadn't accepted his death. She wanted to know if he was all right. She wanted to see him again. She sent her love.

Love? A thrill went through him at Jenny's closing words, then he slapped the letter against his thigh, doubting what she wrote. She couldn't love him—not after she'd been raped, not after he'd groped her and then abandoned her. She'd refused to marry him once. She didn't want him, and they both knew it.

Did he love her? He hadn't been able to admit it to Consuela, but the question crept into his head again now.

"Move on, sir," a man shouted. He pushed a wheelbarrow with wide boards teetering off the sides that was about to careen into Mac.

Mac stepped off the walk and into the muddy street. He thought he'd put Jenny out of his mind after dictating the letter for Consuela to write. It was a struggle now to consider how he felt, another struggle to decide how to respond to her letter.

And he'd just kissed Susan.

Chapter 52:   Memories and Mending

Jenny's school never rebounded after she closed it due to William's smallpox. The other children became accustomed to staying home, and their parents didn't force their children to go to class after Jenny reopened. She continued teaching through the winter, but every day it seemed one or more of the children was sick or was needed at home. The Abercrombie and Bingham families had the worst attendance.

In early February Annabelle Abercrombie told her, "Grandfather Samuel says we can't come to school no more."

"Any more," Jenny said automatically.

"He says we ain't learning anything," Rose Abercrombie added.

Jenny didn't argue with the girls. They weren't learning much, because they only attended school one or two days each week.

"I'm thinking of closing the school early," she told Rachel after the Abercrombie girls talked to her. "Most of the children aren't here regularly."

"But they need the book learning," Rachel said.

"Their parents don't seem to think so." Jenny sighed. "I could earn more raising chickens or making cheese."

"Do you need money?" Rachel asked, sounding surprised.

Jenny shook her head. "I still have most of what Mac left me." Though to her chagrin, she hadn't been able to replace the coins she'd spent. "And I have a credit balance at the Abernethy store for last year's harvest. But I like teaching. It gives me something to do with my time."

"I don't know how you can say you need something to do," Rachel said. "Even when I'm not helping you with school or William, I have plenty to do caring for our tiny house. And in the evenings, Robert and I—" Rachel blushed. "You miss Captain McDougall, don't you? You're lonely."

"Yes," Jenny whispered, glad to speak truthfully to someone. "He's been gone so long. I doubt he's coming back."

A week later, in the afternoon after Jenny's few pupils had gone home, Esther drove a wagon into Jenny's clearing. Jonah and Cordelia played in the back of the wagon, and Samuel lay on a blanket beside them.

"Esther, what are you doing here?" Jenny asked. "And with all the children?"

Esther handed Samuel to Jenny, climbed out of the wagon, and lifted Cordelia to the ground. Jonah clambered down the wagon wheel by himself and raced off to find William. "Rachel told me you don't think Captain McDougall is coming back."

Jenny snuggled her face in Samuel's soft neck. "I worry about it." She'd worried whether he was even alive every moment since receiving the letter.

"Pa had another letter from Joel," Esther said. "Joel didn't say anything about Captain McDougall."

"I haven't heard anything since I heard Mac was ill."

"What's wrong, Jenny?" Esther asked. "I've never thought it right for him to leave you here. William was so young—just a baby. It's one thing if he went to bring his family here. But to abandon you to go prospecting? Without any word? And then he fooled around at politicking." Her tone showed what she thought of politics.

"Lots of men left for the gold mines." Jenny ducked her head as she spoke. How could she get Esther to talk about something else? "Your papa left your mama and all his children when he was in the Army."

"No one knew about the gold when Captain McDougall left. That ain't why he went." Esther reached for Samuel, took Cordelia's hand, and turned to go into Jenny's cabin. "Bring my sewing basket from the wagon, would you please?"

Jenny retrieved the basket and slowly followed Esther into the house. "I'll make some tea," she said, setting Esther's mending on the table.

"So you haven't heard whether he recovered from his illness," Esther said. "Maybe he had a relapse. Maybe that's why he ain't written or come home." Esther made a pallet for Samuel on the floor and took out her sewing. "I can't believe how often Jonah rips his clothes."

"All I know is what I told you, Esther," Jenny said. She wanted to tell her friend the whole sad story, but she'd lived with the lie for so long she couldn't.

Rachel came into the cabin with Jonah and William. "The boys are hungry," she said.

"There's bread and honey on the shelf," Jenny said. "I'll get it."

By the time Jenny fed the children, Esther and Rachel settled in with their mending, and the women's conversation shifted to the lack of provisions in Oregon City stores.

The next afternoon Mrs. Tuller stopped by with her sewing basket. "I was lonely and wanted company while I darn the doctor's socks," she told Jenny.

Jenny waved her into a chair. "I caught up on my mending yesterday with Esther," she said. "But I have some compositions to look over. Please, make yourself at home."

"Oh, my chit-chat will bother you," Mrs. Tuller said.

"No, no," Jenny said, smiling. "I like the company. I'll read the essays out loud, and you can tell me what you think."

She had given the children the topic of "home." The older children wrote of life back East, but the younger ones wrote about Oregon. She and Mrs. Tuller laughed at the children's descriptions of the fireworks in Oregon City, of wading in the summer creeks, of warm fires in small cabins.

"They won't remember life back in the States," Mrs. Tuller said. "Babies born along the way won't even remember our trek across the prairies and mountains. Sometimes it seems so long ago, even to me."

"I remember the journey like yesterday. Almost every day of it." Jenny sighed.

"Why is that?"

Jenny brushed her fingers along the vanes of her feather quill. "Maybe because I was so afraid. Maybe because I was expecting William, and every day was new to me."

"Or maybe because of Captain McDougall?" Mrs. Tuller asked.

"Maybe."

"You wrote him, didn't you? And you asked him to come back?"

Jenny nodded. "No answer. From him or from the woman who wrote me."

"Isn't it too soon to expect anything?"

"Yes. But I still check for mail every time I go into Oregon City."

"When will you give it up?" Mrs. Tuller's question was gentle, but her lips tightened.

"I don't know."

"It's time for you to get on with your life, Jenny. If he's dead. Or even if he's alive and won't come back. Use the letter to put your sham marriage behind you."

"I know." Jenny turned back to the compositions, but tears blurred her vision.

After supper she wrote in her journal:

Tuesday, February 19th—Everyone asks about Mac. There is nothing I can say. Would I be happier if I told them Mac was dead? How could I be?

The following week on a rainy morning, Zeke rode into Jenny's barnyard early, before the students arrived. She stood in the cabin doorway while he approached.

"We need to plant your fields soon," he said, dismounting. "Come the first of March."

"It's still so cold," she said, wiping her hands on her apron.

"What with my farm and yours and helping Pa, I'll have my hands full this year even with O'Neil. Where is he anyway?" Zeke looked around.

"I haven't seen him yet," Jenny said. "He did the barn chores, then went back for breakfast with Rachel. He'll be here soon."

"Is he treating Rachel right?" Zeke asked.

"Like a queen," Jenny said with a smile. "Just like any woman wants to be treated."

Zeke frowned and opened his mouth as if he had something to say. Then he shut it without a word.

"Pershing," O'Neil called as he strode across the yard toward them. "What brings you here so early?"

Zeke turned away from Jenny. "Wanted to talk about planting."

"Ain't it too early?" O'Neil asked.

"Spring'll be here soon, and I have a lot of fields to plant." Zeke pulled his horse toward the barn in the steady rain.

"I'll help you with all of 'em," Jenny heard O'Neil say as the men disappeared into the barn.

Chapter 53:   Mac's Responses

Mac brooded over the letters from Jenny and his father. He knew he had to respond, but he needed to time to think. He worked in his store and made plans to transport gold to Sacramento. He corresponded with Dunbar in San Francisco almost daily and made another trip to see the man personally. It was mid-February before Mac could make himself deal with the letters.

After pontificating on the successes of Mac's older brothers, his father demanded Mac return to Boston by the summer.

> *. . . There are easy routes via Panama now, and the journey is a matter of mere weeks. Traffic is mostly from East to West, so booking return passage should not be difficult.*
>
> *If you are not back by July, your mother and I will conclude you are making your path in California, and will abandon all hope of seeing you again in this lifetime.*
>
> *Please advise.*
>
> *Andrew McDougall*

Mac fumed over what to tell his father. The old banker had no idea of the risks of a Panama crossing. Although traversing the isthmus was quicker than the route around Cape Horn, many travelers to San Francisco said pestilence in the tropics was worse than the danger of stormy seas off South America. Jessie Frémont had almost died in Panama.

He'd heard the overland trail was better marked than in 1847. On horseback, the journey would take three or four months, not the six months of wagon travel it had taken when he and Jenny made the trip. Still, overland travel brought its own perils, as Mac well knew.

He had no interest in joining his brother's law firm, nor in seeking another purpose in Boston. He needed to declare himself to his father—to state his intentions to make his future in the West.

Mac wasn't sure when his desire to remain in the West had become firm. When he bought the store? When he learned of Consuela's pregnancy? When he met Susan?

Or was it because California was nearer to Jenny?

Jenny. He read her letter again, focusing on her doubt that he had died, her desire to see him again, her expression of love.

Mac yearned to see Jenny again also, though he admonished himself he must cut all ties with her. Still, he couldn't help worrying about her. But the differences in their ages and upbringings and Jenny's past suffering stood between them. As did their last night, when he'd given rein to his desire for her.

Whatever Mac's future held, he did not see how Jenny could be a part of it. She should use the letter Consuela had sent to free herself. Only if she extricated herself from their subterfuge could he move on with his life.

So Mac finally braced himself to respond to the letters. He sat in the Golden Nugget, a bottle of whiskey and a glass in front of him. He set out quill pen, ink bottle, and paper, took up Jenny's letter first, and began to write:

February 18, 1850
Dear Jenny,

To answer your question, I am well, but you must construct your life in Oregon without me.

You asked for my sentiments. It is my deepest desire that you use the letter from Señorita Montenegro to remove me from your world, from the fiction I am your husband. The Oregon land is yours—I have no need of it.

You should marry a man who can care for you and William. Zeke Pershing would cherish you and provide you with the security and comfort you deserve. No doubt there are many other men in Oregon who would admire you, if Zeke is not your choice.

I beg you to do as you wrote you would, and let my wishes be your guide. Find another man who will esteem you as much as I do.

I will not write again.

Caleb McDougall

By the time the letter was finished, there were many crumpled drafts on the floor beside him, and the bottle was half empty. Mac poured two fingers of whiskey into the glass and drank it down. Then he staggered up to his room.

The next morning Consuela woke him with a cold, wet rag on his face. "The bartender said you got drunk last night. Now you have vomited in your bed. He sent me to clean you up." She brusquely wiped his chin.

Mac groaned. "Leave me be."

"It is because of this?" she asked, waving a piece of paper in the air.

Mac rose on an elbow and squinted to focus on the paper. "What is it?"

"Another letter."

"Ahh." Mac fell back on the bed, not caring it was damp and fetid.

"Get up," Consuela demanded, pulling him to a seated position. "We must wash you. It is the letter that makes you sick, no?"

"I drank too much."

"You didn't seal it," she said, stripping off his shirt and throwing it into a corner. "So I read it. You tell this Jenny she must find another man, and it drives you to drink. Again."

Mac said nothing.

"I had a letter from Señorita Jenny myself," Consuela said.

Mac widened his eyes in surprise. Then he realized he should have known Jenny wouldn't rely on him to answer her truthfully. "What did she say?"

"She asks if my letter is true. I will not be a part of your lying to her any longer."

"If you read my response, you know I told her the truth."

"Your letter is not the truth. You do not want her to marry this Zeke. Why must you punish yourself so?" Consuela made him stand and pushed him toward the basin of water in the corner. "Clean yourself, then come downstairs to the saloon and eat."

The thought of food made Mac want to retch, but he washed his face and combed his hair. He couldn't bear to shave, so he put on a clean shirt and went to find Consuela.

She waited for him with a plate of eggs and greasy bacon and a mug of coffee. "Eat," she said. "Then come to your store." She flounced out of the saloon as quickly as a heavily pregnant woman could flounce.

After a few bites, the eggs sat easier in his stomach, and Mac finished his breakfast. He knew Consuela was not done chastising him, and he didn't want to listen. He'd made up his mind when he wrote the letter to Jenny the night before. So he asked the cook for a second cup of coffee.

Soon he had no further excuse to avoid his store, and he stumbled outside and down the boardwalk.

"Do you love this Jenny?" Consuela asked, as soon as he walked in.

Mac sighed. "I care about her. But she turned me down once."

"You rescued her from evil men, yes?"

"Yes." Mac wiped his forehead with a handkerchief. "Then I dragged her across deserts and mountains to Oregon."

"Where you gave her a home, yes?"

"Yes."

"And gave her son a name?"

Mac shrugged and turned away. "William is known by my name. I don't mind."

"What man has done more for her than you have?" Consuela moved in front of Mac so he had to look her in the eye.

"Zeke Pershing worships the ground she walks on." It pained Mac to say it, but it was true. Zeke had always been more of a friend to Jenny than Mac had.

"And you do not?" Consuela raised an eyebrow. "I think otherwise, or you would have bedded me. Or one of the other girls."

"I'm not good for women." Mac busied himself lining up the barrels of cornmeal and flour in front of the counter. "Bridget and my child died because I wasn't there when they needed me. Jenny labored in a shed at

Whitman Mission because I took her away from her home. I couldn't keep my hands off her and scared her. She can't love me."

Consuela shook her head. "That is not for you to say."

Mac moved to the bins of nails in the corner. He picked a three-inch nail out of the two-inch bin and put it in its place. He'd wrestled so hard with his response to Jenny. Now Consuela made him doubt his decision.

"If you send this letter," Consuela said, enunciating the English words slowly. "You will come to regret it. You cannot run away from your fears, from the troubles you have caused in this world. If you do not face them, you will die."

"You don't want me to leave California now, do you?" Mac asked. "You need me until your child is born."

Consuela shrugged. "I will survive without you. Jenny and her son manage without you now. It is of your death I speak, not anyone else's."

"Will you address the letter, so it doesn't look like it comes from me?" Mac asked. "Jenny's friends in Oregon need to think I'm dead."

"I will not," she said, straightening her back. "You used me for the earlier letter, and it was wrong."

So Mac convinced Huntington to address the letter to Jenny.

That night he drafted his response to his father:

> *February 19, 1850*
> *Sir,*
> *I have multiple responsibilities in California which preclude me from leaving at this time. I do not know when I will return East.*
>
> > *Respectfully, your son,*
> > *Caleb*

The next morning Mac paused before posting his letters. His last chance to change his mind. About Oregon. About Boston.

He shook his head, paid the postage, and relinquished the letters to the clerk.

Chapter 54: Another Spring Planting

Jenny closed her school for the term on Friday, March 1, about two weeks earlier than the year before. The students' attendance had remained sporadic all winter.

True to his word, O'Neil started planting Jenny's fields on March 1 also. "That forest land I just cleared, it'll be the devil to plow," he told her. "But the winter wheat's showin' in the old fields now, and it's almost time to git the spring wheat planted."

"I thought last year we didn't plant until later in March," Jenny said.

"No sense in waitin'," O'Neil said. He scratched his chest and didn't meet her eye.

Saturday, March 2nd—Mr. O'Neil seems anxious about something. I wonder what it is.

When Zeke came to help the following Tuesday, Jenny asked him if he knew what might be bothering O'Neil.

"Don't know what the man wants," Zeke said, shaking rain off his hat then clapping it back on his head. "Could be he's ready to move on."

"Surely he'd tell me before he makes plans," Jenny said. "Or Rachel would." She didn't feel comfortable asking either O'Neil or Rachel about their future.

"You have a bigger problem than O'Neil," Zeke told her. "Samuel Abercrombie. I saw him and Douglass traipsing through your woodland when I rode over this morning. I asked them what they was doing, but they wouldn't say."

"Why would they come on my land?" Jenny asked, puzzled. "And on such a miserably wet day. Were they talking to Mr. O'Neil?"

"You know old Abercrombie wants your acres," Zeke said with a snort. "Thinks your land is better'n Douglass's. You have a single parcel with both meadowland and good forests. Meadows are easy to farm, and your trees are close by. And you have good water. Mac picked out a prime parcel."

"But Mr. Abercrombie, Douglass, and Daniel all wanted their land next to each other when they chose their claims. They didn't want this piece."

"Seems Abercrombie's changed his mind. Now he thinks his boys got second pickings, particularly Douglass. Ain't nothing wrong with Douglass's claim, except it's in two pieces and the meadows are low and stay damp later in the spring. He ain't near ready to plant yet."

"Well, they can't take my land," Jenny exclaimed. "Can they?"

"Course not. Mac filed the claim proper. Ain't nothing none of the Abercrombies can do so long as you keep proving it up till Mac gets back."

It all came back to whether she could prove up the claim, Jenny realized. But she could only be sure of staying on the land if no one discovered she wasn't Mac's wife.

"I'll put up some boards saying you don't allow no trespassing," Zeke said. "Don't know if Abercrombie'll pay any attention, but it can't hurt."

Tuesday, March 5ᵗʰ—Zeke says Mr. Abercrombie still wants my land. The man truly is my nemesis—as he was Mac's.

The next day Jenny asked O'Neil if he'd seen Samuel Abercrombie on her farm.

"No, ma'am," he said. "But I'll be watchin'. He's an ornery critter, that's for sure."

"He's a neighbor," Jenny said. "And well-liked by the officials in Oregon City. So please don't be rude to him. Just let me know if you see him. I don't want anyone trespassing on my land."

Maybe she could find out from Abercrombie's wife what his intentions were.

The skies had cleared by Thursday, though the yard was still muddy. After the noon meal, Jenny took William by wagon to Esther's cabin.

Once she'd greeted Esther, Jenny suggested they visit Esther's mother-in-law, Samuel Abercrombie's wife. "I have some quilt pieces and thought I'd exchange them for pieces from all our wagon company friends," Jenny said, handing Esther two squares of calico scraps. "Here are two pieces for you."

"How sweet," Esther said. "They're from the drawstring skirt you wore on the trail, ain't they?"

Jenny nodded. "I made the skirt into shirts for William, but he's outgrown them. The fabric is faded, but I cut the shirts for quilt pieces."

Esther rummaged in her own quilting bag and came up with squares she gave to Jenny. "From my blue wedding dress. Remember how bright the flowers were? It didn't last like I'd hoped. Cordelia wears a smock made from it, but these leftover scraps ain't big enough for anything but quilt squares. I have pieces I can give Mother Abercrombie, too," she said. "Let's go."

The young women loaded the children into the wagon and drove to the Abercrombie claim.

"Esther and Jenny," Mrs. Abercrombie said. "What a pleasure to see you. Louisa and I are baking bread."

"Smells mighty fine, Mother Abercrombie," Esther said. "Jenny wanted to share her quilt pieces with you."

The women chatted, and Mrs. Abercrombie found scraps of material to give Esther and Jenny. Louisa Abercrombie, Douglass's wife, promised to find some to exchange also.

"By the way, I hear Mr. Abercrombie has been walking about on my farm," Jenny said when the conversation about quilts ran to an end. "If he has questions about our planting, he should talk to Robert O'Neil. Mr. O'Neil is managing my crops this year, with Zeke's help." She no longer pretended O'Neil worked for Zeke—the hired hand had proved capable of handling the farm work himself.

Mrs. Abercrombie looked surprised. "Captain Abercrombie has been on your land? He didn't mention anything to me. I'll be sure to tell him you suggested he talk to Mr. O'Neil."

Louisa blushed and stared quietly at the quilt pieces in her lap.

Esther frowned at Jenny with a puzzled look, but said nothing.

"Men folk," Mrs. Abercrombie said. "They have their own ways, don't they? I never know what Captain Abercrombie is planning. If I ask, he just tells me I'm to tend to everything in the house, and he'll worry about everything outside. But when it comes time to catch and kill a chicken, he calls that women's work even though it's outside."

The women laughed, and their conversation turned back to quilting and cooking.

When they were in the wagon headed home, Esther asked, "All that talk about Father Abercrombie being on your land, what was that about?"

"Have you heard anything from Daniel about his father and Douglass wanting my claim?"

"Heavens, no," Esther said. "Not even Father Abercrombie can take a claim, no matter who he knows in Oregon City." She was silent a moment. "Can he?"

"I don't see how," Jenny said. "But Zeke says Mr. Abercrombie wants my farm for Douglass. Because my land is better."

"I think Daniel would have told me if he knew anything. But I'll ask him tonight."

"Louisa seemed subdued after I mentioned it," Jenny said.

"She was quiet," Esther agreed. "But how can they take you off the claim your husband filed?"

Chapter 55:   Consuela's Story

Mac traveled the hills beyond Sacramento more frequently in late February and into March, when the winter rains in California ended at last. He rode Valiente into mining territory to talk to storekeepers closer to the goldfields. By working only with established shops, he would be assured the gold he hauled had been weighed properly.

Many assayers were eager to do business with him, and he set up a route for collecting gold to transport to Sacramento. He'd had a new brick safe constructed in his storeroom, where he could keep the bags of flakes and nuggets until Dunbar's men moved them to San Francisco.

When his journeys took him near his old gold claim, he stayed with Joel and the Tanners. He was there on the evening of March 5, when a late snow demonstrated winter was not quite over in the Sierra foothills.

"Sure is good to see you, Captain," Tanner said, while Mac tethered Valiente under a tall aspen. "What brings you here?"

"I could still use more men to help me haul the color from the hill country to Sacramento," Mac said. "Would you be interested?"

Tanner shook his head. "Hatty'd have my head if'n I did somethin' so dangerous. I got plenty of work buildin' sluices and shoein' horses and mendin' tools and wagons. Ain't no call for me to gad about the hillsides."

"How about you, Joel?" Mac asked.

Joel shrugged. "Maybe. I'm getting itchy staying in one place. Might as well see the countryside, find out if there's better spots to dig."

"My gold route starts next week," Mac said. "The teamsters on the first two runs are set, but you'd be welcome to join in later. I plan to have a wagon make the circuit from Sacramento every week. Set out on Tuesday from my store, be back by Saturday or Sunday. Dunbar's boat and crew will pick the loads up on Mondays to take to San Francisco."

"I'll come see you next time I'm in town," Joel said. "Maybe go along on a run or two."

"Any sign of Smith?" Mac asked.

"Ain't seen hide nor hair of him," Joel said. "I think he's left the valley. Maybe even left California. You ain't seen him in town?"

Mac shook his head.

After supper Joel said in a low voice to Mac, "Come walk with me."

The two men strolled away from camp, and Mac asked, "What is it?"

"Didn't want the Tanners to hear, but I got a letter from Miz Jenny."

Mac's heart jumped to his throat. "When was it written?"

"Don't you want to know what she said?"

"Yes," Mac said. "But I need to know when she wrote. I had a letter also. I may have already responded to what she wanted from you."

"She wrote it back in November," Joel said. "I ain't picked it up till I was in Sacramento a week ago. Don't know why it took so long to get here, or maybe it sat waiting for me for a time. She asked me if you was dead or not."

Mac sighed and brushed his hat against his thigh at invisible dust. "She asked me the same thing. And Consuela, too. Jenny didn't believe the letter from Consuela. She didn't think I was really dead, because Esther had a letter from you saying I'd been in Monterey."

"I wrote Esther before you told me your crazy scheme. What you want me to do now?" Joel asked.

"No need to do anything. I wrote Jenny last month—told her I was still alive, but wanted her to be free to live without me. I told her to marry Zeke."

"Marry Zeke," Joel chortled. "You want me to write him to ask her? It wouldn't take him two seconds to hitch up with her."

Mac swallowed. He should say yes. But then Zeke would know he and Jenny hadn't been married. And what if Joel's letter went beyond Zeke? Then everyone would know—the very thing Mac's plan was supposed to avoid. "No," he said. "Let them find their own path, if they are meant to be together."

Back in the shanty beside a dying fire, he wrote:

March 5, 1850. The web I wove grows more

*complicated. All I wanted was to set Jenny free. I still
want what's best for her.*

Mac left the mining claim the next morning to return to Sacramento. He
rode alone, mulling over his new venture. Everything seemed to be in
place, and he thought the enterprise would be successful. It would fill his
days with action and adventure. He would have ample responsibility for
the wealth of miners in the region.

Satisfied with his business plans, his mind turned to Jenny. Would she
use his letter to have him declared dead? It was the only way he could see
to end the fiction they'd created when they set out for Oregon pretending to
be married.

Back in Sacramento, Mac launched the gold transport runs. He'd
commissioned a small wagon built for rugged hauling with a four-mule
harness. He stationed teams of mules at waypoints along the route. The
men he'd hired seemed sober and trustworthy, though he wished he knew
them better.

His schedule allowed for two long days to drive from Sacramento
northeast, then three days to finish the circuit back to Sacramento. The
return trip would take more time, because the wagon would be laden with
bags of gold. He estimated the wagon could haul about a thousand pounds
of gold per trip.

As he'd told Joel, the wagon would set out on Tuesday and return by
Saturday, with Sunday as an extra day if needed. Dunbar's men would pick
up the gold at Mac's store on Mondays to transport to San Francisco.

The first wagon left Mac's store on Tuesday, March 12. Mac drove, and
one of his new guards sat in back with a rifle in his arms, watching behind
them for any trouble. The next week, he sent out two men he'd hired. No
one bothered the wagons on these first two treks through the hills.

"Ain't no problem, Mr. McDougall," his driver told him after the
second run. "Good to have the guard there to provide company. But the
hills seem purty safe."

Mac remembered the ambush on his claim back in 1848. He would
never send a man out alone, just in case. "I need good records, too," he

said. "The ledgers you keep must be as accurate as those in my store. Second man makes sure the account entries stay honest."

"Biggest trouble is the goddamn weather," the driver said. "Been so much rain this year, the wagon wheels sink halfway to the axle in mud. I been in California for years, ain't never seen nothing like this afore. Some miners talking about calling it quits afore they drown."

Mac shrugged. He couldn't control the elements.

March 24, 1850. The gold transports have started well. About 600 pounds of dust in the bags the men brought back yesterday. The first week we hauled 738 pounds.

He wondered how the volume of gold would vary over time. The initial loads might be caused by gold miners had hidden through the winter. But would the weights go up or down in the weeks ahead?

The following Tuesday, after the wagon left his store for its third cycle, Mac sat with Consuela in the kitchen of the store waiting for the noon meal she'd fixed.

"*Tortillas,*" she announced, when she slid what looked like an omelet on Mac's plate.

"An omelet, you mean?" he said, grinning at her.

"*Tortillas,*" she said. "Spanish. With *pollo* and *patatas*. And there is rice."

"Thank you." He decided not to tease her any longer. Her sense of humor had diminished as her waistline grew. Her child could come any day, he guessed.

When Consuela had seated herself across the table from him, he asked. "How did you come to be in California? Were you born here or in Mexico?" He'd known Consuela for two years but had never inquired about her family. He only knew what she'd told him when they first met— she'd been married and her husband died.

"I was born in the hills outside Monterey," she said. "On a ranch near the Rio Carmelo."

"And your parents?"

"My father was a ranchero. He worked on the ranch my mother's father owned. My father was a half-breed—Spanish father and Indian mother." She smiled. "I remember his mother, my *abuela*. A member of the Costanoan people." She spoke with affection.

"Did you visit her?" Mac pictured a childish Consuela with long dark braids sitting on the lap of an old Indian woman.

"*Sí*. When I was little, she lived at the Mission San Carlos Borromeo de Carmelo. The *padres* treated her like a slave until she died." Her smile dimmed.

"Did your mother have Indian blood also?"

"No." Consuela shook her head. "That was the problem. Her parents were both born in Spain, and Mama was born on the ranch. They did not approve of their daughter marrying a half-breed hired hand. But marry they did, secretly in the mission church. There was nothing Mama's parents could do. So I am one-quarter Indian and the rest Spanish."

"Did you grow up on the ranch?"

"*Sí*." Consuela sighed deeply. "Mama and Papa had a small house on the ranch. *Mi esposo* Ramón, he was another ranchero and a half-breed, like Papa. He was so handsome. We fell in love. I was fifteen." Another sigh and a wistful smile touched her lips.

As she told the story, Mac imagined Consuela as a dreamy fifteen-year-old—the age Jenny had been when he'd left her. He was glad Consuela had known love and wished Jenny had had the same experience.

"So you married Ramón?"

"It was not so easy," Consuela said. "They died—my parents and Mama's parents. All of them. Influenza. An epidemic. The ranch was left to my mother's older brother. He did not like Ramón."

Mac waited while Consuela picked at her food.

She continued, "My uncle tried to move me into the hacienda, my grandparents' house, with his family. He wanted me as a maid for his children. Ramón persuaded me to run away with him. Then we married. I was seventeen." She smiled. "For a year, we were so happy. We moved to another ranch, where Ramón found work. I cooked for the rancheros."

"What happened?" Mac knew she was coming to the worst part of her story.

"A fight. A stupid fight over cards among the men. Ramón was shot."

Her eyes filled with tears. "I held him in my arms as he died."

They sat in silence awhile. So many of his friends had known tragedy. Consuela. Jenny. Nate and Susan. Mac had always thought his own life was easy, but even he had lost a child with Bridget. It never helped to compare sorrows, nor to wonder what might have been.

Consuela shrugged. "The ranch owner told me to leave. He did not want a cook without a husband. Not a young woman living alone with the rancheros. I went back to my uncle. He did not want me either."

She looked up at Mac. "I had no choice. I moved to San Francisco, away from everyone I knew. And sold myself. I had nothing else to sell."

Though Mac had told himself not to wonder what might have been, now he did. Consuela was a good cook—couldn't she have found another position? She was attractive—couldn't she have married again? But there was no point in questioning her now. The past could not be changed. "I'm sorry," he said, grateful again he'd rescued Jenny before she was forced into a similar fate.

"No matter," Consuela said. "For eight years now, I answer to no man. They own me only minutes at a time. Not many women can say that."

"After the child comes, you will still have a place in my store."

She shrugged and smiled wistfully. "*Que será será.*"

Chapter 56:   Deserter

Jenny smiled and waved when she saw Zeke ride into her yard on a Wednesday afternoon in mid-March. It was the first sunny day in weeks. She and Rachel had delayed their laundry from Monday until Wednesday, and were now draping wet clothes over a rope hung from a nail on the house to another on the barn.

"I've been to town," Zeke said. "Hear tell men been deserting from the Army. Governor Lane has issued a proclamation to bring 'em in if they're seen."

"The deserters won't stay nearby, will they?" Jenny asked. "Won't they run away?"

"Most likely they'll head for California as fast as they can," Zeke said. "But you be careful. Where's O'Neil?"

"South field," Rachel said. "Planting more wheat."

"I'll go talk to him." Zeke tipped his hat to the women. "He should stick close to the house for a spell."

Poulette and her colt nickered in the paddock as Zeke rode off. Jenny sighed. "I suppose we'll need to keep the horses in the barn when we're not around," she said. "Or the deserters will steal them."

"Why do men desert?" Rachel asked. "They made a promise. Can't they keep it?"

"Ask Mr. O'Neil," Jenny said. "He served his full enlistment. But he must know men who didn't."

Over supper in Jenny's cabin that evening, Rachel did ask her husband.

"Yes, I've known men to desert," O'Neil said, leaning back in his chair. "Not on the trail near Fort Leavenworth. Nowhere to go in those parts. Most left their companies in the mountains. Headed straight for California and warm weather."

"Don't the Army treat 'em right?" Rachel asked.

"Army treats a man fine," O'Neil said. "But some men got a hankerin' to be their own boss. Anyways, you ladies stay near the house. And keep a rifle handy."

Before she went to bed, Jenny wrote:

Wednesday, September 13th—There are evil men everywhere, according to Zeke and Mr. O'Neil. Soldiers are not exempt. I fear for our safety even at home.

When no strangers appeared on her claim over the next several days, Jenny gradually relaxed. The weather stayed dry, and O'Neil spent his time planting. "Got to git the seed in the ground," he said. "Deserters or no deserters."

Zeke fumed when he came by one morning the following week. It was early, and Jenny was still washing breakfast dishes. Rachel had just walked over from her cabin. "Where's that fool O'Neil?" Zeke asked.

"Don't you call him a fool," Rachel said to her brother, her hands on her hips. "He's taking a load off your shoulders, all the planting he's doing on Jenny's farm this year."

"Damn lot of good it'll do her if she's dead," Zeke said. "Or worse."

Jenny gasped.

"What's worse'n dead?" Rachel asked.

Jenny knew what Zeke meant—she'd experienced worse. "We'll be fine, Zeke," she said. "I keep the gun beside me in the house and take it to the barn when I gather eggs or milk the cow. Though it's all I can do to keep William's hands off it."

"'Bout time the boy learned to shoot, ain't it?" Zeke asked.

"He's not quite two-and-a-half," Jenny exclaimed. "He can't even lift a rifle."

"Daniel let Jonah aim a pistol," Zeke said. "I could take William along some day to shoot at targets. Even if he don't hit anything, he'll like it."

Jenny didn't want her boy to grow up so fast. "He's not ready," she said.

Zeke left to find O'Neil, and Jenny went to the barn to check on the horses and chickens. William tagged along behind her, "I wanna shoot, Mama."

"When you're bigger, William," Jenny said, dismissing the child's comments. She'd left the rifle in the cabin, afraid her son would try to play with it after the talk of letting him shoot.

She opened the squeaking barn door. "Guess I'd better ask Mr. O'Neil to grease the hinges," she said, as much to herself as to William.

From the back stall where Shanty was penned came a rustling. The colt whinnied. "Shanty," she said, "what is it?"

Jenny heard the rustling again. Her heart leapt. No rifle. She pushed William behind her. "Run to the house," she said, giving him a soft swat on his rear. "Go see Rachel. Tell her to stay in the cabin with you."

When her son had gone, she turned to the stall. "Who's there?" She grabbed a pitchfork and advanced toward the colt's stall.

A man stood up, visible from his chest up behind the stall door. Jenny screamed.

"Hold on, ma'am," the man said. "I won't hurt nobody."

"Who are you?" Jenny demanded, pitchfork brandished in front of her.

"Name's Adams," he said. "Jeb Adams. Just needed a warm bed for the night. I'll be leavin' now."

Jenny peered at him. He wore a tattered uniform. "You one of the deserters from Fort Walla Walla?" She couldn't see his hands below the wall of the stall.

"Just a man tryin' to find his way in the world, ma'am."

"Are you a deserter?" Jenny repeated. "Put your hands up where I can see them." She gestured with the pitchfork.

"I'll be on my way now." The man pulled the stall door open and rushed toward Jenny, a pistol in his hand.

Jenny screamed and turned to run, but was knocked down when a man rushed past her. Zeke.

Zeke crashed into the deserter, and both men fell to the ground. "Run, Jenny," Zeke shouted as he thrashed the intruder.

Jenny ran to the cabin, yelled at William and Rachel to stay put, grabbed her rifle, and hurried back to the barn. When she returned, the deserter was face down on the ground. Zeke sat on the soldier's back, holding one of the man's arms twisted behind his back.

"I told you to go to the house," Zeke said through his teeth. "Since you're here, find me something to tie him up with."

Jenny tossed him a leather strap she used to lead the colt. Zeke cinched a loop tightly around the deserter's wrists and pulled the man to his knees. "Keep the rifle on him," Zeke said. He found a rope and tied the man to a support beam.

"Now," Zeke said to the intruder, "who are you?"

"Jeb Adams. As I was tellin' the lady, I'm merely passin' through."

"Not through here, you ain't," Zeke said. "I'll be taking you to Oregon City." Zeke turned to Jenny. "Can you keep a gun on him while I find O'Neil? I'm not leaving the farm till he's here to stay with you and Rachel."

Jenny nodded. "He's in the fields. Let Rachel know we're safe now, but tell her to stay in the house with William. I'll handle him," she said, tipping her head at Adams.

"Use his pistol. It's lighter than the rifle." Zeke checked to make certain the pistol was loaded, handed the gun to Jenny, and turned to leave.

She heard Zeke shout at Rachel, and seconds later horse hooves pounded away from her claim. Zeke had gone.

"Now, ma'am, there ain't no need for the gun," Adams said. "I'm tied up. Can't do you no harm."

Jenny stood her ground. "You came at me with this pistol. I'd say that's harm enough."

"If I wanted you dead, ma'am, I would've shot you. I just want to leave Oregon."

The man could talk all he wanted, Jenny thought, she didn't have to answer. Her hands shook, and she could barely keep the pistol aimed at him, but she would protect her child and her farm. She'd shot a man before, back in Arrow Rock, and she'd do it again if she had to.

But the thought of Arrow Rock brought back memories of helplessness she couldn't dispel. Her arms and legs quivered by the time Zeke returned with O'Neil. Grateful, she handed the pistol to Zeke. Then she sank to the ground and inhaled deeply, while the two men debated who would take Adams into town and who would stay on the claim.

"I know the Army sergeant," O'Neil argued. "Let me take him."

Zeke shook his head. "I'm going. You stay with Jenny and Rachel. You're the married man." Zeke won the point and mounted his horse.

O'Neil tied Adams to Zeke's saddle horn, leaving the man's hands bound behind him.

"Better not trip," Zeke said, "or you'll end up under my horse's hooves. Which don't matter none to me."

Jenny worried about Zeke for the rest of the day. He didn't return until sundown, arriving shortly after Jenny, William, Rachel, and O'Neil had begun supper.

"Adams is a deserter, all right, though he ain't one of the ringleaders," Zeke said, joining them at table. "He must've had a falling out with the others, to be on his own. The sergeant was glad enough to lock him up."

"Why'd he desert?" Jenny asked as she filled a plate for Zeke.

"Headed for the gold fields, I suppose," Zeke said, leaning back in his chair. "Another damn fool slavering after gold."

Right after supper, Jenny saw a glance pass from Zeke to O'Neil, then O'Neil stood and ushered Rachel out of the cabin. Zeke remained, saying he would help Jenny wash dishes.

When they were alone, Zeke said, "You can't stay here, Jenny." He dried a plate she handed him. "There's no sign Mac is ever coming back. You should move to town."

Mac's failure to answer her last letter was a good indication he wouldn't return. But she wouldn't admit it to Zeke. "Mr. O'Neil's here."

"And what if he leaves?" Zeke said, drying the last plate and stacking it.

"I'll face that if it happens," Jenny said, wiping her hands on a towel. Her palms broke out in sweat at the thought of living alone with William. What if another deserter attacked? Or a mountain lion prowled again?

"I'll have to insist you leave, if O'Neil don't stay here."

Jenny stuck her chin out stubbornly. "You don't have any right to insist I do anything."

Zeke threw the dish towel he'd been using to the floor, his mouth twisting in an angry grimace. "I don't want to see you hurt."

"I'll be more careful, Zeke." Jenny swallowed. She'd forgotten her rifle today, and she and William were almost killed.

That night her shaking hand caused ink to spatter as she wrote:

Thursday, March 21ˢᵗ—I found a deserter on the claim today. Zeke captured him and took him to the Army garrison in town. How will I manage if Mr. O'Neil and Rachel leave?

Chapter 57: New Business and New Birth

March 27, 1850. Fourth transport run began today. After a dry February, March has been dismal. Ten inches of rain in Sacramento. The mules have had a hard time hauling the wagon through the muck.

Not until the end of March did the rains finally let up, allowing miners to crowd into town for supplies. It was all Mac could do to keep provisions on the shelves. He shifted some of his attention from the gold transport to the store.

Huntington earned his keep with the customers, but Consuela grew uncomfortable standing behind the counter for any length of time. Mac convinced her not to come into the store any longer, and she stayed upstairs, telling Mac she would sew for her baby.

Prospectors entered Mac's store full of tales of treachery and deceit between miners and Indians. "Oughta be a law against foreigners and savages takin' our land," a man from Kentucky told Mac.

"And what's your right to the land?" Mac asked.

"I'm a God-fearin' Christian just tryin' to make my fortune," the man responded. "Not like the heathens and Mexicans."

If Mac turned away all the miners who expressed similar opinions, he'd lose half his customers. So he simply asked, "What can I sell you today?"

On the afternoon of March 28, Joel came into the store to deposit his gold. "Our vein's running out," he told Mac as he plunked a skinny leather bag on the counter. "Weigh my dust, and you can see."

Mac shook the bag's contents onto his scale.

Joel scratched his head. "Might look for another claim higher in the Sierras. Think I'd like to drive one of your transports, do some scouting while I'm out."

"You can go next Tuesday," Mac said. Joel could handle a wagon and team and was a good shot with a rifle. "But there won't be much time for scouting. You need to keep the wagon on its route."

"Got a guard?"

Mac nodded. "I'll have someone to ride with you. Both driver and guard have to watch for trouble and be able to shoot straight."

"What's the pay?"

Mac calculated the weight of Joel's gold flakes, then grinned. "About what you made in this bag."

"And that's two weeks' work." Joel shook his head while he initialed the account Mac handed him. "So I can make the same money driving a wagon for you on a five-day route?"

"Seems right," Mac said. "How are the Tanners?"

"Fine," Joel said. "Hatty has herself a regular business. Men she feeds every day. Does their laundry, too. Hired an Indian girl to help. She could take on twice the customers, if I let her hire another girl."

"Why won't you?"

"Got too many strangers hanging about the camp as it is. More men crowding into the valley, though there's less color. Your teamsters oughta be able to tell you that."

"We haven't hauled as much gold as the wagon can hold. I'd like to add another weekly run, but there's no point until I fill the wagon I have." Mac leaned forward on the counter. "What's Tanner doing?"

"Fixes tools. Hires out to dig in the trenches. He's making as much in wages as I dig out of the ground these days." Then Joel squinted at Mac. "That Smith fellow's been seen again, nosing around some of our neighbors' claims."

"Smith? I thought he'd left the territory."

"Seems not. You tell your men to watch out. He's too lazy to dig, but not to steal."

The next day Mac was surprised to see Smith saunter into the store. Mac wondered whether the man had followed Joel into town.

"Hear you need a guard for your gold," Smith said.

He didn't need Smith, Mac immediately thought. "Got enough men already," he said mildly. He didn't want trouble with Smith, but he would never hire the man. Joel's warning hadn't been necessary—Mac had seen enough of the scoundrel himself.

"Who'd you hire?"

Mac shrugged. "No concern of yours."

"Better make sure you got men who can shoot," Smith said. "Lots of thievin' bastards in these parts now. A wagon full of gold is a damn temptation."

"You wouldn't be tempted to steal it yourself, would you, Smith?"

"If I ain't hired to protect it, it's fair game." Smith grinned and walked out.

Before dawn on Saturday, Huntington burst into Mac's room above the Golden Nugget. "It's comin'," he shouted.

"What?" Mac's head was foggy after too much whiskey the night before.

"Consuela's brat," Huntington said. "What do we do now?"

Mac sat on the side of his bed and reached for a shirt. "I'll ask one of the girls here to stay with her," Mac said. "What time did her pains start?"

"Pains?" Huntington looked dazed. "She didn't tell me nothin' but to fetch you."

"All right," Mac said. "I'll be there shortly."

When he arrived at the store, bringing a hefty saloon girl named Ethel with him, he found Consuela pacing in her room upstairs. "Shouldn't you be in bed?" he asked.

"If she wants to walk, she should walk," Ethel said. "That's what the cows on my pa's farm did. Now, honey, you go on downstairs and leave her to me." Ethel shooed Mac out of the room and down to his store.

Around noon Mac started hearing moans from Consuela's room. As her cries grew louder, customers glanced nervously at the ceiling. "Woman in labor," Mac told them. He, too, was anxious. Jenny had almost died during William's birth. He hadn't wanted to leave her to Doc and Mrs. Tuller's care. He'd forced his way into the room to sit with Jenny.

But he felt no need to be with Consuela. And he had the store to mind.

When Consuela's wails grew more frequent, Mac closed the store early. He went upstairs to check on her, but Ethel wouldn't let him in. "No man should see this," she said. "Or us workin' gals wouldn't git no more customers."

Mac let her push him away. He took Huntington next door to the Golden Nugget for supper. "They don't want us around," he told the older man.

"And I don't want the racket," Huntington said. "You got any cigars with you? Good smoke would help pass the time."

"In the store," Mac said. "When the baby comes, I'll get you one. But it isn't good for your cough."

"I'll put up with a wheezy night for a good cigar." Huntington grinned. "Ain't got no other pleasures I can still indulge in."

They lingered in the saloon, until Ethel came for them late in the evening. "It's a girl," she said. "She's namin' her Maria."

Huntington snorted. "Virgin's name for a whore's daughter. Don't that take the cake?"

"It isn't the child's fault," Mac said.

They went back to the store, and Ethel brought the baby down. "Consuela don't want you visitin' yet," she said, handing the baby to Mac.

Maria was a pretty little thing, he had to admit. Big solemn eyes and lots of dark hair. A rosebud mouth. Tiny fists. Looked better than William had at birth.

"Well, look at that," Huntington said with awe in his voice. "She grabbed my finger. Let me hold her." And the old man wouldn't give Maria back until she started crying. Then he quickly handed her off to Ethel. "I ain't no good with young'uns," he said.

March 30, 1850. Consuela was delivered of her child—a girl, Maria.

The next morning Ethel let Mac see Consuela. "How are you?" he asked.

"Sore." She smiled, looking down at the baby in her arms. "But it was worth the pain to get my *niña*."

"She's as pretty as her mother," Mac said.

"No such talk from you," Consuela said. "You have not flirted with me before. And I'm still fat. I won't be able to work for weeks."

"You don't have to go back to the store until you're ready."

Consuela frowned. "I meant the saloon."

"The saloon?" Mac said in surprise. "Why would you go back there?"

"I cannot take your charity forever," Consuela said. "I had to when I was expecting. But no more. I will care for my *niña*."

Mac shook his head. "You should stay here with the baby. Work for me."

Consuela raised an eyebrow and set her chin stubbornly.

Chapter 58:   Transports and Fire

Mac helped Joel harness the mules on the morning of April 2, as Joel prepared to drive the gold run. "Watch out," Mac told Joel. "Smith came to see me last week. Asked about a job."

"What'd you tell him?"

"No, of course. I don't want him anywhere near my gold."

Joel cocked an eyebrow and grinned. "Maybe it'd be best to have him close at hand. Keep an eye on him."

Mac shook his head. "Not him. You and the guard stay alert."

Then he worried about his men and their load all week.

On Thursday, April 4, fires raged through Sacramento in the commercial area between Mac's store and the Embarcadero. When he heard shouting outside, he called Huntington, and the two men rushed to help quench the flames.

They joined a bucket brigade along with dozens of other men. Without any fire tankers in town, they had to haul water from the river to the flames. Huntington spent as much time coughing and wheezing as carrying buckets.

Mac feared the fire would move toward his store, where Consuela and newborn Maria would be helpless. "Go check on Consuela and the baby," he told Huntington.

"Nah," the old man said, spitting. "We'd best keep fightin' the flames. Consuela's smart enough to run if the fire turns that way."

Mac watched the wind—if it turned toward his store, he'd get them out of harm's way himself. But the men were able to beat the flames back.

After the fire was vanquished, Mac and Huntington went to the Golden Nugget for a beer. "Floods in January, now fires," Huntington said, wheezing. "Seems like this town's doomed."

Mac shook his head. "Just built up too fast. The wood buildings are too close together, and the canvas tents fuel the flames. Some Boston neighborhoods burned frequently. Mostly from carelessness and cooking fires."

"Nope, we're doomed," Huntington replied. "Like Sodom and Gomorrah."

"You think we're sinful here in Sacramento?" Mac asked with a grin.

"Not me," Huntington said, with a cough. "I'm too old for sin. It's you young'uns gotta watch out for the devil."

April 4, 1850. Fought a fire near the store today. Huntington was of little help. Tomorrow is my 29th birthday. Will I be settled by age thirty?

Joel and the guard made it back to Sacramento on schedule on Saturday, April 6, with the load of gold they'd collected.

"Any trouble?" Mac asked.

Joel shook his head. "The road is still sloppy, but no sign of Smith."

"Think I might take a turn," Huntington said to Mac that night while the three former partners ate supper.

Joel guffawed. "You ain't up to driving, old man."

"I can shoot," Huntington protested.

"I have enough men for now." Mac tried to be diplomatic—Huntington had been a good partner, but a week in a wagon would be tough on the aging miner. "I thought you were ready to take it easy now."

"I'm bored," Huntington said. "And Consuela's cookin' is makin' me fat."

Mac thought the skinny old prospector could use a few more pounds. "I'll let you know if I need an extra hand."

He wrote on Sunday morning:

April 7, 1850. How can I tell Huntington he is too old for physical labor? Even sitting as guard on the transport wagon is likely to be hard on him.

Consuela was working in the store again nine days after Maria's birth, as well as cooking for Mac and Huntington. Mac sat in the kitchen with Maria on his lap one evening while Consuela did the dishes.

"Doesn't she ever sleep?" Mac asked. William had done nothing but sleep or cry in the weeks after his birth. Maria slept less, but was serene when awake.

"Not when you're around." Consuela smiled. "She loves your voice."

Mac grinned. "Huntington's jealous. He dotes on her, and she doesn't pay him any mind."

Consuela laughed. "Women are like that. They want the men they can't have and ignore the ones who want them."

April 8, 1850. Maria is a pretty infant who seldom cries. She has luminous eyes like her mother.

In mid-April Mac made a trip to San Francisco to talk to Dunbar about their joint enterprise.

"Business isn't what I expected," the rotund man told Mac. "We'd hoped for a ton a week."

"The gold volume might pick up, now the rains are past," Mac responded. "The wagon is slow in all the mud, and the prospectors haven't been able to dig out much color this year. Some early veins are played out, and the newer lodes take more work."

"The Forty-Niners will be sorry they ever came to California," Dunbar said, grinning. "There's money to be made here—just not in prospecting."

Mac nodded. "San Francisco is large enough now to survive whatever happens with the gold mines."

Dunbar hooked his thumbs in his vest pockets. "County government in place now, and the City of San Francisco incorporated last Monday. Yes, sir, we are here to stay."

That evening Mac dined with Nate and Susan and described his gold hauling business.

"Why, you are a man of commerce," Susan said, smiling. "I'm sure your enterprise will be successful."

"Don't you worry about your schedule becoming known?" Nate asked Mac. "Getting robbed?"

"No trouble so far," Mac said. "But we keep a careful lookout, and I only hire good shots. We should be all right unless a whole gang attacks the wagon."

"Men aren't the only problems you might face," Nate said. "All the rain this winter has set off mudslides everywhere. And have you seen Mount Diablo smoking?"

Susan shuddered. "California is such wild country—volcanoes along with hooligans and drunks. Though I must admit the light from the burning mountain at night is very beautiful."

"I'll have to see it before I leave tomorrow," Mac said.

"Would you care to walk a bit tonight?" Susan asked, smiling.

Mac assented, but Nate declined to accompany them.

Mac escorted Susan up a nearby hill. From the top, he stared at Mount Diablo in the hills on the east side of San Francisco Bay. Smoke billowed from the volcano toward the thin slice of moon in the starlit sky.

He looked down at Susan, who clung to his arm. She smiled at him, her eyes sparkling like the stars.

April 18, 1850. The transport business is going well, and I had pleasant company tonight for dinner. My life is good. How long can I keep it so?

Chapter 59:   Moving On

In early April O'Neil and Zeke were still plowing and sowing the fields. They'd cleared and planted almost twice as much land as the year before. Jenny seldom saw either man before dusk.

> *Friday, April 5ᵗʰ—Rachel, Mr. O'Neil, and I have grown comfortable in one another's company. They break their fast most mornings in their cabin, and William and I eat in ours. Then Rachel and I do chores together, moving between our two homes while Mr. O'Neil is in the fields, sometimes with Zeke's help. Or we visit Esther or Mrs. Tuller. In the evenings, when the men come in dirty from the fields, we have supper ready.*

The men planted even on Sundays. "God don't stop the grass growin' or the rain fallin' on the Sabbath," O'Neil said. "Farmer's got to keep up with the Lord. That's what my pa always said."

But unless rain poured, on Sundays Jenny and Rachel harnessed Poulette to the wagon and rode into Oregon City for church. Sunday, April 7, was a fine morning, and they headed into town.

"William needs to get out," Jenny told Rachel while the two-and-a-half-year-old ran around the churchyard after services with a group of older boys.

"He spends lots of time outside," Rachel said.

"I mean he needs other children. He doesn't see anyone other than Esther's brood."

"Not since your school closed. It was a shame your students didn't come more regularly."

"Yes," Jenny sighed. "I've missed the bartered goods as well as the children's company."

"You have enough, don't you?" Rachel raised her eyebrows at Jenny. "We've never wanted for food this winter."

"Mr. O'Neil hunted when he had time, and Zeke brought us meat as well. And I have my credit in town. So we've done all right." Jenny sighed again. "And I have most of what Mac left me. I've had to spend some, and I might have to use more, if the store wants payment before the crops come in this fall. Plus, there are the taxes, because Mac has not returned."

"Surely the stores will give you more credit," Rachel said. "They're carrying so many emigrants."

"At some point, their credit will stop. I'll have to have the farm paying by then. Or I'll have to go back to teaching school. But I can't do so until fall, when the children are free after the harvest."

Rachel stared at the ground and was silent. Jenny could tell the girl had something to say. "What is it, Rachel?"

"Ro-Robert," Rachel stammered. "He's filed a land claim. We're moving there as soon as your planting is done, so he can clear our land. He says we need our own place. I'm in a family way now." The girl blushed. "We want to raise our baby on our own land. But I feel bad leaving you."

Jenny took a deep breath, closing her eyes. She'd be alone again. Then she smiled and hugged Rachel. "That's wonderful news—both about your claim and your baby. Mr. O'Neil is absolutely right. You should have your own home. You don't owe me anything."

"You gave me a home last year," Rachel said.

"And you helped me, as a good friend does. I'll miss you."

But later Jenny's tears streaked the ink when she wrote:

Sunday, April 7th—Rachel and Mr. O'Neil will move to their own claim soon. I've been alone before, and I can do it again. They won't be too far away to visit.

Writing the words didn't help. She didn't want to live alone again, with only William for company.

"What'll you do when O'Neil leaves?" Zeke asked late one afternoon the following week. "He's filed a claim a few miles south of here."

"He told me he'd still work for me part of the time," Jenny said. "He won't have much of a crop this year. He has to clear his land."

"You could ask Pa about Jonathan and David moving here. They're thirteen now, big enough to be a help with chores. And with farming."

"I won't have those boys doing a man's work in the fields," Jenny said.

"What do you think they're doing for Pa?" Zeke said. "They're helping him and me both."

"And who'll help your papa if the boys live here?" Jenny asked, running the back of her hand over her forehead. "I need another hired hand."

"Won't find one this spring." Zeke snorted. "Every able-bodied man is already working at something. I'll help you two days a week, but that's as much as I can do and manage my own farm, too."

"Thank you," Jenny said meekly.

Zeke hesitated, then said. "Have you written Mac to come home?"

"I've asked." That was mostly true, Jenny thought. She'd told Mac she wanted to see him again. That was the same as asking him to come back.

"What did he say?"

"I haven't heard yet." Jenny stared at the ground, not trusting herself to meet Zeke's eye without crying. "I do miss him, Zeke."

"You know how I feel 'bout him leaving you here alone. It's been more'n two years now." Jenny opened her mouth to speak, but Zeke held up his hand. "I've said it before, but I have to say it again, Jenny. It ain't right."

The next time Zeke came, he brought a wriggling brown dog with him.

"What's that?" Jenny asked.

"I don't want you alone here after O'Neil leaves. The pup's full grown, but not so big you can't handle him. He'll make a good watchdog."

As if to prove his worth, the dog barked. William came running. The dog went straight into William's arms, and the boy giggled when the pup licked his face. Jenny knew she had acquired another animal.

"His tail wags, Mama," William said. And "Wags" the dog became.

"He has to sleep in the barn," Jenny said, wondering if she would be able to enforce that rule.

Jenny tried to keep a smile on her face while she helped Rachel make lists of household items she needed. "We've shared so much the past few months," Rachel said. "I don't know how I'll manage my house all by myself. And the baby needs so much, too."

"Not really," Jenny smiled. "William only had what I could make along the trail. Your mama and Mrs. Tuller told me all I needed was diapers, and lots of them."

Rachel laughed. "We've all seen a lot of diapers since then, haven't we? All the babies born in the last three years. And now it's my turn." Rachel's face beamed when she spoke of having her own home and family.

Jenny tried not to let her own unhappiness show. But in the evenings after William was asleep, she wept into her pillow—the pillow she'd taken off Mac's cot when he left. Sometimes she thought she still smelled him in it. How could she live on her own, without Rachel and O'Neil for assistance and company?

Zeke and O'Neil put the word out in town she needed a hired hand, but she wasn't likely to find anyone. Zeke pressed her to have the twins live on her farm after the O'Neils moved, but she refused.

By April 28, the last Sunday of the month, most of the crops were planted, and Rachel and O'Neil had packed. They planned to move their belongings to their claim on Tuesday and live in a tent while O'Neil built a cabin.

That morning they all went to church together for the last time. Jenny wondered how she and William would fare alone. The boy didn't seem to understand Rachel and O'Neil were leaving. He asked about them frequently when they weren't in sight.

"Where's Rachel?" he asked Jenny several times a day.

"She's at her home. But she'll be back soon," Jenny told her son.

Come Tuesday, Jenny wouldn't be able to tell William that Rachel would be back soon.

After the church service, the congregation held a picnic. The rains had let up enough to sit outside, though the ground was still damp under new grass.

"Spread a blanket," Esther told Daniel. "Here, Rachel, you sit and rest."

"I'm fine," Rachel protested. She hadn't been as sick as either Esther or Jenny had been during their pregnancies.

"It's not fair you're doing so well, when I puked every morning," Esther said, but she smiled at her sister when she spoke. "I'm looking forward to being an auntie. You'll get the work of this baby, not me."

"How you can want another one in the family is beyond me," Amanda Pershing said, shaking her head, as she sat by her stepdaughters with her infant son Franklin on her lap. "We're all tuckered out caring for children. You most of all, Esther."

Esther did look tired these days, Jenny thought. But it wasn't nice of Mrs. Pershing to point it out. "Esther does so well with children," Jenny said, sticking up for her friend.

Rachel, too, defended her sister. "She'll be such a help, when my baby comes."

"I dare say we'll all help," Amanda Pershing said with a sigh. Esther was silent. The sisters and their stepmother still did not get along well.

Zeke came over to the blanket where the women sat. "I picked up the mail yesterday," he said. "Pa got a letter from Joel, and Jenny has one from California." He handed the letter to Jenny.

Jenny didn't recognize the handwriting. Could it be from Mac? She wanted to put it in her pocket for later, but Zeke and the others stared at her expectantly. "Open it," Esther said.

Jenny couldn't refuse with everyone staring at her. She broke the seal, and smiled when she saw it was Mac's handwriting. "It's from Mac," she exclaimed. "He's alive!" The sun broke out above her and shone on the letter in her hand.

"Did you think he wasn't?" Esther laughed. "You'd said he was ill, but you didn't make it sound serious."

"He's well." Then Jenny read on. Her heart fell, and a roaring sound filled her ears. "He's not coming back," she heard herself say, as her world turned dark.

Chapter 60:   Ambush

Mac's gold transport business continued on its weekly schedule. Every Tuesday, two teamsters set out on the run—a driver and a guard. Each man kept two loaded Winchester rifles at his feet and a pistol on his hip. By mid-April Mac had come to trust his employees to drive and guard and keep to the schedule. He preferred to stay with his store and let his hired men make the trip.

But on April 20, one teamster came back from driving the wagon with a sprained shoulder. "Damn mules tried to run away with us," he told Mac. "I pulled a muscle hauling in the traces."

Another man scheduled for the next run had the grippe and couldn't leave his bed. Joel was out in the hills looking for a new place to dig, and two other employees had gone to San Francisco to spend their wages.

Mac had no driver for the April 23 trip. He would have to drive himself. And he had no guards.

"You game to make the transport with me next week?" Mac asked Huntington. "Be my lookout?"

"You ain't got no one else, do you?" Huntington asked, with a grin.

"No, and I need to get the gold to Sacramento. Ships in San Francisco are waiting. I have to keep the Tuesday schedule."

April 22, 1850. I have no choice. Huntington and I leave in the morning.

Before dawn Mac rousted Huntington out of bed. They harnessed two pairs of mules to the wagon, checked their rifles and ammunition, and climbed onto the seat.

Consuela handed them a bag with provisions. "*Tortillas con queso* for your noon meal today," she said. "But then it's hard tack and bacon you must cook yourself."

Mac nodded his thanks, then yelled to the mules, "Hie!" They started out of Sacramento at a fast walk.

Around noon they reached the low foothills of the Sierras and the first stop on their route. Then, as they climbed farther into the mountains, they halted regularly to load gold into the wagon bed and change teams. After heavy rains through winter and early spring, wildflowers now burst out on the hills around the gold fields.

Mac did most of the driving, wanting to spare Huntington the harder role. But they traded places on occasion throughout their two-day journey into the hills.

Concerned about thievery, Mac peered into the forest when trees pressed close to the road. He kept his eye out for men following them and instructed Huntington to do the same.

"We'll see 'em in time to plug 'em," the old prospector said. "No worries there."

But they encountered only a few riders with pack mules in between the gold camps on their route.

After two days they reached the most distant point of the circuit, then turned back toward Sacramento. Now high in mountains, the road they traveled was rougher. Their wagon was partially laden with gold, so they moved slowly. They continued to pick up sacks of gold flakes and nuggets while they descended toward Sacramento.

Lower in the hills, the pines and aspen and scrubby oaks grew farther apart and the land opened up. Mac relaxed with the greater visibility but tried to stay vigilant.

By noon on Saturday, the last day of the trip, they'd finished their stops and had only the final drive to Sacramento. The wagon held many bags of gold and creaked with every turn of the wheels. The mules pulled at a slow pace, straining into their harnesses.

"How much color you think we got back there?" Huntington asked. "I'm thinkin' half a ton."

Mac looked back at the fifty or so bags of gold in the wagon bed. The weight of the bags varied from ten to forty pounds, but he doubted the average reached twenty pounds. He shrugged. "Probably not quite that." But the wagon still carried a fortune.

The road passed through a flat meadow in the foothills. The tall trees gave way to about an acre of grasses sprinkled with a few early wildflowers. Birds chirped from the aspen beyond the open field.

Mac asked, "Shall we rest and eat? Give the mules a chance to breathe. There's a stream over by the trees. Or keep going?"

"Wouldn't mind a chance to piss," Huntington said.

"All right," Mac said, pulling back on the reins. "But we can't tarry. Not and be back by nightfall. No moon tonight."

Mac climbed out of the wagon, then reached for their dwindling bag of food. Huntington urinated against a wagon wheel.

"I'll go fill our canteens," Mac said, scrabbling under the wagon bench to find them.

Rifle shots rang out from the trees beyond the meadow, several rounds close together—more than one man shooting.

"Ambush!" Huntington yelled, scrabbling up the wheel into the wagon bed.

Mac threw himself over the wagon seat into the back beside Huntington.

Three horsemen galloped from the woods, approaching Mac and Huntington from different directions. One man rode straight at the wagon, another circled south and the third around from the north.

"Get down," Mac shouted. "We can't outrun them." They hunkered down behind the bags of gold and pulled out their rifles. "You take north, I'll take south," Mac told Huntington.

The attackers fired pistols as they raced toward the wagon. Mac aimed his Winchester and shot. The rider to their south fell, twitched, then was still. The other two blaggards kept shooting.

When the two assailants came close, Mac whistled in a breath. "Man in the middle is Smith," he whispered to Huntington. "That bastard." He shot at the man, who circled to head back to the trees. Mac reloaded, and shot again when Smith turned back toward them.

"I'm hit," Huntington cried, falling backward.

Mac spared his partner a quick glance. Huntington had a hand on his chest, blood oozing through his fingers. "Can you still shoot?"

"Yeah," Huntington said, wincing.

Smith and the other raider continued to bombard the wagon with bullets, approaching and retreating over and over. The lead team of mules screamed and fell, first one then the other, still in the harness. The other pair whinnied and jumped, trying to escape their fallen companions.

"Christ," Mac hissed when the first mule fell. "We're stuck now." He shot the unidentified rider off his horse, and the mount galloped off. "Smith's the only one left," he told Huntington. "Hang in there."

The huge thief rode straight at the wagon. Mac lifted his head and shoulder above the wooden side, then lurched back at an icy pain. His left arm. He aimed again and shot.

Smith howled and rode off. Mac could see the man in the distance, near the trees, trying to load his pistol with one arm dangling at his side.

"Two down, and Smith is winged," he said. "But I'm hit, too." Mac looked at his arm, which bled and hurt like hell. "It's clean, I think—went straight through." Teeth chattering, he tore off his shirttail and awkwardly tied a strip over the hole in his left bicep.

He inspected Huntington's wound. The older man's chest still bled, and another trickle of blood ran from his mouth.

"I'm gone," Huntington whispered, coughing up red phlegm.

"You'll be fine," Mac said, hoping it was true. He grabbed a rag and stuffed it in Huntington's wound. By now Mac's whole body was shivering, as bad as when he'd had cholera.

"Can you drive?" Huntington rasped.

Mac looked at the mules. The front pair had been killed. The second pair stood, skittish in their traces. "I have to cut the dead team off," Mac said. "Cover me if the bastard comes back. He'll sneak around through the trees, then run in from north or south."

"Better be fast," Huntington said. "I ain't gonna be able to shoot for long." He coughed up more blood.

Mac winced when he crawled out of the wagon. He spoke softly to the live pair to calm them, then stepped on the traces to hold them steady while he used his knife to cut through the leather binding the dead pair. He felt as if Smith's gun were pointed at his back every second. Huntington wheezed noisily, but at least he was breathing.

Mac trembled with fatigue by the time the live mules were free of the bodies of their harness-mates. They tried to buck, but Mac cooed to them again while he clambered back into the wagon. It took him two tries to heave himself onto the bench. "We'll head for Sacramento," he said. "But it'll take till midnight with only one pair of mules. We're likely to be ambushed again."

Huntington pulled himself up to sit in the wagon bed. "Drive," he said. "I'll cover us as long as I can."

Mac lost track of time as the afternoon wore on. Huntington said he thought Smith was tailing them, but Mac saw no one. The spring sun warmed his right side while they headed south toward town. His wound throbbed endlessly. Soon, he slumped forward, barely conscious, unaware of anything but the pain.

The single pair of mules plodded along, pulling the wagon at a snail's pace. They encountered no one along the way.

"Mac," Huntington croaked. "Wake up." Huntington poked Mac in the back with his gun barrel. "I think he's gone."

"Who?" Mac asked.

"Smith. Ain't seen him in an hour."

"How you doing?" Mac managed to say.

"Hurts like the devil. Worse'n a knife wound. I'm still bleedin', I think."

Mac tied the reins to the wagon seat and turned to look at Huntington. The rag in the older man's wound was soaked with blood, and blood also stained the old man's chin. "Let me find you another rag."

"Nah," Huntington groaned. "Leave it be. Less you do, more likely I'll be to make it."

The sun disappeared below the horizon, and a misty rain started. The heat in Mac's arm turned to ice, then it numbed. Shock and blood loss made him so lightheaded he could hardly hold the reins.

Huntington lost consciousness sometime after twilight, and Mac couldn't hear anything but a soft hiss as the man barely breathed.

Later Mac couldn't even hear the hiss. He didn't know if Huntington was dead, or if his own pain kept him from focusing on anything else.

Shortly after full dark, with only a sliver of moon peeking through the cloudy sky, Mac heard a shout. "Who goes there?" a man yelled.

It wasn't Smith, so Mac answered. "Transport to Sacramento," he called back, voice croaking.

"McDougall? What you doing here?" The man rode up out of the darkness. It was a bearded miner Mac had done business with in his store. "You supposed to be back with the gold long afore dark, ain't you?"

"Ambush. We're both shot," Mac said, swaying on the wagon bench.

"Hell and damnation," the miner said. "Let's get you home." He tied his horse to the back of the wagon, and climbed on the seat, taking the reins from Mac. "Lie down."

Mac crawled to lie beside Huntington. The old man's body was warm, and Mac hoped again his partner would live. Then Mac passed out when pain from the jolting wagon on the rough road lanced through his arm, and he dreamed.

Dreamed of Jenny's face smiling over him. Mac felt her hand on his brow, as he had when she nursed him through cholera. He heard her singing as she'd sung along the trail, her soprano voice sweet as a bird's:

> *Amazing Grace, how sweet the sound,*
> *That saved a wretch like me.*
> *I once was lost but now am found,*
> *Was blind, but now, I see.*

Later, much later, he felt gentle hands washing him and coaxing water down his throat. "Jenny," he whispered.

Chapter 61:   Jenny Explains

Jenny awoke, not sure where she was. Esther sat beside her. "Where's William?" Jenny demanded, struggling to sit up.

"Shhh," Esther said, pushing Jenny back to the blanket she lay on. "He's fine. Rachel has the children."

"Where am I?"

"In your wagon. Zeke carried you here. We'll take you home."

"I must have fainted. I haven't fainted since the Barlow Road." That day Mac had scooped her into his arms after she'd carried newborn William through the frozen woods all day and passed out from fatigue.

Mac. The letter. It rushed back to her, and Jenny grabbed Esther's arm. "The letter. Where is it?"

"I have it."

A blush rose from Jenny's heart to face. "Did you read it?"

"Yes."

Jenny lay back with a groan. "Did anyone else?"

"No. I took it." Esther's words were clipped.

"Zeke didn't see it?" Jenny whispered, feeling her blush deepen.

"No. Let's get you home. Then you can tell me what's going on." Esther stood. "She's awake," she called to someone. "Give me Samuel. And William. Daniel, you keep the other children. Zeke and I'll take Jenny home. I'll stay the night with her."

Jenny felt the wagon shake as Esther took Samuel from a pair of hands, and Esther settled down beside her again. William climbed into the wagon also, and they began to move. "Who's driving?" Jenny asked.

"Zeke," Esther said.

Jenny was quiet for the journey home. William patted her cheek.

"Mama better?"

"I'm all right," she whispered, attempting to smile for her son's sake.

When they arrived at her cabin, Zeke lifted William out, then reached to help Jenny down. He placed his hands on her hips and started to lift her, but she stopped him. "I'm fine," she said.

"You said Mac's not coming back?" he asked.

"I'll talk to her, Zeke," Esther said, before Jenny could respond. "You go on home. Rachel and Mr. O'Neil will be here shortly."

Zeke untied his horse from behind Jenny's wagon. "I'll tend to Poulette and the other animals. Take care now," he said, tipping his hat at Jenny.

The women went inside. Esther pushed Jenny to sit in the rocking chair and handed Samuel to her. Esther bustled about, her mouth a thin line, while she found bread and jam for William.

"Esther—"

"We can't talk till William's asleep," Esther said, her voice tight, as if she didn't want to say anything.

A knock sounded on the door. Esther opened it. "Rachel."

"How is she?" Rachel asked.

"She'll be fine," Esther said, and sent Rachel to her cabin across the yard.

Jenny and Esther sat in silence through an early supper, then Esther tucked William in his bed in the loft. The toddler cried, wanting his mother, then his dog Wags, but he finally fell asleep.

Once William was quiet, Esther sat in Jenny's rocking chair nursing Samuel. "Now, what does Captain McDougall mean you need to find a husband?"

"He and I aren't married," Jenny whispered, her face growing red again.

"Not married? But how? . . . William?"

"William isn't Mac's child."

Esther stared.

Jenny took a deep breath. She couldn't avoid this conversation, so she had to plunge forward. "I've wanted to tell you. I've felt so ashamed to lie to you all these years."

"What happened?" Esther asked, her face grim.

"I was hurt—violated—in Missouri. A few months later Mac came to town. He saved me when I was attacked again. He was on his way to Oregon, so he brought me along."

"As his wife," Esther said.

Jenny nodded. "Your papa only wanted married men for the wagon train. I'm sorry."

Esther lifted Samuel to her shoulder and burped him. She buried her face in her son's neck. "William?"

"His father was one of the men who raped me."

Esther gaped at Jenny, startled. "There was more'n one?"

"Three. I don't know who William's father is."

"And Captain McDougall?"

"He never touched me." Esther didn't have to know about the night Mac left. Jenny didn't even know how to describe that night.

"But he took William on as his own."

"While he was here. I always knew Mac would leave."

"I thought you said you asked him to come back." Esther laid Samuel on Jenny's bed, and sat beside the baby, patting his back.

"I did."

"And he's saying he won't."

Jenny nodded and sobbed.

"Do you love Captain McDougall?"

"I think so," Jenny whispered. But today was a day for truth. "Yes."

Esther was silent for a time. "What did he mean about Zeke?"

Jenny shrugged. "Mac told me I should marry Zeke. When I told you someone—this Montenegro woman—had written Mac was ill, really the letter said he was dead. I was supposed to tell everyone here in Oregon Mac had died. So I could marry Zeke. Or some other man, if I wanted."

"Were you planning to tell Zeke all this before you married him? Or were you going to take advantage of him?" Esther was Jenny's friend, but she was Zeke's sister first—Jenny would have to remember that.

Jenny went to stir the fire. "I never planned to marry Zeke. How could I? He thought I was already married." She turned and frowned at Esther. "And don't you tell him what was in the letter. Not about Mac and me not being married. Not about William. And certainly not about Mac telling me to marry him."

"But Zeke knows the Captain ain't coming back," Esther protested. "You told everyone that at the picnic. You have to tell folks something. Or are you going to keep living the lie?"

They talked into the night, but Jenny wouldn't change her mind.

Chapter 62:   Consequences

Jenny spent a sleepless night in her cabin with Esther and Samuel. The next morning as the women and William ate breakfast, Wags started barking outside.

Esther peered out the window. "It's Mrs. Tuller," she said. "Tying up her wagon like she plans to stay a spell. Wonder what she wants"

"She knows," Jenny said. "She and Doc have known since William was born."

"You told them and not me?" Esther's voice rose.

"Doc guessed. Mac told him everything. And I told Mrs. Tuller."

The older woman knocked, and Jenny opened the door.

"Well, you've made a fine kettle of fish now, haven't you, dear?" Mrs. Tuller said, entering the cabin.

"It just came out." Jenny choked back her tears, not wanting to scare William. "When I read Mac's letter."

"How could you keep such a secret from me?" Esther demanded of Mrs. Tuller. "I'm her best friend. And from my father—the leader of our wagon company. Pa let Rachel live here. And my poor ma was so kind to her. You should have told our family."

"Your mama knew something wasn't right," Jenny said. "But she still thought I was steadier than you."

"Steady?" Esther sniffed. "When you lived with Captain McDougall for most of a year. Unmarried."

"Doc and I told you to marry the Captain when he asked," Mrs. Tuller said in a low voice.

Esther gasped and stared at Jenny. "He asked you to marry him and you turned him down? A fine man like him? You are surely addled."

"I couldn't marry him. I kept remembering—" Fear rose again from Jenny's stomach, and she pressed her hand to her mouth.

"Hush, now," Mrs. Tuller said. "William's here. But there are consequences for everything. And you must bear yours now."

Daniel arrived to take Esther and Samuel home. After they'd left, Jenny sent William outside to play with Wags so she could talk with Mrs. Tuller.

Mrs. Tuller sat at the table and took out her knitting. "What are you going to do next?"

"I don't know." Jenny handed her the letter. "Here's what Mac wrote. Esther says I need to tell Zeke. And everyone else."

When Mrs. Tuller had finished reading, she looked at Jenny and sighed. "Lots of folks heard you say Captain McDougall ain't coming back. If you don't tell them you two weren't married, you'll be on your own for the rest of your life. Like the Captain says in his letter. You need to move on."

"But what will people think of me?"

"What do you want them to think of you?"

Jenny paced in the small room. "If I say we weren't married, they'll all think William is Mac's bastard. If I tell them I was violated, they'll think I'm damaged goods. Either way, they'll gossip."

Mrs. Tuller's knitting needles clicked. "Time to worry about that was back in Missouri. Or when you and the Captain could have married. Now you have to live with your choice."

"I can't let William know he was the result of an evil act." Even the thought of William finding out someday caused Jenny to panic.

"Then that tells you what to do. If Captain McDougall ain't returning, he won't care if folks think William is his son."

"I'm not ready to say any more than that Mac isn't coming back. I'll say Mac and I had an argument and that's why he left."

"At some point, it'll come out you weren't married. You should tell a few from our company beyond Esther. At least Rachel and Zeke."

"I don't know how. Will you and Doc Tuller help me?"

Mrs. Tuller smiled. "Of course we will, child."

"And you'll help me stay friends with Esther?"

"Don't you worry. You'n Esther been through a lot together. She'll stand by you."

When she was finally alone, Jenny pulled out her journal and wrote:

Monday, April 29ᵗʰ—Mac is alive! But I will never see him again. Esther knows the truth, and she is angry. How could I have been so stupid?

As she wrote the words, Jenny didn't know if she meant she'd been stupid for agreeing to Mac's scheme back in Missouri or stupid now for letting let the tale slip. Or stupid for having harbored even the slightest hope of Mac's returning.

All she knew was she could easily lose the life she'd carefully built in Oregon because of her foolish outburst.

Jenny spent the next two days helping Rachel and O'Neil move to their new claim. They delayed their departure until Wednesday because of Jenny. Jenny told Rachel only what she and Mrs. Tuller had agreed on—simply that she and Mac had not been married, and that's why he wasn't coming back to Oregon, but she hoped to keep gossip from spreading. Rachel assumed William was Mac's child, and Jenny said nothing to correct Rachel's assumption.

"Are you sure you'll be all right?" Rachel asked. "All alone, and Captain McDougall never coming back?"

"William and I'll be fine." Jenny said, with a brave smile. "You need to start your own home."

Esther helped Rachel load the last bundle into the wagon, and she and Jenny waved while the newlyweds drove off.

"Have you talked to Zeke?" Esther asked.

Jenny shook her head.

"Do you want me to tell him? He asked me why Captain McDougall isn't returning."

Zeke was her friend, Jenny thought. He needed to know something. And with both Esther and Rachel knowing, he was bound to learn the truth. But what would he think of her? "You c-can tell Zeke we weren't m-married," Jenny stammered. "But don't tell anyone else. And don't tell Zeke I was violated. I don't want William to ever know."

"But, Jenny, everyone will think the Captain was William's father."

"Better that than the child of a rapist. At least people will understand why Mac isn't coming back, since we were never married."

Alone that night, Jenny slipped into a black mood, one that consumed her soul. She felt as melancholy as in the days after she'd been raped, as miserable as when she'd first realized she was pregnant, as distraught as she'd been until Mac rescued her.

Wednesday, May 1st—Rachel and Mr. O'Neil have left. William and I are alone. How will I survive?

Chapter 63:   Recovery

When Mac's fever from the gunshot wound broke, he awakened in Huntington's bed in the back room of the store. Consuela bathed his face and neck.

"Huntington?" he croaked, his voice barely audible even to himself.

"Dead," she said. "Lost too much blood. He died in the wagon before you reached town."

Mac closed his eyes and sighed. "Damn." Huntington had been an uncouth windbag, but he had also been a knowledgeable partner. Mac and Joel wouldn't have done nearly so well prospecting without the old man's help. Mac had grown to appreciate the old man's company through the winter in the store. Now Mac's gold hauling enterprise had killed his friend.

"What day is it?" Mac asked, struggling to sit.

"Saturday, May 4. You were shot a week ago." She pushed him down.

"A week?" He sank into his pillow. He'd lost more time than when he had cholera.

"Your fever was very bad."

"Where's Marshal Cunningham? I need to tell him what happened."

"Shhh," she said. "You talked to him the first night. Before the fever hit. You don't remember?"

He shook his head. "Last thing I remember is a man telling me to climb in the back of the wagon. Where's Maria?"

Consuela smiled. "She is fine. An Indian girl cares for her in the saloon."

"You can keep her here."

Consuela shook her head. "When you are well, I will move back to the

Golden Nugget. I've hired the girl to tend my *niña* while I work."

"You can't." Mac tried to sit again. He managed to brace himself on his right elbow and ignored his throbbing head.

"I must."

"I said you could work in the store. I need you now Huntington is gone."

Consuela stood and put the washbasin on a table by the door. Then she turned toward Mac. "I will not keep taking your charity."

"So you'll raise your baby in a whorehouse instead?" Mac didn't understand her logic.

"I've told you, Maria and I are not your problem. I can work again now. It is long enough since Maria was born. The Indian girl helps out in the saloon kitchen. She has a bed there. She can care for Maria." Consuela opened the curtain to let light stream in, then left the room, taking the basin of water.

With his good arm, Mac shielded his eyes against the light. Why was he so bent on keeping Consuela out of the saloon? She was right—she and Maria weren't his responsibility. Bridget and her baby had been Mac's responsibility, but he hadn't protected them. He'd helped Jenny and William, at first to atone for his sins against Bridget, and later because he cared for Jenny. But what more did he owe Consuela, particularly if she refused his help?

And Huntington was dead—killed not by poor health after decades of mining but by the violence of the West and Mac's quest for profit and adventure. Would Mac at some point face the same fate?

It was too much to think about, so Mac slept again.

Mac awoke that evening feeling stronger. He was alone, no sign of Consuela. A plate of food sat on the table next to him, and he ate.

"I'm here, Caleb." Susan's voice sounded from the hall outside his room. "May I come in?"

Mac groaned, not wanting to deal with Susan. "Come in," he said.

"Grandfather and I came as soon as we heard," Susan breezed into the room bringing a flowery scent and wearing a bright yellow dress. Mac closed his eyes. "You poor man." She plumped his pillows.

Nate entered behind her. "What happened, son? All we heard was that you and Huntington were ambushed and he died."

"It was Smith," Mac said. "He and two other men attacked from the woods when we stopped. They must have been following us. The other two died, and Smith was shot. In the arm, I think, like me."

"Does the marshal know?"

Mac shrugged. "Consuela says I told him. I don't remember anything from that night until I woke up this morning."

"Well, you won't need that woman any longer," Susan said. "Grandfather and I can take care of you now. We took rooms in the Golden Nugget so we will be close by, though I cannot abide the noise and smells. We'll stay as long as you need us. Grandfather will mind the store, and I will tend to you."

Over the next few days Mac's health improved. True to her word, Susan organized his meals and spent hours sitting by his bed reading to him. He neither saw nor heard any sign of Consuela or Maria. Nate visited him in the evenings.

"What happened to the wagon of gold after the ambush?" Mac asked Nate.

"Dunbar's men picked it up," Nate said. "Took it to San Francisco as planned. But no one's been willing to make another trip since you were shot. Dunbar has written notes daily asking after your health. He's anxious to resume the route."

After three days of Susan's nursing, Mac protested, "I have to get up. I need to take care of my store."

"Grandfather ran it for two years before selling to you. The store is fine."

"But it's my responsibility now."

"Come now, Caleb. We're practically your family." Susan smiled and brushed his hair from his face. "You need a trim and a shave. Shall I have the barber come this afternoon?"

"I can shave myself, Susan." Mac moved to get out of bed. "Go on now, and let me dress."

Susan looked like she wanted to object, so he stood up in his nightshirt.

"Fine," she said, blushing and looking away. "If you're irritable, you must be feeling better." She rose and walked out of the room.

That evening Mac joined Nate and Susan in the Golden Nugget for supper. "I'm better now," he said. "I appreciate your caring for me, but there's no reason for you to stay any longer."

"No reason, Caleb?" Susan asked, arching an eyebrow.

Mac looked back and forth between Nate and his granddaughter. Susan was clearly setting her cap for him. Did Nate approve? "No," Mac said. "I'll be making another trip to San Francisco when I'm recovered. Need to talk to Dunbar. I'll look in on you both then."

"All right, Mac," Nate said. "We'll head home tomorrow."

Susan pressed her lips together, then said, "I'd better go pack."

Mac stood when Susan did, then watched her cross the room to the stairs. When she'd gone, he sat and sighed. "I hope she doesn't have the wrong impression."

"What impression would that be?" Nate eyed Mac over his brandy. "You've spent a lot of time with her. In Monterey. In San Francisco. And now you've let her nurse you. You could do far worse than Susan."

"I'm not ready to settle down with any woman," Mac said.

"Why not? What are you waiting for?" Nate finished his drink and stood. "Sometimes a man has to take a leap of faith when a good thing stands in front of him."

Chapter 64: Melancholy

Jenny's melancholy deepened after the O'Neils moved away. She missed Rachel's companionship and assistance with housework. And without O'Neil around, Jenny had to handle the outside chores as well as the cooking and cleaning. Not even Wags could bring a smile.

She didn't leave her farm for two weeks. She couldn't bear to face people in church, not after the commotion she'd caused when she read Mac's letter. The only person Jenny saw during those two weeks was Zeke, when he came to work her farm on Tuesdays and Thursdays. She was glad Esther and the Tullers didn't visit—she'd had enough of their advice.

She'd lived alone with William after the Tanners went to California, but this time was different. Then, though she'd lived on the claim with only William for company, she'd had a niggling hope Mac would return. The hope might not have been rational, but still it flickered.

Even when she'd heard from Consuela Montenegro that Mac was dead, she'd hoped. Joel had written about Mac's work on the California Constitution, so she'd had reason to doubt the truth of the Montenegro letter—and she'd been right.

But now—now Mac himself had told her he would not be back. As overjoyed as Jenny was to know he was alive, still she despaired at the thought she would never see him across the table from her, never feel his shoulder and thigh sway against hers on the wagon bench, never taste his lips again.

Monday, May 13th—It is all I can do to finish my chores each day, but I try not to be idle. If I sit for a moment, I think. I eat only

319

so William will eat. As for sleep . . .

Two weeks after the O'Neils moved to their claim, Esther drove a wagon full of children—hers and her younger siblings and stepsiblings—over to Jenny's cabin. "You can't hide on your farm," Esther announced. "We're going berrying. Daniel says the early ones are ripe."

Jenny sighed. It was easier to do what Esther wanted than to object.

The women and children walked in the woodlands searching for salmonberries and thimbleberries, exclaimed over the occasional mushroom and wild onion patches they found.

When they came across bushes to pick, they set the babies to play on a blanket nearby, leaving seven-year-old Noah Pershing to watch them. The older children carried buckets and helped forage. The children ate as many berries as they saved.

"What's wrong, Jenny?" Esther asked her.

"Nothing," Jenny said.

"You've been moping all morning," Esther said, glancing at her baby son. "Sammy's heading off, Noah," she called, then turned back to Jenny. "That child won't stay still no more. Five-and-a-half months old, and he scoots everywhere. He's twice as fast as Cordelia or Jonah ever were."

"Just lonely, I suppose."

"I'd give my eye teeth for a night alone, and my virtue, too." Esther sighed. "It must be so peaceful with only you and William."

A lump rose in Jenny's throat. She couldn't respond. Esther didn't understand Jenny's overwhelming desolation, her sense that nothing would ever be right again. If Esther—her dearest friend—didn't understand, then no one would.

Rage replaced the lump in Jenny's throat, and her fingers grabbed at the branches, stripping fruit mercilessly. She gritted her teeth to keep from weeping.

After Esther and her brood took Jenny and William home and left, Jenny silently made supper for William. She swallowed her fear and resentment—resentment of Esther, of Mac, of her wretched life in Oregon. It hurt too much to acknowledge her bleak future, even to herself.

Jenny put a pulpy mash of berries into sugar and water to stew over the fireplace. Then she made flapjacks. She poured the stewed berries over the flapjacks and set a plate in front of William, placing another plate for herself on the table across from him.

"I don't want berries, Mama," he howled. "I don't like berries."

"You ate plenty this afternoon," she scolded. "Eat your supper."

"No," he shouted. "My tummy hurts." With that, he puked all over the table and his shirt, a deep red vomit no amount of scrubbing would ever remove from his clothes. More work. More thankless work.

"You wicked, wicked boy," she screamed, raising her hand to strike him. "I can't take it anymore. I can't, I can't, I can't!"

His face dissolved into fear and he shrieked as loudly as she had. "Mama," he sobbed. "No, Mama, no." He held his body stiffly, pushing away from the foul-smelling puke.

At the sight of his stinky red face and clothes, she ran across the room and flung herself on her bed.

For a long time, both Jenny and William wailed hysterically. She couldn't deal with him. Not now. Not yet. He was better off without her attention, at least for the moment.

Finally she was cried out, and William's sobs had settled into whimpers.

Knowing she was all the boy had, she sat up and dried her face. She heaved in a breath, then let it out slowly. "Come on, William, let's clean you up."

She bathed her son, dumped his clothes in a bucket of water with lye soap, washed the dishes, and scrubbed the table and floor.

Once William was sleeping in his bed in the loft, she sat at the table with her quill and ink.

> *Wednesday, May 15ᵗʰ—I am so furious I cannot see straight. I am alone in the wilderness, trying to build a home with no one to help me. Not Esther. Not the Tullers. And certainly not Mac, who has abandoned me. I almost hit William today.*

She wept into her pillow until almost dawn.

Jenny woke the next morning to loud sounds from the barn. Poulette and Shanty whinnied and the milk cow mooed. It was full daylight.

William talked softly to himself in the loft—awake, though not demanding yet.

But the animals wouldn't wait.

She dragged herself out of bed and dressed. "Stay in bed," she called to William as she headed to the barn. "I'll be back soon."

She let Poulette and Shanty into the fenced barnyard and mucked out their stalls. Then she turned her attention to the cow.

Sitting on a stool beside the cow, she began to milk, rhythmically pulling on one teat then another. Her breathing matched the cadence of her fingers.

Instead of soothing her, the motion set up waves of sadness. Her throat closed more tightly with every breath.

I cannot do this any longer, she thought. She saw the life ahead of her. One day of drudgery following another. Chores. Field work. Teaching. None of it would change. And no one would share it.

She set her forehead against the cow's flank and cried again.

"Jenny," Zeke's voice said behind her. "You're up late this morning. You're usually finished with the milking by the time I get here."

Jenny kept her tear-streaked face toward the cow. "Didn't sleep well last night. William was sick. I still have to feed him breakfast when I'm done here."

"Well, don't mind me," Zeke said. "I'll just get the hoe and other tools. I'm weeding the south field today. Looks like a fine morning."

Chapter 65:   New Wounds

Consuela and Maria had moved out of Mac's store and into the Golden Nugget when Susan and Nate arrived. After Susan and Nate left, Mac didn't raise the subject of Consuela's work or living arrangements again. Nor did Consuela comment on why she'd left him to Susan's ministrations.

Mac moved from Huntington's bed in the back room of the store to the upstairs room where Consuela had lived. Without either Huntington or Consuela assisting him, the store filled Mac's days. He couldn't lift with his left arm in a sling, so he hired a boy to help him stock the shelves and do the lifting.

After supper at the Golden Nugget each evening, Mac returned to his room.

May 15, 1850. The store is lonely without Consuela and Huntington. Damn that old fool for dying. And damn Consuela for her independence.

Most evenings after he ate, Mac stopped by the kitchen to visit Maria. Her Indian nurse spoke little English, but smiled shyly at Mac. Mac hadn't realized the woman had her own baby. The two infants slept together in a wooden box in the kitchen.

One evening when Consuela served his whiskey, he said, "Maria's nurse has a child also."

Consuela raised an eyebrow. "Yes. How else could she feed Maria?"

Mac stammered, "Y-you're not feeding your baby?" Jenny had been discreet when she nursed William, but he'd been aware of it. Too aware.

"I don't want to nurse Maria and serve my customers," Consuela said

323

patiently. "Some men don't like it."

"You don't have to work upstairs," Mac said.

Consuela shrugged and left him alone.

On Monday, May 20, Mac made a trip to San Francisco to see Dunbar. When Mac asked whether Dunbar thought the hauling of gold should continue, the pompous man said, "It's more important than ever. The *S.S. Panama* left here earlier this month with over a million dollars in gold dust in its hold. Bound for the East Coast. I aim to have a piece of that business, and I need you to bring the gold to me."

"I can't resume the transport runs for a bit," Mac said. Not only was his arm still weak, but until Smith was apprehended, he didn't think it was wise. "It's dangerous to haul so much gold. Killed a good man already, and one of the ambushers is still on the loose."

"Nonsense, sir," Dunbar said, biting on his cigar. "Hire more men on horses to guard the wagon. Even with higher labor costs, there's still a profit to be made for both of us."

Mac told the man he'd consider it, but would need a few weeks to augment his staff.

That evening he had dinner with Nate and Susan. "What do you think?" Mac asked Nate after Susan had left them to port and cigars.

Nate shrugged. "Your call. If you don't haul the gold, someone else will. You have to decide whether you want the risk." Then he raised an eyebrow. "But let your arm heal completely before you ride the route yourself. I have an interest in seeing you stay alive."

Mac wondered whether Nate's interest was for himself or for his granddaughter.

A few days after Mac returned to Sacramento, Joel came to see him. "Why'd you let Huntington die?" were Joel's first words. But he pounded Mac on the back to soften the accusation. "Crazy old coot shoulda kept on fighting."

"Damn it, Joel," Mac said, choking up. "It was Smith. He attacked us."

Joel nodded. "So I hear. Any sign of the devil since?"

Mac shook his head.

"What's happening to the transport route?" Joel asked.

"I haven't been able to make the trip since I was shot. Nor do my men want to handle it. No one will take the risk while Smith is free," Mac said. "But Dunbar wants the business to continue."

"Want to sell the contract to me?" Joel asked.

"What about prospecting?" Mac was surprised. "I thought you were looking for new diggings higher in the Sierras."

Joel shrugged. "Haven't found a site I like in the mountains. Our old claim's all panned out. Most days I make only a few dollars. Some men say they're still digging out a hundred dollars a day, but not many."

"You aren't afraid after what happened to Huntington and me?"

"If I can make money at it, I'll take on the concession."

"Dunbar says to hire more men as outriders."

"I can do that." Joel pulled a stool up to the counter and sat facing Mac. "What's your price?"

"Buy the wagon and mules, and it's yours," Mac said. "Plus a small fee to reserve space for the gold in my safe. Though you'll have to talk to Dunbar to get his approval."

They dickered awhile, then shook hands. "I'll go to San Francisco tomorrow to see Dunbar. If he's agreeable, I'll make the first run next week," Joel said. "Got me some men from the valley who'll guard while I drive, I think. But I'm taking three guards. One in the wagon and two outriders on horseback."

"Smith hasn't been seen, has he?"

"Nope. Marshal Cunningham took out a posse to find him, but weren't no sign of him. Found the other two bodies where you said they was, but not Smith."

With the gold transport off his hands, Mac had little to do other than mind the store. One evening he sat in the saloon after dinner, writing:

May 25, 1850. California has lost its allure. It is a beautiful land, but I have no purpose here. I sold the gold transport concession to Joel. Consuela spends her days with Maria and her nights working. I cannot insist she stop. All I have is the store, and it is not enough to hold me. What, then, should I do?

Lansford Hastings came to Sacramento and met Mac for a late supper on the evening of May 31. Mac's arm was newly out of its sling and still stiff.

"California will be a state by the end of the year," Hastings told Mac. "I'm looking for candidates for the U.S. Congress. Will you run for office?"

Mac thought for a moment. Congress? It would put him back East. His father would be proud, yet would have no control over him.

But when he remembered the social conventions of Boston—no doubt the same in Washington—he soured on the idea. In California, he'd worked with people like Joel and Huntington—men who would be unacceptable to his family in the East. Even Mac's friends in Oregon— Jenny and the Tullers and the Pershings—would be only slightly more satisfactory to his parents. Yet these people and others like them had been his companions for three years.

Only Susan, and maybe Nate, might meet with his family's approval.

Mac shook his head. "I don't think so," he said to Hastings. "I'm honored. But I've decided I'm better suited for life in the West."

"Are you staying in Sacramento then?" Hastings asked. "We could politick for an appointment for you here. A judgeship like Shannon has."

Mac laughed. "I'm afraid I don't have a judicial temperament." He gestured at his arm. "Or I wouldn't have been in another shootout. I've been in three gunfights since leaving Boston. Plus the Oregon militia and a California posse. I don't seem to have found a temperate life."

"Someday you'll be a judge, maybe," Hastings said, flashing a grin. "You're destined for more than running a store." He raised his glass to Mac.

As Mac grinned and clinked his glass to Hastings's, a shriek sounded from above.

"One of the whores sounds unhappy," Hastings said with a chuckle.

More screams followed, and a woman shouted from the top of the stairs, "Consuela! She's been stabbed!"

Mac raced upstairs to Consuela's room, pushing past Ethel and another girl who stood in the doorway. Consuela lay naked to the waist on her bed, bleeding from her abdomen. A small, unkempt man stood over her with a bloody knife in one hand, hitching up his unbuttoned pants with the other.

Mac grabbed the assailant and twisted the man's arm until he dropped the knife. A glance at Consuela showed Mac she was seriously wounded. "Get a doctor," he shouted.

Someone raced down the stairs.

"Bitch laughed at me," the little man said. "Ain't no call for her to laugh." He seemed near tears.

By then a crowd had gathered in the hallway. "Find Marshal Cunningham or a deputy," Mac said. "And someone else take this devil. I can't hold him." His still weak left bicep throbbed viciously.

Another saloon customer took the man downstairs.

Mac turned to Consuela. Ethel knelt by the bed pressing a cloth against Consuela's side.

"How bad is it?" Mac asked, rubbing his left shoulder.

"Bad," Ethel said.

"Doctor should be here soon," Mac said.

"Mac," Consuela whispered.

"I'm here," he said, kneeling beside Ethel.

"Take care of my *niña* for me."

"Hush," he said. "We'll get you patched up."

"Take care of Maria."

Mac remembered the conversation he'd had with Jenny during William's birth. Jenny had demanded he take her child if she died. He hadn't been able to refuse then, and he couldn't now. "All right," he told Consuela.

Chapter 66:   More Death and a Declaration

Consuela survived the night after she was stabbed. The doctor stitched her up and told Mac and Ethel, "Don't know what good my sewing will do. Knife wounds to the belly usually lead to sepsis."

By morning Consuela moaned in pain, barely conscious. The doctor gave her laudanum. "Give her a few drops whenever she's hurting," he said. "No food, only liquids. Call me if she develops a fever."

Ethel nursed her through the day, and Mac took over in the evening. He could hear the raucous sounds from the saloon below.

"Maria?" Consuela whispered.

"The Indian girl has her," Mac said.

"I want to see her."

"I'll get her."

Mac went downstairs to the kitchen and found Maria with her nurse. He motioned that he wanted the baby, and the girl handed Maria to him. She was a small but solid lump in his arms and gurgled in her sleep. He took the baby back to Consuela's room.

Consuela reached to touch Maria's cheek. "So sweet." A tear ran down Consuela's face. "Take her back to Oregon with you."

"Oregon?"

"To your Jenny. I want a good woman to raise my child."

Mac stiffened, pulling Maria away from her mother. "You know I told Jenny I wasn't coming back."

Consuela shook her head. "You were wrong. You love her."

"We've been through this. I can't. She didn't want me." Mac thought of Susan. She was a good woman also. "I'm thinking of marrying Susan Abbott," he said.

Consuela closed her eyes. Mac thought she'd gone to sleep, until she whispered, "When were you happiest in life, Mac?"

"As a boy, perhaps. Summers on the shore." Mac had a fleeting memory of laughing while he raced after his older brothers along a rocky beach. Of holding his grandfather's hand as they traipsed to their favorite fishing hole.

"Since you've been grown?"

He felt the hard wood bench under him as the wagon jolted over prairie grasses. He smelled the fresh scent of pines in the mountains. Jenny sat beside him, swaying into his shoulder while they rode. "On the trip to Oregon," he admitted.

"With Jenny."

"Yes." He'd been happiest with Jenny.

"Not with Susan."

He shook his head. He didn't know if Consuela saw him.

Consuela sighed. "Just say it, Mac. You love Jenny."

Mac thought of Jenny smiling at the Snake River falls, her hand pulling a strand of hair out of her face. She had appeared in his dreams since he'd left her, and running away from her had driven his every action. "I loved her."

"You love her still?"

"Yes."

"Then take Maria and go back to Oregon." A wistful smile fleeted across Consuela's face. "It's too late for me to find happiness. Unless Ramón waits for me in the next world. But you must take my daughter to a better home. You promised you would keep her after I die."

"Don't say that," Mac said. "You'll survive."

Consuela shook her head. "I see it. *La muerte*." And she faded into sleep.

By the following morning, Consuela thrashed in her bed, delirious with fever. "Sepsis," the doctor said. "When the gut is opened up, it can kill off the body from the inside. Nothing I can do."

Mac and Ethel sponged Consuela, trying to bring down her fever, to no avail. She lasted another day, but succumbed on the third day after the knifing.

> *June 3, 1850. Consuela died of her wound, leaving her orphaned child in my care.*

Mac paid for her coffin. He and Ethel and an old Spanish priest were the only ones who attended the burial. Mac had sent word to Joel the day after Consuela was stabbed, but Joel didn't come to Sacramento. He wrote Nate also, but told the old assayer to keep Susan away until after Consuela was laid to rest.

"Will you keep the baby?" the doctor asked when Mac paid him for Consuela's treatment. "If you don't want her, I can find a family to adopt her. She's a comely mite, even with her Indian and Mexican blood."

"I promised Maria's mother I would take care of the baby," Mac said. "I don't know how, but I'll keep her."

"Let me know if you change your mind," the doctor said.

Nate and Susan came to the store a week after Consuela was buried, arriving late in the day on the steamboat from San Francisco. "You poor man," Susan said, rushing across the room to take Mac's hand. "You've had such a time. Well, what can you expect of a woman like that? She was bound to end badly."

"She didn't deserve to be murdered."

Susan brushed aside his comment with a wave of her hand. "Have you found a place for the baby? New York had many foundling homes. Why, there must be one in San Francisco by now. Shall I look for you?"

"No."

"Surely you're not thinking of raising her? With her parentage and history?"

Mac looked at Nate, who cleared his throat and wouldn't meet Mac's eye. "I'm considering it."

"But—" Susan looked at her grandfather and was still.

"Shall we have supper?" Nate said, breaking the awkward silence.

Over their meal in the saloon, Nate asked about the store. Susan said little. After they ate, Susan asked Mac, "I'd like to walk a bit. Will you escort me? Grandfather is probably tired after our travels."

Nate rose and said, "I do think I'll turn in."

Mac offered his arm to Susan and led her outside into the warm evening. The wide road toward the Embarcadero still bustled with wagons, dusk coming late in midsummer.

"I had hoped," Susan said slowly, "we might reach an understanding."

Mac opened his mouth, not knowing what to say, but knowing some response was necessary. "Susan—"

"It's not proper for me to raise the subject. I should wait for you to speak," Susan continued. "But you are faced with a situation which will impact your future wife, and I feel I must say something."

"Susan—" Now Mac knew what she would say, and he had to speak. "Maria is not Consuela, and as her guardian, I must act in the child's best interest."

"No proper woman will want to raise the bastard child of a prostitute," Susan said. "You should consider what is in *your* best interest, as well as that of the child."

Mac nodded.

"I think I've had enough air now," Susan said. "Shall we return?"

Chapter 67:   Proposal

Through the rest of May, Jenny stayed close to her claim. She had to go to Oregon City once for flour and other provisions, but she returned immediately to her cabin.

In late May 1850, five Cayuse Indians were tried in Oregon City for the killings at the Whitman Mission back in November 1847. Jenny shuddered every time she thought of poor Narcissa Whitman. Mac had wanted Jenny and William to stay at the mission that winter. If they had, they might have been killed along with the Whitmans, as other settlers had been. Or captured by the Cayuse, which could have been worse.

She might yet end up like Mrs. Whitman, Jenny thought. She and William lived all alone now—no one would know for days if they were murdered in their beds.

She wasn't completely isolated on her farm. The Tullers and Esther stopped by, and O'Neil and Rachel began visiting Jenny every Tuesday, so O'Neil could help Zeke on Jenny's land.

With the time they had available, O'Neil and Zeke could only maintain half the acres they'd cleared and sown in the spring. The rest of the land was already sprouting weeds and pine seedlings along with wheat and corn.

"Sorry, Miz Jenny," O'Neil said on the first Tuesday of June, when he and Rachel arrived. "Afraid some of your fields are goin' back to wilderness."

"You and Zeke are doing what you can," she said, as Zeke rode up behind the O'Neils.

"Good thing we got those murderin' Cayuse," O'Neil said. "They was hung yesterday."

"Weren't much of a trial," Zeke said, hitching his horse to the fencepost. "No one's sure the witnesses were even at the mission when it happened. Who knows if they tried the right Indians?"

O'Neil snorted. "Right or not, someone's gotta pay. Indians claimed they killed Dr. Whitman because he gave 'em bad medicine. Weren't nothing he could do 'bout savages gittin' the measles."

"Well, it's over," Jenny said. "Can't bring back men who were hung."

"So much time," Rachel said, shaking her head. "So much time before the Whitmans got justice. Mrs. Whitman was such a lovely woman." Rachel and Jenny talked all day about their stay at the mission.

After an early supper, Rachel and O'Neil left. Zeke lingered, washing the dishes while Jenny put William to bed. The boy now scampered up the ladder to the loft, reminding her of the organ grinder's monkey she'd once seen as a child in New Orleans.

Zeke left quickly after Jenny came back downstairs. "I'll be back on Thursday," he said, putting his hat on, then heading to the barn for his horse.

Zeke returned on Thursday, as he said. And he continued to work Jenny's land two days a week into mid-June, with O'Neil helping on Tuesdays.

Jenny made herself get out of bed and do her chores every day. Housework. Caring for the animals. Long hours in the fields, trying to do what Zeke could not finish in his time on her land.

And she willed herself to be patient with her child.

Slowly, as days and weeks passed, her misery lifted. Sunshine helped. Hard work helped, even if the wearying drudgery was part of the reason for her despair.

And William helped—he hugged her and prattled at her all day, showing no signs of fear over her outburst in mid-May. Her son was all she had, and she had to be strong for him.

Meanwhile, Jenny kept expecting Zeke to say something about Mac's letter, but he didn't. Over a month had passed since she'd fainted, and Zeke never mentioned Mac or the letter.

Wednesday, June 19ᵗʰ—I wonder what Esther told Zeke. He farms my land as we agreed, but he leaves each evening with barely a word.

When Zeke still didn't say anything on Thursday, Jenny went to visit Esther in the afternoon and asked, "What did you tell Zeke about Mac?"

Esther looked up from her sewing, her eyebrows raised. "Only what you told me to say. That you and Captain McDougall had never been married, and that's why he wasn't coming back."

"Did he ask about William?"

"No." Esther shook her head. "He just nodded. We haven't talked about it since. Why?"

"Zeke seems uncomfortable around me now." Jenny sighed. "He's been such a help. I'd hate to lose his friendship."

Esther laughed. "You won't lose his friendship. Not Zeke's."

Jenny swallowed hard. "Are other people talking about me?"

"Of course," Esther said. "Other than the Whitman hangings, you're the only interesting news in Oregon City."

"That's not true." Jenny couldn't believe the whole town was gossiping about her. "Governor Lane resigned to go to Washington, and Mr. Prichette is the acting governor. Colonel Estill is making a mail run to Missouri. There's lots going on."

"I'm joshing you," Esther said. "The only people talking are the folks from our wagon company. They're all shocked Captain McDougall ain't coming back. He was so devoted to you on our journey from the States."

"No, he wasn't." Jenny said, sighing. Mac had spent so much time leading his platoon, and then he had responsibility for the whole company. She'd been left to manage their wagon on her own. Or with Zeke's help. "I was glad for Zeke's assistance on many occasions."

"Yes, the Captain *was* devoted to you," Esther insisted. "When Daniel was courting me, I told him to treat me like Captain McDougall treated you. I still tell him that." She shook her head and sighed. "After a time, a couple settles into daily living. Cooking and cleaning and babies. Not much romance in our lives now. Probably would have happened to you if the Captain had stayed. Even if you wasn't married."

Jenny didn't argue. She'd never been romanced, and now it wasn't likely she ever would be. Not with her closest friends thinking she'd behaved immorally with Mac and the rest thinking her husband had abandoned her. She couldn't blame them. She and Mac had made everyone believe they were a family. Their lie was exposed, and she would have to live with it.

"You know," Esther said, "you'll have to watch out for old Samuel Abercrombie. I heard him tell Daniel at dinner last Sunday he wonders if you have a right to your farm. Because Captain McDougall filed the claim, and he ain't coming back."

Jenny gasped. "But Mac said I could stay here. He sent me a deed."

"Old Mr. Abercrombie may be Daniel's father," Esther said, "but I swear he lives to make trouble for folks. He probably don't know about the deed, but he says the land ain't yours if it weren't proved up before the Captain left."

"What did Daniel say?"

"Daniel don't know the law. I ain't sure Father Abercrombie does either, but you'd better find out what's what."

The next Tuesday when Zeke and O'Neil were there, Jenny noticed again that Zeke seemed distant, less friendly than he had been. She caught him eyeing her, then he turned away when she frowned at him. She didn't know what to do, but missed the easy conversations they'd had.

She needed Zeke's help. If he quit working her land, she probably would have to give up the claim. And with Samuel Abercrombie threatening her, she wasn't sure if she could sell the land or not. She might lose the claim, even if Zeke would continue farming for her.

Late on Thursday afternoon, Zeke was mucking out Jenny's barn after hoeing the wheat fields all day. She took him a cup of water flavored with a little mint. His shirt was drenched in sweat.

"This'll help quench your thirst," she said.

Zeke hesitated, then nodded. He took the cup, downing it quickly. "Thank you."

"It's hot for June, isn't it?" Jenny couldn't think of anything to talk about except the weather.

"Yep."

"Thank you for everything you're doing for me."

Zeke looked at her blankly. "You're paying me with my share of the crops."

"Yes, but you don't have to work here. And now, with Samuel Abercrombie threatening—"

Zeke placed a hand on her arm. "You must know how I feel," he said. His face was red even in the shadowy barn. "I've always loved you, Jenny. Now McDougall's gone for good, I want to marry you," Zeke said in a rush.

Surprised at Zeke's declaration, Jenny froze. She couldn't say a word.

"I don't care you weren't married to him," Zeke continued. "I'm glad, so I can have you. I don't care about William, he's—"

"What do you mean, you don't care about William?" William was her life.

"I don't care if he's Mac's son. That you and Mac weren't married."

"It wasn't like that—" Jenny didn't want to tell Zeke the whole story. She only wanted Zeke's friendship. She didn't want to think about marriage. Not to Zeke.

"William's a fine boy. I'll raise him." Zeke took her hand. "Please say yes, Jenny. Please marry me."

Jenny pulled her hand away. She stepped outside and leaned her arms on the barnyard fence. Poulette and Shanty grazed in the paddock beyond the fence, the warm June sun casting a sheen on their coats.

Zeke followed and stood close behind her.

"I wasn't expecting this, Zeke."

"You need someone to take care of you. And William. Why not me? I love you."

Should she say yes? If she couldn't have Mac, wouldn't Zeke do? He was her friend, and Mac had told her to marry Zeke.

He put his hands on her shoulders and turned her to him. "Say yes, Jenny."

But she was silent. "I need time to think," she finally said. She owed Zeke that much.

He sighed, then walked her to the house. "I can wait on your answer.

I've waited a long time to tell you how I feel."

Jenny stood in the cabin doorway while Zeke saddled his horse, mounted, and rode off with a wave. She watched until he was out of sight.

Thursday, June 27ᵗʰ—Zeke asked me to marry him. William would benefit from a father. It's what Mac wanted for me. What do I do now?

Chapter 68:   Jenny's Quandary

Jenny fretted about seeing Zeke at church the Sunday after his proposal. But it was a bright warm day, and she had no excuse to stay home. So she hitched Poulette to the wagon, and she and William rode slowly down the road to town.

What would she say to Zeke? She'd thought of little else since his Thursday declaration. Was she better off married or alone with William?

Every time she thought of Zeke telling her he didn't mind William being Mac's son, she cringed. She couldn't marry Zeke without telling him the truth. She had no idea how he would respond to learning William was the result of rape. And she was uncertain how to tell him.

It had been so easy to tell Mac. She'd only met him the day before, but the gunfight in the Arrow Rock tavern had made them instant comrades. Or so it had seemed. She'd trusted him immediately.

After the church service, Jenny made sure to stay near Esther and her family. She saw Zeke eyeing her, but never let herself be alone for him to approach.

As she talked with Esther and Daniel, Samuel Abercrombie strode over. "Hear tell McDougall ain't coming back," he said to Jenny, without even a nod to anyone in greeting. "How you going to stay on his claim?"

"He g-gave me a letter," Jenny stammered. "And a deed. He wants me to have it."

"Might not be enough for a judge," Abercrombie sneered. "Woman can't own property in Oregon. And what good is his deed to land he ain't owned yet?"

"Father Abercrombie, you mustn't do this to Jenny," Esther said, grabbing her father-in-law's arm.

338

Abercrombie shook her off. "I'm thinking on what I must do," he said, spat on the ground, and turned away.

Jenny barely slept Sunday night. In the morning, she was up at first light, and wrote:

Monday, July 1ˢᵗ—Mr. Abercrombie threatened to take my land claim to a judge. And I feel I must talk to Zeke about William. My life is so unsettled.

After breakfast she saddled Poulette, mounted the little mare, pulled William up in front of her, and rode off to see Esther. She found her friend in the yard washing clothes, surrounded by children.

"Can we talk a spell?" Jenny asked. Her voice cracked as she spoke.

"Are you letting Father Abercrombie worry you?" Esther said, wiping her hands on her apron. "Ruthie," she said to her younger sister, "Take the children to play in the barn." She turned back to Jenny. "Ruthie's here helping me, now Rachel's gone."

Jenny sent William off with the others, then helped Esther pin the wet clothes on the line. "You heard him," she said, when the two young women were alone. "He wants to take my land."

"We'll pull him around," Esther said. "I told Daniel to talk to his pa. It ain't widely known Captain McDougall ain't coming back. Just folks from our wagon company. I don't know if Father Abercrombie knows you weren't married."

"Who does know?" Jenny asked.

"You told Rachel, and you told me to tell Zeke."

Esther didn't seem as concerned as Jenny thought she should be. What would she think of the next news Jenny had to tell? "There's more," Jenny said.

"What?"

"Zeke proposed."

Esther's face broke into a smile. "At last. I wondered when he would, once he found out you weren't married. We'll be sisters. Don't that solve all your problems?"

"But how can I marry Zeke if I don't tell everyone either that Mac is dead or that we were never married? And Zeke doesn't know everything. Not about William."

Esther raised an eyebrow. "You told me not to tell him."

"But I didn't know he wanted to marry me," Jenny wailed.

"How could you not?" Esther lifted a sopping shirt and snapped it before hanging it on the line. "He's been mooning over you since we left Missouri. He thought you were married to Captain McDougall, or he'd have spoken up long before now."

"I can't marry Zeke without telling him everything."

"So tell him."

"But what will he think of me?"

Esther shrugged. "You won't know till you tell him. But I'm guessing it won't make a hill of beans difference to Zeke."

"I can't marry any man who doesn't love William."

"Zeke's a good man. You know that. Talk to him."

Jenny worked in silence with Esther until all the clothes were hung. Then she said, "Will you mind William awhile? I want to talk to the Tullers."

"They won't tell you any different."

"Probably not, but I want to see what Doc says."

Jenny rode to the Tullers' homestead and found the doctor's wife doing laundry also. "Jenny," the older woman said with a smile, "where's William?"

"I left him with Esther. I need to talk to you and Doc."

"I'm about to set out some dinner," Mrs. Tuller said. "It's leftover meat and potatoes from last night. Too hot to cook after washing all morning. Will you have a bite with us?"

"Yes, ma'am," Jenny said. "I'll dump your wash water while you fix the meal."

Mrs. Tuller bustled into her cabin, and Jenny dragged the tub to the downhill slope of the yard and emptied it toward the creek.

Doc came around the side of the barn. "Hello, Jenny. What brings you here?"

"I need to talk to you and Mrs. Tuller."

Doc frowned at her with his bushy eyebrows. "Well, come in," he said, holding the door open for Jenny. "I suspect Mrs. Tuller has asked you to stay for dinner."

"Yes, sir." Jenny preceded the doctor into the cabin.

Over smoked venison, she haltingly told the Tullers about Zeke's proposal and about what Mr. Abercrombie had said on Sunday.

"My lands," Mrs. Tuller said. "Don't that solve all your troubles. Zeke knows your farm like the back of his hand, and he has his own claim if Samuel Abercrombie gets you thrown off Captain McDougall's."

"But Zeke doesn't know about William."

"What doesn't he know?" Doc said.

"That William isn't Mac's son."

"What difference does that make? Zeke knows William ain't his own son, and he's ready to take you anyway." The doctor helped himself to more potato salad. "A man's only concern is whether a child is his or not. Don't matter who else's it is."

"Now that's not true, Doc," Mrs. Tuller said. "Captain McDougall is a fine man. Like Zeke. William's father wasn't, whoever he was. Blood do tell sometimes."

Doc snorted. "You're asking for trouble if you tell young Pershing more'n he needs to know."

"But what's fair to Zeke?" Jenny asked, as much to herself as to the Tullers.

"Here's another thing to think about," Doc said. "Legislature's likely to change the land laws. There's rumblings now."

"What do you mean?"

"It's too early to say, but if the laws change, folks might have to refile their claims. You can't file on the land without McDougall. And he won't be here to file for you. So it might not matter what Abercrombie does."

"You think I'll lose the farm?" A pang of fear surged through Jenny's gut. Hearing Doc talk about the legislature was worse than fretting about Mr. Abercrombie's meanness.

"You might need Zeke Pershing more'n you think." Doc's eyebrows met in a frown. "Consider what's best for you and your boy."

Chapter 69: Drifting

Consuela's murderer was quickly brought to justice. Within days after her death, the attacker was tried and hung. Mac sat through the brief trial and went to the hanging, though he had little desire to attend any execution. As Maria's guardian, he wanted justice for his ward's mother. And Consuela had been his friend, though not always a comfortable confidante.

By late June, three weeks after Consuela's death, Mac had made no decision about his next move. It had been almost two months since he'd been shot, but he told himself his arm was still too weak. The truth was he didn't know what to do.

June 24, 1850. I shall remain in the West.

After writing that one sentence, Mac stopped to sharpen his nib. He couldn't think what more to write—a desire to remain in the West was the most he could declare, even to himself.

He'd proven his independence from his father—made a fortune from prospecting, contributed to the Constitutional Convention, managed a thriving store, and started the transport business. Hauling gold had proven dangerous, but he still thought it was a promising enterprise. Through all these ventures, he'd tried to behave with integrity, loyalty, and industry.

Mac hungered for action, more than he could get in Boston. Nevertheless, the brush with his own mortality and losing Huntington and Consuela had sobered him.

He wanted more than adventure. He wanted more than self-respect. He wanted a place to call home. He wanted to build a future, to leave a legacy to mark his time on earth.

But a legacy of what? A home where?

He could stay in Sacramento, run his store, and help transform California into a prosperous state. William Shannon had offered him a place in his law practice. Practicing law in California would be more exciting than his brother's staid firm in Boston.

And Susan had made her position clear. She would marry him, provided he didn't have Maria as baggage. To be close to her grandfather, she would likely settle happily with Mac in San Francisco or Sacramento.

Or—and he let the idea slowly creep into his mind—he could follow Consuela's advice. He could return to Oregon to see if Jenny would have him.

Yet, Susan thought they were close to an engagement. Susan could help him build a place for himself in California, but she didn't want Maria.

How would *Jenny* feel about the baby?

Could he and Jenny build a future in Oregon?

Mac slammed his journal shut, unwilling to make any decision.

After Consuela's death, Mac had moved Maria and her nurse into the back room of his store. He lived in the room above but took his meals in the Golden Nugget.

Maria grew prettier when she began to smile. At three months old, she cooed and waved her arms whenever she saw Mac. She rarely cried when he held her.

Mac's parents hadn't spent time with him when he was a child. He'd mostly left William to Jenny's care, and the nurse tended to most of Maria's needs. He didn't know if he could be a good father, but he cherished Maria, and softened in her presence as he hadn't since he'd played with his kitten as a boy.

Mac couldn't turn the baby over to the doctor to adopt out. Without discussing the matter with Susan, he told the doctor he wanted to be declared the child's legal guardian.

"Most folks out here don't bother with legalities," the doctor said. "But being as you're a lawyer, write up an affidavit for me to sign saying the child's mother asked you to be guardian. I heard her. So did that whore

Ethel. You won't be questioned."

So Mac drafted the affidavit, had it signed and notarized, then kept it with the important papers for his store. For better or worse, Maria was his ward.

Mac tried to make the best of life in Sacramento while struggling to decide his future. He hired an impoverished teacher from Connecticut as a clerk to replace Huntington. The young man wanted to earn a stake to buy into a mine. He was good at handling money and inventory, but he knew less than Consuela about outfitting a prospector.

Through July Mac made weekly trips to San Francisco to buy goods for the store. On one trip he called on Dunbar to see how the gold transport business was faring.

"Doing quite well, McDougall," Dunbar told him. "Your friend Pershing is an industrious lad. He doesn't have the brains you do, but he hustles."

"Yes, sir, he does," Mac said. "Joel will do a fine job."

"You don't regret selling him the business?"

"No. I'm not embarrassed to say I'd rather avoid the danger. I have a daughter now, an orphan I've adopted."

"Well, having a family does make a man more cautious." Dunbar slid his fingers into his vest pockets. "Then one must find one's excitement in making another dollar."

In the evening Mac dined with Nate. He asked Susan to accompany them, but she planned to attend a Daughters of Temperance meeting.

"What does Susan say about your drinking?" he asked Nate while they lingered over cigars and whiskey.

Nate chuckled. "Says I'm too old to change." Then he raised an eyebrow. "What does she say about yours? You've spent a fair amount of time with her."

Mac shook his head. "She hasn't talked to me about drinking. But she told me to give up Maria."

"Why did Susan feel the need to speak to you about the child?" Nate asked. "She's my granddaughter. I don't want her hurt."

Mac stared into the amber liquid in his glass. "I'm committed to Maria.

I've made that decision. But otherwise I'm drifting," he confessed, ignoring the implications of Nate's statement. "The store is merely a way to fill my days."

Nate blew a ring of smoke and his gaze sharpened on Mac. "I can't condemn you for raising the child, not after I fostered my own to my sister. But what will you do if not keep the transport business?"

"I could practice law here. I've had an offer." Mac paused and sipped his drink. "Consuela told me to go back to Oregon."

Nate coughed on his whiskey. "What about Susan?"

Mac couldn't ignore the direct question from Nate. "I haven't mentioned Oregon to her. I have no commitment to her."

"What's waiting for you in Oregon?"

"Maybe nothing. Maybe a woman. I don't even know if I'd be welcome."

Nate leaned forward. "I said I don't want Susan hurt. Better you break it off with her now than regret you didn't later."

"There's nothing to break off, sir."

"Maybe not in your mind, but what about in hers?"

"I have no intention of harming Susan." Mac stubbed out his cigar and stood. "I have an early morning steamboat to catch. Please give her my regards."

When Mac returned to Sacramento, Joel was waiting in the store. "They found Smith," he told Mac. "High in the hills behind the valley where we mined. One of the prospectors brought food to him."

"Where is he now?" Mac asked.

"Marshal Cunningham took another posse out. You plugged Smith in his right arm. It didn't heal right, and he couldn't shoot straight. They brought him back without much trouble."

"He's here?"

"Yep. Hauled him in last night. He's sitting in the jailhouse here in Sacramento. Gonna be a trial next week. Your pal William Shannon's the judge, and you're the lead witness. Smith'll hang for sure."

An eye for an eye, Mac thought. The miscreant had left a trail of death for as long as Mac had known him—from the dandy Tobias Jones with the beaver hat, to the posse avenging Murderer's Bar, to Huntington and the two reprobates who'd accompanied Smith on the attempted gold robbery.

July 21, 1850. Smith has been captured and will stand trial. At least the violence of one murdering fiend will end.

Chapter 70:   Courting and Independence

After visiting with Esther and the Tullers, Jenny continued to mull over Zeke's proposal. Her conversations with her friends hadn't helped. Esther and Mrs. Tuller thought she should tell Zeke about William's parentage. Doc didn't think it was necessary. Jenny was inclined to agree with Esther and Mrs. Tuller, but she didn't know how Zeke would react. Maybe Doc was right. Maybe a man didn't care who fathered a child he had to rear.

As for the land—it had kept Jenny and William alive since Mac left. With Tanner gone and with only limited help from O'Neil, she needed Zeke to maintain the farm. And if Mr. Abercrombie followed through on his threat, she might not be able to keep her home even with Zeke's help.

Mac had wanted her to marry Zeke. He'd said so in his letters.

Everything seemed to be pointing Jenny toward Zeke. But in her heart she knew she couldn't marry him unless she told him the truth about William.

Did she even want to marry Zeke? Did she want to live with him for the rest of her life? To let him bed her? It wouldn't feel like a violation with Zeke. Would it?

Jenny remembered Mac's kiss the night before he left. It had frightened her, but thrilled her, too. Would kissing Zeke be like that?

She didn't know. All she knew was that Zeke would want an answer to his proposal.

Wags's barking early Tuesday morning let Jenny know Zeke had arrived. She was thankful William was crying about a splinter in his knee, so conversation with Zeke would be impossible. While the boy wailed loudly, Jenny called out from her cabin doorway, "I can't talk now, Zeke. I need to calm William down."

"O'Neil and I are working in the south field today," Zeke said.

She smiled. "I'll bring you some ginger tea later on."

Zeke eyed her, but she went back inside.

Throughout the day Jenny managed to avoid Zeke except when O'Neil was around. She took the tea and biscuits with ham and butter out to the men at midday, but didn't stay. Zeke kept their discussion to the work he and O'Neil were doing.

At the end of the day, she went to the barnyard to bid them good-bye. Zeke lingered when O'Neil saddled his horse. "I'm going to work on the broken harness," Zeke told her.

"Then you'll stay for supper, too?" she asked.

"Thank you. I will."

She waved to O'Neil when he rode off, then sighed and went inside to fry a chicken for their meal. She couldn't put off the conversation with Zeke any longer.

They ate in silence, responding only to William's childish questions. After supper Zeke helped Jenny wash and dry the dishes. William played in the corner of the cabin with whittled animal figures O'Neil had carved for him.

Zeke said, "I think I frightened you last week, Jenny. I didn't mean to."

She glanced at him over the bucket of suds. "You surprised me, that's all."

"I guess you haven't been thinking of me the same way I've been thinking of you."

She shook her head. "Zeke, I need to tell you—" If she was going to tell him about William, she should do it soon. But how could she now, with the boy nearby?

"I'm not going to press you for an answer right away, Jenny." Zeke took her soapy hand. "But can I court you?"

"Court me?"

"You can get used to the idea. See if you think I can make you happy."

Jenny's heart melted at his thoughtfulness. "Yes, Zeke. You can court me."

"And will you let me take you to the Independence Day celebration in town next week?

Jenny nodded and smiled.

On Thursday, July 4, a wagon arrived at Jenny's cabin shortly after breakfast. Not only Zeke, but Esther and her family greeted Jenny. Jenny hadn't expected a crowd to go with them to Oregon City.

"We're here to chaperon," Esther announced. "I've packed a picnic."

A chaperon. What a silly notion after she'd lived with Mac for a year and been independent for two more years. Jenny grimaced and shook her head. "I have food also," she said and brought out her basket.

Zeke jumped out of the wagon and stowed the basket in the back with Esther's provisions and the children. Then he lifted William in beside the food, helped Jenny into the back also, and climbed in himself.

Jenny sat on a barrel in the wagon bed. Zeke sat on the floor across from her, gazing at her the whole time it took Daniel to drive them to Oregon City.

The celebration in town was similar to those of earlier years—an invocation, political speakers, a parade, and a picnic. Through the whole morning, Zeke never left Jenny's side.

When it came time to set up their food, Esther shooed her brother away. "Let us have a little women-folk time, Zeke," she said. "Jenny don't need you around every minute." She turned to her husband, "Daniel, you and Zeke take the children off to see the soldiers."

Jenny let out a breath she hadn't realized she'd been holding. "Thank you," she said to Esther. "I didn't know courting could be so overpowering."

Esther laughed. "Don't you worry. I'll give my big brother a little talk on how to let a lady be."

"I've never been courted before."

"Just smile and flirt a little. That's all it takes."

Jenny swallowed. This all felt wrong. Flirt? "I don't know how to flirt. And most people still think I'm married to Mac."

"Of course you know how to flirt. Every woman does. Just let Zeke know you like him. And that's why I'm chaperoning you—so no one will say anything till you're ready."

"I do like Zeke, but—"

"It ain't hard, Jenny. It's just putting your best foot forward. Letting a man know you need him."

Jenny shook her head. She would try.

But when Zeke asked her to walk with him later, she was tongue-tied. She'd always been able to talk to Zeke before. Why was courting so difficult?

Thursday, July 4th—Another Independence Day celebration. Esther says to let Zeke know I need him. Do I? I need a farm hand—Zeke can do that. I want someone to hold me. Do I want Zeke?

Chapter 71:   More Courting

Zeke kept working Jenny's land two days a week through the stifling July heat.

"Don't you need to spend time on your own claim more?" she asked.

He shrugged. "If we marry, this farm will be mine as much as the claim I have."

"Mr. Abercrombie is trying to take the land away from me. He says Douglass should have it."

"Over my dead body," Zeke said. "As long as the land is being improved—and that's what I'm doing—we can pay the taxes and McDougall's filing will stand. You don't have to worry about Abercrombie."

He seemed so sure. Maybe it was a help to have Zeke on her side.

Jenny found it odd to have Zeke courting her. After the Fourth of July celebration, she rarely made it into Oregon City during the busy summer, even for church on Sunday. But Jenny noticed Zeke watching her whenever he was on her farm, and he was quick to assist with any lifting she needed done.

"You don't have to leave what you're doing to help me, Zeke," she told him one day. "I can carry the water bucket, and you're busy."

"Now, Jenny, you let me help you." Zeke wiped his arm across his sweaty brow. "That's what courting is."

It wasn't like courting in New Orleans, at least not what Jenny remembered of her mama's sisters when she was a child. The young ladies in New Orleans sat in the parlor, waiting for debonair men in flashy suits and oiled hair to call on them, chaperoned by Jenny's married mother or her grandmama. No beau in New Orleans ever sweated through courtship, toting buckets of oats and water for the women they wooed.

And it wasn't like Mr. Peterson courting her mama after Jenny's papa died either. That courtship had been sudden and short—Jenny had seen no romance between her mama and Mr. Peterson.

In fact, the man had been as likely to touch Jenny as her mother. Jenny shivered at the remembered feel of Peterson's wandering fingers. She still had nightmares about the day when Peterson and the Arrow Rock sheriff and his son all attacked her.

It didn't do any good to remember that attack, Jenny chided herself as she considered marriage to Zeke. She'd always been comfortable around Zeke. She'd known him for three years, and he'd never done anything improper. He'd been courteous and kind to her—in fact, more attentive than Mac had been. She shouldn't be so reluctant to marry him, she scolded herself.

She wished Zeke would try to kiss her. She needed to know if she liked his touch.

How did a girl ask a man to kiss her? Her mama had never raised the subject of kissing. Even if Mama was here now, Jenny wasn't sure she could talk to her.

Mac had kissed her—the once—then seemed to regret it. Rachel had managed to get O'Neil to kiss her before they were married—and enjoyed it. Should she ask Rachel? Or maybe Esther, who had flirted openly with Daniel when they were courting—surely Esther and Daniel had kissed before they were married.

But she and Zeke were rarely alone. Even when no other adults were on the claim, William was there. She couldn't let a man kiss her in front of her son. Not a man she wasn't sure she would marry.

And Jenny still hadn't talked to Zeke about William's father. She knew she must, but that conversation couldn't happen with William around either.

So all she did to show an interest in Zeke was to cook his supper at the end of the long summer days. But most evenings they were both too tired to talk while they ate.

Thursday, July 18th—Zeke has been such a help. I almost think I must marry him. Yet isn't that why Mama married Mr. Peterson—

simply to have a man around? Better no man than the wrong man, it seems to me.

Jenny made time one morning in late July to visit Mrs. Tuller. She hitched Poulette to the wagon and loaded William and a bowl of blackberries to take to the Tullers.

"How lovely, Jenny," Mrs. Tuller said. "It's been too hot for me to go berrying. These will be a treat."

"I can't stay long, Mrs. Tuller," Jenny said. "I only wanted some company. I haven't seen anyone but Zeke and Mr. O'Neil since the Fourth of July."

Mrs. Tuller sent William into the barn to look at the new kittens. "Have you told your young man you'd marry him yet?" she asked Jenny.

Jenny shook her head.

"What's keeping you, dear?"

"I want to be sure."

Mrs. Tuller laughed. "No one's ever sure, Jenny. No matter what you might read in those silly novels."

"I don't read Gothic novels. I've never even seen one, and I wouldn't have time if I had one." Jenny sighed. "I'm not looking for romance like most young girls. I have a son to think of. I need to be certain of Zeke for William's sake as well as my own."

Mrs. Tuller clucked her teeth. "You've seen how Zeke helps his pa, how he looks after his twin brothers, how he treats Rachel—he made sure Mr. O'Neil was right for her. He won't do no less for you and William."

"I'm being silly, I suppose," Jenny said. "But I don't know if I even want to be married at all."

"It's what you need, girl, so don't let this man go."

Doc came in for dinner, William in tow. "Jenny," he said. "I found this youngster in the barn. Will you take a kitten home?"

William's face shone, "Can we, Mama?"

"What will Wags think?" she asked. But at William's bright-eyed face, she could only nod. "We'll just hope the two of them get along. And the cat has to stay in the barn as a mouser."

"Hear tell there's been trouble with mail deliveries in town," Doc said, plunking his black bag down on the table. "Postmaster can't keep a regular schedule on the routes to Portland and Astoria. Heaven only knows when our mail will be sent, or when letters from the States will arrive here."

"I haven't sent anything," Jenny said. "And I'm not expecting any letters either. Still, it's a shame to know we're so far removed from home."

Chapter 72:   A Letter From Oregon

Smith's trial was set for Monday, August 5. The Honorable William Shannon presided.

The trial took less than a day. Mac testified he had recognized Smith during the transport robbery attempt. The marshal and two deputies testified Smith had shot at them when they went to bring him in. A lawyer Mac didn't know attempted to represent Smith, but there was little he could argue to defend the scoundrel. The jury found Smith guilty within an hour after beginning their deliberations.

"I hereby sentence you to death by hanging," Shannon said, with a pound of his gavel. "Said sentence to be carried out as expeditiously as the marshal can arrange." Apparently, Lansford Hastings's arguments during the Constitutional Convention had not convinced Shannon of the evils of the death penalty.

Smith sobbed at the judge's pronouncement, and Mac exhaled in relief. He'd expected both the verdict and the sentence, but he felt better knowing Smith would no longer threaten the mining district. And Huntington's death had been avenged.

When the courtroom cleared, Shannon asked Mac to dine with him that evening.

Over beefsteak, Mac asked Shannon. "How's your law practice?"

"Growing." Shannon tipped his wine glass at Mac. "There'd be room for you to join me, if you want. I know you're not eager to take up lawyering, at least not in Boston, but I can promise you some interesting cases." He winked at Mac. "You could defend murderers like the one today."

Chuckling, Mac replied, "That's not a tempting offer."

"And how is the lovely Miss Abbott?"

Mac shrugged. "Still lovely. But she's unhappy I've adopted a Mexican child."

"You're committed to the little girl?"

"I won't permit her to go homeless."

"Well, let me know about joining my practice," Shannon said. "In the meantime, don't get into any trouble, or I'll have you in chains in my courtroom. I won't go easy on you either."

Mac grinned. "Not much chance of that. I lead a boring life."

"Are you recovered from your wound?" Shannon asked.

"After almost three months, it still aches at times. But I'm well enough. Unlike Smith, I was fortunate to have a doctor dig the bullet out. And friends to nurse me."

The days after the trial returned to monotony. Mac could feel himself drifting toward a life in California.

> *August 7, 1850. I could split my time between the store and practicing with Shannon. Surely, I could convince Susan to accept Maria. It wouldn't be a bad life.*

But even as he wrote the words, his description of the future felt like settling, not like a life he'd relish.

One afternoon Mac took Valiente out for a long ride along the American River. He wanted to escape town, and the stallion needed exercise. His arm complained, but it felt good to stretch it.

The river was as blue as the sky above it, and wild golden daisies lined the banks. A few late cottonwood seeds floated in a warm summer breeze.

"What do you think, boy?" he asked when he stopped to let Valiente drink. "Shall we stay here? I could find you a filly like Poulette? We could both be happy."

An image of Jenny riding Poulette across the prairie flashed through his head. What was she doing right now? he wondered, turning Valiente back toward town.

That Friday Joel rushed into Mac's store waving a letter. "You're in a heap of trouble now, Mac," he crowed. "I just got my mail. Listen to this. It's from Esther." Joel read from the letter:

July 5, 1850
Dear Joel,
    I hope this letter finds you happy and healthy. We are all fine here. Jonah, Cordelia, and Samuel are growing like weeds. Pa and Mother Amanda are well also, as is the rest of our family, including our youngest brother, Franklin, Jr.
    Jenny surprised us all with her story. Perhaps you've heard it from Captain McDougall. They were never married.
    Now Zeke has offered for her, and they are courting. They spent the whole day together during our Independence Day celebration yesterday. She's bound to marry him soon.
                    Your loving sister,
                    Esther

"Your secret's out," Joel said with a smirk on his face. "Zeke'll get Miz Jenny after all."

Mac grabbed the letter. Dated early July—Zeke had proposed to Jenny over a month ago.

Throwing the letter to the ground, Mac slammed one fist into his other palm. Rage flashed from his gut to his head. Rage at Joel. At Zeke. At himself for dithering. Zeke couldn't have Jenny—she was Mac's. "Not if I can help it," he gritted through his teeth. "I'm going to Oregon."

Chapter 73:   Talking to Susan

*August 10, 1850. It is harder to leave California than
I would like. I must dispose of the store and find a way
to care for Maria on the journey. I am on my way to San
Francisco to talk to Nate about the store.*
And I must talk with Susan.

Immediately after reading Joel's letter from Esther, Mac made
arrangements to leave Maria with her Indian nursemaid for a few days and
booked passage on the next steamboat to San Francisco. He met Nate for
supper the night he arrived.

"I'm selling out and going to Oregon," Mac told Nate.

"Have you told Susan?" was the older man's first reaction.

Mac shook his head. "I will. Know anyone who might buy my store?"

Nate frowned. "She talks like the two of you have an understanding."

Mac sat back in his seat, stunned. "No, sir. I told you, I have made no
commitment to her." He wouldn't let Susan interfere with his decision to
marry Jenny. But he didn't want to hurt Susan.

"Oh, she doesn't say you asked her to marry you. But she smiles and
says she talked you out of ruining your life with the Indian baby."

"I told you last time we met, I've adopted Maria."

"Susan won't like that." Nate's frown became a glower. "She's a
headstrong young woman, but she's all I have. You clear the air with her
before I advise you about the store."

Nate rebuffed all Mac's efforts to discuss the store. Mac was chagrined
to know he'd disappointed Nate, who reacted as Mac's old tutor had when

Mac failed to complete a lesson. He was uncomfortable through the rest of their dinner, knowing he needed to have an even more uncomfortable conversation with Susan.

The next morning after breakfast, Mac called on Susan. They met in a small parlor in the hotel where Nate and Susan lived. Mac didn't know if it was his imagination, but her greeting sounded strained.

"Did your grandfather tell you I'm heading to Oregon?" Mac asked.

She pursed her lips for a moment, then looked at her lap and said, "That's a surprise. He said you wanted to talk to me about your plans. But he didn't say anything more. I thought perhaps—" She shook her head. "Why Oregon?"

"You know I traveled there in forty-seven."

She nodded.

"I left many friends there from the wagon company I rode with. One friend in particular. A young woman."

Susan stood abruptly and moved to look out the window. "You've never mentioned her."

"No." Mac took a deep breath. "Her name is Jenny. We traveled together from Missouri. I'm in love with her."

Susan's back grew rigid.

"People in the wagon company believed we were married. That her child was mine. I want to do right by her, if she'll have me."

"Of course, she'll have you. A wealthy, well-educated Bostonian?" Her voice was bitter. "Any woman would have you."

"She turned me down before."

Susan whirled around. "Why are you doing this, Caleb? I thought you cared for me."

"I do—"

"If you cared for me, you'd abandon this silly notion of returning to Oregon. Of doing right by some hussy who is no better than Consuela—"

"Be careful, Susan—"

"—A girl who only wants your money," she continued angrily. "If you cared for me, you'd send the baby away, as I asked. If you cared for me, you wouldn't have let me come to care for you." Her voice broke.

"I'm sorry, Susan, I truly am." Mac raked his fingers through his hair. "I wish I'd recognized how I felt about Jenny years ago. But I didn't. I haven't treated you well. I'm not sure we would have been well suited. But I'm sorry."

"Not well suited?" She sniffed. "I should have realized your drinking and carrying on with prostitutes were ingrained in your character. But I thought I could change you."

"Susan—"

"Please leave, Mr. McDougall. I don't think we have anything more to talk about."

"Susan—"

"I think it would be best if you returned to calling me 'Miss Abbott.' Although I doubt we will see much of each other in the future." Susan made a brief curtsy. "Good day." She stalked from the room.

Mac was silent as he watched her leave. It was best to let her have the last word. He'd known as soon as she called Jenny a hussy he was getting off easy.

He breathed a sigh of relief and went to find Nate.

"What'd she say?" Nate asked.

"She was upset," Mac said. "I'm sorry. I told her I was sorry."

"Well, I won't say I'm not disappointed. I thought the two of you would make a fine match. You'd never seemed serious about that girl in Oregon."

"I told myself I wasn't, but I am," Mac said. "I hope I'm not too late." He swallowed hard at the thought Jenny might already have married Zeke. "Now, will you help me sell my store?"

"You sure that's what you want?"

"Yes."

"Sell off your inventory at rock bottom prices," Nate said. "Other merchants will buy it from you, just to keep the cheap goods out of people's hands. Then they'll mark it up come winter when new things are scarce. You get rid of the merchandise, and they make a profit."

"That works for the dry goods," Mac said. "But I'm stuck with the building."

"I'll look for a buyer for you." Nate blew a ring of smoke. "Or take both the inventory and building and manage it myself again."

"I thought you were done with working." Mac grinned. "You told me you were ready for a life of luxury."

"Turns out luxury is a might too peaceful," Nate said. "Body can only eat so much. And Susan won't let me drink all I want."

"She said she thought she could change me."

Nate harrumphed, but otherwise ignored Mac's comment.

"I can leave you my power of attorney. You can run the store as my agent, then sell it later," Mac offered.

"That'll work. But if you find another buyer, go ahead and sell." Nate smoked silently a moment, then asked, "What made you decide on this Oregon girl anyhow?"

Mac ground his cigar in the ashtray. "The thought of another man having her. Even the man I told her to marry."

"Damn foolish of you to take so long to figure it out."

"Yes, it was." Mac exhaled. He itched to begin the journey to Oregon.

"Have you written her to tell her you're coming?"

"I'd hoped to be on the next boat north. So I'd be in Oregon as quickly as a letter could get there. But if I can't leave for another couple of weeks, a letter makes sense."

"You taking the Mexican brat with you?"

Mac's eyes narrowed at Nate's description of Maria, but he held his temper. "You mean my daughter? Yes."

"What if your gal in Oregon doesn't want her?"

Jenny had traded with the Indian women along the trail, exchanging smiles as well as food. He thought of her love for William, despite not knowing which despicable man had fathered the boy. "She'll take Maria." Mac was certain of that. "It's whether she'll take me I worry about."

"Well, Maria's prettier than you, that's for sure." Nate said, chuckling. "There are hundreds of ships in the harbor. Maybe one of them is going north. Write your letter quickly and send it on the boat. Then settle your affairs in California in an orderly manner."

Chapter 74:   Confession

Jenny's summer days were hectic from first light until full dark, in the cabin, in the barn, and in the fields. Zeke labored on both her farm and his own. Rachel and O'Neil, who had no crops on their land this year, returned to help with the harvest.

The winter wheat was ready to reap in mid-July. From that point on, Jenny spent most of her time working with the men. As soon as the winter wheat was harvested, the oats and barley were ripe, followed soon by the spring wheat. They rushed from one acre to the next, working as long as the daylight lasted.

Rachel's baby was due at the end of September, and Jenny refused to let her work on the grain harvest. So Rachel spent her days tending William and cooking for those who slaved in the fields.

In addition to crop work, Jenny made jam out of the wild berries she gathered and put up beans and cucumbers from her garden. Rachel and Esther often helped with these tasks, and the young women shared their preserved fruits and vegetables.

Zeke, Rachel and O'Neil often stayed for supper, but after the meal Zeke always left when the others did. "Won't do to have people talking," he told Jenny. They'd walked to the yard as he took his leave one night. "I don't want to make trouble for you."

She shook her head. "We wouldn't want any more trouble, would we?"

"What's wrong, Jenny?" Zeke asked. He clapped his hat on his head and untethered his horse from the fence rail.

Jenny shrugged. "I don't know." She knew she had to talk to Zeke about William, but she was uncertain how to raise the topic.

"We'll talk about our wedding after the harvest. I'll give you time to think till then."

She smiled. "Thank you, Zeke. I appreciate your patience with me." She kept trying to convince herself she should marry him.

Zeke grinned and rode off.

That evening she fashioned a new tip on her quill and wrote:

> *Thursday, August 22ⁿᵈ—Zeke is a kind beau, eager to please me. But I cannot marry him without revealing all my secrets. How will I tell him?*

Jenny put aside the journal and mulled over what she should say to Zeke about William.

The next day Jenny packed up her sewing and William and rode Poulette to Mrs. Tuller's house.

"Jenny," the older woman exclaimed. "Whatever are you doing here in the middle of harvest?"

Jenny lifted William off Poulette into Mrs. Tuller's waiting arms and dismounted. After the boy ran off to play with the cats in the barn, Jenny said, "I don't know what to do about Zeke."

Mrs. Tuller laughed. "Just tell the man you'll marry him."

"But he hasn't even kissed me," Jenny whispered, a warm blush rising on her neck and cheeks.

Mrs. Tuller patted her arm. "That comes natural, child. Don't worry about kissing and such."

"But I do. Because of—" Her voice trailed off.

"Oh, dear, of course you worry." Mrs. Tuller hugged Jenny and sighed. "So you haven't told Zeke?"

"No." Jenny took her sewing out of the saddlebag. "Not yet. I don't know how. And I can't talk to him when William is around." She gestured at her son giggling as he brought a striped kitten over to her.

"Come on in," Mrs. Tuller said. "I'm pickling beets today. William," she said to the boy, "you put that cat back in the barn, and I'll give you a piece of pie."

While the women worked, William ate. When he rubbed his eyes, Jenny settled him on the Tullers' bed, then returned to help pickle the vegetables.

"I've been thinking," Mrs. Tuller said. "Zeke works your land on Tuesdays and Thursdays, right?"

"Yes, ma'am."

"Next Tuesday, I'll come for William in the afternoon, when the men are back in the fields. He can spend the night with Doc and me. Doc won't mind. That'll give you and Zeke a chance to talk after supper."

"Would you, Mrs. Tuller?" Jenny smiled, but inside her heart sank. By Tuesday she would have to know what to tell Zeke.

Tuesday came quickly. Jenny had lain awake every night for hours thinking about how to tell Zeke about William's father. There was no easy way to describe the most painful, horrific day of her life. No matter how she tried to word it in her mind, she was sure she would blurt it out when the time came.

Tuesday, August 27ᵗʰ—Tonight I will talk to Zeke.

Strange, she thought, putting the diary away. She hadn't had any trouble telling Mac so long ago in Missouri. The story spilled out of her. Maybe it would again, once Zeke sat in front of her.

Mrs. Tuller picked up William as planned, and Zeke and O'Neil returned to the cabin just an hour later, their labors halted by a heavy rainstorm. Both men came to the cabin to wash up before O'Neil left.

"How's Rachel?" Jenny asked.

"Mighty uncomfortable," O'Neil said. "Can't sleep. She's hopin' the baby comes soon."

Jenny smiled. "The last month will pass in no time. Then neither of you will sleep much."

O'Neil laughed as he mounted his horse. "See you next week, Miz Jenny. If my child don't interfere." He tipped his hat and rode away.

"Where's William?" Zeke asked, looking around the clearing.

"He's with the Tullers tonight," Jenny said.

"Maybe I shouldn't stay," Zeke said. "'Tain't proper without even the boy here."

Jenny twisted her hands in her apron. "I need to tell you something," she said, her voice quavering.

"Whatever's the matter, Jenny?" Zeke took her arm and led her into the cabin.

"Let's eat first," she said, and turned to dish up the stew from the fireplace.

She couldn't swallow a bite. Zeke ate two platefuls of stew and sopped up the gravy with a biscuit. He scowled at her in silence while he ate.

When his plate was empty, Zeke leaned back in his chair like the man of the house he hoped to be. "Mighty fine biscuits," he said. "Now, what is it you want to tell me?"

"It's about William," Jenny began.

"I've told you I'll do right by the boy," Zeke said. "I'll treat him like he was my own."

"Mac isn't his father," Jenny said.

Zeke gaped at her, his eyebrows raised. "Who is?" he asked in a harsh voice.

Jenny stood and turned to take the stew pot off the fire. She set it on the hearth beside the fireplace. "Back in Missouri . . . three men."

"Three!" Zeke shot out of his chair so quickly it tipped over. "You were with three men?"

She shook her head. "It wasn't like that. They raped me."

"How . . . ?"

"In my stepfather's tavern."

"Why didn't he stop it?"

"He was one of them."

"Where was your mother?"

"At home. I was alone with them. I couldn't do anything to stop it." Tears streamed down Jenny's face. It wasn't like telling Mac. Mac had listened to her, letting her tell the tale in her own way. Zeke questioned her, dragging the facts from her, not allowing her to describe how she'd felt.

Zeke picked up his chair and sat in it heavily. "Who were the other men? Besides your stepfather?"

"The sheriff and his son."

"All at the same time?"

Jenny nodded.

Zeke groaned. "Just one time?"

She nodded again.

"So you don't know which man fathered William?" Zeke asked, his voice strangled.

Jenny shook her head and sobbed, staring into the fireplace. She felt Zeke come near her. He turned her around to face to him.

"It's all right, Jenny. It wasn't your fault." He wiped a tear from her cheek with his thumb. "I have to go."

And he left.

Chapter 75:   A Letter and a Bill of Sale

Mac worried how Jenny would respond to his proposal. He'd taken her into the wilderness away from her mother, abandoned her in Oregon, thrown her at Zeke, told her he'd never return. And now? Now he wanted her beside him for the rest of his life.

He'd always wanted her, he realized to his chagrin, almost since the day they'd met. She first attracted him with her bravery despite the stones life had thrown at her. Then she captivated him with her cheerfulness and calm amidst their struggles to survive in the desert and mountains. He'd tamped down his desire for her in response to her declarations of independence. He hadn't understood how much he wanted her until he'd been forced to picture her marrying Zeke.

He hoped he wouldn't be too late.

That evening Mac wrote his letter:

> *August 11, 1850*
> *Dear Jenny,*
>
>   *I'm heading to Oregon as soon as I can. I have a store to sell, but then I will return.*
>
>   *If you will have me, I want to marry you. In truth, this time. I want to live with you and William and any children we might have in happiness and love.*
>
>   *I also bring an adopted daughter, Maria, whom I hope you will welcome into your heart.*
>
>   *Wait for me. Please.*
>
>   *My deepest affections,*

367

Mac

In the morning he delivered his letter to the captain of the *Robert Samuels*, a schooner bound for Oregon. He also booked passage for himself, Maria, and Valiente on another ship scheduled to head north from San Francisco within weeks. He still had to sell his store and figure out how to care for Maria on the voyage.

But he would be anxious every moment until he saw Jenny again.

Back in Sacramento, Mac had supper with Joel in the Golden Nugget. He asked Joel if he wanted to buy the store.

"No, indeed," Joel said. "Don't want to be tied down. Taking on the gold transport is a great adventure, but you won't find me spending my days behind a counter."

"Would you sell the store to me?" Ethel asked, when she brought them a bottle of whiskey.

"You want it?" Mac looked up in surprise.

"Never saw myself growin' old as a whore," Ethel said. "Consuela should have taken you up on your offer to keep workin' for you. She'd be alive if she had."

"What do you know about accounts?" Mac asked.

Ethel shrugged. "I can add and subtract. What more do I need to know?"

"How much can you pay?" Truth be told, Mac didn't care. Nate had indicated a willingness to take the store off his hands if need be, but Mac liked Ethel. He'd appreciated her straight-forward bluntness ever since she helped Consucla during Maria's birth. He'd gladly give her the store to get rid of it.

The saloon manager motioned Ethel to return to work. "I can't talk now, but I'll come see you in the mornin'," she said.

Ethel was at the store promptly when it opened. "What are you askin' for the buildin' and goods?"

"I figure it's worth twenty-five thousand dollars. How much can you pay down?"

"Five thousand."

Mac raised his eyebrows, surprised she'd saved that much at the Golden Nugget.

"I know the value of a dollar, Mr. McDougall, even if most miners in these parts don't."

He did a quick calculation. "Pay me your five thousand down, and four hundred per month for five years."

"Five thousand now, then two hundred a month over ten years," she countered.

Mac didn't care what Ethel paid but enjoyed the dickering. He questioned her about her knowledge of bookkeeping and the goods in the store. His young clerk now handled the books and inventory pretty well, but she would need to provide oversight.

Once he confirmed she understood the basics of maintaining inventory and accounts, he decided not to press hard on the terms. "Your down payment and three hundred dollars over seven years."

"Two-seventy-five over the seven years," she responded immediately. "I'm good for the money, you stingy Bostonian."

Mac grinned, stuck out his hand, and she shook it. "Sold," he said. "I'll draft up a contract. Now help me figure out what to do about Maria."

"That's a harder problem than runnin' a damn store," Ethel said. "Indian woman carin' for her now don't speak English. You don't want to take her to Oregon, do you?"

"It doesn't seem right to take her so far away from her tribe," Mac said. "Can we find another wet nurse willing to go to Oregon?"

"How old is Maria now? Could she do without milk?"

Mac had no idea how long babies needed milk. "She'll be about five-and-a-half months when we leave. She'd do best on milk, wouldn't she?"

"Be easier to buy a cow than find a wet nurse," Ethel said. "With the cow around, any woman can care for her."

"Or I could tend to her myself," Mac said.

Ethel looked at him in surprise. "You'd change her diapers? Wash her laundry? Feed her from a bottle?"

"If I had to."

"You done it before?"

"I've changed diapers. Though not very often." Mac had mostly left William to Jenny. And the Indian girl took care of Maria's needs.

"Best let me see if I can find a cow. And a woman goin' to Oregon." Ethel's voice showed her skepticism of Mac's ability to care for an infant.

That evening Mac wrote:

August 16, 1850. I have sold my store to Ethel. I am eager to leave California, but still must provide for Maria.

Over the next two weeks, while he waited for his ship, Mac taught Ethel how to run the store. They signed the bill of sale he drafted, then he bought her dinner at the Golden Nugget to celebrate, smoking cigars with her after the meal, like he had with Nate.

Mac also took a last trip out to the mining camp where the Tanners lived and Joel still prospected part-time.

"I'm returning to Oregon," Mac told Tanner and Hatty, who was obviously with child again. Mac refrained from any comment, not wanting to remind her of her earlier losses.

"I always knew you would," Hatty said with a grin. "But it sure took you long enough to git around to it. Miz Jenny and your boy will be mighty glad to see you."

"Now, Hatty," Mac said. "You know I'm not as smart as you."

"You surely ain't, Captain McDougall. Or you'd never have left your wife alone so long."

"Do you think she'll have me back?"

"What choice do a woman got?" Hatty said. "If her husband come home, what can she do if she don't want him?"

So Hatty didn't know Mac and Jenny weren't married. He'd wondered if Joel had told them. Mac kept his mouth shut. The fewer people who knew, the better. He hoped to remedy his past failure immediately upon reaching Oregon.

"If you ever need anything, you let me know," he told Tanner, holding out his hand for the man to shake. "I'll help you however I can."

"Since Negroes can't own property in California, no more'n in Oregon," Tanner said. "I'm obliged to you and Joel Pershing for givin' me a place and not chargin' me rent."

"You earned our support on our journey west," Mac said. "And you're earning your way here in California, you and Hatty."

"I wish you and Miz Jenny much happiness," Hatty said, while Mac saddled Valiente to return to Sacramento. "You and your children."

Children, Mac thought, beginning the long ride back to town. He and Jenny would start their life together with two children—William who was Jenny's only, and Maria who was an orphan. What other children might they have together? Several, he hoped, and he smiled all day thinking about building a family with Jenny.

Chapter 76: A Ship Is Lost

Ethel found a sturdy young woman named Helga Larson wanting to go to Astoria in Oregon. "She can care for Maria," Ethel told Mac. "Seems like a sensible woman."

"Me and Sven, my husband, we come from Sweden," Helga said when Mac interviewed her. The Larsons had arrived in San Francisco in 1849 to seek their fortune in the gold fields, but had run out of money before they found riches. "Sven, he go to Oregon. Find work in Astoria. On the docks, like in Sweden. I stay here until he send for me. He write me now to come." Helga worked as a laundress and maid for a boardinghouse in Sacramento.

"Have you cared for babies before?" Mac asked.

"*Ja*," Helga said. "I watch little brothers and sisters. Back in Sweden. I go to Astoria with you. I take care of your *flicka*, your little girl."

"No children of your own?"

"No." She smiled, which made her round face pretty. "But I hope when I see Sven."

"Can you start immediately?" Mac asked. "I have passage on the next ship to Oregon."

"*Ja*," she said. "I want see Sven soon."

He hired Helga on September 3 and immediately launched into his final preparations for the voyage. He paid the Indian nurse and sent her back to her tribe. Then Mac moved himself, Helga, and Maria to San Francisco, taking two rooms in a hotel. He bought a nanny goat from a Mexican herder in the hills above town. Then he was ready to leave, but his ship was delayed in reaching San Francisco. All he could do was wait.

"I tell men mining no good," Helga told Mac one afternoon when she

372

brought Maria to see him. "Mines are dirty. Food costs too much. But they don't listen."

"Every man needs to learn the lesson himself," Mac said. He thought of his good luck in beating the rush to California. San Francisco had been so different in 1848—a sleepy village with a beautiful harbor. Now enterprises of every sort lined its streets. He'd been there for the rising of California from pastureland to land of plenty, from Mexican territory to birth of a state.

He reflected that evening on his experiences, on his attempts to prove himself since he left Boston—along the trail, in the mines, at the Constitutional Convention. He'd had financial success, but hadn't found a calling, as Consuela had urged him to do. Nor had he followed her advice to seek happiness. He hoped to find his calling in Oregon, and he knew he'd never find happiness without Jenny.

He wrote in his journal:

September 11, 1850. I am ready to leave California. I was never eager to settle here, though I might have defaulted to it. I have sought adventure for three years, but I've not found a place to call home.

He hoped to find his place with Jenny. Surely he could discover a challenge worthy of his efforts in Oregon, but that mattered less than being with Jenny.

Convincing her to love him would be challenge enough. Mac thought of Jenny constantly now, wondering what she might think of him after almost three years apart. She might hate him for leaving her or for sending her word he'd died. Could she accept him as a husband and as a father to William?

The boy had only been a baby when Mac left. Mac hadn't paid much attention to him, because he'd had no intention of remaining with Jenny. Now William was almost three. Old enough to need a father.

And Maria. Mac was bringing his own baggage home to Jenny. Jenny would accept Maria, he was confident. Would she accept him?

It all came back to that.

Mac wrote his parents before he left for Oregon. They deserved to know at least some of his plans. He had last written them in March to tell them he wasn't returning. He'd had no word from them since, but out of filial duty he wanted to let them know he was leaving California.

> *September 13, 1850*
> *Dear Mother and Father,*
> *I am returning to Oregon, and have sold my business*
> *in California. My ship to Astoria is due on the 17th, and*
> *I sail as soon thereafter as the captain will leave.*

Mac decided not to mention Jenny to his parents. If she would not have him, there was no need for them to know. And he couldn't adequately explain his past with Jenny—nor his hoped-for future—in a letter. He would write them again if she accepted him.

> *I have personal matters in Oregon to attend to, and*
> *will let you know of my future plans once my affairs are*
> *resolved. In the meantime, send any correspondence to*
> *me care of the Abernethy store in Oregon City.*

But Maria. His parents should know they had another granddaughter. She wasn't the grandson his father had long desired, but she might someday have need of his parents' protection. If they would give it to a child of mixed blood.

> *I have adopted an orphan girl, Maria, the*
> *granddaughter of a Spanish rancher. Her mother was an*
> *acquaintance in Sacramento whose dying request was*
> *that I care for her child. Maria is a beautiful baby, now*
> *over five months old, and she engages my affections*
> *more deeply each day.*

He had little other news to share. But perhaps this letter would begin to thaw the differences between him and his parents.

> *Until I reach Oregon and write you again, may God's providence rest on both of you and on my brothers and their families.*
>
> *Affectionately, your son,*
> *Caleb*

Mac sealed the letter and posted it the next morning.

On September 24, a week later than expected, the clipper ship on which Mac had booked passage reached San Francisco. He'd spent the week pacing the docks, calling at all the shipping offices for news, and walking with Maria in the autumn afternoons.

When the ship arrived, he took a ferry out to its moorage and introduced himself to the captain.

"Why the delay?" he asked.

"Our cargo was slow to load in Panama, and the passengers and baggage weighed us down," the captain said. "Our profit is in conveying emigrants to the gold fields, and we must accommodate as much of this traffic as we can."

"I need to arrange passage for a nanny goat and a second stateroom in addition to the space I've already reserved."

The captain gave him a price, and Mac paid.

"The cook can have any milk left over after the baby has what she needs," Mac told the captain. "Or give it to any other passengers on board. I just want my daughter well fed."

"For what you're paying, Mr. McDougall, your daughter can bathe in it," the captain said. "Have your passengers here at dawn next Monday. The animals and any baggage can be loaded on Sunday."

"What do you hear in port from Oregon?" Mac asked.

"Very little," the captain replied. "Most traffic to San Francisco still comes north from Panama or the Horn, then returns south. Only a few boats call at San Francisco from Oregon." He shook his head. "I did hear of one ship bound for Oregon sinking near the mouth of the Rogue River last month."

"Which ship was it?" Mac asked out of idle curiosity.

"The *Robert Samuels*."

"The *Samuels*?" Mac's heart plummeted. "I'd sent a letter to Oregon on the *Samuels*."

The captain shrugged. "Doubt it got there. The crew and passengers survived, but most of the cargo was lost." He grinned. "Other than some whiskey the crew salvaged."

Mac's stomach churned. Had Jenny received his letter? Was she waiting for him, or had she married Zeke already? He kicked himself for planning his departure from California so methodically. He and Maria should have ridden Valiente hell-bent to Oregon as soon as he'd seen Esther's letter to Joel.

"Can we leave sooner than next Monday?" Mac urged the captain.

"I'm waiting for freight from the mines. It's not scheduled to arrive till Monday. We'll leave once the goods are on board."

"I'll pay you double my fare," Mac said.

But the captain was firm. "I have commitments. I can't be at the beck and call of one passenger."

Mac made the rounds of shipping offices in San Francisco, seeking further information about the *Robert Samuels*. But no one knew any more than the captain Mac talked to.

All Mac could do was wait.

Sunday night before he left, Mac had dinner with Nate. Mac had invited Susan also, but Nate said she was indisposed. "Are you really leaving California?" the older man asked. "Not too late to change your mind."

"Yes, it is," Mac said. "I loaded Valiente and the goat on board this afternoon. I'd abandon the goat, but not Valiente."

"I wish you and Susan had reached an understanding. But here's to you," Nate said, raising his glass. "To our friendship, and to your happiness."

"To Jenny," Mac replied, and raised his glass also. "I won't be happy if she hasn't waited for me."

Nate said nothing while he sipped his whiskey.

"And I hope for Susan's happiness as well," Mac said, raising his glass again. "The West needs more women like her."

Nate cocked his eyebrow and said, "To Susan."

When Monday finally arrived, Mac had Helga and Maria at the dock before first light. He settled them in their cabin and checked on Valiente. The Andalusian stallion, now a mature eight-year-old, was restless in the cargo hold, but calmed when the goat was tethered nearby.

"Ain't never had such a fine horse on board," the crewman in the hold said.

Mac patted Valiente's nose and offered him an apple. "He's sailed before," Mac said. "Down the Ohio River in forty-seven, and from Oregon to San Francisco in forty-eight."

"Well, he's forgotten his manners," the sailor said, as Valiente pawed and whinnied. "Hope he don't break his ropes."

"I'll check on him when we're out of the harbor," Mac said. "He'll probably settle down."

Mac stood on deck while the ship sailed toward the Golden Gate in early afternoon. He stared back at San Francisco, the harbor now crowded with boats, unlike when he'd arrived in forty-eight. The growing city climbed the hills above the bay.

Then Mac turned west toward the open sea. The ocean glinted gold with the morning sun behind him, and the wide expanse of open water beckoned.

Would Jenny be waiting?

Chapter 77: Threats

Jenny's conversation with Zeke about William hadn't comforted her. Zeke hadn't blamed her for what happened, but she sensed his opinion of her had changed. She didn't regret telling him, though now she doubted even more whether she should marry him.

On the last Thursday of August, two days after she'd talked to Zeke, he sent his younger brothers to say he couldn't work on her farm that day—he was harvesting his own fields. The twins did chores for Jenny and picked beans in her garden.

"Zeke told us to do what we can to help," Jonathan said. "He'll be back next Tuesday."

On Sunday Jenny took William to church. Zeke was there, despite the busy harvest season, and he eyed Jenny with a determined expression. He stayed close to Esther and her family or to Captain and Amanda Pershing, and merely nodded at Jenny as they passed outside the church.

Jenny's heart sank. If Zeke was willing to spend time with his stepmother, he must be set on avoiding her.

After the church service and summer picnic, Zeke approached her. "May I drive you and William home?" he asked.

Jenny nodded.

Zeke tied his horse to the back of her wagon, assisted Jenny and William onto the seat, then vaulted beside Jenny, all in silence. He took the reins.

As they drove toward the cabin, only William's chatter and the sound of katydids broke the still heat of the late summer afternoon.

When they arrived at Jenny's claim, Zeke put the horses and wagon in the barn, then knocked on the cabin door.

"Come outside with me, Jenny," Zeke said, glancing at William playing in the corner. "I want to talk."

She followed him, leaving the door open so she could keep an eye on William.

"W-what you told me don't matter," Zeke stammered. "I been thinking on it. We'll have to watch the boy, see how he turns out. But I'll do my best by him. I've loved you since the first time I saw you. I can't change that."

Something sank in Jenny's heart when Zeke said he'd have to watch William. She sighed and nodded.

"So what's your answer?" Zeke said, taking her hand.

She let him hold her hand, then swallowed and said, "I'm still considering, Zeke."

"How much time do you need?"

The harvest dance was coming up in a few weeks. "I'll give you my answer at the dance."

Sunday, September 1ˢᵗ—How will I decide? Zeke says he'll have to watch William. I've been watching my son since the day he was born. He's perfect.

Monday afternoon Doc rode into Jenny's yard when she was outside doing laundry. His face was grim.

"It's Samuel Abercrombie," he said. "He's threatening to tell the authorities you're not McDougall's wife."

Jenny gasped. "I thought all he knew was Mac wasn't coming back."

Doc shook his head. "Don't know how he heard. I suspect Daniel told his pa whatever Esther told him."

"Esther wouldn't—"

"You know that girl can't keep her tongue in her head. And Daniel don't hardly ever stand up to his pa. Not unless Esther makes him."

"What can Mr. Abercrombie do?"

"He can make a lot of trouble for you, girl, that's what." Doc's bushy eyebrows drew together in a frown. "As McDougall's wife, you could stay on the land. You might have rights as his widow, though the law ain't clear on that. But you ain't wife nor widow. And now Abercrombie knows."

"Why would he do this?" Jenny whispered. But Samuel Abercrombie had never liked Mac. And he hadn't liked the way Jenny treated his granddaughters in school—even blaming her for Annabelle's smallpox.

Doc snorted. "He's always wanted this piece of land. You got better water and drainage than his son Douglass has got. And this section joins up with Daniel's. Abercrombie's been saying he thinks Douglass should have this section. Says he'll take it to court."

"Will a judge listen to him?"

"He's been buttering up all the officials in town since he got to Oregon. They'd listen to him, though I don't know how they'd decide."

"What can I do?"

"Lay low. He ain't talked to anyone yet. His wife—she's a good woman—is telling him to leave well enough alone. Maybe he's only spouting off to me. But you'd best marry young Zeke Pershing. That'll make sure you and your boy have a home."

As soon as Zeke arrived on Tuesday morning, Jenny ran outside to ask if he'd heard rumors about Samuel Abercrombie wanting her land.

"I ain't heard a word," Zeke said. "But it'd be just like the bastard." His face reddened. "Sorry, Jenny. I don't mean to cuss, and 'specially 'bout bastards."

It took Jenny a moment to realize Zeke was referring to William. Then, enraged at the vile epithet about her child, she rebuked him. "I will not—I will never—let you refer to my son that way. If I marry you—and I don't know that I will—I will expect you to be his father in every way. I will expect you to defend him against the rest of the world."

"Jenny, I said I was sorry—"

"And I will expect you to care for him as much as I do. If you can't, then tell me now." Jenny drew in a long breath. "Now, will you please saddle Poulette for me? I need to talk to Esther."

She had William ready to leave when Zeke brought the mare out of the barn. She seethed as she rode Poulette to Esther's claim. She didn't know whether she was angriest at Zeke, at Samuel Abercrombie, or at Esther.

When she arrived in Esther's yard, she dismounted, threw Poulette's reins over the paddock post, and lifted William down. She knocked once, barely paused before opening the door, then entered the cabin and demanded, "What did you tell Daniel about Mac and me? And what did he tell his papa?"

Esther looked up from washing her breakfast dishes, her face drawn. Jonah and Cordelia squabbled on the floor, and Samuel squalled in his cradle. "Jenny, what a surprise. Why are you here so early?"

"What does Mr. Abercrombie know? He's threatening to take my claim away."

"How can he? Captain McDougall filed it proper, didn't he?"

"Doc says Mr. Abercrombie is making trouble, because I'm not—" Jenny stopped. Jonah and William stared at her. "I'm sorry," she said. "I'm so mad I'm spitting, but I don't want to upset the children."

"Jonah, take William and Cordelia out to the garden," Esther said. "See if there's any new beans to pick."

The children ran outside. Jenny picked up baby Samuel and put him to her shoulder, rubbing his back to soothe him. He struggled, but she needed the contact to soothe herself.

"Now what are you talking about?" Esther asked.

Jenny explained what Doc had said. "What does Daniel's father know?" she asked again.

"I told Daniel everything," Esther said, wiping her soapy hands on a towel. "I always do. Except about you being raped—I didn't tell him that. I told him you and Captain McDougall ain't married. Just what Zeke and Rachel know. I don't know what Daniel told his pa."

"How could you? Didn't you know he'd tell Mr. Abercrombie?" Jenny raged at Esther. "Did you tell Daniel that William isn't Mac's son?"

Esther shook her head. "I couldn't tell him that without talking about you being violated."

"So all Mr. Abercrombie knows is I'm not Mac's wife. And Mac isn't coming back."

Esther nodded. "That ain't so bad, is it?"

Only God knew what old Samuel Abercrombie would do to hurt her. Jenny buried her face in baby Samuel's soft neck, wishing she could hide from his grandfather forever. "It's enough."

Chapter 78:   Is It Love?

Jenny had little time to think over the next week while the harvest continued. Not only were the grain crops ripe, but her garden produced more vegetables every day to gather and preserve. But whenever she sat for a moment, Samuel Abercrombie's threat filled her mind.

She tried to tell herself Esther had only done what most wives would do and the gossip between Esther and Daniel wouldn't harm her. But she couldn't convince herself that Esther's loose tongue wouldn't cause Mr. Abercrombie to make good on his threat to throw her off the land.

On Tuesday, September 10, when Zeke and O'Neil were supposed to be harvesting Jenny's fields, only Zeke showed up, and he was late. As he rode into the yard, Zeke shouted, "Rachel's having her baby. It's coming early. That's why O'Neil ain't here. Esther's gone to help. She needs you to mind her children. I'm off to tell Doc Tuller, soon as I saddle your mare for you. Then I'll be back to harvest your wheat."

"I can manage Poulette," Jenny said. "You get Doc." No matter her anger toward Esther, she had to help out now.

Zeke rode off.

Jenny gathered a bag of mending to take, readied William, saddled Poulette, and rode to Esther's house. Esther was gone when Jenny arrived, and Daniel was with the children.

"I hate to leave you with our three young'uns plus William," Daniel said, a harried expression on his face. "But it's harvest. I have to get our crops in."

"We'll be fine," Jenny said, smiling. "The older ones can play, and I'll enjoy snuggling Samuel."

But Samuel was toddling now and didn't want to snuggle. Jenny had forgotten how active a year-old baby could be. She couldn't do any mending, between supervising four children—all under four years old—and cooking first the noon meal and later supper.

Jenny's mind wandered while she peeled potatoes. This is what her life would be like if she married Zeke. They'd have more children probably. It would be nice for William to have younger brothers and sisters. Could she handle a houseful of babies and a husband—keeping them fed and clothed—even when she was huge with child?

She'd been *enceinte* for most of the journey to Oregon, then had a newborn, yet she'd cooked and washed and minded the wagon the entire trip. Other women—Esther's mother for one—had handled many children and been expecting another baby also. But then Mrs. Pershing died of childbirth fever, Jenny remembered with a pang of sorrow. Family life brought risks and burdens along with happiness.

Dusk had descended over the valley when Esther returned. "It's a boy," Esther announced with a smile. "Tiny thing, but seems healthy. Named Robert after his pa. Mr. O'Neil's busting with pride. You'd think no man ever fathered a son before."

Jenny laughed. "Mr. O'Neil probably never thought he'd be a papa. How's Rachel?"

"That girl was born to be a mother," Esther said shaking her head. "Easy pregnancy, easy childbirth, even though it was her first and he came early. Mrs. Tuller's staying with her tonight. Shall we visit tomorrow?"

Jenny nodded. "I can't go for long. I didn't finish my mending today, and I have tomatoes and beans to put up at home. But I want to see Rachel and her baby."

Esther grinned as she sank into a chair and picked up Samuel. "Now you see what my life's like. All these children. I'm frazzled by day's end." She nuzzled the baby's nose with hers. "But I love 'em all."

The next morning Jenny and William returned to Esther's with the wagon. Esther climbed on the seat beside Jenny and took Samuel on her lap. The other children scrambled into the back with William. The wagon rolled along the rough road toward Rachel's cabin.

"Visitors," Mrs. Tuller exclaimed when they arrived. "Just what the new mother needs."

Rachel was up, though she walked gingerly and had dark shadows under her eyes. She showed the baby off to Jenny. Jenny's eyes welled with tears when she took the newborn into her arms. "So sweet," she whispered. "Little Robert."

"We're calling him 'Bobby,'" Rachel said. "So's not to confuse him with his pa."

"No one's going to confuse this mite with his big old pa for a long time," Esther said, giggling.

Mrs. Tuller bustled near the fireplace preparing meals to leave for Rachel's family. She and ten-year-old Ruthie Pershing kept the toddlers busy so Jenny, Esther, and Rachel could talk.

"I'm so happy," Rachel murmured, but Jenny would have known that even if she hadn't spoken. The new mother looked bloated and worn after labor, but her face beamed with love and joy.

Esther smiled and touched her sister's arm. "As you should be," she said to Rachel. "Enjoy it now, before the cares of mothering wear you out."

"Are you worn out?" Jenny asked Esther.

"How could I not be?" Esther said. "Three babes, and another on the way."

Jenny gasped.

"Yes, another." Esther grimaced. "At this rate, I'll die younger'n Ma."

"Esther, don't say such a thing," Mrs. Tuller said sharply from the other side of the room. "You have a good husband and lovely children." Jenny remembered Mrs. Tuller had lost all her sons back in the States.

"Yes'm, I do," Esther said with a sigh. "But I'm plumb tuckered out caring for 'em. Wish Daniel'd go off soldiering like Pa did, so I could have a rest from birthing. Or to California like Captain McDougall—" Esther stopped suddenly. "I'm sorry, Jenny. I forgot."

"Never mind, Esther," Jenny said. "I'm past caring about Mac." She was lying to her friends and to herself, but Mac had made his feelings clear—he didn't want her.

"What are you going to tell Zeke?" Esther asked. "He's fretting about your answer, I know."

"I told him I'd decide by the harvest dance," Jenny said. "I want to be certain I'm making the right decision."

"How can you have any doubt, Jenny?" Mrs. Tuller said. "You need a husband, and William needs a father."

Jenny glanced over at William and the other children playing across the room. "I can't talk about it here," she said. She wasn't sure she could tell Esther that Zeke had referred to William as a bastard. Esther might side with her brother, rather than with Jenny.

When they were ready to leave, Mrs. Tuller asked for a ride back to her cabin. Jenny drove with Mrs. Tuller on the wagon seat beside her. Esther sat in back with the children.

"Are you really not settled about marrying Zeke Pershing?" Mrs. Tuller asked Jenny quietly.

"I'm not sure I love him, Mrs. Tuller," Jenny said. "Not like Esther loves Daniel." She heard Esther snort behind her. "Or like Rachel loves Mr. O'Neil."

Mrs. Tuller patted her hand. "Love comes, Jenny. When a woman marries a good man, love comes. You don't have anything to worry about with Zeke."

"Maybe not," Jenny said. "But I wish I were sure."

That evening as she thought over everything her friends had said, Jenny wrote:

> *Wednesday, September 11th—The Tullers and Esther and Rachel all tell me to marry Zeke. There are many good reasons to do so, but something is holding me back. Is it only that he isn't Mac?*

It dawned on Jenny that her mama must have been in a similar situation after Papa died. Mama had had a child and a farm to manage and no man around to help. Mama had chosen to marry Bart Peterson.

In Jenny's mind, her mama had made a terrible decision. Mr. Peterson had been a depraved villain—emboldened perhaps by Sheriff Johnson and his son, but every man is accountable for his own actions.

Zeke was not wicked like Bart Peterson. He'd been loyal to Jenny for years. She might not like what he said about William, but he'd never hurt the boy.

Oh, Mama, Jenny thought, what should I do?

William's third birthday was September 16, a Monday. The day before, despite the busy harvest season, Jenny took a pound cake and berry compote to the picnic after the church service in Oregon City. She invited all their friends to share the cake, and they all congratulated William.

Zeke stood beside Jenny while everyone sang "For He's a Jolly Good Fellow" to the boy. Like a father would do, Jenny thought, tears creeping into her eyes. But Zeke rarely touched William, other than to lift him into or out of a wagon. She'd never seen him hug William.

Would Zeke be a good father to her son? That was the most important question in her mind. She didn't want her decision to hurt William.

Zeke took Jenny and William home after church. "Won't you give me an answer, Jenny?" he asked, when he untied his horse from behind the wagon in her cabin yard.

"You said I could have until the dance." Jenny knew she sounded curt, but she wanted the full time to consider.

"I hate not knowing," Zeke said, taking her hand. "I want to make plans with you. Where we'll live. How we'll handle both farms."

"I think of little else," Jenny said. That much was true. "Will Mr. Abercrombie let me keep Mac's claim, do you think?"

Zeke shrugged. "If not, one farm is enough. It may be all I can manage, with helping Pa also." He rubbed her palm. "Just let me know you won't turn me down," Zeke said.

She smiled at him. "I'm still thinking."

Zeke leaned over and kissed Jenny softly on the lips. "Think harder," he said with a grin. Then he swung into the saddle and left her.

Jenny touched her mouth as she watched Zeke ride off.

Chapter 79:   Storm at Sea

"How long will our voyage take?" Mac asked the captain shortly after he boarded with Helga and Maria. It had taken Mac three weeks to travel south from Oregon in March 1848, but the heavy seas had still carried winter storms on that voyage.

"This ship usually takes ten days or so to the mouth of the Columbia, barring bad weather. I need to offload cargo at the Rogue River, so could be a day or two more. Then we have the river currents to contend with before we reach Astoria."

Mac spent the first few days after they left port walking the decks of the clipper ship. He checked on Valiente and the nanny goat each morning, but even they didn't need him. The crew fed the animals, and the ship's cook milked the goat and bottled the milk Maria needed, using the rest in meals.

Seasickness hit Helga as soon as they reached the open ocean. "It will pass in a few days," she assured Mac when he knocked on her cabin door the first morning out. "Like when Sven and I cross the Atlantic."

Maria didn't seem affected by the motion of the waves, so Mac took her on deck each morning and afternoon, shielding her from the wet ocean spray. But the six-month-old baby tired quickly, and Mac took her back to his cabin.

By the third day Helga had her sea legs and was able to walk about the ship. Then Mac could leave Maria with her.

The Pacific didn't live up to its name—its autumn waves pitched and careened. Still, sailing up the California coast was not so bad as Mac's trip south to California. And the seas had also been rough on the occasions when he'd sailed the Atlantic off the coast of New England, particularly during winter gales.

When he wasn't walking the deck, Mac paced the narrow floor of his small cabin and fidgeted on his bunk. He thought about writing his parents again. But he couldn't post a letter until he reached Astoria, and he had nothing to tell them. Yet. If Jenny would have him, he would inform them of his marriage. If she would not . . .

October 3, 1850. If Jenny will not marry me, I will leave Oregon. I cannot watch her build a life with Zeke. Where might I best raise Maria? She will need a woman's care.

Mac berated himself for his delays in leaving California.

As the captain had told Mac, the ship stopped at a couple of small ports along the coast, including at the mouth of the Rogue River, where the *Robert Samuels* had sunk. Mac's letter to Jenny was probably at the bottom of the sea nearby.

A new town of gold seekers sprouted beside the Rogue just upstream from the estuary where the clipper anchored. Men flocked to the new gold finds along the river's banks, like they had rushed to California in 1848.

Mac fumed at the delay in their journey while he stood on deck and waited for their ship to ferry food and tools into the settlement. The rocky shoals off the mouth of the Rogue meant an extra day to find anchorage and another day to offload the cargo.

October 5, 1850. The untamed land around the Rogue resembles California when I first arrived. The gold mines will need experienced prospectors, but it is no place for me to bring Maria. I wish we were already in Astoria.

Two mornings later the ship anchored again off the Umpqua estuary.

Sand dunes rose on the shore, but Mac couldn't see much else at the river's mouth. Yet the crew lowered two small launches off the side of the ship.

"Why are we stopping?" he asked the captain.

"Water barrels sprang leaks. We need fresh water. Maybe trade with Indians for fish. Cook says he could use fresh provisions."

"There's no town here?" Mac asked.

The captain shook his head. "Nothing but Indians. Umpqua tribe. River's named after them."

"Mind if I go along?" Mac asked. He didn't like delaying the journey, but if they were stopping, he might as well see some of this primeval land.

"Can you shoot?" the captain asked.

Mac nodded.

"Tell the mate to give you a rifle from the locker in the foc'sle, then climb down the ladder."

Mac clambered down the rope ladder after the first mate to the bow of the dory, then watched the shore approach while the seamen heaved on the oars. They steered the boat into a cove in the dunes and jumped off into shallow, brackish water. Tree-covered hills rose behind the dunes.

"How do we know the Indians are here?" Mac asked.

The mate pointed. "See the fire pits? They're here."

Just as the mate spoke, three Indians stepped out from the scrubby pines beyond the dunes. The mate and one of the sailors approached the natives and motioned in trade, as Mac had with the Indians he'd met along the wagon trail and on his gold claim. The sailor filled an oilskin bag with dried fish from the Indians, and the mate handed one of the Umpqua a bolt of bright calico.

"Be quick," the mate said when he returned. "Big storm's brewing. We need to move the ship away from the beach."

They filled their barrels with fresh water from a spring and loaded them into the dories. The small boats sat low in the water as they headed back to the clipper. Mac smelled the smoky scent of the fish with every slap of the dory in the surf. Waves slopped over the gunwales, and they made sluggish progress through the choppy seas.

Mac searched for Helga and Maria when he was back on board.

"There's a storm coming," he told Helga. "Stay in your cabin."

Mac went back on deck. Once the crew weighed anchor, the clipper pitched and rolled. Mac staggered to maintain his balance. The crew unfurled the sails and took the ship out to open water. Wind whipped through the rigging, and waves crashed over the bow and swept the deck. The wooden beams creaked each time the ship plunged into a trough.

"Storm's a strong 'un," the captain said, when he paused for a moment to talk to Mac. "I know you're a good sailor, but I need all passengers below decks. I'm running her away from the coast. Going to be rough."

Mac returned to his cabin. The ship's motion slung his box of books from table to floor. He repacked them and tied the box to his bunk.

He was too uneasy to stay in his cabin, so he reeled down the passageway to check on Maria and Helga.

"No milk," Helga told him. "And I am sick again."

"I'll go to the galley for more," Mac said. "Then I'll feed Maria."

The cook had doused the galley fire and was spreading cheese on hardtack. "No hot meals today," he said. "Grab a biscuit for you and the girl."

"Do you have milk for the baby?"

The cook shook his head. "Ain't had time to milk the goat." He gestured to the corner. "Take the bucket and get it yourself."

Mac had never milked a goat and hadn't milked a cow since leaving Oregon. But how hard could it be? He picked up the wooden bucket. He barely managed to stay upright as he made his way down a ladder to the hold where Valiente and the goat were tied.

As he stepped off the ladder into the hold, Mac heard Valiente shriek in fear. He turned and saw a crew member bludgeoning the horse. Valiente neighed again when Mac raced forward, the whites of the stallion's eyes showing terror. In the next stall over, the nanny goat bleated.

"Get the hell away from my horse," Mac shouted as he pulled the sailor away from Valiente. He dodged the man's cudgel and slammed a fist into the sailor's jaw.

Shaking his head and roaring, the sailor swung his club wildly. Mac ducked it, grabbed the man's arm, and banged it against the bulkhead. The sailor's forearm snapped. He screamed and dropped his weapon.

Though tied to his stall, Valiente tried to rear. Mac worried the horse would hurt himself. He cared little about the sailor moaning on the floor.

He kicked at the man. "Get out," he shouted, then turned to the stallion.

The man scrambled to his feet and lurched away, clutching his arm.

Mac tried to calm Valiente, but the horse continued to pull against his restraints. Finally, at Mac's soothing tone, the stallion stilled, and Mac ran his hands over the horse's flanks. He didn't see any blood, though Valiente shied when Mac touched his left rump where a large welt rose.

"Whoa, boy," Mac soothed. "You're all right now. Let me milk the nanny, then I'll find you some salve."

The skittish goat would not stand still, so Mac tethered her head and back legs to nails in her stall. He tried to milk her, but with the ship's motion he couldn't balance on the stool. When he had an inch of milk in the bucket, he stopped, not wanting to risk spilling it on his way back to Maria.

Mac looped a rope through the bucket handle and tied it around his waist to leave both hands free to hang on to the rolling ship. He clumsily made his way up the ladder toward Helga's cabin.

When he arrived, Helga sat retching into a basin while Maria fussed on the bunk. "Is she ill?" he asked Helga, breathing heavily after the ordeal in the hold.

"Little *flicka*, she fine. Just hungry. It's me sick."

"I'm sorry," Mac said, picking up Maria and patting her on the back. "I spilled some of the milk, but I think there's enough for her now."

"I have biscuit, too. Baby make do." Helga tried to stand.

"I'll do it," Mac said. He took Maria and the milk and biscuit back to his cabin and prepared a bottle.

The ship continued to roll with the waves while he fed the baby. When she slept, Mac took her back to Helga and went to the hold to treat Valiente's rump with an odiferous salve.

Then he found the captain to report the sailor's attack on his horse.

"I told the man to check the cargo, but that's all," the captain said, as furious as Mac was at the sailor's mistreatment of Valiente.

Later, after the captain had questioned the sailor, he told Mac, "He says the horse was thrashing about. Thought the animal would break loose and damage the cargo." The captain snorted. "No excuse for bludgeoning your mount and attacking you. I'll have the man flogged."

"If I'd had a gun in the hold, you wouldn't have to whip him," Mac said. "I'd have killed him."

Mac wrote that evening:

October 8, 1850. Lansford Hastings might not approve of the death penalty, but there are times when killing is required. I'd defend Valiente as staunchly as I would myself or Jenny.

Chapter 80:   Harvest Dance

Zeke's kiss hadn't helped Jenny decide whether to marry him. The kiss had been pleasant, but had not stirred her emotions. The kiss hadn't scared her or reminded her of the rape. But then, Zeke never scared her. In fact, he'd calmed her through many a river crossing when she'd feared drowning. Zeke had always been kind to her, whatever he said about William.

It didn't seem enough to build a marriage on—not being scared of a man, thinking of him as kind.

While she fretted about Zeke, Jenny also made plans to open a school again the Monday after the harvest dance, when the older children would be done in the fields. The Pershing, Purcell, and Bingham children would return. The prior year's failure because of the smallpox epidemic was behind them.

"What about the Abercrombie girls?" Esther asked Jenny. "Will Father Abercrombie let them come?"

"I don't know," Jenny said. "I haven't heard yet. If they don't attend, I won't mind. Without Rachel to help, I'll have plenty of pupils to keep me busy."

When Zeke heard about the school, he asked, "How can you be my wife if you're teaching children all day?"

"Even if we marry," Jenny said, "I want to be able to take care of myself. And William."

"As your husband, I will be responsible for taking care of you," Zeke said. "You only need to take care of me. And our children. I won't have my wife teaching school."

When Zeke talked like that, Jenny wondered all the more if she could marry him. She bit her lip to stay silent.

Sunday, September 22nd—Zeke doesn't want me to teach. I cannot marry him until the spring then, because I promised my students I'd teach this winter. I am used to managing my own life, and do not relish turning it over to Zeke.

Would Mac have acted any differently? All good, strong men want to care for their families.

Jenny and Esther worked together, preserving vegetables from their gardens. Tomatoes, squash, corn—each year the garden produced more than the year before. Jenny's grain crops would be smaller this autumn, because Zeke and O'Neil hadn't been able to till as much land as the year before, nor to harvest everything they'd planted. But she would have plenty of vegetables.

Still, this winter would be easier than the last, Jenny thought. She would have bartered goods from her students' families, unlike the winter before when her school closed for weeks due to smallpox. She sent a prayer heavenward there would be no epidemics this year.

And prayed also that Mr. Abercrombie wouldn't make a fuss about her claim. Even if she married Zeke, she wanted to keep the land. It was all she had left of Mac.

"What're you going to tell Zeke?" Esther asked.

Jenny still didn't know the answer to that question herself.

"Well?" Esther asked again, when Jenny didn't respond.

"I don't know," Jenny said.

"You ain't dragging this out to tease him, are you? He's my brother—you better treat him right."

"I'm not teasing, but I need to be sure," Jenny said. "How'd you know Daniel was the man for you?"

"He was so handsome." Esther sighed and smiled into the distance.

"He's still a nice looking man," Jenny said.

"I never thought you'd noticed." Esther flashed a grin at Jenny, then sighed. "But that don't matter so much now. We've built a life. The children. The farm." She turned to Jenny. "And you and Zeke will build a life, too."

"He kissed me," Jenny confessed.

"Zeke? Well, it's about time." Esther laughed. "You mean he hadn't before? I didn't think my big brother was so slow."

Jenny shook her head. "But I didn't feel anything."

Esther turned serious. "It didn't remind you of . . . of Missouri, did it?"

"No," Jenny said. "But it wasn't like Mac—"

"Captain McDougall kissed you?" Esther looked surprised. "I thought you said you and he never—"

"It was only a kiss. Just one kiss." It had scared her at the time, but now Jenny smiled at the memory of Mac's embrace.

Esther grasped Jenny's arm. "Jenny," she began slowly. "A marriage is more than bedding. It's also working together. And raising the children that come."

"I know that—" Jenny started.

Esther interrupted. "I wish I'd known how hard it would be before I married Daniel. I might have waited. But then, after Ma died, if we hadn't been married already, we might never would have. Daniel wasn't happy taking in Jonah, particularly when Cordelia came so quick."

"I never knew," Jenny said. Esther had endured so much since her mama died—mothering Jonah and her own babies, helping with her younger siblings, and tolerating a stepmother she disliked.

"What I'm saying," Esther continued, "is Daniel and me, we've made a home together. It ain't all flowers and ribbons like I thought it would be when we was courting. But I love him, no matter how hard life is sometimes. And he'll stick by me. I know he will. And Zeke'll do the same for you. He's that kind of man."

So is Mac! Jenny's soul cried. Mac had stuck by her all the way from Missouri. "It's not Zeke I'm troubled about," she said to Esther. "It's me."

As the harvest celebration drew near, Jenny continued to ponder whether to marry Zeke. She knew all the reasons she should, but in the end, her heart wasn't in it.

The night before the dance, Jenny lay awake waiting for sleep to bring to an end to her anxiety. She cradled her pillow in her arms—the pillow she'd taken from Mac's bed after he left—and imagined she still could catch his scent in it.

When she couldn't sleep, she lit a candle and wrote:

> *Friday, October 4ᵗʰ—I turn eighteen today. I am grown now and must build a good life for William and myself.*

She sighed, then dipped her quill in the inkpot and continued,

> *I cannot marry Zeke. He has always been my friend, but I do not love him the way a wife should love a husband. I would be settling for second best. He isn't Mac.*

That was the only answer she could give herself. She knew Mac wasn't coming back, even if she wished it were otherwise. But she wasn't ready to commit herself to another man. She'd be better off alone with William than thinking after a year or two she'd made a mistake marrying Zeke.

She would have to tell Zeke no.

The dance was late Saturday afternoon and included a picnic supper. Zeke said he would come for her and William in midafternoon.

Jenny was too nervous to eat the noon meal. As William ate, he prattled on about the rocks in the creek he'd picked up that morning while they searched for mint leaves and crawdads. Jenny barely heard him.

"Go find your coat," she told William, as she finished packing her basket with fried chicken and greens with bacon for supper. "Zeke'll be here soon."

"We goin' to the dance, Mama?" William asked her, hopping from foot to foot.

"Yes," she said. "You can play with Jonah and the other children."

William followed Jonah everywhere.

Zeke arrived with his wagon. He helped Jenny and William climb in, then loaded the picnic basket. He glanced at Jenny while they rode away from her cabin.

When they were almost to Oregon City, Zeke took her hand in his callused one.

"When will we talk?" he asked, squeezing her fingers gently. He sounded confident.

"Let me start William playing with his friends," Jenny said, pulling her hand away. "Then I'll walk with you."

Zeke nodded, and they rode the rest of the way in silence.

Crowds of wagons and horses and people thronged Abernethy Green, where new emigrants made camp when they first reached Oregon City. The dwindling number of settlers in Oregon since the California gold discovery left plenty of room on the green for residents to gather.

Zeke found a spot for the wagon and hobbled his team. "Come on," he said, lifting Jenny down. William held out his hands for help, and Zeke set the boy on the ground.

William ran over to Jonah, who sat with Esther and her family. Esther waved at Jenny and Zeke, and they walked over to Esther's blanket.

"Will you watch William?" Zeke asked. "I want to talk with Jenny." He clasped Jenny's hand again.

Esther grinned. "Of course. You two lovebirds go spooning."

Jenny slipped her hand out of Zeke's, but took his arm. They walked toward the Willamette River banks, not far from the green.

"Remember when we got here three years ago?" Zeke asked. "How happy we were?"

Jenny nodded. "I was so glad the journey was over."

Zeke turned to her. "Will you make me happy again, Jenny? Marry me."

Jenny shook her head. "I can't, Zeke." She swallowed hard, watching his face fall. "I wish I could, but I don't love you. Not the way you deserve."

Zeke took her shoulders, shaking her a little. "But I love you, Jenny. You care for me, I know you do."

"I do care for you, Zeke. But I can't marry you."

"Why not? Is it McDougall?" Zeke asked. His hands squeezed her shoulders. "He ain't coming back."

"I know." Tears welled in Jenny's eyes. "I'm sorry, Zeke. But I still

397

love him, and I can't marry you."

"Someday?" Zeke's voice was harsh. She wondered whether pain or anger caused his tone.

Jenny looked out over the river. "I don't know, Zeke. But I don't want you waiting. That's not right."

"What will you do? You can't run the farm by yourself."

"You won't keep working it for shares?" Jenny asked.

"Damn it, Jenny, I have my own land to manage. I can't keep tilling yours if it won't be mine someday. And what if Abercrombie tells the land office you ain't been married to McDougall?"

Jenny sighed. "I'll find a hired hand in the spring. Or sell the land, if I can. Or move to town. You told me once I should run a school in town."

They stood for a moment, looking out over the river, each lost in thought. Jenny had first stood on the bank of the Willamette with Mac, shortly after they reached Oregon City and their journey ended. Then she'd felt such hope for the future. Now? Her future was blank. She was relieved to have told Zeke her decision and did not regret it, but she had no idea what to do next.

"Shall we go back?" Zeke asked. "Will you at least dance with me?"

Jenny smiled. "Yes, Zeke. I'll dance with you."

Chapter 81:   Delays in Astoria

The captain scheduled the sailor's flogging for the next morning.

"I suppose it's necessary," Mac said when the captain informed him. He'd been ready to kill the sailor in the heat of the moment, although now the idea of flaying a man's back was difficult to stomach.

"It's the only way to maintain discipline at sea, Mr. McDougall," the captain replied. "Men must obey, even during a crisis like that storm. The crew must know there are consequences to breaking the rules."

Mac attended the sailor's flogging. The man cried out each time the cat o' nine tails left a bloody welt on his back, worse than the damage he'd done to Valiente.

Consequences, Mac thought. There are consequences to everything. He didn't want to dwell on the consequences of his dithering in California for three years—it might have cost him Jenny.

The clipper continued north toward Astoria. Their progress was slow in rough seas.

"I need to keep the ship far off the coast in this weather," the captain told Mac. "Too many vessels run aground on rocks close to shore."

"Are there still no charts of the Pacific?" Mac asked, thinking of the detailed charts he'd seen of the Atlantic coast.

"Not accurate ones. Can't tell where we are when we can't see the shore or the stars. Best to keep out to sea."

At last they reached the mouth of the great Columbia River. They dropped anchor so the crew could prepare the ship to enter the estuary. Sailors hurried about, coiling lines and tending sails. The mate bellowed orders, telling his men where to stow the sails and how they would approach the harbor depending on winds and currents.

Mac stood on deck and watched the sailors work. Gulls screamed overhead, fighting for detritus thrown overboard from the ship's galley. The skies were so gloomy with fog he couldn't see the gulls until they dove for floating morsels near the hull.

"Why are we stopping?" Mac asked the mate.

"Waters at the mouth of the Columbia are treacherous," the mate responded. "We must wait for good visibility and tides in our favor. Can't see the sand bars now. And we need the tides to push us upstream. Otherwise, the river current is too strong to counter."

"How long until we can proceed?" Mac peered into the fog. The skies were as dense as his apprehension about the future.

"Tomorrow at the earliest. If the skies clear. Still won't be easy. The prevailing winds are north to south, and we need to head east. We'll be crosswise to the wind."

Mac paced the deck in frustration and played cards with the officers to take his mind off the delays. When he couldn't bear the lack of progress any longer, he went to his cabin and wrote:

> *October 11, 1850. I fritter away the daytime hours, then toss and turn in my bunk all night. So close, and yet still I must wait before I can make my way home to Jenny.*
>
> *I hope it will be home.*

The ship remained anchored beyond the river's current for two days in rolling ocean waves. Finally, the sun shone palely through high clouds. "Next turn of the tide," the captain said. "We'll push through, God willing. Ready the sails."

When the captain gave the order to raise anchor and set the sails, the ship leapt forward like Valiente starting a good run. The clipper lurched from crest to trough in the waves and gathered momentum as it passed a sandbar in the middle of the estuary. The skeleton of a ship rose from the bar.

"The *Isabella*," the captain said, pointing at the wreck. "She went down twenty years ago. In another few years, she'll be covered by sand."

After passing the sandbar, the clipper turned toward the south bank of the Columbia to anchor off Astoria.

"What's the fastest way to Oregon City?" Mac asked the mate. "It's been almost three years since I left."

"You got your mount, so you can ride. Maybe four days on horseback. Or there's a steamship now, takes two days, for fifty dollars. Don't know what they'll charge for the horse."

"I'll look into it," Mac said. "I need to settle Helga with her husband before I can leave." Another delay, he fumed.

After the ship anchored, Mac made arrangements for Valiente and the nanny goat to be transported with the cargo to a warehouse in Astoria. He would need the goat to feed Maria until he reached Oregon City. Finally, on Monday, October 14, he and Helga, who held Maria, boarded a boat going to shore.

Once they arrived at the docks, Mac asked for Sven Larson. "He used to work here," a warehouse manager told him. "But he's got his own fishing boat now."

"His own boat," Helga exclaimed, clapping her hands.

"Don't know where he docks it. Most of the Finns and Swedes are gillnet fishermen. Their docks are west." The man gestured.

Mac escorted Helga in the direction indicated, and they made further inquiries.

"*Ja,*" another Swede told them. "I know Sven Larson. He out two week now. Be back soon." But he could not tell them more.

There was nothing Mac could do but find rooms in a boardinghouse, despite the urgency he felt to reach Oregon City. For the next two days, he looked for Sven Larson in the dank, foggy autumn weather, leaving Helga and Maria at their lodgings.

October 16, 1850. I cannot leave Helga alone in

*Astoria, so I pray we find her husband soon. I am eager
to be on my way to Oregon City. To Jenny.*

On the third morning Mac was successful. "*Ja,* I am Sven Larson," a
blond man said in response to Mac's inquiry. Sven's strong physique led
Mac to believe he was in his late twenties, like Mac, but the man's cheeks
were weathered and ruddy from years at sea.

"Your wife Helga accompanied me from San Francisco," Mac said.

"Helga? She here?" Sven's eyes lit up, then just as quickly his face
shadowed. "Why she with you?"

"I hired her to care for my daughter while we traveled," Mac replied.
"Come with me, and you can fetch her back with you."

Mac and Sven returned to the hotel. "Helga," he said. "I found Sven."

Helga beamed and threw herself into her husband's arms, crying,
"Sven! Sven!"

Sven hugged and kissed his wife, and Helga clung to his arm, chattering
in Swedish.

Mac smiled as he watched the couple reunite, but felt a pang of fear.
Would Jenny greet him as enthusiastically when he arrived at the farm? Or
would she be married to Zeke and lost to him?

"*Tack för allting.* Thank you," Helga said. She hugged Maria, curtsied
to Mac, and said her good-byes. Then she and Sven left.

Mac sat in the hotel lobby holding Maria. "Well, daughter," Mac said.
"Let's go find Jenny. Shall we book passage on the steamboat to Oregon
City?"

Maria looked up at him with solemn eyes that matched the deep brown
hue of Consuela's. Then her face lit up with a smile. That was enough
encouragement for Mac.

Chapter 82:   Alone

Monday, October 7th—School started today.
I will teach by myself this year. Rachel is too
busy with her own house and child.
I hurt Zeke, I know. Perhaps in time he will
agree I made the right decision. Esther, too, is
angry with me. I hope we can still be friends.

Jenny felt as alone as she had when Mac first left and almost as melancholy as after the O'Neils moved. Esther and the Tullers did not understand why she had rejected Zeke's proposal.

Now she would have to make her own way in the world. After leaving Missouri, she'd depended on Mac during the trip across the plains and mountains. Then she'd waited for Mac after he left, hoping he would return. She leaned on Zeke to help her and considered marrying him for the security he could offer.

But she couldn't bring herself to marry without love, particularly when she wasn't certain of Zeke's affection for William. And she was done with relying on men.

Perhaps someday a man would come along who wouldn't make her feel like she was settling for someone less than Mac, who would make her want to lean on him. So far, that hadn't happened.

She would face her future alone. She could manage, she told herself each morning. But she sobbed into Mac's pillow each night, bereft and empty.

Autumn rains began the same week Jenny's school did. Her students arrived damp, and their cloaks and coats steamed when she set them by the fire to dry during class.

Although the Abercrombie girls did not attend Jenny's school, two new pupils from a family just arrived from Missouri did. Established households had taken up a collection of money and clothes to help the new family. Early snows had caught them and many other emigrant families east of the Cascades. The wretched weather slowed their travel and made both the Columbia River and the mountain passages even more treacherous than what Jenny and her companions had faced in 1847.

"They got here with nothing," Esther whispered to Jenny. "Had no food their last week on the trail, other than berries which made them sick."

Jenny sighed, remembering the trek around Mount Hood where she'd collapsed and where the Abercrombies lost half their belongings when a wagon careened down the mountain slope.

"I'll teach their children for free this year," she told Esther. "The rest of you give me enough."

During one rainy school day that week, William played on Jenny's buffalo robe by the fire while she taught her students their lessons. Jenny noticed him listening when the younger children recited the alphabet and numbers.

The Bingham boy stumbled over the primer, and Jenny turned to her son. "What comes after P, William?" she asked.

"Q, R, S," he crowed. "T, U, V. Then double-you for William."

So at three years of age, William became Jenny's youngest pupil. He still sat on the buffalo skin, because his short legs couldn't reach the floor from the school benches.

Now that the crops were harvested, Zeke only stopped by occasionally, but on Thursday he brought his younger siblings to school. Jenny felt guilty asking him to do any work for her. As he'd said, she couldn't depend on him, not when she wouldn't marry him.

That morning he started chopping logs in her barnyard. She protested, but he replied, "It's all right, Jenny. I'll still chop your firewood."

She shook her head. "I can do it. Or I'll ask the twins. I've talked to your papa about trading their work for lessons. I have to make it on my own."

Zeke muttered, "It doesn't have to be this way."

But Jenny believed it did.

That evening after she reviewed essays her students had written about where their families came from, Jenny thought again about her mother. By turning Zeke down, she'd decided on a different future than Mama had—Jenny wouldn't take just any man, no matter how lonely she was, nor how hard a life she faced. Mama might not have been willing—or able—to raise a child and manage a farm alone, but Jenny was determined to stand on her own to provide for William and herself. She was eighteen now—full grown—and she had to act like it.

She didn't begrudge her mama deciding differently, even though Mama's decision to marry Bart Peterson had caused Jenny such terrible pain. In her last letter, Mama had not shown an inclination to continue corresponding, but Jenny now felt an overwhelming desire to talk to her mother.

She took out a sheet of paper and began to write:

> *October 10, 1850*
> *Chère Maman,*
>
> *I have thought of you often in recent months, and I hope you and my brother Jacques are well and happy.*
>
> *Your grandson William is three now. I cherish every minute with him. He had smallpox last year, but recovered with few ill effects.*
>
> *I am alone with William now. Mr. McDougall is away, and I manage his land as best I can. I teach school also. William*

knows his letters and can recognize some primer words already.

I am thankful for the fine education you and Papa gave me. You raised me in a loving home, and I will always be grateful.

She chose to keep silent about what happened after Mama married Mr. Peterson. She now understood her mother's need for a husband's support, but she had no desire to offer civil greetings to a man who'd abused her— she wouldn't mention him in the letter.

You and Jacques are in my prayers. I hope to hear from you soon,
Your devoted daughter,
Geneviève

The following Saturday, as she listened to her students recite their lessons, Jenny fretted over Samuel Abercrombie's threats. She decided she'd had enough of worrying, enough of wondering what trouble Samuel Abercrombie might make for her.

She didn't know whether he had any legal right to interfere, but he surely had no moral right. She'd managed the farm through its first three harvests and kept her house and barn in good order. No one had more right to the land than she did. Not even Mac.

On Sunday she left William with Mrs. Tuller after the service and strode over to Mr. Abercrombie. "Might I have a word, sir?" she asked.

Mr. Abercrombie crossed his arms over his barrel stomach and cocked an eyebrow.

"It's about my land," Jenny said.

The large man snorted. "Your land? McDougall filed the claim. He ain't coming back, and you ain't his wife. You got no rights."

"I've seen to the planting and the reaping. I've fought intruders and wild animals. Seems to me it's my land," Jenny said. She hid her hands in her skirts with fists clenched. "Mac gave me a deed to the claim, and I'll fight anyone who tries to take it from me."

"Unmarried females can't own nothing."

"Is that how you want your granddaughters treated, sir?" Jenny asked, hands moving to her hips, arms akimbo. "What if one of them is without a man's protection some day? Should she be thrown out of her home?"

"They's respectable young girls. Excepting for what they may have learned in your school. From you and from the Tanner boy and Pershing lads. My son Douglass can make better use of that land than you can."

"Douglass has his own house and land." Tears filled Jenny's eyes, due to anger not fear. "This is the only home my son and I have."

"Your son." Abercrombie spat on the ground. "Your bastard, you mean."

Without thinking, Jenny slapped Mr. Abercrombie's cheek, feeling his rough beard against her palm. "My son is smarter and better behaved than your two granddaughters put together."

She turned and stalked off, her legs trembling with every step. Confronting Samuel Abercrombie had only made her situation worse. Now he would almost certainly ask a judge to rule the claim was not hers. She could only hope the deed Mac had given her was sufficient. And in the meantime, her reputation would be ruined. The whole county would learn she and Mac had not been married.

The second week of classes continued dank and wet. Jenny loved her students, but she wouldn't let them outside in the middle of the day, no matter how they fidgeted. She didn't want to scrub the cabin floor every time they came back inside with muddy boots and shoes. Each day seemed longer than the last.

On Saturday, October 19, at noon, when she released her students at the end of the second week of school, the children raced away. "Good-bye, Miz McDougall," they called. "See you Monday."

The rainy skies lightened and the downpour decreased to a thin mist. William fretted when the older children left. "Wanna play with Wags," he whined.

"It's too wet for that dog to come inside."

"Wanna play with Jonah."

Jenny had had enough of children for the week. "Shall we go visit the

Tullers?" she asked.

William smiled and nodded. "Wanna see the kittens."

Jenny saddled Poulette, hoisted William on the mare's back, and packed a jar of gooseberry preserves into a saddlebag.

"Congress is about to make California a state," Doc Tuller told her when she arrived. "Word could come any day now."

"A state," Jenny said. "It must be growing so fast."

"More people there than in Oregon now," Doc said. "I don't expect we'll see many of our folks return here."

"But some Oregon men came back," Mrs. Tuller said. "Most didn't find a single nugget in the mines." She clucked her tongue. "Or they found gold, then lost it gambling."

"Do you think Joel Pershing will return?" Jenny asked.

"Has Esther or Captain Pershing heard anything?" Mrs. Tuller asked. "Seems they're the only ones Joel has written. Rachel never did hear from him after she married."

"Not that Esther has mentioned," Jenny said. She hadn't heard any news of anyone in California since Mac had written he would not return. "But surely Joel will write soon." And Joel would mention what happened to Mac—she would hear news of Mac someday.

Why did she want to know about his future? she wondered. He wasn't coming back.

"There's more news," Doc told Jenny. "Congress passed a Land Donation Act. Folks here been thinking it would happen."

"What's it say?" Jenny asked.

"Men can only claim half a section of land now, not a full section like we did. Married men can file on another half section, so they can still get six hundred and forty acres for a family." Doc picked up his pipe and primed it. "But it complicates how you pay the tax on the old claims. Ain't no provision for how to do that now."

"Then what happens to the old claims? What do I do?"

"Legislature says they'll honor them under the new land law."

Jenny sighed. "That's good news."

Doc shrugged. "It's only good news if no one objects to your claim. Esther and Zeke and the rest of the Pershings won't tell. Neither will Mrs. Tuller and me. But you know you can't rely on Abercrombie."

"I won't move unless I'm forced to," Jenny said.

"Well, don't give anyone reason to question you," Doc said. "Since you ain't McDougall's wife, you don't have clear right to the farm. Be hard to refile the claim without him."

"It's too late," Jenny said. "I argued with Mr. Abercrombie last Sunday."

Mrs. Tuller shook her head. "You wouldn't have this problem if you'd married Zeke Pershing. You'd have his land."

Jenny sighed. "I couldn't. I'll have to manage."

And somehow she would manage—she had no choice but to find a way to provide for William. But it would be easier if she could stay on the farm.

Jenny worried about her land while she did the evening chores in the barn. It seemed increasingly likely she would lose the land. If she had to move, she would need a place big enough to teach school. The school would be her only source of income. She could probably make do on what she earned from teaching, if she found a few more pupils. Maybe the Tullers would let her build a cabin on a corner of their claim.

As Jenny collected eggs for supper from the nests in the barn, Poulette whinnied in her stall.

"What is it, girl?" Jenny said, stroking the mare's nose.

Poulette snorted and nickered again. Two-year old Shanty grew restless at his mother's anxiety and pranced in the next stall.

Jenny heard another horse in the barnyard neigh back at Poulette. Who would call on her this late in the day? She looked outside the barn door, gasped, and dropped the eggs.

Chapter 83:   Return to the Homestead

Mac embarked with Maria, Valiente, and the nanny goat onto yet another boat, this time the sidewheeler *Columbia* bound from Astoria to Oregon City. He'd stored his belongings in a warehouse in Astoria, other than food for the journey and what he needed for Maria. These items he stashed in Valiente's saddlebags. He would deal with his possessions later. First he had to see Jenny.

"Trip'll take two days," the captain told Mac. "Depending on the wind. We ride up the Columbia all day and put in at Portland tonight. Tomorrow we head up the Willamette."

Mac fretted at the slow churning of the steamship's wheel, but it was faster and easier than riding Valiente the hundred miles to Oregon City with Maria in a sling across his chest and the goat tethered behind.

The *Columbia* had no galley or cook, but he had goat's milk, porridge, and applesauce for Maria, as well as provisions for himself and feed for the animals. He could make do for two days.

Several women eyed Mac and Maria while he stood on deck holding the infant. One older woman with a buxom daughter came over to him. "Is that baby your child, sir?" she asked.

"Yes, ma'am," he said.

"And where's her mother?"

"She died."

"What a pity," the woman said. "You must feel the want of your wife, sir. Carin' for your daughter on your own."

"I'm hoping to remedy the situation," Mac said, without thinking. "I'm on my way to ask a woman to marry me."

"Heavens," the woman said. As she bustled her daughter off, Mac heard her mutter, "His first wife can't have been dead more'n six months."

"Well, Ma," the daughter said. "You were fixin' to hitch him to me."

Mac smiled. He hoped Jenny would be so amenable to marriage.

October 18, 1850. We reached Portland this evening, and will arrive in Oregon City tomorrow. Caring for Maria fully occupies my time on the steamboat. She fusses when I don't let her crawl, but she could be trampled or fall overboard. This morning she almost rolled underneath a mule tied nearby.

On the afternoon of the second day, a Saturday, the *Columbia* docked in Oregon City. Maria looked rather disheveled, her clothing wrinkled and damp and her face dirty. Mac wanted to clean her up before they rode to the claim, but his hands shook, worrying about what Jenny would say when he returned. And with a baby—if she hadn't received his letter, she would know nothing of Maria's existence.

Mac had fought thieves and Indians with courage. He'd navigated politics in Monterey with confidence. But thoughts of his coming reunion with Jenny made his palms sweat.

As they disembarked, Mac hoped he wouldn't run into people he knew. He wanted to see Jenny before he talked to anyone else. Whether he and Maria would stay depended on Jenny.

He was committed to raising Maria, and he was ready to settle down. If Jenny didn't want him, he'd have to decide between Boston and California. What kind of life would a Mexican-Indian child have in Boston? California would be better.

But he didn't want Boston or California. He wanted a life with Jenny.

Mac carried Maria and steered Valiente and the goat off the steamship. After tying the goat's lead rope to the saddle horn, he mounted Valiente. They headed through town and up the bluff east of Oregon City. The town had grown in three years. It wasn't as big as San Francisco, but the streets bustled with commerce and everyday life.

He remembered standing on the bluff with Jenny when they first approached Oregon City in 1847. Jenny had looked up at him that day, smiling her thanks that he'd led her and William safely to their destination. It had felt like arriving home when they gazed out over the town.

Oregon had become Jenny's home. Now he wanted it to be his.

Mac steered Valiente on the route they'd taken in March 1848, when he left Jenny. In truth, he knew now, he'd run away from his feelings for her, from the life they could have had. He hadn't been ready to admit he loved her.

Now all he wanted was to build a life with her.

The trail to the cabin was both too long and too short. Too long to wait to see Jenny. Too short to convince himself all would be well.

The land around him was as beautiful as he remembered—forested, fertile where cleared, October leaves brilliant in the setting sun. A cool breeze sifted Mac's hair, and he hugged Maria against his chest. They could have a good life here.

As sunset darkened into twilight, Mac stopped Valiente within sight of the cabin. Maria wriggled and fussed in the sling, protesting her long confinement.

The small house looked neat, the barnyard clean, a fenced paddock of grass beside the barn. It looked like a comfortable farm in the States, except the clearing was surrounded with the tall pines and alders of Oregon. Jenny had cared for the land well.

Valiente neighed and pranced, as if recognizing he was home at last.

Another horse whinnied in response. Poulette?

A woman came to the barn door. She dropped her apron full of eggs. "Mac!" she screamed and ran toward him.

Jenny.

Chapter 84: Reunion

Jenny heard the eggs splat as they hit the ground. "Mac!" she cried. Her shoes slipped on the crushed shells and slime when she ran toward the man on horseback. Pure joy danced in her soul—Mac was here.

She stopped when she neared the stallion. Mac had a baby with him, strapped to his chest like she used to carry the infant William, and a nanny goat was tied to Mac's saddle.

"Mac," she said in a whisper this time, wondering who the child was to him.

"Whoa." Mac reined in Valiente whose hooves pawed at the ground. The stallion quieted, but the baby cried.

"Would you take Maria?" Mac asked, removing the infant from the sling.

Jenny's arms reached naturally for the child, but her eyes never left Mac's face. As she took the baby, Jenny's fingers met Mac's and her heart jumped. She cuddled the little girl against her shoulder. The sweet sour scent of dirty baby met her nose. "Shhh," she whispered to the squalling infant.

She said nothing while Mac dismounted and hitched Valiente to a fencepost. But she watched him, unable to turn her eyes away, even to the infant in her arms. He was more muscular than she remembered, a firmer cast to his jaw, but still handsome. Her eyes drank him in and she wanted to touch him, to be sure he was really here.

The baby screamed and arched her back, fighting Jenny's attempts at comfort. The poor child must be exhausted.

Mac turned to Jenny when he'd dealt with the horse. "Jenny," Mac said and opened his arms.

She rushed into Mac's embrace, the baby calming between them. He smelled of horse and milk and sweat. She sobbed, just once, when Mac closed his arms around her and the child. Just for a moment she let herself savor the comfort and delight of his strength.

"I should never have left you," Mac said.

The baby fussed, and Jenny pulled back. "Why are you here now?" she asked.

"You didn't receive my letter?" Despite the question, he didn't sound surprised.

"Your last letter said you were never coming back." Jenny's voice was flat, despite her joy at seeing Mac. She needed to know what he intended before she revealed how she felt. She couldn't bear it if he left again.

"I sent another letter. I said I was coming." Mac's shoulders sagged. "I asked you to wait for me. But I fear the letter was lost in a shipwreck."

"A shipwreck?" She didn't know whether to believe him. Mac had been honest with her in the past, but almost three years had passed.

"You haven't married Zeke, have you?" Mac asked. "Esther wrote Joel you were going to marry Zeke."

"He asked me."

"Am I too late, Jenny?" Mac took her hand.

She grasped the baby closer with the other arm. "Too late for what?"

"For you to marry me. I asked you in the letter."

Stunned, Jenny removed her hand from Mac's and turned toward the cabin. Her heart soared at the sight and sound and scent of Mac, but he'd appeared out of nowhere with a baby in his arms. Saying he wanted to marry her. "You've been gone almost three years."

A part of her wanted to shout "yes!" in response to his proposal and throw herself into his arms again. But she had too many questions. She'd been alone too long, been too independent, too responsible for William. She had to understand why Mac talked of marrying her. "Come have supper," she said, needing time to think.

"Where's William?" Mac asked, entering the small house behind Jenny.

"Playing in the loft." She called her son down to supper like she did every evening. "William, come downstairs." But how could she and Mac talk with the boy around?

William clambered down the ladder. "Who's that man?" he asked.

Mac knelt in front of William. "I'm Mac," he said, holding out his hand.

The boy shook Mac's hand, but eyed him suspiciously. "Who's that baby?"

"That's Maria," Mac said. "My daughter."

Jenny stared at the baby she still held. The child looked Mexican, dark eyes and black, straight hair. "Your daughter?"

"My adopted daughter," Mac added. "I'll tell you the story."

She was curious, but feared what he might say. "Supper first," she told Mac, then handed Maria back to him. "The food isn't fancy, but there's plenty."

"I'll wash her up," Mac said. "Her things are in my saddlebag."

"Set her on the buffalo skin while you fetch them," Jenny said, nodding at the pelt Mac had given her so long ago. "It's clean enough."

Mac put Maria on the rug, and went outside. William squatted beside Maria, gazing at the baby's face. "She's pretty," he said.

"Yes," Jenny said. "She's a lovely baby." She smiled at William, though her throat choked shut. Mac had a daughter. A Mexican child, apparently. Was Consuela Montenegro the child's mother?

Mac came back inside with a saddlebag. He fumbled with its laces and pulled out a bottle. He changed the baby's diaper, then went outside to wash his hands.

When he returned, Jenny told him, "There's milk in the bucket the baby can have."

"Thank you." He filled the bottle, then sat at the table with Maria in his lap and began to feed her.

Jenny's hands shook as she fried ham and eggs and sliced cornbread. "William, please set the table. For three." The boy had learned to count out the cutlery.

William did his chore, then he watched Mac feed Maria.

"Sit down, William," Jenny said, putting plates on the table, then taking her seat. She gave thanks for the food, and William started to eat.

Jenny wasn't hungry. She held out her arms for the baby. "I'll finish her bottle. You eat," she said to Mac.

Mac looked around the room while he ate. "The cabin looks comfortable," he said.

Jenny smiled. "It's home."

"What are those for?" Mac gestured at the benches stacked against one wall.

"I teach a school for the nearby children." She was proud of her teaching. She wondered how Mac would react. "The Pershings and others."

"I can count to twenty," William said. "And say my letters." He proceeded to demonstrate.

"Bright lad," Mac said, ruffling William's hair. "What else can you do?"

William and Mac talked while Jenny finished feeding the baby. She inspected the child's face as she held Maria. Jenny didn't see any of Mac in the infant. He'd said she was adopted, and Jenny wondered again whether Maria was the Montenegro woman's daughter.

She and Mac said little to each other while Mac ate and Jenny picked at her food. She glanced surreptitiously at him. Every time she looked up, he was staring at her. William babbled on about horses and kittens and babies and school. Mac responded, grinning at the boy.

After the meal, Jenny washed up. "Let William show you the barn," she said. "You can stable Valiente. I'll watch the baby."

Mac and William went outside. Jenny stood at the wash bucket, tears streaming down her cheeks, wondering about Mac's motives. Did he want to marry her for Maria's sake or for his own?

Chapter 85: Telling Their Stories

Mac and William explored the barn thoroughly. William talked the whole time and squealed with delight when the goat butted him softly in the stomach. He called Wags and searched for his cat, then brought them both to Mac to show off proudly.

Mac chuckled as he responded to the boy's incessant questions. The infant he remembered was gone, and an inquisitive young lad had emerged. The child looked like Jenny.

Mac moved Valiente into his former stall next to Poulette. A fine spotted black colt occupied the stall on the other side of the mare, and a pair of mules filled two other stalls. Mac filled all the animals' feed bins with hay, including the nanny goat's. The farm was indeed prospering under Jenny's care.

As Mac milked the goat, William asked, "Why don't you have a cow?"

"The goat travels better," Mac replied.

William wanted to know why, and Mac answered as best he could.

The simple barn chores eased his anxiety, until his mind wandered from William's chatter, and he wondered what Jenny was thinking. She'd said so little since he arrived. She'd come into his arms easily, but hadn't responded when he proposed marriage. He'd hoped she would immediately accept, smiling her joy.

Had he already bungled their reunion? But he hadn't even started to tell her how he felt. At least she wasn't married.

When they returned to the cabin, Jenny told William, "Bedtime," and the boy slowly climbed the ladder to the sleeping loft, peering down at Mac from every step. A few minutes later, William popped his head over the edge of the ladder and asked, "Where will that baby sleep?"

Jenny sighed and said, "Go to bed."

"Is William in my old bed upstairs?" Mac asked Jenny.

Jenny nodded.

"I'll sleep in the barn tonight. May Maria stay in the cabin with you? She sleeps through the night. If I give her more milk before I go to bed, she shouldn't bother you."

"The cradle's in the loft." Jenny gestured toward the ladder.

"I'll bring it down."

"Bring a blanket, too. So she won't be cold. And one for yourself."

Mac climbed the ladder and saw the cradle he and Tanner had made three winters ago. It sat in a corner, filled with blankets and old clothes. William watched him cross the loft.

Mac emptied the cradle except for two blankets, and felt his way back down, grasping his load in one arm and hanging onto the ladder with the other. He set the cradle near the foot of Jenny's bed. "She can turn over, but I don't think she'll fall out," he said.

Jenny tucked Maria into the cradle, nestled the blanket around the sleeping baby, and set the cradle rocking gently. Then she sat at the table and asked, "Why are you here, Mac?"

Mac took a deep breath. The time had come to plead his case. Could he convince Jenny to marry him? "I missed you. I've realized I was happiest when we were together. I want to marry you." He sat in a chair beside Jenny and took her hand. "A real marriage, if you'll have me."

"You left me."

"I'm sorry, Jenny. About how I behaved that night." He rubbed her fingers. She didn't pull away. "About frightening you. And leaving you."

She shook her head at him. "I wasn't scared of you. Not after the first surprise. I was only afraid of being alone." Then she looked at him. "I came to understand why you left. And I learned I can take care of William and myself without you. Without Zeke. Without anyone."

"Don't you want me here? Wouldn't your life be easier if we were together?"

"If I wanted easy, I would have married Zeke." Now she did pull her hand away.

Mac swallowed hard. She still wasn't responding like he'd hoped. "But you didn't marry him. Do you want to be alone?"

"No," she said. "But I'd rather be alone than live without love." She frowned. "You always said you'd leave. I knew you would. But how could you tell me you were dead? That I cannot excuse."

"I wanted you to be free of me. I hadn't yet admitted to myself that I love you, Jenny. It took me time to realize it." Too much time, he thought, gritting his teeth.

"How do I know you won't leave me again?" She looked down at her hands, but Mac saw her eyes brimmed with tears.

He tipped her chin up so she looked at him, then he brushed a tear off her cheek. "I love you, Jenny," he repeated. "I won't leave. If you say you'll have me, I'll never leave again."

Jenny stared at him for two long breaths, then broke their gaze and pulled away. "What have you been doing all these years?"

Mac touched Jenny's cheek again, wanting to touch far more, but knowing it wasn't time yet. Then he stood and paced the room. "Mined for gold with Joel and a man named Huntington. We did all right. Worked for Lansford Hastings drafting the California Constitution. Opened a store. That did all right, too. Tried hauling gold to market. I have plenty of my own money now. I'm not dependent on my father or my brothers."

"And Maria?"

"Her mother was Consuela Montenegro. The woman who wrote you. A friend. She worked in my store for a bit."

Jenny paused, then asked in a tight voice, "Did you lie with her?"

Was she jealous? he wondered. "No."

"So Maria isn't yours?"

"No. Consuela was a prostitute. Maria's father could be any of dozens of men, even Joel Pershing. But not me." Mac hesitated, but he wanted Jenny to know how he felt about Consuela. "Despite her profession, she was a good woman, and I won't hear ill spoken of her. But you deserve to know the truth."

Jenny's shoulders relaxed, and her voice was softer when she asked, "Why do you have Maria now?"

"Consuela died. Stabbed by a customer."

He heard the harsh hiss of Jenny's inhale. "Poor woman."

"Before she died, she asked me to take her baby. I couldn't say no."

"Like I asked you to take William if I died?" she whispered.

Mac nodded and grinned. At least she remembered his promise to her at Whitman Mission. "I'm a sucker for a pretty lady with a baby." He took a deep breath. "And you, Jenny, what have you done for three years? Besides raise William. He's a clever boy."

"Managed the farm. Taught school in the winters. I had help in the fields. First Tanner. Then Zeke, after Tanner left. And Robert O'Neil—an ex-soldier who worked for me until he married Rachel Pershing. Doc and Mrs. Tuller are nearby, and Esther and Daniel. They have two children now, plus Jonah. I managed."

"So many changes," Mac murmured. "Yet our friends are still here."

"We had some hard times. William had smallpox. I was so afraid I'd lose him." Jenny sighed, then shrugged. "The farm provides most of our food. The crops did well, and I sold the grain. The students pay in kind also. Your money helped, but I've replaced nearly all I took."

"I left the money for you."

Jenny stuck her chin in the air. She'd always done that when she was being stubborn. "I didn't want anything from you. Not if you weren't here."

"So you've built a home in Oregon, like you wanted."

"It's a good life."

"Aren't you lonely?"

"Lonely? All my friends are here."

"Did you miss me?"

Jenny's eyes filled with tears again, and she rose to face the fire. "It isn't fair for you to ask that," she said into the flames. "You weren't mine to miss."

"I missed you."

"Why did you come back, Mac?"

Mac frowned. She kept asking—she didn't believe him. Mac searched his mind for a way to convince her he meant what he said. He reached in his pocket, felt William's tattered bootie, and pulled it out. He handed it to Jenny.

She gasped. "William's baby sock."

"I picked it up the night I left," he said. "I've carried it with me always. And now I've brought it back. Will you marry me, Jenny?"

"You never wanted to marry me before."

"I was a fool, Jenny. Such a fool. I did want to marry you when I asked the first time. But you turned me down, and I didn't want to push you." Mac moved to stand beside her at the fireplace. His hands gently turned her to face him. Again, he wanted to touch more of her. "I can't stay the way we were. The last night before I left proved that. If I stay, we have to marry. I want you as my lover and my wife."

Jenny caught her breath and stared at him, her eyes searching his.

"If you won't marry me," Mac continued, "then Maria and I will leave—Boston, or back to California, it doesn't matter if I'm not with you. But I can't stay here without having you. I love you, and I want to marry you." He tightened his grip on her shoulders. "Will you have me, Jenny? Can we put the past three years behind us?"

"Maybe," she whispered.

"Can you have me as a husband after what happened to you in Missouri? After I left you here alone for all this time?"

Mac felt Jenny's tension ebb away and she softened in his hands. "I've always loved you, Mac," she said in a rush. "Before I knew what love was. From the first day we met and you saved me."

Jenny stepped into Mac's embrace. His heart swelled when she continued, "That night three years ago, I knew as soon as you'd gone. I'd rather have you as my lover than have you leave." Her voice was muffled in his shoulder, but he heard every word. "You surprised me then. Scared me a little. But I've always loved you," she repeated. "I trust you, body and soul. So yes, I'll marry you."

Mac raised her face to his and kissed her deeply. She fit so well in his arms, and her mouth tasted sweet and soft. He was home.

Chapter 86:   Union

She'd waited for this for so long, Jenny thought when Mac's lips touched hers. This was where she was destined to be. In Oregon. In Mac's arms. This was why she hadn't felt anything when Zeke kissed her. Because she was meant to be with Mac. Her fingers squeezed the silly gray sock he'd given her.

His arms tightened around her, holding her close. For one moment, she recalled the men who'd attacked her so long ago, but only for a moment. Then the love in Mac's kiss pushed all memory aside, and she clung to him as tightly as he held her. The kiss deepened and blotted out all other thought.

"Mac," she whispered, when she could take a breath.

"How soon will you marry me, Jenny?" he whispered back.

"Tomorrow."

"And tonight?" At Mac's rough, deep voice, Jenny felt a flare from her breasts to her womb.

There was only one answer. "Tonight I am yours," she murmured and led him to the bed.

And it was true. Through the night, Mac made sweet, careful love to her, with Maria nearby and William snoring softly in the loft overhead. In between lovings, they talked. They told tales from their pasts and built dreams for their future.

As she drifted into sleep in Mac's arms, Jenny's memories of past troubles faded and her doubts vanished. She had everything she wanted in this small cabin in Oregon. She basked in the joy and contentment of knowing she'd found her place in the world.

In the morning Jenny woke to see her son beside the bed peering at her and Mac. "That man still here," William said. "And that baby."

Beside her, Mac lifted himself on an elbow. "I'm staying," he told the boy. "I'm your father."

"I don't got a papa," William said. "He's in Cali . . . Cali . . ." His face wrinkled.

"California," Mac said. "I was in California, but I'm home now."

"Come," Jenny said, hearing Maria fuss in her cradle. "We have to dress for church. We need to be there early." Then she whispered to Mac, "To talk to the preacher about marrying us."

Mac leaned over and kissed her. "We'll be there in time."

Jenny bustled about the cabin. She told William to put his clothes on, while she bathed Maria, laughing at the baby's splashing in the wash bucket. She thought blissfully of the passion she and Mac had shared during the night. She wished they could have stayed in bed all day, but she had a family to care for.

A family.

From being alone with William to having a family in one night. Her mind could not take it in, and she hummed every sweet song she knew. She patted Maria dry and held the baby close before digging out the prettiest dress she could find in Mac's saddlebag.

Two children were a lot more work than one, Jenny realized, and she smiled thinking of Esther's brood. Mac brought in wood and water and harnessed Poulette to the wagon, while Jenny clothed and fed Maria. Somehow, they were ready early. As a family, they could manage life well together—she was sure of it.

"Let's stop by the Tullers' farm on the way," Jenny said, when Mac lifted Maria up for Jenny to hold in the wagon. "They can stand up with us before the service."

Mac grinned, jumped to the wagon bench, and tapped the reins on Poulette's back to get the mare moving. They rode side by side as they had on the six month journey to Oregon, though now Mac pressed his thigh against hers and planted a kiss on her temple. And she smiled at him brightly.

"For God's sake, McDougall, where the hell have you been?" Doc Tuller shouted when they pulled into the Tullers' yard.

"Doesn't matter," Mac said. "I'm back now. Ready to do what I should have done three years ago. We're getting married."

"She'll have you now?" Doc asked in his gruff voice.

Jenny blushed and nodded. "We're headed to the church. We'd like you there with us."

Mrs. Tuller clapped her hands. "My stars, child, I'm so happy for you. Of course, we'll come."

"A baby?" Doc asked, his eyebrows coming together in a frown at the sight of Maria on Jenny's lap.

"My adopted daughter, sir," Mac said.

The doctor raised one shaggy eyebrow, but said nothing.

Jenny's back stiffened and she lifted her chin. "Her name is Maria," she said.

Mrs. Tuller pulled back a corner of Maria's blanket to reveal her face. "Such dark eyes," she exclaimed. "How precious."

"We'll be right behind you," Doc said. "Soon as I harness the mules."

The two wagons rolled into Oregon City and entered the churchyard. Jenny led Mac to meet with the minister in the parsonage, while the Tullers minded the children.

It took a while to explain their story to the minister's satisfaction.

"Are you certain this is what you want, Jenny?" The preacher steepled his fingers in front of his face. "I've never heard such a tale. You lived together pretending to be man and wife, then parted. And now you want to marry after three years' separation?"

"Yes, Reverend," Jenny said. "I'm sure. I've always loved Mac. Though perhaps I was too young to know it before."

"You're putting right what God wanted long ago, I suppose," the man said doubtfully. "But what if Mr. McDougall leaves again?" He frowned at Mac.

"I won't leave," Mac said, taking Jenny's hand. "I've lived with Jenny and apart from her, and now I know—I want to spend the rest of my days with her. There's nothing that means so much to me anywhere else on earth."

"Those words are as good as any vows I've heard," the minister said, standing. "Call in your witnesses, and I'll bless your union."

Mac brought the Tullers and children into the parsonage. The minister conducted the brief ceremony, while Mrs. Tuller wiped her eyes. As they recited their vows, Mac held Maria, and William leaned against Jenny.

"I now pronounce you man and wife," the preacher concluded.

Mac kissed Jenny as tenderly as he had the night before. They signed the registry and filed into church for the Sunday service.

As the prayers began, Jenny heard whispers all around. Zeke slouched frowning in the back of the church. Esther leaned forward from the row behind and tapped Jenny's shoulder. "Do tell, what has happened?"

"Mac is home," Jenny said, and she couldn't keep the grin off her face. "To stay."

Around her the music rose, and Jenny sang, Mac's voice harmonizing with hers,

> *Amazing Grace, how sweet the sound,*
> *That saved a wretch like me.*
> *I once was lost but now am found, . . .*

Found, Jenny thought. Mac had found her so long ago, and now they'd found each other again. Whatever came next, they would face it together. Her hand reached out to clasp Mac's.

He squeezed her fingers gently. "Found," Mac whispered.

Jenny smiled while their voices soared together.

THE END

Author's Note and Research Methods

This book is a work of fiction, but is based on the facts of the California Gold Rush and the settlement of both Oregon and California between 1848 and 1850.

Many of the events depicted in these pages are historical, including the dates the San Francisco papers announced the gold discovery in March 1848, the events at Murderer's Bar and the posse that followed, the topics discussed at the California Constitution Convention and the attitudes of the delegates, the Independence Day celebrations in Oregon City, the hangings of Native Americans for the murder of Marcus and Narcissa Whitman, the fires in San Francisco and Sacramento, the eruption of Mt. Diablo, and the Oregon City smallpox epidemic. Many of the anecdotes about mining life came from prospectors' diaries.

I have tried to be faithful to the development of San Francisco, Sacramento, and Oregon City, though I have fudged some dates to fit my story. For example, Oregonians learned about the discovery of gold in California sometime in July 1848, but probably later than the July 4 celebration when I show the news reaching Oregon.

Also, I have used my imagination in describing banking procedures and the transportation of gold from the mines to Sacramento and San Francisco for shipment back East. I spent significant time researching these topics, and I hope my conjectures are reasonable. I have tried to be true to the land laws in Oregon as they evolved during these years, but I cannot verify whether the deed Mac sent Jenny would have given her legal right to his claim, so I left this an open question in the novel.

A ship named the *Samuel Roberts* went down near the mouth of the Rogue River in 1850, but the date didn't quite fit my story. So I changed the name to the *Robert Samuels* and sank a fictional ship.

Real places in the Sacramento area mentioned in this book include Sutter's Fort, the Embarcadero, and the hotels. The Golden Nugget is a figment of my imagination. In fact, newspaper descriptions of Sacramento in 1849 describe it as a "proper" town, but I have prostitutes and gambling halls arriving in mid-1848, soon after the miners did. In San Francisco, the Exchange, the Post Office, the Parker House, and other buildings are historical.

Real places in Oregon include the Abernethy store, the Methodist Church, Rose Farm, and Willamette Falls. The locations of all the characters' land claims are fictional.

Most of the characters in this book are fictional, though several historical personalities pass through these pages. Most notably, General Bennett Riley, Thomas Butler King, the delegates at the Constitutional Convention (Lansford Hastings, William Shannon, John Frémont, and others mentioned), Jessie Benton Frémont, and Governor Lane in Oregon are all real people. Francis Pettygrove was one of the founders of Portland, Oregon, and Edward Dunbar did own a bank (consisting of a large brick safe) in San Francisco in 1850. I have placed all these historical characters in scenes of my own imagination.

A real McDougall (John McDougall, later the first lieutenant governor of California) was a delegate at the California Constitutional Convention in 1849, but he was no relation of Mac's.

There are numerous books and online resources available on the California Gold Rush. The 19th century accounts of the Gold Rush I relied on included:

- *A Year of American Travel,* by Jessie Benton Frémont (1878)
- *Report of the Debates in the Convention of California, on the Formation of the State Constitution, in September and October, 1849,* by John Ross Browne (1850)
- Hubert Howe Bancroft's multi-volume *History of California* and *History of Oregon*
- Newspapers of the period, which can be found online in the California Digital Newspaper Collection and Historic Oregon Newspapers
- Many prospector diaries and letters

I also recommend the following recent books:

- *The Age of Gold: The California Gold Rush and the New American Dream*, by H.W. Brands (2002)
- *A Year of Mud and Gold: San Francisco in Letters and Diaries, 1849-1850*, by William Benemann (Editor) (2003)
- *The California Gold Rush and the Coming of the Civil War*, by Leonard L. Richards (2007)

I take responsibility for any historical errors in *Now I'm Found*.

If you enjoyed **Now I'm Found**, *consider reading* **Lead Me Home**, *Book 1 of this series, which tells the story of Mac's and Jenny's journey on the Oregon Trail. Available at bit.ly/LeadMeHomeAmazon*

or

bit.ly/LeadMeHomeNook.

Discussion Guide

These questions are intended to help book clubs and other reading groups discuss *Now I'm Found*. They might also help students writing essays about the Gold Rush years.

1. What interested you the most in reading about the early Gold Rush years? Were there topics you wanted to know more about?

2. Would you have stayed in Oregon to farm or left for California to search for gold? Why?

3. What did you learn about travel in the 1840s?

4. How did the difficulties of long-distance communication in the West during this time period contribute to the plot?

5. How did Jenny's age make a difference in the story?

6. What choices did Mac and Jenny make that you disagree with? Why?

7. What do various characters think about marriage? What were marriages based on in the mid-19th century?

8. How did Mac and Jenny change and develop while they were apart?

9. Which issues debated in the California Constitutional Convention

are still with us today, and which have been resolved?

10. How accurately do you think the author depicted prejudice against Native Americans, African Americans, and other minorities in this book?

11. Who was found in *Now I'm Found*? Why do you think so?

12. How do you feel about the relationship between Mac and Jenny at the end of the book?

13. What do you think happened to some of the other characters?

Acknowledgments

Many thanks to my diligent and supportive critique partners in the Sedulous Writers Group and in Homer's Orphans, to Tom who read an early draft, and to my recent readers, including Al, Dane, Irma, and Sylvia.

I also appreciate the help of members of Write Brain Trust, who have taught me much about publishing and marketing.

I am grateful to you all for your input and encouragement.

About the Author

Theresa Hupp grew up in Eastern Washington State, except for two years in the Willamette Valley in Oregon. Her ancestors include early emigrants to Oregon and immigrants to Sacramento, California (though her California forebearers arrived after the Gold Rush). Theresa now lives in Kansas City, Missouri, near the beginning of the Oregon Trail.

Theresa is the award-winning author of novels, short stories, essays, and poetry, and has worked as an attorney, mediator, and human resources executive.

Lead Me Home, Theresa's first novel about Mac McDougall and Jenny Calhoun, was published in 2015. It has been a #1 bestselling novel about the Oregon Trail in Amazon's Kindle Store.

She has also published another novel—a bestselling financial thriller—under a pseudonym, as well as an anthology under her own name, *Family Recipe: Sweet and saucy stories, essays, and poems about family life*. In addition, Theresa has published short works in *Chicken Soup for the Soul*, *Mozark Press*, and *Kansas City Voices*. She is a member of the Kansas City Writers Group, Missouri Writers Guild, Oklahoma Writers Federation, Inc., and Write Brain Trust.

Theresa's blog is *Story & History: One writer's journey through life and time*, http://mthupp.wordpress.com, where she often posts about the Oregon Trail and the California Gold Rush. You can also follow her on her Facebook Author page, http://facebook.com/TheresaHuppAuthor, and her Amazon page at http://www.amazon.com/Theresa-Hupp/e/B009H8QIT8.

Praise for *Lead Me Home*

From reviews on Amazon and Goodreads:

. . . Not only did I vicariously sweat during the trip across the western deserts, grow nervous about river crossings, feel the dust in my face behind the animals, and mourn the loss of wagon train members, but also I empathized with the emotional ups and downs of the main characters.

. . . on the challenging Oregon Trail of 1847 . . . the going is slow and scary and dusty behind a team of oxen. With well-researched attention to detail, [Hupp] takes us on this journey and shows how her characters cope and grow under these difficult circumstances.

. . . so realistic that the reader might believe the diary entries . . . came from a real traveler.

. . . an incredible story, amazingly and beautifully written.

. . . compellingly entertaining and marvelously instructive.

. . . remarkable! A great read.

. . . Hupp drew me in . . . . I can't wait for the sequel.

Lead Me Home is available online at Amazon or Barnes & Noble, in paperback or ebook formats, at bit.ly/LeadMeHomeAmazon or bit.ly/LeadMeHomeNook.

Made in the USA
Las Vegas, NV
09 November 2023

80526322R00243